Sources of American Indian Oral Literature

This series offers new editions of works previously published,
as well as works never before published,
on Native American oral tradition

Mythology of the Blackfoot Indians

SECOND EDITION

Compiled and translated by

Clark Wissler and D. C. Duvall

Introduction to the Bison Books edition by
Alice Beck Kehoe

Introduction to the new Bison Books edition by
Darrell Kipp

UNIVERSITY OF NEBRASKA PRESS

LINCOLN AND LONDON

Originally published in 1908 in the Anthropological Papers series of
the American Museum of Natural History, New York, vol. 2, part 1.

The University of Nebraska Press is grateful to the James M. Milne
Library, State University College at Oneonta, New York, for loaning
a copy for reproduction.

Library of Congress Cataloging-in-Publication Data
Wissler, Clark, 1870–1947.
Mythology of the Blackfoot Indians / compiled and translated by
Clark Wissler and D. C. Duvall; introduction to the Bison Books
edition by Alice Beck Kehoe; introduction to the new Bison Books
edition by Darrell Kipp. — 2nd ed., new Bison Books ed.
p. cm. — (Sources of American Indian oral literature)
Includes bibliographical references and index.
ISBN 978-0-8032-6023-8 (pbk.: alk. paper)
1. Siksika mythology. I. Duval, D. C. II. Title.
E99.S54W525 2007
299.7'8352013—dc22
2007027615

INTRODUCTION TO THE NEW BISON BOOKS EDITION
Darrell Kipp

Apiniokio Peta in the Blackfoot language translates into English as "Morning Eagle." It is the name my grandmother Esquee Pisaki (Yellow Hawk Woman) christened me with at my birth in 1944. It was the name of her uncle, a man noted for his clairvoyant abilities, who passed on in 1882. The stories in *Mythology of the Blackfoot Indians* were the standard oral literature of my relatives' day. They are the Blackfoot Long Ago Stories (*Amskapi Pikuni Aa'ksikaitapiitsinikiwa*) my grandmother knew about the Blackfoot as told by people of the tribe—stories she learned from her uncle the all-seeing Morning Eagle and those around her who spoke the Blackfoot language.

Yellow Hawk Woman passed on in 1958 at the age of ninety-eight. Born in 1860, she was a young woman in the waning days of the buffalo hunt, when the camp still moved with the seasons. She also was very much part of an emerging dark period for the Blackfoot, marked by the infamous 1870 Bear River Winter Massacre and the bleakness of the 1884 Starvation Winter, when buffalo could no longer be found in her once bountiful homeland. During the advent of the reservation period in the mid-1880s she married my grandfather Sako' Naa'maa (Last Gun), who as a seven-year-old was one of the few survivors of the 1870 massacre. They moved into a two-story frame house and had seven children. Yellow Hawk Woman never learned to speak English, but she adapted well into so-called modern life, especially after the death of her husband in 1936. It is doubtful that she ever heard the English word *mythology*, but if it had been explained to her in Blackfoot as denoting the old stories of her people, she surely would have accepted it to the same extent I do today, despite my once questioning the meaning of the word.

In 1983, in a one-in-a-million chance opportunity, I was fortunate to obtain a mint copy of Clark Wissler and D. C. Duvall's *Mythology of the Blackfoot Indians*. My first reaction was to recoil from the title, despite the fact that at the time I was desperately searching for any and all written materials about my tribe. The word *mythology* dampened my elation at discovering the book because my sense of the term paralleled the bulk of dictionary definitions: false beliefs, fabricated and imaginary stories, or events akin to nonverifiable history. I was not prepared (nor would have been my grandmother) to accept our tribe's origin stories, events of historical heritage, and people as imaginary, false, and nonverifiable. I only came to acknowledge the word after extended review in numerous dictionaries, finally accepting a definition of "a traditional narrative of an early history of a people" as that intended in Wissler and Duvall's day and age. The word *mythology* still strikes me as a less-than-perfect means to embody the intricate nature of the contents of this book, but I leave it to readers to peruse Wissler's own introduction to the collection for clarification of his decision to utilize the term.

As a long-time student and scholar of the English language with an undergraduate minor in English and an MFA in writing, I understand that the definitions of even common words are an ever-changing landscape in a dynamic society, so today I am willing to let the issue be. Also, as a student of the Blackfoot language for the past twenty-four years, I am aware of major transitions within our words imposed by the changing times, and I accept the shifts although they are departures from old forms that have been lost for posterity. In the orthodox Blackfoot language form, *ai'samoyi*, for example, translates as "a long time ago in olden times," and *misamipaitapi'sinna* translates as "people of long ago," from the root forms *misam* and *isamo*, meaning simply "a long time."

A long time since when? Since the youthful days of Morning Eagle and his inheriting of the stories in this collection from his older relatives? *Mythology of the Blackfoot Indians*, originally published in 1908, caught my attention because it was an old book—an ancient text—when I first saw it in 1983, a seemingly long time ago in itself. Does not the contemporary generation's version of "a long time ago" change as we move further away from the present? When David Charles Duvall was collecting these narratives between 1903 and 1907, my father, who passed on twenty-two years ago, was a mere child. I would surmise, since our tribal population at the time was less than two thousand, that my grandparents likely knew of Duvall and most certainly of his family.

Duvall was positioned to record the pathway of information that linked generations. His decision to set the highest standards for his translating and recording goals assures the reader that his classic work remains legitimate scholarship today. It is clear Wissler had great faith in the talents of Duvall as a chronicler, writer, and translator of the narratives. He was confidant in Duvall's understanding of the nature of the collection work and in his ability to elicit the best the interviewees had to offer. The quality of the scholarship was increased further by Wissler's insistence that Duvall's written accounts keep to the translated narratives of the interviews as closely as possible. So, although the word *mythology* conjures up a sense of a long time ago while, at least to some of us, hinting inadvertently at an unverifiable oral history, *Mythology of the Blackfoot Indians* is an excellent resource describing authentic *ai'samoyi* about *misamipatapi'sinna* still embraced by self-respecting and knowledgeable Blackfoot people today.

As each year passes and the collective tribal memory ascends away from *ai'samoyi*, or "the long ago," the collection serves more and more as the established record of a literature important to the heritage of the tribes. That it was collected by a Blackfoot-speaking chronicler assures and enhances the authentic nature of the accounts. Making it readily available to the public, especially members of the Blackfoot tribes, is of crucial, if not paramount, importance. I have every reason to believe that D. C. Duvall's contributions to the heritage of the Blackfoot people will ultimately be noted for what they represent, and he will be honored with a long-overdue tribute of acknowledgment for his work.

I do not attribute a stamp of authenticity lightly to *Mythology of the Blackfoot Indians*. My knowledge pertaining to the collection did not come about in a purposeful fashion but through a series of fortunate events. In 1987 tribal members founded the Piegan Institute in Browning, Montana (headquarters of the Blackfeet Indian Reservation), to research, promote, and preserve the Blackfoot language. As one of the founders of the institute I was drawn into a full-scale study of the language and formal contact with a significant number of representatives of the older generations of my tribe. Approaching them not as a visiting scholar but as one of their own was unusual enough, and although I was born and raised within the extended family of the tribe, my twenty-year absence, formal education, and inability to speak the language made for an inauspicious start. Were it not for the kindness and patience embodied in their sense of loyalty to our tribal family, I surely would have been dismissed as a mercenary.

It is an obvious fact, supported by a formal survey, that the Blackfoot language was in a fragile state by 1980. With the advent of the reservation period, the language had been outlawed as the spoken word of the tribe, and all the first speakers of the language—those who had learned it as children—were well into their sixth decade. Most telling, it was not being taught to children within the tribe. Several individuals over the years taught interested members as personal tutors but were never able to generate a larger interest among the membership. Those of us involved in the infancy of the revitalization movement soon discovered, as the previous teachers had, that an indoctrination deeming the language as worthless was well imbedded within the contemporary tribal mind view. Early participants were fraught with doubt at the mere notion of studying, learning, and teaching the language and, as I observed, rethinking many of the heritage elements it contained. Younger members—community college students—remained skeptical they could master the language, and the older generations seemed reluctant to break the learned taboo associated with speaking the language.

George and Molly Kicking Woman, Keepers of the Long Time Pipe; Joe Bear Medicine; Francis Potts; Margaret Running Crane; Gertie Heavy Runner; Clara LaPlant; Donald and Lena Little Bull; Dan Bull Plume, a noted artist; Clarence Home Gun; Percy Bull Child, the author of *The Sun Came Down*, an important chronicle itself of the genesis of the Blackfoot people; Thomas Edward Little Plume, acknowledged as a gifted speaker of the language; and significant others over the ensuing years represented authentic connections to our Blackfoot origins in every way. Yet, during the early study period they were often reluctant to discuss a spectrum of heritage items. Many responses came slowly and often with qualification: "Those were the old days . . .," or, "Maybe, it would be

better to ask so and so . . ." It dawned on me that they were simply
being protective and did not want us to get involved in something
we could ultimately pay a social price for. Not until I explained,
for example, that comparative theology simply provided information on religions without proselytizing did they agree to discuss
the holy ceremonies, Old Man, and other stories of the tribe.

As mentioned, during this formative time I obtained a copy of
Mythology of the Blackfoot Indians. My hesitancy to embrace a
book with the word *mythology* in the title was dispelled after a
quick read. Despite my limited, but growing, knowledge of the
contents, I quickly ascertained a certain ring of authenticity
about the work. I immediately brought the book to the group, and
as might be expected there was a casual dismissal since it was
thought to have been written by a non-Blackfoot, or *Napikwan*.
Due to my pitiful knowledge base about tribal family histories, I
did not note D. C. Duvall's tribal membership and failed to mention this important detail. Thankfully, within a short time the
fact was pointed out to me by members of the group. Several of
Duvall's handwritten notes to Wissler were also photocopied at
a Canadian archive, and they enhanced my already deep respect
for his timely endeavor. Ultimately, the assembled granted nodding approval to the stories recorded in *Mythology of the Blackfoot
Indians* for the tales' familiar content and sheer resemblance to
their own versions. Wissler, in his introduction, best serves my
description of this nodding approval with his mention of a conversation he had with a Blood Indian. The man displayed a common
ragweed plant to him and explained, "The parts of this weed all
branch off from the stem. They go different ways, but all come
from the same root." The metaphor illustrates the notion that,
while the stories may vary to a degree, they must remain true to
the root.

Although years have passed since those days of study with the
older people of my tribe (patient as they were with their young
relative), numerous reflections remain fresh in my mind since our
review of *Mythology of the Blackfoot Indians*. One account, number 7 in "Tales of the Old Man" entitled "Old Man and the Great
Spirit," drew extra attention due to the appearance of a cross. In
the story the Great Spirit says to Old Man, "I will make a big
cross for you to carry." Napi, or Old Man, being who he is, natu-

rally comes up with an alternative and tells the Great Spirit, "No, you make another man so that he can carry it." Although Old Man carries the cross for a while, he gets his wish and is sent away to teach the people how to live. The other man, who also gets tired of carrying the cross, turns out to be a *Napikwan*. The Great Spirit sends him off alone to become a traveler. This infusion of a distinct Christian symbol was at first treated with bemusement; it was later attributed to the influence of the church on a particular informant of Duvall's and deemed a contemporary innovation to the story.

It was once common for Blackfoot people to be presented with examples of how their tribal belief systems were compatible with various modern-day activities by well-meaning but obviously misinformed individuals. My sense is that the practice was a misguided form of inclusion, a conversion technique, or an attempt to negotiate some acceptable middle ground within a dichotomy of belief systems. It struck me how the older people, including the devote Christians, would acknowledge the premise, as with the cross in the Old Man story, yet graciously avoid acquiescence. There were the Blackfoot ways and there were others, and although a similar sense of altruism might exist it was not appropriate to merge them. This is an important factor since it is clear even assimilated Blackfoot people preferred the pristine nature of their stories; *Mythology of the Blackfoot Indians* assured them of a standing semblance of order. Is it not then, as the tribal authorities assert, more important to accept the purist nature of origin stories (knowing the shortcomings of translated literature) and derive from them what one can rather than dilute their content to fit into a contemporary viewpoint?

The best way of knowing the quintessential nature of these stories remains, if one is able (*and it is becoming increasingly less likely as tribal languages irretrievably come to their end*), to review them alongside first speakers of the language. For example, in number 17 in "Tales of the Old Man" entitled "Old Man cooks Two Babies" readers surely note the abhorrent and disgustful act of cooking two babies. The story's actual intent, as explained by a fluent Blackfoot speaker with his grandmother advising, concerns the onset of menopause in women or why old women cannot (or should not) have babies. Another common theme is Old Man forever tricking various animals into allowing him to kill, cook, or eat them. Invariably, a pregnant female is spared and survival of the species is assured. This speaks to the rigors of tribal life ways, where the communal clan could perish in a variety of manners, and why a promise for survival was paramount in the wake of pending disaster.

The origin languages of tribes are capable of illustrating these nuances, often lost in the translation, and this is why Wissler's charge to D. C. Duvall to stay as close to the origin language idiom or form as possible is so important. The genius and tenacity of Duvall, and his gift as a first speaker of the language, render his translations as close to the heart as his command of English could bring them. It is apparent that it was more than Clark Wissler expected, and his long-time reliance upon Duvall's recording abilities is evident in all of his major works on the Blackfoot people. *Mythology of the Blackfoot Indians* speaks well of an enduring collaboration chronicling the many lifetimes and stories of the Blackfoot people—much to everyone's good fortune.

INTRODUCTION TO THE BISON BOOKS EDITION
Alice Beck Kehoe

"Why a reservation, what was it that urged the writer to visit and revisit these out-of-the-way-places?" Clark Wissler (1971:9) realized it seemed strange that an educated man from Muncie, Indiana, should choose to spend so many months, again and again, in the log cabins of dusty Plains hamlets. Why a reservation? "The Indian is perpetuated in memory as the most original and conspicuous feature of our romantic history" (Wissler 1971:10). Wissler had seen boys "playing Indian" even in Australia. Were the Indians wilderness savages? Deeply fascinated by human behavior, Clark Wissler (1870–1947) felt drawn to the reservations, where he could find men and women who had lived in societies radically different from the agricultural states of his own heritage. A boyhood tramping fields collecting Indian artifacts, a youth teaching in rural schools, and formal education in the new field of psychology led Wissler into anthropology in 1902. James McKeen Cattell, director of Wissler's doctoral dissertation in psychology, headed a Columbia University joint department of psychology and anthropology until 1902. Cattell and Franz Boas, who took over the newly separated department of anthropology, enjoyed adjoining offices. Wissler took courses from Boas and the other anthropologist, Livingston Farrand. Wissler's fellow graduate student Alfred L. Kroeber claimed the shift from psychology to anthropology as a profession was a practical choice—in 1902, the jobs for young doctorates were in anthropology.

Also in 1902 the American Museum of Natural History separated its archaeology program from ethnology, naming Franz Boas the curator of ethnology (simultaneous with his teaching position at Columbia) and authorizing him to hire an assistant. Boas selected Clark Wissler, whom he sent in the summer to the northern plains to conduct fieldwork and retained in the winter to carry out museum duties. Boas left the American Museum in 1905 after quarreling with wealthy patron Morris Jesup. Marshall Saville, the curator of archaeology, left the same year and, like Boas, took a full-time position at Columbia (McVicker 1992:149). Clark Wissler first became acting curator of ethnology, then curator the next year. In 1907 he became curator of a recombined Department of Anthropology, which he administered most ably and amiably until his retirement in 1942 (Freed and Freed 1983:808).

Wissler's fieldwork was concentrated in the years 1902–5, when he was assistant in ethnology. For the museum he collected artifacts and ethnographic information on various Sioux reservations, but his major accomplishment was a magnificent series of monographs on the Blackfoot. That series, beginning with *Mythology of the Blackfoot* in 1908, is a collaborative work with D. C. Duvall. In 1909, Wissler suffered an illness that kept him frail until 1928, when he was nearly sixty. By that time, administrative duties and service as officer in a number of learned and professional organizations, as well as teaching one day a week at Yale University from 1924 to 1940, precluded fieldwork. Perhaps the loss in 1911 of his gifted and dedicated Blackfoot collaborator also discouraged Wissler from attempting later fieldwork; Wissler was reticent about his personal feelings, but his correspondence with James Eagle Child, engaged to carry on after Duvall's death, reveals great frustration with the less committed younger man.

D. C. (David Charles) Duvall (1877–1911) was the son of the French Canadian Charles Duvall, who died when David was about six, and Yellow Bird (Louise Big Plume), daughter of the Pikuni Big Plume and Kills At Night. Charles was employed at Fort Benton, where he married Yellow Bird, and she remained there for about three years after her husband died, then returned to the Blackfeet Reservation. Duvall was called Tanatski (*anátsski*), "Pretty Face." His sisters were Lillie Bennett, who had been kidnapped by a friend of her father's when he died and was brought up in Missouri; Minnie Huffman, who married a non-Indian, living off the reservation until her death in 1910; and half-sister Margaret Eagle Head, married to Hart Merriam Schultz (son of the popular writer James Willard Schultz and his Pikuni first wife Fine Shield Woman). In 1900 Duvall married Gretchen, daughter of Good Gun (Running Wolf) and Lone Woman. They eventually divorced, and he married Cecile Trombley in January 1911. He had no children

Blackfeet (Southern Piegan) guides Tom Sanderville and No Coat Running Crane overlooking Badger Creek, 1921. There is a *piskun* (bison pound) below the valley rim on which the men sit. Duvall and Wissler traveled about the reservation in a similar manner. Courtesy Milwaukee Public Museum (103917).

(DeMarce 1980:93, 95). At the time of his suicide, he was separated from Cecile (letter from Superintendent McFatridge to Wissler, 20 July 1911, Wissler papers, AMNH).

Yellow Bird's brother was Eagle Child, one of Wissler's principal informants and father of James. Yellow Bird married Jappy Takes Gun on Top about 1894 after living for three years with Eagle Head and bearing him a daughter, Margaret. Yellow Bird had four children with Jappy, none surviving infancy. The census recorded that after Charlie Duvall died, she had lived two years with a Homer Gregg before her common-law marriage with Eagle Head. Her son David spent some boyhood years at Fort Hall Indian School, Idaho.

Clark Wissler met Dave Duvall in 1903 at Browning, the agency town of the Blackfeet Reservation. Duvall worked there as a blacksmith in his own shop located a block west of the town square, and rented a home in town. He considered the Pikunis "his people" and Wissler engaged him to interpret, which soon excited in the young man "an ambition to become [the Blackfoot language's] most accurate translator into English. . . . On his own initiative he set out to master the more obscure and less used parts of his mother tongue. . . . As time went on, he began to assist in collecting narratives and statements from the older people" ("In Memoriam," *Social Life of the Blackfoot Indians* [1912, p. ii]). During the half-dozen years of his intensive collaboration with Wissler, Duvall's skill in writing English, as well as his understanding of Blackfoot, grew rapidly until he felt competent to embark on his own lengthy manuscript of Blackfoot mythology, which he sent in chapters to his mentor but was left unpublished at his death.

Asking about Duvall fifty years after his death, Robert Scriver, a lifelong resident of Browning, was told he was called "that 'French Man' who was always asking a lot of questions about the old Indian ways, always carried a notebook with him, the old people were apparently eager to have him record their culture. Duvall of course spoke Blackfeet fluently and was educated enough to translate what he was told so that Wissler could put it down in his reports" (personal communication, Robert Scriver, 14 April 1994). In January 1911, Duvall asked Wissler for "one of those talking machines" to "get the songs" of the elders he interviewed. Wissler replied on 7 January: "I . . . will think the matter over. One trouble is that owing to the delicacy of the mechanism, considerable experience is necessary to operate it" (Wissler papers, American Museum of Natural History, hereafter AMNH).

Early in their collaboration, Wissler commissioned Duvall principally to collect items of material culture. Duvall frequently engaged craftspeople to make the requested items for Wissler—for example, a "Baby Board." On 12 October 1904, Duvall wrote Wissler that "Mrs. Yellow Wolf is making the Baby Board and her mother is making the dog travois," then on 10 November, "Mrs. Yellow Wolf, and Boy, also failed to make some of the things. . . . Gretchen will make [the baby board] as soon as we can get the material" (Wissler papers, AMNH). What made Duvall invaluable to Wissler was his understanding of the scientific nature of the ethnographic enterprise. Duvall wrote on 24 November 1905: "Dr. Clark Wissler . . . I got your other letter and check. I will have those other thing[s] in a week or more. About that travois I think I will have it made a little different from the one I send to you. Some says that they are two ways making them. One like the one you have and another like this one I have drawing on the back of this letter. this is the only change the round cross pace [piece] the rest is all alike" (Wissler papers, AMNH).

That understanding of the importance of checking with more than one informant, and recording variance in detail, encouraged Wissler to work by correspondence with Duvall over the winters. By 27 January 1906, Wissler's confidence in Duvall led him to write

> I have looked over the story you sent as a sample and find it quite satisfactorily done. Now, the kind of stories that I want are a little different although I can use the one you sent very well. The kind I want are such as I took when we were working together. For all such stories as well written as the one you sent me I can pay at a rate of about ten cents per hundred words. At this rate the one you sent would amount to something over $2.00. . . . I send you a copy of one that I took with you that you may have in hand one of the kind that we can use and also I should like if you would make such changes in it as may be necessary so as to make it as much like the real story as possible. Of course in rewriting this I have put in our own style, but should like your own copy to be written as nearly in the Indian style as possible. If you care to go on with this work I should like to have you go over all the stories I took in the same way." (Wissler papers, AMNH)

Typically, Duvall would interview elders in their homes and then send Wissler the manuscript. Wissler would critically review the material and return to Duvall a number of sheets, each with a query written in longhand, or a set of queries (with spaces between them for the answers) typed on one sheet. Duvall was to take the queries to informants and fill in or clarify the points raised and later return the completed sheets to Wissler. In a letter to Wissler dated 10 March 1911, Duvall remarked: "I can get in more time and do better when I have a number of different papers to work on, as the people are liveing far a part and I may put in a whole day in getting to one man, and then the man may only know a little about one thing. now when I have more papers I can always find some one to work with every day and work more steadily" (Wissler papers, AMNH).

This mode of collaboration, with the half-Indian resident ethnographer taking considerable initiative in developing the inquiries and the academically credentialed anthropologist an exacting editor organizing the data to facilitate comparative studies, was modeled for Wissler by his teacher Boas, who worked thus with his Scots-Tlingit collaborator George Hunt residing in Prince Rupert with the Kwakwaka'wakw (Kwakiutl). Duvall kept account of the time and postage he spent on Wissler's assignments, sending weekly itemized bills.

In May 1911, Duvall asked Wissler whether he would be requiring his services as interpreter during the coming summer; if not, ethnologist Walter McClintock wished to hire him. Duvall had sold his blacksmith shop the previous year and needed work (letter of 3 October 1910, Wissler papers, AMNH). Wissler replied that he didn't expect to be out that summer, nor was he planning active correspondence: "I shall have nothing for you after the first of May until next winter." He encouraged "Mr. Duvall" (who always signed himself "D. C. Duvall") to accept McClintock's employment. (McClintock had himself inquired of Wissler in April whether he would be requiring Duvall's assistance.) By June, Wissler was planning ahead: "I am not sure of our plans for next year [but] should like to arrange with you to go to the Northern Blackfoot and the Blood Reservation, starting at such time in the fall as may be convenient to you. . . . [S]pend at least two months working on such points as I may direct you . . . [and] at least a month on the Blood Reservation on similar work" (letter 9 June 1911, Wissler papers, AMNH). Duvall wrote in reply from Badger Creek on 19 June that he had been a foreman for the past month and a half on a project digging irrigation ditches in the Heart Butte district. He expected to work on the ditch crew until July haying time, then to spend a month working with Walter McClintock and his brother (Wissler papers, AMNH).

But within a month Wissler received a letter from Duvall's nephew, James Eagle Child, with shocking news (dated 18 July): "Dav. committed suicide. Shoot him self in head. . . . [We] could not be learn what he had done such a thing as he did. . . . He never said he was going to do it or write any note. I think a little trouble over his wife. . . . His people here are all taking it pertty hard" (Wissler papers, AMNH). Duvall was buried in the Browning Catholic cemetery, in the section for unbaptized children and suicides. Robert

Scriver was unable to locate the grave (personal communication, 14 April 1994).

Wissler wrote to the Indian agent at Browning, 21 July 1911: "Whatever weaknesses Duvall may have had he took a deep interest in recording the history of the Blackfoot tribes and so far as we know, faithfully discharged all his obligations to us. He had linguistic ability of a high order. May he rest in peace!" (undated letter draft, Wissler papers, AMNH). To the director of the American Museum, Wissler wrote of Duvall: "For many years he was one of our most productive non-resident field workers. Jointly with me he published in our series a work on the Mythology of the Blackfoot Indians and made important contributions to two others. There are now on file about 750 pages of unpublished manuscript contributed by him during the past year, all containing hitherto unknown data on the anthropology of the Blackfoot" (Wissler papers, AMNH).

In his semifictionalized memoirs of his ethnographic work, Wissler described Duvall under the pseudonym of "Sunray":

He also had a white father whose memory he cherished as a successful gambler, a career he secretly envied but could not follow. Sunray was bright, had done fairly well in an Indian boarding school, and learned to make harness, a trade which gave him part-time employment around the agency. But he really enjoyed taking me about and took an intelligent interest in helping me with my notes. Often around the camp-fire he opened his mind. He saw no future in his trade. What galled him most was that no one trusted him. He was loyal to me but I heard that he was tricky at times and grasping. His favorite game was to over-charge for his services. When I parted from him the last time, he seemed melancholy.

"You are a white man," he said. "You have a place among your people, you count for something. Around us here are Indians, they revere their past, they have the respect of their fellows. Here I am, neither an Indian nor a white man—just nothing."

I did what I could to encourage him, to suggest that he could be a white man if he set out to be, though I had secret misgivings about the soundness of this advice. We parted and Sunray returned to his job. But a year or two later he blew out his brains. Poor Sunray! Our ethical code frowns upon such a deed, but there always rises the question, "What else could he do?" [Wissler 1971:194–95]

Wissler prepared the wealth of data recorded by Duvall for serial publication in the *Anthropological Papers of the American Museum of Natural History,* under the titles "Material Culture of the Blackfoot Indians" (1910), "Social Life of the Blackfoot Indians" (1911), "Ceremonial Bundles of the Blackfoot Indians" (1912), and "Societies and Dance Associations of the Blackfoot Indians" (1913). Only the first volume, this 1908 publication on mythology, lists Duvall as coauthor, but it is clear from the 1912 correspondence between Wissler and James Eagle Child that Duvall alone had the intelligence and diplomacy to elicit from the elder men and women the data on nineteenth-century Blackfoot culture that Wissler would publish.

THE BLACKFOOT STUDIED BY WISSLER AND DUVALL

The Blackfoot[1] comprise three allied nations on the northwestern plains of southern Alberta and southwestern Saskatchewan, Canada, and adjacent north-central Montana. They speak a distinctive language of the Central Algonquian stock. In their own language, the Blackfoot call themselves *niitsítapii,* 'Indian, real people.' The members of the confederation are the *káínaa* 'many chiefs,' but called in English "Bloods"; *siksiká,* 'black foot'; *piikánii,* divided into two groups, *aamsskáapipiikánii* 'south Pikunis' and *aapátuxsipiikánii,* 'north Pikunis.' The Kainaa's name for themselves is self-explanatory. The Siksikas' name refers to people whose moccasin soles were blackened. Pikunis—the closer English spelling, formerly spelled Peigans (in Canada) or Piegans (in the United States)—were said to take their name from wearing scruffy robes scraped too hastily to be properly finished. Each nation was a loose set of autonomous bands making a living by hunting bison.

In 1691 the young Hudson's Bay Company explorer Henry Kelsey, traveling from York Factory on Hudson's Bay, reached in south-central Saskatchewan the frontier between Indians willing to trade directly with his employers, and Archithinue to the west. Archithinue did not use canoes, disliked eating fish, would not trap

[1]Black*foot* is the Canadian and preferred scholarly spelling, Black*feet* the U.S. reservation name and common usage.

beaver, and saw no reason to undertake the months-long journey to the posts at the Bay. The name "Archithinue," applied by Kelsey's Cree and Assiniboine companions, is a Cree word that means "foreigner, stranger, enemy": the people probably were Blackfoot and their Algonquian-speaking allies the Gros Ventres (Atsina, or 'white clay people').

At this historic contact in 1691, Blackfoot dominated the territory from longitude 105°, near Regina in central Saskatchewan, west to the Front Range of the Rockies in Alberta and Montana, and from the Red Deer River, halfway between Edmonton and Calgary in Alberta, south to the Yellowstone in southern Montana. Their allies the Gros Ventres were their eastern flank, in Saskatchewan, and an allied Dené group, the Sarsis, buffered their northwestern border. Distinctive pottery found in late prehistoric-protohistoric sites and boulder constructions historically built by Blackfoot, of which one example has been radiocarbon-dated to the fifteenth century, suggest continuous occupation of their territory by Blackfoot since the fifteenth century; whether their ancestors were in the territory earlier is controversial (Duke 1991).

Whoever was in the northwestern plains before the fifteenth century—and possibilities include the Kutenais, who historically took refuge in the mountain valleys west of the Front Range, and the ancestors of the Apacheans (Navajos and Apaches) of the American Southwest, as well as Blackfoot—the people adapted to the high, windy prairie by perfecting the skill of impounding bison herds and using every part of the slaughtered animals. Bison hides were sewn to make wind-resistant, portable tipis, or, with the hair left on, they were made into bedding and robes; bones were chopped up and boiled to extract nutritious marrow and fat; meat was boiled or wind-dried for later consumption; tools were manufactured from bones; hair was mixed with plant fibers for weaving or braided into rope; horns were made into ladles; rawhide and paunches served as containers; and of course buffalo chips gathered on the prairies were used as fuel for fires. Essential as the bison herds were, camas (*misisǽǽ* in Blackfoot; *Camassia quamash*) and prairie turnips (*má's* in Blackfoot, Indian breadroot, *Psoralea esculenta*) were necessary carbohydrate foods. Both were harvested with knowledgeable care so that the uprooting of those selected for harvest enhanced the growing conditions for the remaining plants. Women were in charge of the harvesting and taught their daughters to sustain responsibly the species used by the people. Berries were gathered in season by picnicking parties of women and children and were dried in quantity to add important vitamins to the diet. They were eaten mixed with pounded dried meat and fat as pemmican, or with ground root flour to make thick soup or pudding. Blackfoot bands moved camp about twenty times each year in a carefully scheduled round of peak harvests of bison and plants, winter shelter, and trading post visit (Kehoe 1993:89).

To live on the high plains, the Blackfoot spent most of the year in camps of from ten to twenty lodges, numbering about 80 to 160 people. This band size had enough able-bodied men and women to operate the bison drive lane and pound and process the carcasses. For much of the year, the bison herds, ranging from twenty to seventy adult females with their calves and bulls, were roughly similar in size to the camps of their human predators. Both bison and humans wintered in sheltered valleys, and both congregated in summer into concourses of thousands, the bison feeding on the thick-growing grasses and the humans on the bison. Humans and bison alike found mates in the big summer rendezvous camps, where people indulged in trading, feasting, gambling, adjudication of disputes, strategic planning among allies, and religious ceremonies. The summer rendezvous camps were a kind of town that, like villages in fantasy, came alive periodically and then disappeared as into mists. Being able to join together in communities of thousands, if only for a few weeks each year, enabled the Blackfoot to maintain a sense of nationhood and appropriate civil institutions.

Although Plains Indians are conventionally pictured as subsistence hunters, trade played a major role in their economies. Alberta archaeologist Jack Brink, noting that the largest bison pounds seem to be located reasonably near rivers, inferred that the processed yields from these kills were transported downriver to be traded for maize, Knife River flint, ornamental shells, and, by the early seventeenth century, European goods. The European fur trade directly reached the northwestern plains with Buckingham House on the North Saskatchewan River in 1780 and then Rocky Mountain House in 1799 on the upper reach of the North Saskatchewan, and Fort George and Fort Vermillion farther east on it, all just beyond Blackfoot territory; then in 1800, Chesterfield

House was established within it, where the Red Deer River meets the South Saskatchewan. A typical Blackfoot trading party brought, as to Fort George in 1794, eight hundred pounds of pounded dried meat and more than enough fat to mix with it to produce pemmican, plus skins of eight hundred wolves and twelve bears, and twenty bison robes (Morgan 1991:165). Blackfoot refused to meet the demands of European traders for beaver; Morgan (1991:179) suggests the Indians realized the crucial role played by beaver dams in maintaining sources of water in the dry months on the northwestern plains. Throughout the nineteenth century until the bison herds were exterminated, Blackfoot supplied commercial quantities of pemmican and bison robes to the trading posts vying for their custom.

With trade went intimate knowledge of a extensive section of western North America. Positioned as they were at the Front Range of the Rockies, the Blackfoot participated in the trade of the Missouri and Saskatchewan basins to the east and the transmontane trade down the Snake and Columbia rivers to the west. They also traveled along the Old North Trail, just east of the foothills of the Rockies, from the edge of the Subarctic tundra to Mexico (McClintock 1910:434–40). The map that Lewis and Clark used for the Missouri Basin and west to the Columbia was based on cartograms drawn for Hudson's Bay Company factor Peter Fidler in 1801 and 1802 by the Blackfoot leader Ac ko mok ki ("The Feathers") (Kehoe 1993:94).

Horses and guns shifted balances of power throughout the plains during the eighteenth and early nineteenth century. Blackfoot refer to the times before they owned horses as the "dog days," for then they depended on a sturdy breed of dog as pack and draft animal. Dogs continued to be bred to carry backpacks and pull small travois well into the nineteenth century. However, after the Blackfoot had seen their rivals to the southwest, the Shoshones (Snakes), riding horses into battle about 1730, the Blackfoot, too, needed these superior animals that could dash in and out of fights as well as carry loads several times heavier than any dog could bear. By 1754, "Archithinue" in southern Alberta, who most likely were Blackfoot, kept herds of horses trained to maneuver in hunting bison. At that time, these Archithinue obtained guns in trade from the Assiniboines, the vanguard of the European trade on the Canadian prairies. The range permitted by guns gave the Blackfoot the advantage over the Shoshones, who had only bows. With firearms, the eighteenth-century Blackfoot conquered central Montana—as their rivals to the east, Crees and Assiniboines supplied with guns and ammunition directly from the European posts, pushed them and the Gros Ventres out of central Saskatchewan. The opening of the nineteenth century saw the Blackfoot holding the high plains of southern Alberta and Montana to the Front Range, contesting the Saskatchewan border with Crees and Assiniboines, the Rocky Mountain passes with Kutenais, Salish, and Shoshones, and the Yellowstone headwaters with Crows.

Ac ko mok ki's maps revealed Blackfoot territory to Americans, but he and his countrymen resolutely held off invading trappers and traders. Meriwether Lewis in 1806, searching for the head of the Marias River, had entered what is now the Blackfeet Reservation, met a group of Blackfoot, and killed two who tried to steal a gun from his party during the night. Lewis and his men escaped retribution, but Blackfoot took the lives of dozens of Euroamerican trappers, whose activities threatened Blackfoot political economy. By 1832, the American Fur Company had negotiated the establishment of a trading post near the mouth of the Marias, and it was here that Prince Maximilian of Wied and his companion, the artist Karl Bodmer, studied and depicted Blackfoot in 1833. Maximilian estimated the number of Blackfoot at nearly twenty thousand persons. They were sharply reduced by a smallpox epidemic carried on the riverboat to the fort in 1837. Ten years later, the American Fur Company built Fort Benton on the Missouri, the southern border of Blackfoot country. Fort Benton became the principal American trading post in the northwestern plains, competing with the Hudson's Bay Company posts along the Saskatchewan and its tributaries. Advantaged by cheaper steamboat transportation on the Missouri, in contrast to the canoe brigades used by the Hudson's Bay posts, Fort Benton could buy thousands of bison hides from the Blackfoot and sell imported goods at appealing prices. Yellow Bird's marriage to Fort Benton employee Charlie Duvall was one consequence.

The first treaty between the United States and Blackfoot was signed in 1855. It was intended to inaugurate a shift in Blackfoot life from nomadic bison hunting to sedentary farming with cattle raised on pastures. "Civilization and Christianization" would be promoted—and, not incidentally, roads, garrisons, and whatever else might consolidate U.S. control over the territory. Canada was a generation later in treaty making. It was only in 1877 that the calamitous disappearance of the bison herds forced the Indian peoples to accept Euroamerican domination. An astute observer would have noted that the herds seemed to have retreated westward for fifty years, from the eastern plains borderlands by 1830, to the eastern prairies and hilly refugia in the 1860s, to the western prairies—Blackfoot territory—in the 1870s. By late 1878, no more pemmican was available to Hudson's Bay Company posts and thousands of Indians in the northwestern plains faced starvation (Carter 1990:35–36,80). Two dozen Canadian Blackfoot starved to death in 1879 (Ewers 1958:279), and over the winter of 1883–84, nearly six hundred Pikunis were reported to have starved to death, their destitution exacerbated by a Congressional committee's decision that the appropriation for rations be reduced by the $100,000 allocated for irrigation projects (Ewers 1958:294; Samek 1987: 41,72).

Starvation had capped a decade of horror that began with the third of the major smallpox epidemics suffered by the Blackfoot (the first was in 1781, the second 1837). During the winter of the 1869–70 epidemic, a U.S. Army force assaulted a Pikuni camp on the Marias River, seeking revenge for the murder of a Euroamerican rancher married to a Pikuni. Though the camp was the band led by the cooperative chief Heavy Runner, more than a hundred men and at least fifty-five women and children were massacred (Ewers 1958:250). The 1870s was the decade of whisky forts, unregulated posts built just north of the Canadian border after the Hudson's Bay Company had ceded its domain to the newly created Dominion of Canada. Freely selling liquor in the Blackfoot heartland, the whisky forts were responsible for the intoxication that resulted in hundreds of fatal brawls or drunken collapse often ending in death from exposure. Euroamerican settlers infiltrated Blackfoot country on both sides of the international border during this decade. The Great Northern Reservation, created for Montana Plains Indians in 1873, reached from the Missouri River to the Canadian border; but then, under protest from settlers, its southern portion was rescinded in 1874. Even the appointed Indian agent resisted the restriction of the Blackfoot to the northern sector of the territory; for his principled stand, he was dismissed. Extinction of the bison herds was the final blow to the Indian nations of the northwestern plains.

Some two thousand Pikunis survived the Starvation Winter of 1883–84 and settled into villages within a day's ride of the agency on Badger Creek (Ewers 1958:298). A commission negotiated a further reduction of the reservation in 1886, releasing its eastern portion to settlers. Cattle were issued to replace bison hunting with ranching, more feasible than farming on the high plains. From the construction of the Great Northern Railroad across the reservation in the 1890s, which enabled steers to be shipped to Midwest markets, some of the Pikuni families became relatively prosperous. Schools were built, most operated by Christian missions; European clothing ("citizens dress") replaced the indigenous; craftwork—even women's beadwork—was discouraged; and native religious practices were forbidden. Domination reached to the dead, who were ordered to be interred rather than wrapped and placed on high places (a compromise was wooden grave houses, the corpse wrapped within and a hole left for the spirit to pass through). Mourners who rent their garments and cut off finger joints, a traditional expression of grief, were jailed by Captain L. W. Cook, the acting agent in 1894 (Ewers 1958:311). Fortunately for Wissler's researches, twentieth-century agents were less fanatic in "civilizing" their charges, and rituals and crafts persisted.

Wissler first visited the Blackfeet Reservation in 1903. Four years later, the Bureau of Indian Affairs decreed that the common land must be allotted in severalty to individual Indians, who would reside in monogamous households (a policy established by the Dawes Act of 1887). Under the Dawes Act, "surplus" land remaining after a formula allocation per enrolled Indian could be sold to non-Indian settlers. The Euroamerican conviction that the road to civilization was a straight and narrow one through agriculture motivated the BIA to encourage Indian families to take allotments of farmland, rather than ranchland. Extensive irrigation ditches dug beginning in the 1880s were supposed to be the key to agriculture. On the Blackfeet Reservation, Indian agents pragmatically continued them as the only source of wage employment for most

Buffalo Body, his wife (Shield Woman?), and daughter, photographed in 1921 when Buffalo Body was about sixty-three. The cabin is typical of reservation housing at the time of Duvall and Wissler's collaboration. Buffalo Body was half-brother to Heavy Gun's two wives. Courtesy Milwaukee Public Museum (103892).

men of the tribe. Duvall was a foreman on one of these ditch proj-
ects in the spring before his suicide in July 1911. After 1918, many
Pikunis were declared competent to decide to sell their allotments,
a measure taken after the 1919 drought, followed by a severe winter, killed thousands of livestock (Ewers 1958:319)—and the
1918–19 influenza pandemic killed Blackfoot, though historians
have neglected to mention this. From the nadir of 1919 began a
slow rebuilding of ranching, aided by the 1934 Indian Reorganiza-
tion Act of Roosevelt's New Deal administration. Today the Blackfoot, on both sides of the international border, remain generally
impoverished, but they remain Blackfoot: the language is still
widely spoken, tribal colleges have been created to combine formal
education with heritage programs, and the stories recorded by Duvall for Wissler and the American Museum's research program are
still told.

THE BLACKFOOT AS SUBJECTS OF STUDY

The Blackfoot typified the historical Plains Indians—they were
nomadic bison hunters who lived in portable tipis. When that way
of life disappeared with the extinction of the wild bison herds, anthropologists felt obligated to record descriptions of the vanished
life from the survivors on the reservations. George Bird Grinnell,
naturalist and editor of the magazine *Forest and Stream,* collected
notes and stories from Blackfoot as well as Pawnees and Chey-
ennes along with his observations on wildlife; *Blackfoot Lodge
Tales* (1892) remains a sound volume of well-told stories. Among
Grinnell's acquaintances in the field was James Willard Schultz,
who came west to Montana in 1877 and worked for Joe Kipp, the
trader on the Blackfeet Reservation. Schultz married a Pikuni who
bore him a son, Hart; left the reservation upon being widowed in
1903; and by his death in 1947 had written thirty-seven books,
many centering on the Pikunis. His most famous, *My Life as an Indian* (1907), romanticized his involvement with the Blackfoot; he
has been praised as a "born storyteller," but born storytellers are
not scrupulous about historical facts. The Reverend John Maclean,
a Methodist missionary in Alberta, published a series of notes from
his work with the Canadian Blackfoot in the 1890s, culminating in
Canadian Savage Folk (1896); the general tone of his volume is indicated by its title. Quite the opposite was Walter McClintock, a

young American employed in 1896 on a U.S. Forest Service project to determine forest preserves. McClintock was impressed by the Blackfoot with whom he camped in subsequent summers, recorded his observations and stories told him, checked his notes with the counsel of several leading scholars including Clark Wissler, and in 1910, published his ethnography in a lively narrative framework with copious photographs he had taken. Where Schultz reveled in his role as squaw-man, McClintock wryly noted, "It was necessary to do my own cooking . . . I had not taken a wife" (McClintock 1910:23).

Professional anthropologists after Clark Wissler included the Dutch linguist C. C. Uhlenbeck, who transcribed a series of myths and reminiscences from May to August 1910, mostly around Holy Family Mission on Two Medicine River. Uhlenbeck relied on Joe Tatsey, whose father was a Blood and mother half Pikuni. Tatsey had married a Pikuni and was living on Birch Creek, the southern border of the Blackfeet Reservation. With the bilingual Tatsey's close collaboration, Uhlenbeck published two volumes of texts, Blackfoot and English translation on facing pages (1911, 1912). Uhlenbeck's translations are the closest we have to Blackfoot narrative style in the early reservation period, and he identifies the narrators. There was then a hiatus of sorts in anthropological study, filled instead with the collecting of artifacts and their use, together with depictions of their former owners posed in elaborate regalia, to publicize the Great Northern Railroad's tourist hotels in Glacier National Park (Walton, Ewers, and Hassrick 1985). Study by anthropologists resumed in 1938 and 1939, this time by a group of graduate students brought from Columbia University by their professor, Ruth Benedict. Out of Benedict's loosely supervised on-the-job training program came a set of published monographs by Lucien and Jane Richardson Hanks (1945, 1950), Esther Goldfrank (1945), and Oscar Lewis (1942). Next was John C. Ewers, a student of Wissler at Yale, who in 1941 began a four-year residence in Browning as first curator of the Museum of the Plains Indian. Ewers published a series of papers, books, and popular articles on the Blackfoot, of which the most notable is his broadly conceived *The Horse in Blackfoot Indian Culture* (1955).

The second half of the twentieth century has seen a variety of studies from Blackfoot data. Claude Schaeffer followed Ewers as

Curator of the Museum of the Plains Indian; he collected texts but published little. Hugh A. Dempsey, a British-born historian who married into the prominent Blood family of James Gladstone, has published many scholarly articles and biographies of Blackfoot individuals ranging from the chiefs Crowfoot and Red Crow to the tragic Charcoal, driven to suicide after he killed his younger wife's lover. George and Louise Spindler carried out psychological anthropological research on the Blood Reserve, published in the 1960s; and their student Malcolm McFee in the same period, 1959–60, observed the contemporary Pikunis, publishing *Modern Blackfeet: Montanans on a Reservation* (1972). Blackfoot data have been used for examinations of feminist issues (e.g., Kehoe 1976, 1983), to illuminate cosmological constructions (Kehoe 1991, 1992), and to demolish stereotypes of Indian life (Kehoe 1993). Popular thirst for romanticized Indian lore has been catered to by Adolf Gutohrlein, an Austrian-born Californian whose odyssey as a 1960s hippie led him to the Blood Reserve, where he was tagged "Hungry Wolf." Assisted by his Blood wife Beverly Little Bear, Adolf Hungry Wolf cobbled together the couple's own ethnographic work with excerpts from published works. By the 1980s, the creation of Native American Studies programs in universities and of tribal colleges on reservations, in tandem with the development of contemporary American Indian literature and a shift in anthropology toward recognizing Indian-language narrators and poets as literary creators worthy of analysis, have produced a rapidly growing body of texts in both English and indigenous languages. Of these, the Pikuni-Gros Ventre novelist James Welch is particularly to be noted here, his works including *Fools Crow* (1986), a story of the dramatic year 1870, and *The Indian Lawyer* (1990), in contrast a realistic study of a successful contemporary Pikuni.

WISSLER AND DUVALL'S MONOGRAPH

Wissler intended to present the culture of the Blackfoot as it was held in common. He realized that in actuality each individual held a somewhat idiosyncratic variation, that a canonical corpus neither existed nor was desired by the Blackfoot (p. 5). Although recognizing the nonexistence of a standard version, Wissler did not question that his goal should be the resolution of the variants into, as it were, a set of type specimens of myths, to be placed in the American Museum collections along with the type specimens of travois, medicine bundles, and moccasins. The concept that each society has "a" culture, and anthropologists seek to discover "the" culture, derived from early nineteenth century Romanticism closely tied to nationalist movements—that is, repudiation of imperial control by burgeoning regional political economies was legitimated by claiming empires repressed the true cultural souls of their constituent indigenous nations. By the later nineteenth century, the overseas conquests of imperial powers, as well as their oppression of their own peasantries, were phrased as the White Man's Burden, to "civilize" the millions said to be mired in "backward" cultures. A dichotomy was set up contrasting alleged static, unchanging "traditional" cultures of "primitives" and peasants against the dynamic, inventive bourgeois culture of the imperial West. The conquest and degradation of American Indians called for a salvage ethnography to collect the memories of the culture-bearers now adapting to reservations, a salvage comparable to the collection of fauna and flora likely to go extinct as the "wilderness" was cleared for agriculture and cities: having existed on God's earth, they should not be wholly obliterated, but specimens should be preserved in museums for comparative scientific study. Thus Wissler began, in 1903, to collect artifacts and then myths from the reservation Blackfoot. Dave Duvall initially worked as an interpreter, scrabbling to supplement the meager income from his blacksmith shop. His unusual intelligence and gift for ethnographic interviewing allowed Wissler to commission him to work on his own. With relatively little formal education, Duvall did not question the goals presented by Dr. Wissler the trained scientist. Because Wissler had met many Blackfoot during the months he had himself worked on the reservation, the correspondence between him and Duvall seldom required much identification of Duvall's informants. The goal of discovering and recording "the" culture and "the" mythology meant that the informants need only be reasonably respected, articulate adult participants in pre-reservation life. Variation in their reminiscences should be recorded only as examples of the raw data reworked into single exemplary narratives in good English. Where Uhlenbeck and Joe Tatsey labored to transcribe and translate as closely as possible to

Tribal council meeting at Heart Butte, 1921. "Citizens dress" was normally worn
by Southern Piegan men in Duvall's time. Courtesy Milwaukee Public Museum
(104451).

idiomatic Blackfoot, Duvall wrote his notes in good English style.
If he took notes in Blackfoot, they have not been recovered; possi-
bly he translated as he wrote in the cabins of his informants. Seldom were data precisely attributed: the best clue to who told what
is in the weekly ledger accounts Duvall mailed to Wissler, detail-
ing the hours with Big-brave, Red-plume, etc., and the fees paid to
them.

Checking Duvall's account sheets against the 1907–8 Allotment
Census published in 1980 as *Blackfeet Heritage,* it appears that
most of his informants were middle-aged men between forty and
sixty, veterans of the last decades of Blackfoot independence. Set-
tlement was initially largely by bands, so Duvall's informants, living in the hamlet of Heart Butte and along the creeks south of
Browning, tended to cluster both geographically and through kinship. Big-brave's aunts, two sisters, were wives of Heavy-gun;
Black-bear was first cousin to Heavy-gun; and these men, as well
as Red-plume, were members of the band led in 1869 by Big-brave's

father, Mountain Chief. (Red-plume and Big-brave star in a story published by Schultz [1962:271–81].) When Duvall journeyed to Heart Butte, he could interview Big-brave, Heavy-gun, and several other men, including Owl Top Feathers and Tom Kiyo.

Of all the informants listed frequently in Duvall's accounts, the most favored seems to have been Tom Kiyo, owner of Head Carrier's Beaver Bundle, which he ceremonially opened in 1911 so that Duvall could take notes on the ritual (Wissler 1912:177). Tom Kiyo (*kiááyo,* 'bear') is listed in the 1890 census as twenty-eight years old and married to the nineteen-year-old Good Medicine. Neither Grinnell nor McClintock mentions a Tom Kiyo/Kyaiyo among his informants. Inquiry in Browning brought recollections that he lived in Heart Butte in the 1920s. His name evokes a story frequently told around that village, of Father Le Seuer, a Catholic mission priest, intruding upon a bundle-opening ceremony conducted in Kiyo's home. The priest, who spoke Blackfoot, lashed out at the crowd and kicked the holy bundle. Tom Kiyo said to him, "You'll pay for this!" Returning to the mission, the horse pulling the priest's buggy stampeded, the buggy tipped over, and the priest's leg—the leg with which he kicked the bundle—was broken. Later, the priest cursed Tom Kiyo, "You'll never get another wife," and Tom Kiyo never did (personal communication, Darrell Kipp, 10 June 1994; Robert Scriver, 4 June 1994).

Other informants whom Wissler named in later monographs are New-breast, Mad-plume (uncle to New-breast's wife), Curley-bear, and Jappy Takes-gun-on-top, who, although only six years older than Dave Duvall, was married to Duvall's mother, Yellow Bird. Duvall's account ledgers sent to Wissler list these men with whom he worked: White Man, White Quiver, Chief Crow, Three Bears, Flat Tail, Heavy Breast, The Boy, Lazy Boy, Bull Child, Elkhorn, Bear Skin, Shorty White Grass, Bad Old Man, Comes at Night, Steep Short Face (nephew of Comes at Night), Sam Many Guns, Talieu Ashley, Eagle Child, Henry No Bear, Heavy Runner, Last Star, Boy Chief, and these four women: Mrs. No Chief, Mrs. Strangle Wolf, Mrs. Wolf Plume, and Mistaken Buffalo Rock. In 1911, Duvall prepared his own manuscript on myths, this time identifying the tellers: "The Ghost Woman," by Jappy [Takes-Gun-on-Top]; "A Man With his Hands Cut Off," by Comes at Night; "The Woman Who Married a Star" by Mrs. W. P. [Wolf Plume], "Scabby Round

Robe and the Beavers" and "How Horses Came About," by Tom Kiyo; "How the Black and Yellow Buffalo Lodge Came About" and "Horse Medicine Owners," by Red Plume; "Snake Lodge," by Heavy Gun; "How the White Lodge Came About," by Three Bears; "Crow Water Medicine," by Owl Top Feathers, "People Sacrificing Flesh to Sun," by Split Ears; and "When Transferring Hair Lock Fringe Suits," by Shorty White Grass. But for the 1908 *Mythology of the Blackfoot,* we have no such list, only the occasional note in the Wissler-Duvall correspondence, such as a letter of 1907 from Duvall transmitting "The Buffalos' Adopted Child, or the Iron Horns" taken from "an old woman Mistaken Buffalo Rock."

MYTHOLOGY OF THE BLACKFOOT

Mythology of the Blackfoot is an important collection for several reasons. For anthropologists, it was for its time a model of "scientific" ethnography, systematic, consciously unbiased, and carried out with a gifted, dedicated native collaborator. For folklorists, it is a carefully organized, conscientiously annotated corpus of great value for comparative as well as aesthetic studies. For the Blackfoot people, it is an extensive, honest compendium of much of their traditional history. Uhlenbeck's and de Jong's texts in Blackfoot with close translation are more useful for the modern scholar concerned with exact transcription, but *Mythology of the Blackfoot* is accessible to general readers beyond its scholarship. Both Wissler and Duvall were genuinely interested in the stories, and in spite of its mode of publication in a drab gray monograph, life abounds in the tales. Later collections of Blackfoot mythology (Black Boy 1973; Bullchild 1985; Fraser 1990; the Blackfeet Heritage Program series—e.g., Ground 1978; Rides At The Door 1979)—like those earlier by Grinnell, McClintock, and Schultz, add little not included in *Mythology of the Blackfoot.*

Wissler's own introduction to the volume thoroughly documents the literature on Blackfoot myths available to 1908, compares Blackfoot myths to those of other Plains peoples, brings out the unique (for example, page 15 on the role of women) and unusual aspects of the collection, and discusses the role of stories in Blackfoot life. To appreciate the material fully, readers should examine also the *Ceremonial Bundles of the Blackfoot Indians* (1912), the mature fruit of the Wissler-Duvall collaboration, where Duvall's increased expertise in interviewing, observing, and translating, and Wissler's confidence in his work, combine to present Blackfoot religious knowledge and behavior in a manner reasonably true to the Blackfoot point of view, yet "scientific" enough in its mode of description and discussion to be well comprehended by the Western reader. As Wissler himself notes (p. 17), the ceremonies connected with the medicine bundles constitute the praxis for the myths (and conversely, the myths are the ground for the ritual practices).

It is above all required of Western readers that they suspend their accustomed division between the supernatural and history, for the Blackfoot were not worried about establishing a long duration of time or pinpointing events in a sequence before the memories of those still living. They had a sensible understanding of linear time, but a heightened sensibility, compared to most Westerners, of the continuity of life in nature. Insofar as men today are impulsive and foolish, the character Napi lives as he lived in the dawn of the world; insofar as the animal nations on the prairies carry on their species' societies, the animal people in the myths are still around. There is not so much a contrast between Western concern with exact history and Indian awareness of the cycles of life, as shared actual experience highlighted for the Westerners by the punctuations of great events and personalities, while for Indians, ongoing relationships are emphasized.

The Blackfoot saw themselves as one among many forms of sentient life, all ultimately invigorated by cosmic Almighty Power. Several forms of being are manifestly more powerful than humans, for example, the fearsome grizzly bear, the heavy-horned bison, and beavers and otters who are able to live under water as well as on land. Those beings have on occasion pitied or been attracted to a human and bestowed a fetish or empowering song upon him or, more often, her. Most young Blackfoot men and many women went to lonely places at least once in their lives to fast and pray continuously until a pitying being appeared, vision-like, promising aid in living a satisfying life. When the gift was strong enough to aid the community, the fortunate recipient's tale became part of history, the history of the medicine bundles that served as portable shrines for these nomadic people.

For Wissler, the supernatural elements in these histories meant

they should be termed *myths*. Wissler distinguishes, in this monograph, between Duvall's collection of tales illustrating men's nature (in the person of Napi, Man since the dawn of the world), the
histories of the origins of recognized stars and constellations and of
holy rituals and objects, more mundane origin stories, and a set of
popular tales. Wissler's footnotes indicate tales and motifs wide-
spread in North America, or even farther; the specialist will be interested in, for example, how the Maya Hero Twins become Ashes-
Chief and Stuck-Behind-the-Lodge-Poles in Blackfoot telling.
Blood-Clot is not only told elsewhere in the Plains, he resembles
the miraculous Japanese boy found in a peach pit. Aesthetically,
many of the myths are well structured and engrossingly told, although readers must go to Uhlenbeck and Tatsey's somewhat for-
bidding collections to see the actual narrative form and phrases.
Within the stories in Wissler and Duvall's monograph are
glimpses of the passions, the fears, and sometimes noble actions
vivifying Blackfoot community life—jealous husbands, children
abandoned and saved by old ladies braving mean-spirited men,
cliff-hanging episodes where evil or imprudence threatens to over-
come good people. A relish of being alive, of taking up challenges,
proving one's worth—whether man or woman—comes through
this collection.

Indian life before European invasions was as dynamic, changing, and political as life in any Western country. These Blackfoot
myths should be read as legendary history. They are not fairy tales
and not always parables. They give the reader, fundamentally, a
feel for a way of life nearly extinguished by incredible epidemics
and massive invasions, now slowly reconstituted in its homeland,
in part through the enlightened labor of Mr. Duvall and his part-
ner in New York, Dr. Wissler.

ACKNOWLEDGMENTS

I am most appreciative of the unstinting assistance from the staff
of the American Museum of Natural History, especially Stanley
Freed, Belinda Kaye, and Anibal Rodriguez; to the Glenbow-Al-
berta Institute for access to the manuscript notes of Claude Schaeffer; and to Darrell Kipp of the Piegan Institute, Browning, Montana; Loretta Pepion of the Museum of the Plains Indian,

Browning; and Robert Scriver, Browning. Allan R. Taylor, University of Colorado, kindly provided phonemic transcriptions of the Blackfoot words. (For the writing system adopted by the Alberta Blackfoot reserves, see Frantz and Russell, 1989.)

REFERENCES

Black Boy, Cecile
1973   "Blackfeet Tipi Legends." In *Painted Tipis*. Exhibition catalog, Oklahoma Indian Arts and Crafts Cooperative. Anadarko: Southern Plains Indian Museum and Crafts Center.

Brink, Jack
1990   "Bison Butchering and Food Processing at Head-Smashed-In Buffalo Jump, Alberta." Presented at the 48th Plains Conference, Oklahoma City.

Bullchild, Percy
1985   *The Sun Came Down*. San Francisco: Harper and Row.

Carter, Sarah
1990   *Lost Harvests*. Montreal: McGill/Queen's University Press.

de Jong, Josselin
1914   *Blackfoot Texts*. Verhandelingen der Koninklijke Akademie van Wetenschappen te Amsterdam, Afdeeling Letterkunde n. r. 14 (4). Amsterdam: Johannes Muller.

DeMarce, Roxanne, ed.
1980   *Blackfeet Heritage, 1907–1908*. Browning MT: Blackfeet Heritage Program.

Duke, Philip G.
1991   *Points in Time*. Niwot: University Press of Colorado.

Epp, Henry, ed.
1993   *Three Hundred Prairie Years: Henry Kelsey's "Indland Country of Good Report."* Regina SK: Canadian Plains Research Center.

Ewers, John C.
1955   *The Horse in Blackfoot Indian Culture*. Smithsonian Institution, Bureau of American Ethnology Bulletin, no. 159. Washington DC.
1958   *The Blackfeet: Raiders on the Northwestern Plains*. Norman: University of Oklahoma Press.

Farr, William E.
1984   *The Reservation Blackfeet, 1882–1945*. Seattle: University of Washington Press.

Frantz, Donald G., and Norma Jean Russell
1989   *Blackfoot Dictionary of Stems, Roots, and Affixes*. Toronto: University of Toronto Press.

Fraser, Frances
1990   *The Bear Who Stole the Chinook: Tales from the Blackfoot*. Vancouver: Douglas and McIntyre. First published as *Bear and Other Stories* and *The Wind along the River,* Toronto: Macmillan of Canada, 1959, 1968.

Freed, Stanley A., and Ruth S. Freed
1983   "Clark Wissler and the Development of Anthropology in the United States," *American Anthropologist* 85:800–825.

Goldfrank, Esther S.
1945   *Changing Configurations in the Social Organization of a Blackfoot Tribe during the Reserve Period (The Blood of Alberta, Canada)*. Monograph 8, American Ethnological Society. Seattle: University of Washington Press.

Grinnell, George Bird
1892   *Blackfoot Lodge Tales*. New York: Charles Scribner's Sons.
1913   *Blackfeet Indian Stories*. New York: Charles Scribner's Sons.
1961   *Pawnee, Blackfoot and Cheyenne*. Selected by Dee Brown. New York: Charles Scribner's Sons.

Ground, Mary
1978   *Grass Woman Stories*. Browning MT: Blackfeet Heritage Program.

Hanks, Lucien M., Jr., and Jane Richardson Hanks
1945   *Observations on Northern Blackfoot Kinship*. Monograph 9, American Ethnological Society. Seattle: University of Washington Press.
1950   *Tribe under Trust: A Study of the Blackfoot Reserve of Alberta*. Toronto: University of Toronto Press.

Hungry Wolf, Adolf [Gutohrlein]
1977   *The Blood People: A Division of the Blackfoot Confederacy*. New York: Harper & Row.

Hungry Wolf, Beverly [Little Bear]
1984   *The Ways of My Grandmothers*. New York: William Morrow.

Johnston, Alex
1987   *Plants and the Blackfoot*. Lethbridge AB: Lethbridge Historical Society.

Judy, Mark A.
1987   "Powder Keg on the Upper Missouri: Sources of Blackfeet Hostility, 1730–1810." *American Indian Quarterly* 11:127–44.

Kehoe, Alice B.
1976   "Old Woman Had Great Power." *Western Canadian Journal of Anthropology* 6:68–76.
1983   "The Shackles of Tradition." In *The Hidden Half,* edited by Patricia Albers and Beatrice Medicine, pp. 53–73. Washington DC: University Press of America.
1991   "Contests of Power in Blackfoot Life and Mythology." In *Contests,* edited by Andrew Duff-Cooper, pp. 115–24. Cosmos 6. Edinburgh: Edinburgh University Press.
1992   "Clot-of-Blood." In *Earth and Sky,* edited by Claire R. Farrer and Ray A. Williamson, pp. 207–14. Albuquerque: University of New Mexico Press.
1993   "How the Ancient Peigans Lived." *Research in Economic Anthropology* 14:87–105.

Lewis, Oscar
1941   "Manly-Hearted Women among the North Piegan." *American Anthropologist* 43:173-87.
1942   *The Effects of White Contact upon Blackfoot Culture.* Monograph 6, American Ethnological Society. Seattle: University of Washington Press.

Lewis, Oscar, and Ruth Maslow Lewis
1939   Field Notes, Brocket Reserve, Alberta [North Piegan]. Columbia University Laboratory directed by Ruth Benedict.

McClintock, Walter
1910   *The Old North Trail, or, Life, Legends and Religion of the Blackfeet Indians.* London: MacMillan. Reprinted by University of Nebraska Press (Lincoln, 1968).

McFee, Malcolm
1972   *Modern Blackfeet: Montanans on a Reservation.* New York: Holt, Rinehart and Winston.

McVicker, Donald E.
1992   "The Matter of Saville: Franz Boas and the Anthropological Definition of Archaeology." In *Rediscovering Our Past: Essays on the History of American Archaeology,* edited by Jonathan E. Reyman, pp. 144–59. Aldershot: Avebury.

Morgan, R. Grace
1991	"Beaver Ecology/Beaver Mythology." Ph.D. dissertation, University of Alberta, Edmonton.

Murdock, George Peter
1948	"Clark Wissler, 1870–1947." *American Anthropologist* 50:292–304.

Rides At The Door, Darnell Davis
1979	*Napi Stories*. Browning MT: Blackfeet Heritage Program.

Samek, Hana
1987	*The Blackfoot Confederacy 1880–1920*. Albuquerque: University of New Mexico Press.

Schaeffer, Claude
n.d.	Manuscript notes from Blackfoot Informants. Archives, Glenbow-Alberta Institute, Calgary.

Schultz, James Willard (Apikuni)
1907	*My Life as an Indian*. New York: Forest and Stream.
1962	*Blackfeet and Buffalo*. Edited by Keith C. Seele. Norman: University of Oklahoma Press.
1974	*Why Gone Those Times? Blackfoot Tales*. Edited by Eugene Lee Silliman. Norman: University of Oklahoma Press.

Uhlenbeck, C. C.
1911	*Original Blackfoot Texts*. Verhandelingen der Koninklijke Akademie van Wetenschappen te Amsterdam, Afdeeling Letterkunde n. r. 12 (1). Amsterdam: Johannes Muller.
1912	*A New Series of Blackfoot Texts*. Verhandelingen der Koninklijke Akademie van Wetenschappen te Amsterdam, Afdeeling Letterkunde n. r. 13 (1). Amsterdam: Johannes Muller.

Walton, Ann T., John C. Ewers, and Royal B. Hassrick
1985	*After the Buffalo Were Gone: The Louis Warren Hill, Sr., Collection of Indian Art*. St. Paul: Northwest Area Association.

Welch, James
1986	*Fools Crow*. New York: Viking Penguin.
1990	*The Indian Lawyer*. New York: Viking Penguin.

Wissler, Clark
1911	*The Social Life of the Blackfoot Indians*. Anthropological Papers, vol. 7, part 1. New York: American Museum of Natural History.
1912	*Ceremonial Bundles of the Blackfoot Indians*. Anthropological Papers, vol. 7, part 2. New York: American Museum of Natural History.

1971 *Red Man Reservations*. New York: Collier. First published as *Indian Cavalcade or Life on the Old-Time Indian Reservations* by Sheridan House (New York, 1938).

Wissler, Clark, and D. C. Duvall
1908 *Mythology of the Blackfoot Indians*. Anthropological Papers, vol. 2, part 1. New York: American Museum of Natural History.

Mythology of the Blackfoot Indians

CONTENTS

INTRODUCTION.

This collection of narratives was made among the several divisions of the Blackfoot Indians during the years 1903–07. Unless otherwise stated, the translations were made by D. C. Duvall, and revised by Clark Wissler. The usual method was to record literal oral translations, which were in turn rendered with some freedom, though the translator's idiom has been retained wherever feasible. In every case, however, both the translator and the editor have sought to reproduce the narrative with the original sequence of incidents and explanatory ideas. In narration the Blackfoot often repeat sentences at irregular intervals, as if they wished to prevent the listener from forgetting their import. Naturally such repetitions were eliminated in the translations. A few narratives were recorded as texts. While texts will be indispensable for linguistic research, the present condition of Blackfoot mythology is such that its comparative study would not be materially facilitated by such records. Each narrator has his own version, in the telling of which he is usually consistent; and, while the main features of the myths are the same for all, the minor differences are so great that extreme accuracy of detail with one individual would avail little. The method pursued with the most important myths was to discuss them with different individuals, so as to form an opinion as to the most common arrangement of incidents; a statement of such opinions being given as footnotes to those narrations in which great variations were observed. This variable condition may be interpreted as a breaking-down of Blackfoot mythology, but there is another factor to be considered. Myths are told by a few individuals, who take pride in their ability and knowledge, and usually impress their own individuality upon the form of the narrative. Thus it seems equally probable that the various versions represent individual contributions, and, in a certain sense, are the ownership-marks of the narrators. Once when discussing this matter with a Blood Indian, the venerable old man pulled up a common ragweed, saying, "The parts of this weed all branch off from the stem. They go different ways, but all come from the same root. So it is with the different versions of a myth." Hence, to say that any one version of these myths is correct would be preposterous, because they have not now, and probably never did have, an absolutely fixed form. The only rational criterion seems to be the approximate form in which the myth is most often encountered. So far as practicable, we have made this the basis of selection; but doubtless many narratives containing unusual features have passed into our collection unobserved. In some instances we have given exceptional versions, because they contained important cultural data, exercising due care by duplication or otherwise that no essential incidents should be omitted. In a few cases we have given versions from the various divisions of the Blackfoot. So far as our observation goes the differences between versions from these divisions are no greater than between individual versions within a single division.

While the greater part of these narratives were collected among the Piegan in Montana, the North Piegan, Blood, and Northern Blackfoot in Canada are well represented. As may be expected under conditions just stated, the contributors were relatively few,— twenty-one in all. No claim for completeness is made. Our effort has been to present narratives in which the tone of the mythical age predominated, or in which the supernatural was the main interest. In a future paper we hope to present some typical tales of adventure, and a collection of esoteric narratives in connection with a discussion of certain aspects of Blackfoot culture. We made no effort to collect ordinary humorous tales (of which there are a great number, chiefly obscene), because none of those encountered contained mythical or supernatural elements.

A number of Blackfoot myths have been recorded elsewhere. The first to mention the subject seems to have been the younger Henry, whose journal (1808), together with that of Thompson's, contains a brief though somewhat confused statement of the Old Man, the Moon, and the Sun.[1] In 1884 Clark reported briefly some observations on mythology in his well-known work[2] on the sign language. A year or two later appeared a collection of traditions from various Canadian tribes by Father Petitot,[3] in which a few references were made to Blackfoot mythology. The next observer appears to have been John Maclean, who from time to time published abstracts and versions of various myths.[4] By far the most complete collection was made by George Bird Grinnell, containing in all something over thirty narratives.[5] A few myths have been published by R. N. Wilson.[6] So far no other publications giving first-hand data have come to our attention.

---

[1] New Light on the Early History of the Greater Northwest. Edited by Elliott Coues, 1897, p. 528.
[2] Indian Sign Language, 1885.
[3] Traditions Indiennes du Canada Nord-ouest, 1886.
[4] Journal of American Folk-Lore (Vol. III, 1890, p. 296; Vol. VI, 1893, p. 165); The Indians of Canada, 1892; Canadian Savage Folk, 1896.
[5] Blackfoot Lodge Tales, 1892, revised 1903; Journal of American Folk-Lore (Vol. VI, 1893, p. 44).
[6] The American Antiquarian, Vol. XV, 1893, pp. 149, 150, 200–203: Report of the British Association for the Advancement of Science, Vol. LXVII, 1898, pp. 788, 789.

The narratives collected by us contain incidentally and otherwise a great deal of important data on the culture of the Blackfoot Indians, which we expect to use in the future. Accordingly the senior author has classified and arranged them to facilitate such use. Those of our readers interested solely in comparative mythology will doubtless not be hampered by this, if they ignore the main headings. Proceeding from the point of view just stated, it appears that according to association, content, and function, the narratives fall into four groups, — Tales of the Old Man, Star Myths, Ritualistic Origin, and Cultural or other Origins. To this may be added a miscellaneous collection in which, for the most part, each narrative is its own excuse for being. A brief discussion of these groups may serve as a characterization of Blackfoot mythology.

The Old Man, or Napiw[a], has been given the first place in our collection. The collection of Grinnell contains several adventures not found in ours. One of these is characterized by the following:

> Old Man goes out to hunt with the wolves. When sleeping with them at night, he is kept warm by lying under their tails. The next day, Old Man disregards an injunction against opening his eyes, and is hit on the nose with a bone. Later he retaliates, and kills the wolf who threw the bone. In this story, also occurs the only known case in which Old Man becomes an animal. By request he is transformed into a wolf; but this seems to be lost sight of in the course of the narrative, where he appears in his true form. Later he encounters Chief Bear, and shoots arrows into him and several other bears. Then he meets Frog going for medicine, takes Frog's skin, puts it on, and, so disguised, goes in and kills the bears.[1]

This last incident bears a striking similarity to part of an Algonkin myth recorded among the Sauk and Fox by Dr. William Jones.[2] Grinnell also records an incident in which Old Man plucks the hair from a fox and sends him out to attract buffalo. The buffalo are killed with laughing at the antics of the fox. While Old Man is butchering, it becomes cold and the fox freezes stiff. The buffalo laughing himself to death occurs in our collection, but is due to the Old Man's acts.

According to Maclean, the Old Man was a party to the stealing of bags containing summer and winter.[3]

Petitot says that by tradition the three divisions of the people — Northern Blackfoot, Bloods, and Piegan — are the respective offspring of the Old Man's three sons.[4]

The creation of the world from mud brought to the surface by a diving

[1] Blackfoot Lodge Tales, op. cit., p. 149.
[2] Culture-Hero Myth of the Sauks and Foxes (Journal of American Folk-Lore, Vol. XIV, p. 225).
[3] Journal of American Folk-Lore, Vol. VI, p. 166.
[4] Petitot, Traditions Indiennes du Canada Nord-ouest, p. 493.

animal is a frequent incident in the mythology of central North America. In addition to the fragment in our collection, Blackfoot versions have been recorded elsewhere. Maclean makes use of them in several publications, one of which runs as follows: —

"The aged men of the camps tell us of the time when there was nothing but water, and the Old Man was sitting upon a log, with four animals. Pondering over his situation, he thought that there must be something under the water, and, anxious to learn what might be there, he sent the animals down after each other, till the last to descend was the muskrat, and he alone returned to tell the story of his explorations, bearing in his mouth some mud, which the Old Man took, and rolling it in the palm of his hand, it grew rapidly and fell into the water. Soon it assumed such dimensions that he stepped upon it, and placing there a wolf, this animal ran swiftly over the plastic matter, and wherever he stepped an indentation was made, which became a valley, and where he placed not his foot the plains and mountains appeared. The water rushed into some of the indentations, and these became lakes." [1]

In confirmation of this the following may be noted: —

"At a certain time, it happened that all the earth was covered with water. The 'Old Man' (Napiw) was in a canoe, and he thought of causing the earth to come up from the abyss. To put this project into execution he used the aid of four animals, — the duck, the otter, the badger and the muskrat. The muskrat proved to be the best diver. He remained so long under water that when he came to the surface he was fainting, but he had succeeded in getting a little particle of earth, which he brought between the toes of his paw. This particle of earth the "Old Man" took, and blowing on it he swelled it to such an extent as to make the whole earth of it. Then it took him four days to complete his work, and make the mountains, rivers, plants, and beasts." [2]

The myth was also known to the Sarcee in the same form as above.[3] The writer once asked a well-informed old Piegan man if such a story was known to his people. His reply was to the effect that he had heard of it, but regarded it as a white man's tale. This may be an error, for Henry wrote about a century ago as follows: —

"At first the world was one body of water inhabited by only one great white man and his wife, who had no children. This man, in the course of time, made the earth, divided the waters into lakes and rivers," [4] etc.

Thus there seems no reason to doubt but that this myth was known to the Blackfoot in the same general form as was current among the numerous tribes of the Algonkin group. It may not have been current among the

[1] Canadian Savage Folk, p. 51.
[2] Hale, Report of the British Association for the Advancement of Science, 1886, p. 704.
[3] Wilson, Report of the British Association for the Advancement of Science, 1889, p. 224.
[4] New Light on the Early History of the Greater Northwest, p. 528.

Piegan, since Henry was among the Northern Blackfoot (from whom our version was obtained), and Maclean seems to have secured his data from the Bloods. That the Blackfoot formerly had a well-defined creation myth, in which the Old Man took the initiative in producing and transforming the world, is indicated by several writers. Those noted above give more or less in detail a running account of the peopling of the earth and the instruction of mankind in the art of living. While these incidents do not occur in detail in the Old Man myths recorded in this paper, they are occasionally implied. Such origins are at present often assigned to the Old Man without the formality of a myth. It will be noted that the greater part of the tales collected by us recite the absurd, humorous, obscene, and brutal incidents in the Old Man's career. No ritualistic or ceremonial practices appear to be based upon any of these narratives, though it may have been otherwise in the past. On the other hand, connected with them are the suggestions of origins for many aspects of material culture, such as the buffalo-drive, the making of weapons, methods of dressing skins, etc. A considerable number of places and topographical features were associated with his adventures; as Old Man's River, Tongue Flag River, Old Man's Gambling-Place, Old Man's Sliding-Place, Rolling-Stone Creek, etc. In fact, there seems a tendency to give all of his adventures a definite location in what is now Alberta.

From the accounts of all observers, it appears that confusion exists in assigning some myths. Thus Grinnell records as adventures of the Old Man our myths containing the incident of the dog and the stick (p. 52), the placing of the crow in the smoke-hole (p. 51), the woman with a snake-lover (p. 150), and the rolling head (p. 154). We found differences of opinion on these and other tales, but have in our list the ones rarely if ever challenged. Taking into consideration all the data at hand, we are of the opinion that there has been a disintegration of the creative and cultural origin myths concerning the Old Man. This opinion is partly based upon the agreement of these myths with those attributed to similar characters among the Cree, Ojibwa, Fox, and other divisions of the Algonkin stock, for which a common origin is assumed, and also partly on the present attitude of the Blackfoot themselves toward these myths.

For several decades at least, the Blackfoot have considered the Old Man as an evil character, in most respects trivial, who long ago passed on to other countries. Whenever the writer asked if the Old Man was ever prayed to, the absurdity of the question provoked merriment. The usual reply was, that no one had enough confidence in him to make such an appeal. In daily conversation his name is often used as a synonyme for immorality. However, it must not be implied that he is regarded as an evil spirit. His name is especially associated with things obscene, and pertaining to sexual immorality. I have heard the Piegan say that so and so "must be trying to be like the Old Man; he cannot be trusted with women."

We have occasionally noted a tendency to assign modern obscene anecdotes to this character, and it may well be that many of the tales long attributed to him have been accumulated by the laws of association. The unfortunate human tendency to appreciate keenly the humor in such anecdotes seems sufficient to account for their survival and accumulation long after belief in and respect for the Old Man as a creator, teacher, and transformer, has passed the verge of extinction.

Certain differences of opinion among former observers make it desirable to reconsider our assumption that these myths are survivals from a much larger group constituting the ancient basic beliefs of the Blackfoot. The first account we find bearing upon this point was written by Alexander Henry in 1809.[1] He speaks of "one first great white man and his wife" to whom all things are due, but states that he went to live in the sun and is called Nah-toos, while his wife went to the moon. Unfortunately, Henry is not sufficiently specific for the identification of the "one first great white man." Among the present Blackfoot people, Natos refers to the Sun-Man, whose consort is the Moon-Woman, a character regarded as distinct from the Old Man. The term used by Henry is probably a translation; for, in his comparative vocabularies, "Nappeekoon" is given as the equivalent of "white man," the term still applied to members of our race. This of itself makes it probable that Napiw[a] is the character referred to in the above.

Later, about 1874, R. P. Lacombe writes that Napiw[a] went to live in the Sun.[2] M. Lacombe is quoted by Hale (1885) to the effect that Napiw[a] and Natos are distinct, and that the former is a secondary character.[3] Maclean also states that Napiw[a] is a secondary character.[4] Grinnell (1892) expresses the opinion that Napiw[a] and Natos are the same and that the latter is a more recent conception.[5] It is of interest to note that the earlier writers are disposed to treat Natos, the Sun, as the home of the Old Man, while the later ones make each a character. My own information is emphatic in indicating a present distinction between the two. This is supported by the following statement from a man for many years an interested observer of Blackfoot customs: —

"The Sun is then the principal deity. . . . Equally erroneous is the view that they addressed prayers to, or in any manner worshipped, 'Napi,' the Old Man of the legends, the blunderer, the immoral mischief-maker." [6]

---

[1] New Light on the Early History of the Greater Northwest, op. cit., pp. 527, 528.
[2] Petitot, op. cit., p. 504.
[3] Hale, op. cit., p. 704.
[4] Canadian Savage Folk, p. 52.
[5] Grinnell, op. cit., p. 258.
[6] R. N. Wilson, Report of the British Association for the Advancement of Science, 1898, p. 789.

There are several obvious ways in which the different statements recorded above can be interpreted. It may be reasonable to assume that the later writers were better informed, and therefore able to distinguish between two mythical characters having some things in common. On the other hand, the observations may be of equal weight, and so represent a change of belief. While the means are not at hand for the solution of this question, it may be noted that the myths so far recorded are quite consistent with the modern Blackfoot belief that Napiw[a] and Natos are distinct characters. For example, in Grinnell's version of the theft of the fire-leggings, Napiw[a] steals them from Natos. Again, the Old Woman, or Moon-Woman, is practically always associated with Natos as his respected and honored consort; while mention of such a character seldom occurs in the myths of the Old Man group. Further, in ceremonies Natos is often addressed as Napiwa, but, so it was stated to us, in the sense of old and venerable man. This suggests that the sole difficulty may be due to verbal confusion in the native tongue, obscuring a former distinction between Napiw[a] and Natos. However this may be, the import of the preceding seems to be, that, for a number of years at least, the Old Man has been a secondary mythological character. The problem is, then, to determine whether this secondary relation is due to gradual displacement by intrusive beliefs, or to the fact that the belief in the Old Man is in itself of recent introduction.

While we have no intention of making a comparative study of these myths, a few statements may not come amiss. The Old Man of the Thompson Indians, is, like the Old Man of the Blackfoot, a secondary character, though relatively less prominent, and, according to Boas, he is not made an object of prayer, and not held in particular reverence.[1] In the Plains, it appears that the Old Man of the Crow, Nih'a[n]ca[n] of the Arapaho, Nix'a[n]t of the Gros Ventre, and Napiw[a] of the Blackfoot, have a great deal in common. They were in certain respects creators, but also tricksters; and many vile pranks were common to all. The general impression one gets from comparative reading of all these tales is that the Blackfoot and the Crow stand in close relation as opposed to the Arapaho and the Gros Ventre. However, the collections from the Crow and Gros Ventre are not complete. It is interesting to note that the Arapaho Nih'a[n]ca[n] is the word for "white man," as is also the Cheyenne Vihuk and the Blackfoot Napiw[a]. The Arapaho Hixtcaba Nih'a[n]ca[n] (Above-White-Man, God) is identical in meaning with Spo[x]toom Napiwa. Again, the statement of Kroeber, that "in none of the Arapaho myths is there the slightest trace of any animal or spider-like qualities attributed to Nih'a[n]ca[n]," [2] applies equally well to

---

[1] Thompson River Indian Traditions, p. 7.
[2] George A. Dorsey and Alfred L. Kroeber Traditions of the Arapaho. (Field Columbian Museum Publication 81, 1903, footnote, p. 7).

Napiw[a], also entirely human. This is certainly in contrast to many of the surrounding tribes in whose mythologies similar antics are attributed to a rabbit, coyote, or spider-like person. Thus we have another of those frequent suggestions that the Algonkin tribes of the Plains themselves constitute a sub-group.

It is unfortunate that so little Cree mythology has been recorded, as the few narratives published by Russell [1] suggest the closest relation to those of the Blackfoot so far encountered. Similarities to Fox and Ojibwa myths seem much more numerous among the Blackfoot than among the Arapaho, Gros Ventre, or Cheyenne. Thus, the wide distribution of these characteristics among the various Algonkin speaking tribes of the Missouri-Saskatchewan area, seems to favor the view that the Old Man myths represent the older basic beliefs of the Blackfoot. In this connection the failure to find in the present mythological beliefs evidence of the identity of the Old Man and the Sun, justifies the assumption that the secondary character of the former is due to the intrusion of the latter.

According to the testimony of many writers, the Blackfoot Indians took great interest in the heavens, and possessed considerable astronomical knowledge. However that may be, this collection contains an unusual number of Star Myths. We have considered them as such because the chief characters either appear as heavenly bodies (though sometimes in disguise), or become such at the end of their earthly careers. In many cases this transformation forms no essential part of the narrative, being a mere incident, or as it were an afterthought by the narrator. This is especially noticeable in the Twin-Stars, or Brothers, where we find an elaborate myth composed primarily of the widely distributed Found-in-the-Grass. The same may be said of Blood-Clot or Smoking-Star. On the other hand, we find the Morning-Star as an important character in a number of myths, where he appears as the son of the Sun and Moon. In Blackfoot religion these three are in many respects a sacred trio to whom prayers are addressed individually and collectively. Again, in the Morning-Star myths we find the well-known incident of a woman marrying a star, in this case the Morning-Star himself, whose son by this union becomes the Fixed-Star. Taking the entire eight Star Myths as a whole, but three appear to be original with the Blackfoot, — Cuts-Wood, Scar-Face, and the Bunched-Stars.

A large number of myths function as ritualistic origins, the rituals themselves being in part dramatic interpretations of the narratives. Yet, while the rituals are fixed and rigidly adhered to, the myths show the same wide variations in detail as those of other groups. This is contrary to expectation.

---

[1] Frank Russell, Explorations in the Far North, 1898, pp. 201–220.

We cannot at present decide whether this is best explained by assuming these myths to be secondary popular accounts of the ceremonies composing the rituals, or otherwise. In most ceremonies the origin of the ritual is regarded as the result of a personal relation between its first owner and its supernatural giver; each ceremony, or demonstration of the ritual, being a reproduction of this formal transfer. Thus the myths are, in a sense, preludes to the rituals; yet, when one asks for the reason or significance of a specific part of a ritual, he is referred at once to the myth. Thus the great variation in these narratives is difficult to interpret.

In passing, one important aspect of this group deserves attention. It will be seen that these narratives can be placed in two divisions, according to the relation between the incidents and the rituals associated therewith. In many cases the relation is primary, or the myth itself recounts the incidents leading directly to the transfer. Also this transfer is the main incident or climax of the narrative. In other cases the myth stands apart, having its own culminating incident, after which we are informed, parenthetically as it were, that one of the characters came into the possession of a ritual. Rarely are we told in such cases that a definite relation exists between the origin of this ritual and the incidents composing the narrative, though some kind of relation is always implied. In this collection there are twenty myths bearing the primary relation, and eleven bearing the secondary. To be exact, five of the Star Myths show ritualistic functions, one of which may be considered primary, and four secondary. Thus, in a total of thirty-six ritualistic myths, twenty-one appear to bear the primary relation, and fifteen the secondary. Thus we are safe in assuming that at least a third of all Blackfoot ritualistic origin myths belong to the secondary division. As may be anticipated, the character of the myths in one division differs considerably from that of the other. Those of the secondary type are decidedly classical, and show greater art in composition than those of the primary. The people seem to appreciate them for the sake of their power to charm, while the sacred associations of the primary myths are sufficient to make them respected.

The most suggestive difference, however, appears when a comparative view of these divisions is made. Those in the primary group are not often found in the mythologies of other tribes: in fact the incident of a woman with beaver-children is the only certain exception we have so far encountered. On the other hand, many myths of the secondary division are widely distributed among other tribes. Here we find the well-known Blood-Clot, Found-in-the-Grass (Twin-Stars), The Woman-who-Married a Star, The Girl with a Dog for a Lover (No. 25), The Woman who Married a Bull (Nos. 26, 27), The Buffalo-Boy (No. 28), The Child Reared by the Buffalo

(No. 31), The Brother on the Desert Island (No. 18), not to mention minor incidents of these and other narratives.

There are, however, exceptions, the chief of which are Scar-Face and Scabby-Round-Robe, to which we have so far found no parallels. The natural inference from the foregoing is, that in the primary division the myths and the rituals had a common origin, while in the secondary they have come into association, by accident or otherwise, long after their respective forms became fixed.[1] The intrusion of rituals practised by other tribes may have been the occasion of many such associations. Thus we find that the secondary character of the Origin Myths for the societies of high rank — as the Bulls, Horns, Dogs, etc. — is most pronounced in those societies derived, according to Blackfoot tradition, from other tribes. That the traditions in these instances are founded upon fact is rendered exceedingly probable by the peculiar distribution of these same societies among the tribes of the Missouri basin.[2] With one exception, the myths associated with the sun-dance are also secondary. While there are no traditions indicating foreign origin for this ceremony as a whole, its general distribution makes such an origin probable. Yet it is with this ceremony that the highly original Scar-Face myth is secondarily associated. This exception in the case of a very important myth indicates that the cause of the secondary association cannot be wholly due to a tendency to assimilate foreign tales. Such inference is sustained by the presence of a considerable number of foreign tales without ritualistic associations of any kind, and by the entire absence of such associations in the Old Man group, which we have shown to be a very important part of the older Blackfoot mythology.

The discussion of this problem would carry us into a study of the rituals themselves, a subject we propose to take up in a future publication. We may, however, offer a tentative interpretation of the preceding peculiarities. Assuming the tales of the Old Man as older and fundamental, the absence of ritualistic associations among them may be due to the more recent development of the present ceremonies. The beaver-medicine, seemingly one of the oldest rituals, and apparently the creation of a single shaman, set the type to which all other rituals tended to conform. In this case the myths still tend to the primary association, or to conserve the type. Later rituals were brought in from other tribes and adjusted to the prevailing type, even to the introduction of new myths, that would also tend to be foreign, though not necessarily. Further, according to our data, rituals originating in shamanistic dreams have sometimes been attributed to heroes in well-known

---

[1] For an example of a myth incorporated in a ritual, see Franz Boas, The Social Organization and the Secret Societies of the Kwakiutl Indians, 1897, p. 662.

[2] A. I., Kroeber in the Proceedings of the International Congress of Americanists, 1906, Vol. II, pp. 53–64.

myths, the hero having appeared and transferred the ritual. Thus we have the functioning of a well-known factor in primitive speculative thought. The tendency to find a mythical origin for every important ceremonial practice is common to all peoples, as is also the tendency to conventionalize the kind of associations formed.

Another characteristic of this group is the frequency with which a woman plays an important part in the transfer of rituals and other powers, — the Elk-Woman, the Otter-Woman, the Woman-who-Married-the-Buffalo, the Woman-who brought-the-Pipe, etc. In almost every case the woman has sexual relations with a male being from whom, or by virtue of whom, the ritual or power comes, and such grant is often manifestly to appease a wronged husband or parents. However, this may be a more or less conventional mode of constructing a myth, based upon the same human interests that make the love-passion the core of all novels.

Now we may consider myths of cultural and other origins. In the first place, these narratives are such as account for certain conditions in humanity and nature, and certain folk-practices. In the second place, the origins and transformations are primary rather than secondary parts of the narratives, in which respect they stand in opposition to a large part of the preceding group. Such a distinction is by no means absolute, and some of the narratives in this group will doubtless impress the reader as not quite within the bounds of the above characterization; yet he should not forget that we have also been influenced in the selection by the attitude of the narrators and others toward the tales themselves.[1] One of the chief points of note in this group is the lack of correspondence to the mythology of the Plains. In most cases the narratives seem to be original with the Blackfoot, yet this is relative, since here and there are suggestions of parts of other myths. Again, these narratives are relatively few in number, and in most cases lack the classical ring of other groups.

The miscellaneous group contains various elements. Some are recognizable as Plains and Eastern tales; while others, again, seem to be original. The definite intrusion of what are regarded as Kutenai myths is a matter of interest, because the narrator, a Piegan, is credited with the chief responsibility of their introduction in association with the Black-Tail deer-dance. Narratives Nos. 19, 20, deserve special mention, because they are told as ethical puzzles usually exciting discussion, different persons having more or less fixed opinions about the matter. So far as known to the writer, such narratives have not been reported by other observers. A large part of this

---

[1] In the case of the Medicine-Hat tale, the origin of the name is to a degree secondary; but the real significance of the narrative is that it accounts for the origin of a special method for trapping eagles.

miscellaneous group is made up of narratives for children, though all tales of the Old Man are told even to the youngest children, and often recited as lullabies for infants.

No effort has been made to determine the place of the Blackfoot in the mythology of the Plains; but in the various footnotes, references to such parallels among neighboring tribes as came to our notice have been made. Many of the myths generally distributed throughout the central parts of North America appear in our collection and among the works of other writers. Some rather striking exceptions are the well-known Imitations of the Host, Vaginal Teeth, and The Dancing Ducks. All of these appear in the Arapaho collections, and, with the exception of the second, in the Gros Ventre. By inquiry we found individuals who claimed to have heard the following narratives, but were unable to render them: The Dancing Ducks, Vaginal Teeth, The Man who Received a Flageolet from an Elk, The Man who Played Dead and Deceived a Bear,[1] The Recovery of Water by Stealing the Vessels in which it was Concealed, and the Wounded Man Carried Home by a Bear. Among those for which no recognition was observed may be mentioned the Imitation of the Host, Raven Creating the World and People, The Tar-Baby and the Recovery of the Daylight by Theft. However, without going into details, certain tentative similarities may be noted between the mythology of the Blackfoot and that of neighboring tribes, though the material at hand is very unsatisfactory. There is the appearance of close similarity to the mythology of the western Cree and an almost equal degree of similarity to that of the Crow. To come to a definite conclusion on this point, we need larger collections from these tribes, and also data on the mythology of the Assiniboine, who were allied with the western Cree living along the edge of the forest. Again, the similarities in Gros Ventre mythology are numerous, though, as may be expected, the myths of this tribe bear much greater resemblance to those of the Arapaho. On the other hand, there are a number of similarities between the Blackfoot and the Arapaho not paralleled in the Gros Ventre. However, our collection from the latter is probably not so complete as from the former. While these similarities taken together include many of the more widely distributed North American myths, they include others apparently restricted to these three tribes. In this connection we need more data from the Cheyenne, Kiowa, and Shoshone, especially the former, who are members of the Plains Algonkin group. There are also a number of Blackfoot similarities to Arikara incidents, that seem less definite among the collections from other Caddoan tribes. Perhaps these Arikara incidents are characteristic of Upper Missouri mythology. Here we need data from the Hidatsa.

---

[1] Dorsey and Kroeber, Traditions of the Arapaho, op. cit., p. 451.

It may not be out of place to give our impression of the position these tales occupy in Blackfoot culture. While their mythology certainly stands for a part of what we know as the literature of a people, it does not by any means comprise the larger part; for historical, military, adventurous, ceremonial, and other forms of narratives there are in profusion. It will be noticed that the narratives in our collection correspond in general style to what we recognize as fiction. The attitude of the Blackfoot people toward these narratives is difficult to reduce to accurate statement, but one gets the impression that they are often valued more for their æsthetic factors than otherwise. Yet the active elements of this mythology seem to function in mythical characters so firmly fixed in folk-thought, that each may. be regarded as a reality. One also gets the impression, after some familiarity with the serious life of these people, that mythical characters are generally accorded the same reality as pertains to a deceased friend. The most venerated of these are Sun-Man, Moon-Woman, Morning-Star, the Thunder, Scar-Face, the Seven-Stars, the Pleiades (Bunched stars), Otter-Woman, Elk-Woman, the Old Man, Blood-Clot, Scabby-Round-Robe, the Woman-who-Married-the-Star, and the Woman-who-Married-the-Buffalo. All are regarded as having made at least some important contribution to the welfare of the people. Naturally, not all are of equal rank; the Sun, Moon, Thunder, and Morning-Star being of very great power and supernatural significance. An exhaustive collection of Blackfoot narratives would doubtless contain numerous and various versions of the doings of these and other minor characters. Taken collectively, these characters give the sanctions for many practices and beliefs. That they are strictly moral sanctions is doubtful, since they seem to have prescribed the formal parts of ceremonies and worship rather than ethical procedure. Anyway, to the present Blackfoot mind, the moral lives of these characters are not always exemplary. The Old Man is held in contempt, and one may hear such expessions as "I do not hold Scar-Face in esteem, because, while he did a great thing, he did it for spite." However, a full discussion of these characters must be deferred until we have presented the details of ceremonial practices and beliefs.

So far as we know there are no restrictions against the telling of myths at certain times of the year. There is no detailed myth which can be narrated only to select audiences, as among the Arapaho, Cheyenne, and Dakota, — myths that have so far not been recorded. Neither are their myths peculiar to women or men, as the case may be, any one being at liberty to render any myth whatsoever. However, persons not versed in a ritual are often reluctant to narrate the myth accounting for its origin, because in a general way it is improper for one to speak in detail of medicines concerning which they have little knowledge.   As women take important parts in most ritualistic ceremonies, such restrictions are not correlated with sex differences. Then, again, all elderly persons are assumed to have had considerable experience in ritualistic ceremonies; hence young people usually hesitate to narrate myths in deference to the rights of their elders.

CLARK WISSLER.

NEW YORK CITY,
    July 11, 1908.

I. TALES OF THE OLD MAN.

1. The Making of the Earth.

During the flood, Old Man was sitting on the highest mountain with all the beasts. The flood was caused by the above people, because the baby (a fungus) [1] of the woman who married a star was heedlessly torn in pieces by an Indian child. [2] Old Man sent the Otter down to get some earth. For a long time he waited, then the Otter came up dead. Old Man examined its feet, but found nothing on them. Next he sent Beaver down, but after a long time he also came up drowned. Again nothing was found on his feet. He sent Muskrat to dive next. Muskrat also was drowned. At length he sent the Duck (?). It was drowned, but in its paw held some earth. Old Man saw it, put it in his hand, feigned putting it on the water three times, and at last dropped it. Then the above-people sent rain, and everything grew on the earth. [3]

2. Languages Confused on a Mountain.

After the flood, Old Man mixed water with different colors. He whistled, and all the people came together. He gave one man a cup of one kind of water, saying, "You will be chief of these people here." To another man he gave differently colored water, and so on. The Blackfoot, Piegan, and Blood all received black water. Then he said to the people, "Talk," and they all talked differently; but those who drank black water spoke the same. This happened on the highest mountain in the Montana Reservation [Chief Mountain?]. [4]

3. Order of Life and Death.

There was once a time when there were but two persons in the world, Old Man and Old Woman. One time, when they were travelling about,

---

[1] In rendering these narratives explanatory matter supplied by the narrator is indicated by parenthesis, that supplied by the translator or editor is indicated by brackets.

[2] See Narrative of the Fixed Star, p. 58.

[3] A North Blackfoot version, collected by Dr. R. H. Lowie. For another version, see Maclean, Canadian Savage Folk, p. 51; Also Hale, Report of the British Association, 1886, p. 704. For a Sarcee version, see Wilson, Report of the British Association, 1889, p. 224. For note on the distribution of this myth, see G. A. Dorsey and A. L. Kroeber, Traditions of the Arapaho (Field Columbian Museum Publication 81, p. 20).

[4] A North Blackfoot version, collected by Dr. R. H. Lowie. In this connection note the following: "Au commencement, on habitait sur une montagne, et tous les hommes parlaient la même langue." — Petitot, op. cit., p. 383. See also pp. 130 and 332. For a second mention of this incident in our collection, see p. 23.

Old Man met Old Woman, who said, "Now, let us come to an agreement of some kind; let us decide how the people shall live." "Well," said Old Man, " I am to have the first say in everything." To this Old Woman agreed, provided she had the second say.[1]

Then Old Man began, "The women are to tan the hides. When they do this, they are to rub brains on them to make them soft; they are to scrape them well with scraping-tools, etc. But all this they are to do very quickly, for it will not be very hard work." "No, I will not agree to this," said Old Woman. "They must tan the hide in the way you say; but it must be made very hard work, and take a long time, so that the good workers may be found out."

"Well," said Old Man, "let the people have eyes and mouths in their faces; but they shall be straight up and down." "No," said Old Woman, "we will not have them that way. We will have the eyes and mouth in the faces, as you say; but they shall all be set crosswise." [2]

"Well," said Old Man, "the people shall have ten fingers on each hand." "Oh, no!" said Old Woman, "that will be too many. They will be in the way. There shall be four fingers and one thumb on each hand."

"Well," said Old Man, "we shall beget children. The genitals shall be at our navels." "No," said Old Woman, "that will make child-bearing too easy; the people will not care for their children. The genitals shall be at the pubes."

So they went on until they had provided for everything in the lives of the people that were to be. Then Old Woman asked what they should do about life and death; should the people always live, or should they die? They had some difficulty in agreeing on this; but finally Old Man said, "I will tell you what I will do. I will throw a buffalo-chip into the water, and, if it floats, the people die for four days and live again; but, if it sinks, they will die forever." So he threw it in, and it floated. "No," said Old Woman, "we will not decide in that way. I will throw in this rock. If it floats, the people will die for four days: if it sinks, the people will die forever." Then Old Woman threw the rock out into the water, and it sank to the bottom.[3] "There," said she, "it is better for the people to die forever; for, if they did not die forever, they would never feel sorry for each other, and there would be no sympathy in the world." "Well," said Old Man, "let it be that way." [4]

---

[1] See Hale, Report of the British Association for the Advancement of Science, 1886, p. 705.
[2] "Old Man made some women .... As the mouths of the women were opened vertically, so he closed them up again and cut them anew." — Maclean, Canadian Savage Folk, 1896, p. 52.
[3] This part of the myth is analogous to a Cheyenne version, for which see Kroeber, Journal of American Folk-Lore, Vol. XIII, p. 161. For a similar incident, in which the stone is thrown by Nih'ā°ça°, see Dorsey and Kroeber, op. cit., pp. 17, 81.
[4] For a comparative statement of mythical accounts of the origin of death, see Dorsey and Kroeber, op. cit., p. 20.

After a time Old Woman had a daughter, who died. She was very sorry now that it had been fixed so that people died forever. So she said to Old Man, "Let us have our say over again." "No," said he, "we fixed it once."

4. WHY PEOPLE DIE FOREVER.

One time Old Man said to Old Woman, "People will never die." "Oh!" said Old Woman, "that will never do; because, if people live always, there will be too many people in the world." [1] "Well," said Old Man, "we do not want to die forever. We shall die for four days and then come to life again." "Oh, no!" said Old Woman, "it will be better to die forever, so that we shall be sorry for each other." "Well," said Old Man, "we will decide this way. We will throw a buffalo-chip into the water: if it sinks, we will die forever; if it floats, we shall live again." "Well," said Old Woman, "throw it in." Now, Old Woman had great power, and she caused the chip to turn into a stone, so it sank.

So when we die, we die forever. [2]

5. THE FIRST MARRIAGE.

Now in those days, the men and the women did not live together. [3] The men lived in one camp and the women in the other. The men lived in lodges made of skin with the hair on; the women, in good lodges. [The idea is, that the women dress the skins, hence the men could not live in dressed-skin lodges.] One day Old Man came to the camp of the men, and, when he was there, a woman came over from the camp of the women. She said she had been sent by the chief of the women to invite all the men, because the women were going to pick out husbands.

Now the men began to get ready, and Old Man dressed himself up in his finest clothes: he was always fine looking. Then they started out, and, when they came to the women's camp, they all stood up in a row. Now the chief of the women came out to make the first choice. She had on very dirty clothes, and none of the men knew who she was. She went along the line, looked them over, and finally picked out Old Man, because of his fine appearance. Now Old Man saw many nicely dressed women waiting their turn, and, when the chief of the women took him by the hand, he

---

[1] See Dorsey and Kroeber, op. cit. p. 17.
[2] This version was received from a North Piegan. For a third version, see Grinnell, Blackfoot Lodge Tales, pp. 138–139.
[3] Rev. E. F. Wilson writes, "The Sarcee have a tradition similar to that of the Blackfoot about men and women being first made separately, and then being brought together through the action of the mythical being 'Napiw.' " — Report of the British Association, 1889, p. 244.

pulled back and broke away. He did this because he thought her a very common woman. When he pulled away, the chief of the women went back to her lodge and instructed the other women not to choose Old Man. While the other women were picking out their husbands, the chief of the women put on her best costume. When she came out, she looked very fine, and, as soon as Old Man saw her, he thought, "Oh! there is the chief of the women. I wish to be her husband." He did not know that it was the same woman.[1]

Now the chief of the women came down once more to pick out a husband, and, as she went around, Old Man kept stepping in front of her, so that she might see him; but she paid no attention to him, finally picking out another for her husband.

After a while all the men had been picked out, except Old Man. Now he was very angry; but the chief of the women said to him, "After this you are to be a tree, and stand just where you are now." Then he became a tree, and he is mad yet, because he is always caving down the bank.[2]

6. Old Man Leads a Migration.

The first Indians were on the other side of the ocean, and Old Man decided to lead them to a better place. So he brought them over the ice to the far north. When they were crossing the ice, the Sarcee[3] were in the middle and there was a boy riding on a dog travois. As they were going along, this boy saw a horn of some animal sticking up through the ice. Now the boy wanted this horn, and began to cry. So his mother took an ax and cut it off. As she did so, the ice gave way and only those on this side of the place where the horn was will ever get here.[4]

---

[1] Arapaho Tale No. 51 (Dorsey and Kroeber, op. cit.) has a few of the minor characteristics of this tale, but the plot is different.

[2] For another version of this incident, see No. 23. The following was collected among the Northern Blackfoot by Dr. R. H. Lowie: —

Women were living on one side of Little Bow River, the men on the other side (northwest of Calgary). They killed coyotes, using skins for blankets. Old Man came to the women's buffalo-drive. The women asked, "Whence come you?" "From men's camp." The women told Old Man to go there and tell the men to come. "We'll choose husbands," they said. The women asked for the chief's color. Old Man said, "He wears a wolf blanket with the tail on." The men arrived at the women's buffalo-drive. The chieftainess wearing bad clothes went out to the men. She selected Old Man; but he did not want her on account of her ugly appearance. Then the chieftainess said to the women, "You see that tall man; don't choose him." She then put on good clothes, and Old Man tried to get her; but she chose another. He was left unchosen. He stamped his foot, and made the earth fill the enclosure of the buffalo-drive.

[3] The following version was found among the Sarcee, — Another Indian told us how the Sarcee were at one time one people with the Chipewyans, and gave us the myth which accounts for their separation. "Formerly," he said, "we lived in the north country. We were many thousands in number. We were travelling south. It was winter, and we had to cross a big lake on the ice. There was an elk's horn sticking out of the ice. A squaw went and struck the horn with an axe. The elk raised himself from the ice and shook his head. The people were all frightened and ran away. Those that ran toward the north became the Chipewyans, and we who ran toward the south are the Soténna or Sarcee. — Rev. E. F. Wilson, Report of the British Association for the Advancement of Science, 1889, p. 243.

[4] This is said to have happened on a lake in Alberta, called Buffalo Lake by the Indians, because its shape is like a buffalo lying down. See Kroeber, Gros Ventre Myths and Tales (Anthropological Papers of the American Museum of Natural History, Vol. I, Part III, p. 112). Also known to the Arapaho and Cheyenne.

Now Old Man led these people down to where the Blood Reserve now is, and told them that this would be a fine country for them, and that they would be very rich. He said, "I will get all the people here." All the people living there ate and lived like wild animals; but Old Man went among them and taught them all the arts of civilization.[1] (When crossing the ice, only about thirty lodges succeeded in getting across, and among these were the representatives of all the tribes now in this country. At that time the Blackfoot were just one tribe.) When he was through teaching them, he did not die, but went among the Sioux, where he remained for a time, but finally disappeared.[2] He took his wife with him. He had no children.

7. OLD MAN AND THE GREAT SPIRIT.

There was once a Great Spirit who was good. He made a man and a woman. Then Old Man came along. No one made Old Man; he always existed. The Great Spirit said to him, "Old Man, have you any power?" "Yes," said Old Man, "I am very strong." "Well," said the Great Spirit, "suppose you make some mountains." So Old Man set to work and made the Sweet-Grass Hills.[3] To do this he took a piece of Chief Mountain. He brought Chief Mountain up to its present location, shaped it up, and named it. The other mountains were called blood colts. "Well," said the Great Spirit, "you are strong."

"Now," said Old Man, "there are four of us, — the man and woman, you and I." The Great Spirit said, "All right."

The Great Spirit said, "I will make a big cross for you to carry." Old Man said "No, you make another man so that he can carry it." The Great Spirit made another man. Old Man carried the cross a while, but soon got tired and wanted to go. The Great Spirit told him that he could go, but he should go out among the people and the animals, and teach them how to live, etc.

Now the other man got tired of carrying the cross. He was a white man. The Great Spirit sent him off as a traveller. So he wandered on alone. The man and woman who had been created wandered off down towards Mexico, where they tried to build a mountain in order to get to the

---

[1] See Grinnell, op. cit., p. 139. The following fragment also, from the Northern Blackfoot, was collected by Dr. R. H. Lowie, — On the other side of the High River, the Blackfoot were living on grass. Old Man saw them, and saw buffalo driving them. "What are you doing?" he asked. "The buffalo kill and eat us," they said. "You are foolish; you ought to eat buffalo," he replied. So he made arrows for them with which to shoot the buffalo. The Indians now made buffalo-drives.
   The idea that buffalo formerly ate men is found in Cheyenne Myths, Kroeber (Journal of American Folk-Lore, Vol. XIII, p. 161).
[2] See Macean, Canadian Savage Folk, op. cit., p. 444.
[3] See Grinnell, op. cit., p. 137; also the Old Man and the Coyote, Teit, Traditions of the Thompson River Indians of British Columbia, 1898, pp. 48, 109.

sky to be with their children; but the people got mixed up until they came to have many different languages.[1]

8. OLD MAN GAMBLES.

Far up in the north there is a place known as Old Man's Gambling-Place.[2] There is where Old Man played the game of the arrows and the rolling wheel. Once when he came to this place, he found some people playing at the game. He joined them, and lost his robe and moccasins. As soon as he took them off, the robe became back-fat, and the moccasins buffalo-tongues. As the winner had no use for such things, he gave them back at once. Then Old Man put the tongues on his feet, and they became moccasins, and, putting the back-fat on his shoulders, it became a robe. So he gambled again and again, always with the same result.

9. OLD MAN AND THE ROLLING STONE.

One time Old Man went out with the Fox. This Fox was his little brother, or chum. It was a very hot day, and, when they came to a large rock, Old Man took off his robe and threw it over the rock, saying, "Here, brother: I make you a present of this robe." Then Old Man went on, but presently saw a heavy cloud coming up: so he sent his little brother back to get the robe. So he went back to the rock, and said, "Rock, Old Man wants his robe." "No," said the Rock, "he gave it to me as a present. I shall keep it. You tell him that he cannot have it." So the Fox went back and told Old Man what the Rock had said. Then Old Man said, "My little brother, you go back and tell him again. Tell him I must have that robe." So the Fox went back to the Rock, and said, "Rock, Old Man sent me for his robe." The Rock replied, "No, no! Rocks never give back presents. If you give anything to a Rock, you cannot take it back." So the Fox returned to Old Man and told him what the Rock had said. Now Old Man was very angry. He said, "Now there is that Rock. It has been there for years and years with nothing over it; but it refuses to let me have my robe." So he rushed up to the Rock and snatched off the robe, saying, "I need this for myself."

Then Old Man started on, but presently, hearing a great noise behind him, said to the Fox, "My little brother, you go back and see what is making that noise." Then the Fox returned, saying, "Let us hurry, for that Rock is after us." When Old Man looked back, he saw the Rock coming. It was rolling along. So they both ran; but all the time the Rock was getting closer. As he went along, Old Man saw some bears, and called upon them for help. The Bears went to fight the Rock; but they could do nothing, for it rolled over them, crushing them. Again as Old Man was running along, he saw some Buffalo-bulls and called upon them for help. "Here," he said, "this Rock is chasing me. I want you to stop it." So the Bulls rushed upon the Rock; but the Rock crushed them. Then as he went on he saw some Night-hawks, and called upon them for help. "Here," he said, "is a Rock chasing me, I want you to stop it." Then the Night-hawks flew down and discharged flatus at the Rock, and each time they did so, pieces flew off. Finally it was broken to pieces.[1]

Then Old Man went on, and finally came to a nest of Night-hawks. There were young ones in it. Going up to the nest, he said, "Where are your parents?" "They have gone for some meat," replied the young ones. "Well," said Old Man, "I guess your parents are the ones that spoiled my fun. I was having a lot of fun with a Rock that was running after me, and they spoiled it:[2] so I am going to tear your mouths out." So he took hold of their bills, and split their mouths back to their necks.

Now, after Old Man had gone on, the Night-hawks came back to feed their young ones. They said to them, "You have been eating. Where did you get the meat that made your mouths bloody?" Then the young Night-hawks told them how Old Man had been there, and how he had treated them. Then the Night-hawks went in pursuit of Old Man. When they overtook him, they flew around overhead, defecating on his robe. Each time they did so, he cut off the soiled portion and threw it away. As the robe became smaller, the filth fell upon his body. At last he sought relief by plunging into the river. In this way he lost his robe.[3]

10. OLD MAN ROASTS SQUIRRELS IN HOT ASHES.

One time as Old Man was going along, he came to a place where there were many Squirrels. These Squirrels were playing in hot ashes. Some of them would lie down in the ashes, while the others would cover them

---

[1] A similar incident occurs in the Gros Ventre myth of the Bird with the Large Arrow, Kroeber, op. cit., p. 70. Also see a Cree tale, Russell, Explorations in the Far North, p. 210.

[2] A similar sentiment is expressed in a Gros Ventre myth, Kroeber, op. cit., p. 70.

[3] For other versions see Grinnell, Blackfoot Lodge Tales, p. 165, and Maclean, Journal of American Folk Lore, Vol. III, p. 296. A similar incident is known to the Arapaho, Dorsey and Kroeber, op. cit. pp. 66-70. The incidents in the Arapaho tale agree quite closely with the preceding version and also with an Arikara version, Dorsey, Traditions of the Arikara, p. 147. Also see Ute Tales, Kroeber, Journal of American Folk-Lore, December, 1901, p. 261.

over. When it became so hot that they could stand it no longer, they would call out to the others, who would take them out at once. Old Man watched the game a while, and then insisted that he be allowed to try. He asked them if he could be baked first. "No," said the Squirrels, "we are afraid you do not know how to play, and that you will be burned. Let us be baked first to show you how." Old Man asked them again, but they still refused. Finally Old Man agreed, provided they would let him cover up all the Squirrels at once. At last this was agreed to. Then Old Man began to cover up the Squirrels in the hot ashes. One of the Squirrels, who was about to become a mother, begged so pitifully not to be put into the ashes that Old Man said, "Well, you may go." When they were all covered up with the ashes, some of them became too warm, and called out to Old Man to take them out; but, instead of doing this, he heaped on more ashes as fast as he could, and finally the Squirrels were roasted to death.[1]

Then Old Man took some red willows and made a scaffold upon which to put his squirrel-meat. On this he laid the roasted squirrels. This made the willows greasy, and this is why the red willow is greasy even to this day.[2] Now Old Man had so much meat that he could not eat all of it. So he ate what he could, and, being tired, he lay down by a tree to rest. He had a little brown eye [anus] that always watched for him when he slept. So when he lay down to sleep he told Little Brown-Eye to keep watch, and to wake him if anything came around. Just as Old Man was about asleep, Little Brown-Eye gave the warning note (flatus). Old Man got up and looked around, but saw only a crow on a tree near by. This disgusted him so that he went to sleep at once. Not long after this a lynx came around. Old Man was now sound asleep. Little Brown-Eye roared away, but he could not wake him up. So the lynx ate up all the squirrels on the scaffold. After a while, Old Man woke up and went to his scaffold to eat. When he found that the meat was all gone, he was very angry, and said, "Little Brown-Eye, I told you to wake me up if anything came around. Here you let a lynx eat all of my meat." With that he caught up a stick from the fire and rubbed it into Little Brown-Eye.[3] The wood was a kind of willow, and ever since that time this willow has been called "stinking wood."

Then Old Man started out to trail the lynx. He could follow him easily because his tracks were greasy. At last he found him asleep on a large flat rock. Old Man rushed up, caught him, and said, "You are the thief who stole my meat. Now I am going to punish you." So he broke off a part

---

[1] See a Crow tale, Simms, Field Columbian Museum Publication 85, p. 285.
[2] A similar version by Grinnell, op. cit., p. 155.
[3] See Arapaho tale, Dorsey and Kroeber, op. cit., p. 60, footnote; also a parallel in the Gros Ventre, Kroeber, op. cit., p. 71. A similar incident occurs in a Dakota myth, Riggs, Contributions to North American Ethnology, Vol. IX, p. 114; Jones, Fox Texts, p. 289; and Russell Cree Myths, op. cit., p. 213.

of his tail and threw it away. Then he stood on the hind legs, and, pulling by the fore legs, stretched the lynx out to a great length. Next he took the lynx by the ears, and bumped his nose against a rock until it became flat. Then he jerked a handful of hair from the pubes, which he stuck on his nose for whiskers. He took up the lynx, and, holding him over a fire, scorched him on the sides. This is how the lynx came to have his present form.[1]

Now Little Brown-Eye had been badly burned by the stick, and was very sore. When Old Man lay down to rest, he happened to turn Little Brown-Eye toward the wind, and as the wind blew it cooled it, making him comfortable. Yet Little Brown-Eye was still painful, and Old Man called on the wind to blow harder. It did so; but as there was yet pain he called out again and again. Then a terrible storm came up. It blew harder and harder, and finally began to carry Old Man away head over heels, down the hills and over the mountains. As he was going tumbling along, he caught hold of everything he passed; but all the bushes and trees gave way before the terrible wind. At last Old Man caught hold of the birch.[2] Now the birch is very tough, and will not break easily. Old Man held on to it while the wind tossed him up and down, up and down. At last the wind died down. Old Man got down from the birch-tree and became very angry. He said, "Here, you old birch-tree! You spoiled all my fun. I was having a fine time playing with the wind. We were running over the hills and the mountains and through the woods, until you caught hold of me. Now I am going to punish you." So Old Man took out his knife, and gashed savagely at the tree. Now the marks you see on the birch-tree at the present time are the scars made by Old Man's knife.[3]

11. Old Man makes a Drive, and loses Meat in a Race.

Now Old Man went on and came to a place where deer and elk were playing a game called "Follow your leader." Old Man watched the game a while. Then he asked permission to play. He took the lead, sang a song, and ran about this way and that, and finally led them up to the edge of a cliff. Old Man jumped down and was knocked senseless. After a while he got up and called to the rest to follow. "No, we might hurt ourselves." "Oh!" said Old Man, "it is nice and soft here, and I had to sleep

---

[1] This incident and some other parts of the tale bear some resemblance to Arapaho Tales Nos. 24, 26, and 27. Dorsey and Kroeber, op. cit. Also the incident of changing the form of an animal is found in Ute Tales, Kroeber, op.·cit., p. 268.
[2] See a Crow Tale, Simms, op. cit., p. 287.
[3] This version is in general agreement with one by Grinnell, op. cit, p. 171. The differences in the details are doubtless due to the popular nature of the publication in which they are found.

a while." Then the elk all jumped down and were killed. Then Old Man said to the deer, "Now, you jump." "No," said the deer, "we shall not jump down, because the elk are all killed." "No," said Old Man, "they are only laughing." So the deer jumped down and were all killed. Now, when the elk were about to jump over, there was a female elk about to become a mother, and she begged Old Man not to make her jump, so he let her go. A few of the deer were also let go for the same reason. If he had not done this, all the elk and deer would have been killed.[1]

Old Man was now busy butchering the animals that had been killed by falling over the cliff. When he was through butchering, he went out and found a place to camp. Then he carried his meat there and hung it up to dry. When he was all alone, a Coyote came to him. This Coyote had a shell on his neck, and one leg was tied up as if badly hurt. The Coyote said to Old Man, "Give me something to eat." Old Man said to the Coyote, "You get out of here, or I will take up my genitals and beat you over the head." [2]

But Coyote did not go away. Old Man said to him, "Give me that shell on your neck to skim the soup, and I will give you something to eat." "No," said Coyote, "that shell is my medicine." Then Old Man noticed that the Coyote had his leg tied up, and said, "Well, brother, I will run you a race for a meal." "Well," said Coyote, "I am hurt. I cannot run." "That makes no difference," said Old Man, "run anyway." "Well," said Coyote, "I will run for a short distance." "No," said Old Man, "you have to run a long distance." Finally Coyote agreed. They were to run to a distant point, then back again. Coyote started out very slow, and kept crying for Old Man to wait, to wait. At last Coyote and Old Man came to the turning-point. Then Coyote took the bandage off his leg, began to run fast, and soon left Old Man far behind. He began to call out to all the coyotes, the animals, and mice, and they all came rushing up to Old Man's camp and began to eat his meat. It was a long time before Old Man reached the camp; but he kept calling out, "Leave me some meat, leave me some meat."[3]

Now, Old Man had hung all the tongues of the animals on poles, and when he got to the camp he saw them still hanging there; but, when he took them down, he found that they were nothing but shells, for mice had eaten out the inside.[4] The place where this happened was on Tongue Flag River

---

[1] For another version of the preceding, see Grinnell, op. cit., p. 158. A somewhat similar tale is given by Dorsey and Kroeber, op. cit., p. 60.

[2] Old Man's genitals are also spoken of as a lariat. The rainbow is often designated as such, using either term apparently at random. However, the usual idea is, that his genitals are used as a lariat to rope the clouds.

[3] For a similar incident, see Grinnell, op. cit., p. 157. Also Maclean, Journal of American Folk-Lore, Vol. III, p. 297.

[4] See Grinnell, op. cit., p. 158.

and Old Man had three names; Old Man, Painted-Dried-Meat, and Fooled-a-Little [meaning the opposite].[1]

12. OLD MAN SEES BERRIES IN THE WATER.

One day Old Man, standing on the bank of a stream, saw in the water some reflections of berries growing on the bank. He thought them to be real berries: so he dived into the water, but could find no berries. As soon as he was back upon the bank again, he saw them: so he dived one time after another, and finally tied rocks to his legs, that he might stay down longer. Then he nearly drowned. At last he was very tired, and, finding a shady place under a bush, he lay down to rest. Now, looking up, he saw the berries hanging over his head. Now he was very angry. He picked up a club and beat the berry-bushes until there was but one berry left. This is the reason why the people to this day beat berries from the bushes.[2]

13. OLD MAN LOSES HIS EYES.

Once there was a bird that had power to throw its eyes into a tree and call them back again. Now, Old Man came along one day and saw the bird throw its eyes up into a tree and call them back again. He said, "I should like to do this." So he began to cry, and asked the bird for some of its power. At last the bird took pity on him. It told him that, when he came to straight standing trees, all he had to do was to wish his eyes to go up, and then to wish them down again. However, he was warned not to wish it when among crooked trees.

Then Old Man went on and came to some nice straight trees. Then he wished his eyes up in the tree, and at once they were up there. Then he wished they were back again, and at once they were back again. Now, Old Man was greatly pleased. Then he came to some thick brush, and he said to himself, "Now I wonder how it will work if I try it on this brush. I wonder why the bird told me not to send my eyes into crooked trees." So out of curiosity he wished his eyes in the brush, and as he did so they went down into the brush and disappeared. All his wishing would not bring them back again. Now Old Man could not see, and he went along making signs for some one to come to his aid. Finally a coyote who was

---

[1] For a similar tale, see Dorsey and Kroeber, op. cit., p. 62.

[2] An incident closely agreeing with this is found in combination with an Arapaho tale in which Nih'ăⁿçaⁿ cooks babies, Dorsey and Kroeber, op. cit., p. 101. It is interesting to find the Arapaho sequence of these incidents in a Cegiha myth, J. O. Dorsey, Contributions to North American Ethnology, Vol. VI, p. 562.

passing that way came up and looked at Old Man. The coyote saw that his eyes were gone. Now this coyote had a festered foot, and he held this up to Old Man's nose. "My," said Old Man, "that smells like a buffalo-drive. I must be near a camp." Then the coyote stole away, leaving Old Man hurrying on.[1]

After a while, as Old Man was walking along, a girl saw him, and, as he was making queer signs, she went toward him. "What do you want?" she said. When Old Man heard the voice, he said, "I want you to come over here." Now Old Man tied up his eyes, and, when the girl came over, he said, "I wish you to lead me, for my eyes are sore." They went on until they came to some thick brush. Then Old Man said, "I will make a camp here." So he set up some poles as if to make a lodge. Then he went after more poles but, being unable to find the ones just set up, he started another shelter, and so on. Finally the girl said, "What are you doing?" Old Man said, "I am making several lodges, so you can have your choice." After a while he began to tie a rattle, made of hoofs, to the girl's dress. "What are you doing now?" she said. "Oh," said he, "I am putting preventive medicine on you." Then they camped together. Old Man had hung the hoof-rattles on the girl to act as a bell, so that he could hear her and follow her. One day the bandage came off his eyes, and the girl saw that he had no eyes. When she found this out, she tried to run away from him. Old Man followed her by the sound of the rattles; but, when she discovered this, she took them off and threw them out from a steep bank over the river. Then Old Man followed the rattling that they made, and fell head first into the water.[2]

Now Old Man met Coyote, and said to him, "Brother, you loan me one of your eyes, and I will go and get some meat for both of us." Coyote agreed to this, and gave Old Man one of his eyes. Then Old Man went into a camp where there were people; but when they saw that one socket was empty, they were frightened and began to run away. Old Man ran after them, calling, "I will not hurt you; come back." But this only frightened them the more. At last, finding that he had scared the people, he was very angry, and, going back to Coyote said, "Here, you are to blame for this. You only gave me one eye, and scared all the people away." So then he took the other eye from Coyote.[3]

---

[1] For a similar version, see Grinnell, op. cit., p. 153.
[2] See Maclean, Journal of American Folk-Lore, Vol. VI, p. 168.
[3] See Grinnell, op. cit., p. 154. In the Arapaho tale, Dorsey and Kroeber, op. cit., pp. 50–52, Nih'ä°ça° loses his eyes in the same general manner as indicated above, but borrows eyes from small animals. The adventures with the girl and the coyote do not occur. In the Gros Ventre tale the incidents are somewhat similar to the Arapaho; Kroeber, op. cit., p. 70.

14. Old Man and the Fire-Leggings.

One day Old Man was going along. He came to a lodge standing all by itself, and when he looked in he saw a great deal of dried meat. Looking around he saw hanging up a pair of leggings, which were made of rough buffalo-hide with many crow-feathers on the sides. Then he saw the owner [1] of the lodge, and said to him, "My friend, give me those leggings." "No," said the stranger, "I will not give them to you." "Yes, I must have them," said Old Man. "No," replied the stranger, "these old leggings are of no use to you." "Well, then," said Old Man, "let me sleep here." "Well," said the stranger, "you may do that." Now, that night, when the man was asleep, Old Man watched his chance, stole the leggings, tied them on his back, and ran off as fast as he could. He ran and ran until he was a great way off. "Now, then," thought he, "I am so far away that they cannot overtake me: so I will lie down and sleep." All this time the leggings were on his back. After a while he woke up, and when he looked around, he saw that he was back in the lodge again.

It seems that the owner of the lodge, on awakening in the morning, saw Old Man sleeping with the leggings on his back: so he called to his wife and told her about it. The woman cooked some food, and, when all was ready, the man called out, "My friend, get up and eat!" Now, when Old Man awoke, he was surprised to find himself back where he started from. The man said, "Oh, my friend, what are you doing with my leggings on your back?" Old Man got up, felt on his back, and, finding the leggings, said, "Well, I don't know how they came there, unless it is because your leggings like me." So he took the leggings off and gave them back to the man.[2]

Now Old Man wanted those leggings very much, so he decided to try again. The next night, as soon as every one in the lodge was asleep, he took the leggings, tied them on his back, and travelled as fast as he could until morning; then he lay down to sleep. After a while, he heard some one calling, and, when he looked around he was again back in the lodge. "Here," said the man, "what are you doing with my leggings on your back?" Now Old Man felt around in apparent surprise, and said, "Well, I do not know how they got there, unless your leggings like me so well that they get on my back during the night." "Well," said the man, "if the leggings like you so well I will give them to you. But they are not ordinary leggings: they are medicine-leggings. You must not wear them every day,

---

[1] In a version by Grinnell, the leggings were said to belong to the Sun.   op. cit., p. 167.
[2] For a similar incident with Turtle and the magic robe, see Jones, Fox-texts, p. 301; also a magic quiver, Russell, op. cit., p. 215.

but take them out with you when you go to hunt.   Whenever you find game
in the brush, put on these leggings and run round and round.   As you do
this, the brush will take fire; but I warn you that you must never wear them
except when you have use for them."

Now Old Man was greatly pleased, so he took his leggings and started
out.   After a time he came to the camp of the Piegan.   All the people were
watching him.   So he began to dress himself up to look fine.   He said to
himself, "Now, here are those leggings.   I think I will wear them."   So
he put them on.   Now he started out, and at the first step, fire started in the
grass.   This frightened him very much, and he began to run, setting fire
to everything.   The faster he ran, the more fire there was.   The people
began to call out that Old Man was trying to burn them up.   He ran as
fast as he could, and at last succeeded in getting the leggings off.   He threw
them down on the ground, where they burned up.   Then the fire went out.

So Old Man lost his leggings.

15. Old Man frightens a Bear.

One day, as Old Man was going along, he saw a bear digging roots.
Then he hid behind a hill where the bear could not see him, and called out,
"You dirty anus bear!"   When the bear looked up, he saw nothing, and
went on digging roots.   Then Old Man called out again, "Oh, you dirty
anus bear!"   This time the bear looked around quickly and saw Old Man
get behind the hill.   He took after him at once.   Old Man ran away as
fast as he could with the bear at his heels.   Finally he came to a large tree,
and began to run round the tree with the bear after him.   They kept on
around the tree so long that a deep trail was worn in the ground.   At last
a buffalo-horn was uncovered in the trail.   When Old Man saw this, he
picked it up, held it on his forehead, and, turning, rushed at the bear.   This
frightened the bear so much that he turned to run, and as he did so he
defecated all over Old Man.[1]

16. Old Man gets fast in an Elk-Skull, and Loses his Hair.

One day Old Man was going along, when he came to an elk-skull on the
ground.   Inside of it were some white mice dancing.   Old Man began to
cry, because he wanted to go in and dance with the mice.   The Mice told
him that he was too big to get in to dance, but that he could stick his head

---

[1] For another version see Grinnell, op. cit., p. 157.   A similar incident occurs among the
Arikara, Dorsey, op. cit., p. 139, and the Cree, Russell, op. cit., p. 210.

inside, and shake it which would be the same as dancing. "However," they said, "whatever you do, you must not go to sleep." So Old Man stuck his head into the skull; but he forgot and went to sleep, and, while he slept, the Mice chewed all his hair off. When Old Man awoke, he could not get the skull off his head, so he went into the river and swam along with the antlers sticking out of the water. In this way he passed a camp of Indians. Then he made a noise like an elk. The people shot at him, went into the water and dragged him out; but when they had him on shore they saw that it was Old Man. Then they took a stone and broke the skull, that he might get his head out again.[1]

17. Old Man cooks Two Babies.

Old Man came to a lodge in which there were some old women and two babies. The women asked him to get some meat for them. So he went out into the brush. He pulled hair out of his robe and scattered it around. Then he rubbed his buttocks on the snow until they bled, making the snow bloody. Then he returned to the lodge and told the women that he had killed something, and asked them to go out and bring in the meat. So they started out, leaving their babies in the cradles.

As soon as the women had gone, Old Man took out his knife, cut off the heads of the babies, and put their bodies into the pot. Then he put their heads back into the cradles, and fixed them as before.

When the women came back they said, "We cannot find the meat. The snow was all bloody, with hair scattered around. The coyotes must have eaten it."

"Oh," said Old Man, "while you were gone, I got an antelope. It is cooking in the pot. Now be careful; don't wake the babies. I shall go after some wood." So Old Man went out, gathered a pile of wood, and blocked the door with it. Then he called out to the women, "Your babies are cooking in the pot."

The women rushed to the cradles and found it was true. Now they were very angry, and tried to get out by the door; but the wood was in the way. Old Man ran off.[2] However, the old women soon got out of the lodge, and pursued him. When they were about to overtake him, he ran into a hole in the ground. Then the women sat down and cried.

While they were crying, Old Man came out of another hole, disguised

---

[1] Similar tales are known to the Arapaho (Dorsey and Kroeber, op. cit., pp. 107–111). The Gros Ventre version is similar only in the main incident of the mice dancing in the skull (Kroeber, op. cit., p. 68). The Arikara have a similar tale (Dorsey, op. cit., p. 137).
[2] This incident is found among the Gros Ventre (Kroeber, op. cit., p. 71).

himself, and came around to the women.   "Well, my grandmothers," said he, "why are you sitting here?"   Then the women related to him all that had happened.   Then Old Man appeared to be very angry, and said, "I will go into that hole and kill him."   Then he went into the hole, and while he was inside he made a great noise, as if a terrible fight was going on.   At last everything was quiet, and after a time Old Man came out, saying, "Now he is dead."

Then Old Man requested the women to go down into the hole to bring out the body; but, as soon as they were under, he stopped up the entrance, made a fire, and suffocated them with smoke.[1]

18.   OLD MAN'S ESCAPE.

Old Man came to a camp of the Piegan.   He went up to a lodge.   It was a chief's lodge.   Looking in he saw no one but a girl asleep.   He stole up and put excrement on her dress.   The smell of it wakened her, and she requested Old Man to remove it.[2]

"Well," said Old Man, "I must have pay.   I do not work for nothing."

The girl offered bows, arrows, and everything in the lodge; but Old Man refused each offer.   Then she offered him her mother, sisters, etc.; but still he refused.   Then she offered him her robe, her leggings, moccasins, etc.; but he refused each in turn.   Finally she had nothing but herself to offer.   Old Man said he would be satisfied with that.

When the girl saw the size and length of Old Man's lariat, she was troubled, and asked him to tie a stick across it, near the end.   This he did. While they embraced, he removed the stick.   The girl was torn in pieces.[3]

Then Old Man went into the lodge of some old women.   He tied up his head and pretended to be very sick.   They cared for him.

When the chief returned to his lodge, he found his daughter dead, and from her condition knew that Old Man must have been there.   He searched, and found him with the old women.   When Old Man was accused, he pleaded sickness as a proof of innocence.   Now the chief was suspicious. He decided to try an ordeal.   Every one was to be required to jump a ditch, and the one who failed was to be considered guilty of the crime.   As they were going out to the place of trial, Old Man met a bird, and induced it to exchange genitals with him.[4]   Then they went on to the place.   When it

---

[1] This tale agrees generally with two Arapaho versions (Dorsey and Kroeber op. cit., pp. 101–105).   A general statement of its distribution is given in a footnote, ibid. p. 103.   The last incident is found in a Gros Ventre tale (Kroeber, op. cit., p. 43).
[2] See Gros Ventre version (Kroeber, op. cit., p. 74).
[3] See note p. 28.
[4] According to a Northern Blackfoot version, he concealed his guilt by placing them in the sky as a rainbow.   See footnote p. 28.

came the turn of the bird, he could not jump because of the unusual weight he carried. So he fell into the ditch. When they were about to execute the bird, he told what had been done. Then they were about to kill Old Man, but he offered to bring the girl to life again. The chief agreed to give him a trial.[1]

When all was ready, Old Man placed two women at the door of the lodge, one on each side. They held stone mauls in their hands. On the outside he placed two men with spears. The other people were sitting around inside of the lodge. Then Old Man put two pieces of fat on the fire, and when they were hot he took one in each hand and whirled about, causing the hot grease to fly into their eyes. Then he sprang out of the door. As he passed, the women with mauls struck at him, but killed each other. The same thing happened to the two men with spears.

Old Man ran, but he was pursued by the men of the camp. After a time, the chase led by a place where some women were dressing hides. They caught him. Now Old Man was good at promising. He promised them elk-teeth, and they let him go. Soon the chase passed some young men playing the wheel-game. They caught him. He told them that he was not being pursued, but was running a race for some arrows. So they let him go. At last he got away.[2]

19. OLD MAN DECEIVED BY TWO WOMEN.

Now all the women knew that Old Man was a very bad character, and they always tried to avoid him. One day two women out picking berries saw Old Man coming, but saw no way to avoid him. So they decided to play dead. As Old Man was going along, he saw the two women lying on the ground, stopped, and said, "Poor women! These are nice women. It is too bad they are dead." Then he touched one of them, "Oh, they have just died! They are still warm; something must have killed them. I wonder what it was." So he turned them over and over, but found no wounds. Then he began to remove their clothes, examining their bodies carefully. Finally he saw the vulva. "Oh!" said he, "no wonder they died. Here are the wounds. They have been stabbed by a dagger." Then he put his finger in one of the wounds, took it out and smelled it. "No," he said, "it was not by a dagger that they were killed. They were shot by a gun, because I smell the burnt powder. Well," said he, "I pity these poor women. They were too young to die. I must try to doctor them

---

[1] For a tale almost identical with the preceding see Dorsey and Kroeber, op. cit, p. 73.
[2] For another version, see Grinnell, op. cit., p. 159.

back to life again." So he took one of them on his back to carry her away to the doctoring place. One of her arms hung over his shoulder, and as she pretended to be dead, she allowed it to swing freely so that, as they went along, her hand beat his nose, making it bleed. At last, when Old Man came to a suitable place for doctoring, he put the woman down, and started back for the other one; but when he was halfway, both women jumped up and ran away. Then Old Man called out, "Oh, I thought you were dead! Don't run away. Come, play dead again."[1]

20. Old Man sees Girls picking Strawberries.

One day as Old Man was going along, he saw some girls picking berries at a distance. So he insinuated his long lariat along under the ground and up among the strawberries, the juice of which stained the protruding end.[2] As the girls were picking, one of them came to the protruding part, and exclaimed, "Oh, here is a big one!" She tried to pick it, but it could not be moved. The she called her companions to her aid, but without avail. They tried to eat it. At last one of them sat on it. Suddenly she was raised up and killed.[3]

21. Old Man penem trans flumen mittit.

Old Man went on. After a time he saw a female beaver on the other side of the river asleep. He called the muskrat, and requested him to carry his lariat across and place it to the beaver. He directed the muskrat to pinch the end when properly placed. Now the muskrat began to swim across with his burden. The current was swift, and carried him down. At this Old Man scolded harshly, which made the muskrat very angry; so when he landed, he sought out a thicket of thorns in which he deposited his burden and did as directed. Old Man thrust with all his might. He ploughed out a deep trail.[4]

22. Old Man makes Buffalo laugh.

Old Man looked from Red Deer River over to Little Bow River. He saw some buffalo. He tied up his hair in knots, and crawled along on hands

---

[1] Parts of this tale are known to the Crow (Simms, op. cit., p. 284).
[2] See part of a Crow tale (Simms, op. cit., p. 284).
[3] See note p. 28.
[4] For similar tales, see Dorsey and Kroeber, Arapaho Myths, op. cit., pp. 63–64.

and knees. The sight made the buffalo laugh. One of them laughed himself to death, and the Old Man butchered him.[1]

23. ADVENTURES OF OLD MAN.

As Old Man was travelling along, he saw a rock, and said, "Now I shall give you this robe." So he took off his robe and put it over the rock.[2] Now Old Man was travelling with his little brother the Fox, and as they went on it began to look like rain, so Old Man sent his little brother back to get the robe. But when Fox came to the rock, and said that Old Man sent him for the robe because it was going to rain, the Rock said, "No, he gave it to me." Then Fox returned, and reported to Old Man. This made Old Man very mad. He hurried back to the rock, and jerked off the robe, saying, "You have been here many years without a robe, and now you will not give it back to me when I need it." Then Old Man went on. Presently he heard thunder. After a time Fox looked back and saw the rock rolling after them. Then they began to run. They ran as fast as they could. Presently Old Man saw some buffalo-bulls, and called on them for help. The bulls tried to stop the rock, but they were crushed. Then Old Man saw some bears, and called to them for help, but the bears could not stop the rock. Then Old Man saw some night-hawks, and called out to them for help. Then the night-hawks flew down, and each time they came near the rock they discharged their flatus, causing pieces to fly off. Finally the rock was broken to pieces, and from the inside came a bear and a bull [buffalo].[3]

Now old Man came to a river where he saw some young night-hawks in a nest. "Oh, yes!" said he, "it was your father and mother who spoiled all my fun. They broke to pieces the rock that was chasing me. Now I shall tear your mouths." So he widened their mouths. When the old birds came back, the young ones told them what Old Man had said. So they pursued him. When they overtook him, they circled around and defecated over him.

As Old Man ran to escape them, he met a man with leggings made of calf-skin. Old Man called out to him for help. Now those leggings were medicine, and the owner caused them to make a fire, which frightened the night-hawks away. Then the two men sat down. Old Man said, "Stranger, give me your leggings." "Well," said the man, "I will give them to you in winter. You will not need them in summer." Old Man insisted, and

---

[1] Recorded among the Northern Blackfoot by Dr. R. H. Lowie. For another version see Grinnell, op. cit., p. 170.

[2] This account is in the form of a continuous narrative, repeating most of the incidents contained in the preceding tales. It was narrated by a North Piegan Indian.

[3] This incident does not occur in other versions.

finally the man said he would give them to him after a while.[1] "Well," said Old Man, "I am going over to the lodges you see yonder."

Now when Old Man came to the lodges, he said to the people, "Let us have a game." (This is a game in which the players move in a row. The leader carries a stick one end of which is on fire, and he strikes the stick, causing the sparks to fly around.) Now in this game Old Man led, and carried the stick. The people who were playing were deer and elk people. Then Old Man suggested that they play another game, "Wherever the leader goes." [In this game the players all follow the leader.] They played this until night. Finally they came to a very high bank. Now Old Man played a trick. He said, "Wait!" and crept down at another place; then, running up to the foot of the cliff, called out, "You have not heard me for a while because I have been laughing. I found a nice soft place when I jumped down." So all the animals jumped down and were killed. There were some females among them about to become mothers, who begged Old Man to be allowed to go. At last he granted their request.

Then Old Man dried the meat and kept it. After it was all eaten up, he travelled on again. Finally he came to a place where some squirrels were playing at a game. The squirrels would be covered up by one of them with hot ashes. Old Man asked them to let him play, but they declined. At length they agreed. Finally Old Man requested that he be allowed to cover them all up at once. Now there was one female squirrel who was about to become a mother, and she begged so pitifully of Old Man to let her go, that he consented. As he did so he said, "I will do this that there may be more squirrels in the world." Then he covered all the squirrels with the ashes, and when they became too hot, they called out to be uncovered; but Old Man paid no attention to this. So they died. Then Old Man brought some red willows and made a scaffold upon which to put his meat. Hence, the red willow is greasy to this day. When he had put all the squirrels out on the scaffold, he began to eat. Finally he could eat no more, but there were still many squirrels left. Now he went to sleep, and said to his anus, "If any one comes along, you make a noise and wake me up." So, whenever a bird or an insect came along, the anus made a noise, waking Old Man. This made him tired. Finally he was so sound asleep that he did not waken when the noise was made. Then a lynx came. He soon found the squirrels, and began to eat them.

Now when Old Man awoke, he was hungry, but found his meat gone. Then he was very angry. So he followed the tracks of the lynx, and soon found him sleeping on a flat stone. He caught the lynx, and tried to tear

---

[1] Comparison with the preceding narrative (No. 14) will show how the story of the fire-leggings is made a part of the plot in this continuous narrative.

him in two by pulling on his front and hind legs, but did not succeed.   Then he banged his nose on the rock, so that the lynx has a flat nose even to this day.   Then he pulled out a bunch of hair from the pubes, and put it on the nose of the lynx for whiskers.   Now Old Man was mad at his anus for all this.   So he took a stick from the fire and rubbed it.   This wood smells bad to this day.

Then Old Man started out but the burn was painful and he went up on a hill that the wind might fan it.   There was no wind, so he rolled buffalo-chips down the hill in order to produce wind.   At last the wind began to blow very hard, and he was carried along, bouncing up and down.   He caught hold of bushes and trees, but none of them were strong enough to hold him.   At last he caught hold of the birch.   This did not break, but held him bouncing up and down.   When the wind went down, Old Man was very angry.   He scolded the birch for being so strong.   Then he took out his knife and slashed the bark.   [The cause of the markings on the bark.]

Now the man who promised the leggings to Old Man came with them. He said, "You must not use them every day.   Do not put them on unless you want to set things on fire.   Wear them on the ice, and when you are hungry, dance and sing, and up will come food.   But you must not do these things often."   Old Man paid no attention to what was said, took the leggings, put them on, and began to dance, and when he did so they took fire; so he took them off as quickly as he could, and gave them back to their owner.

At this time the women and the men were not married, and Old Man came to a place where the women were going to pick out husbands.   Old Man stood among the men, but no one picked him out.   This took place in a buffalo-drive.   When Old Man found that he had not been chosen, he was very angry.   He began to tear down the cliff; then he turned into a pine-tree, and has been there ever since.

II. STAR MYTHS.

1. The Twin Brothers, or Stars.[1]

A long time ago there was a man by the name of Smart-Crow. When he travelled, he always went by himself. One day after he was married he told his wife that in the future two children would be born to them, both boys. He predicted that one of them would be an outlaw (?) and the other a good man. Smart Crow knew this, because a Crow had given him the information in a dream. This Crow also told him, that, before his two children were born, an evil man would try to kill their mother. The Crow told the man that he must warn his wife. It said, "This man will come to the lodge when you are away, and ask to come inside. Your wife must say nothing to him. He will repeat the visit four nights." The next time Smart-Crow went out to hunt, he told his wife about this dream, and warned her not to speak to the strange man.

While Smart-Crow was away, the strange man came and stood before the lodge. After a while the woman thought to herself, "Why does not this man come in?" Now, the stranger had great power. He read the woman's thoughts, and, as soon as she thought this, the man answered by saying, "I will tell you why." So he entered the lodge and sat down, saying as he did so, "I knew you wished me to come in." Now the woman began to cook some meat for the stranger, and when it was ready, she put it in some wooden bowls, and placed it before him. There were four kinds of bowls in the house. Some were made of hard knots of wood; some, of bark; some, of buffalo-horn; and some, of mountain-sheep horn. After the woman had cooked the meat, she placed it before the stranger in a wooden bowl. The stranger looked at it and said, "That is not the kind of bowl from which I take my food." Then the woman took the food, and, putting it into a bark bowl, offered it to him again. "No," he said, "I do not take my food from bark." So the woman took the food, placed it in a bowl of buffalo-horn, and offered it to him for the third time. Again he refused, saying that he did not take food from horns. The woman took back the food, and, putting it in a bowl of sheep horn placed it before him; but he refused to take food in such a dish. Now the woman was troubled, and looked about the lodge for something in which to serve the food. Finally she saw a piece from the horn of a moose, and offered him food upon it

---

[1] Sometimes spoken of as the Origin of the Four-Tail Lodge; also spoken of as the Dusty Stars, or Puff-Balls. The Blackfoot have a curious belief that certain kinds of fungi are associated with the stars. Sometimes these fungi are spoken of as the "fallen stars." See pp. 19, 42, 44, 60.

This he refused also. As she looked about for something else, she happened to see a blanket. "That will not do, either," said the stranger. Then she offered her dress. "That is nearer the kind I must have," he said. Then the woman said, "Oh, well, I will put the meat on my belly." "All right," said the stranger. The woman then lay down on her back, and placed the meat on her belly. She was heavy with child. The stranger had a white stone knife, which he sharpened and began to cut the meat. Three times he cut the meat; but the fourth time he said, "I came near cutting you." The fifth time he cut the woman open. Then twin boys came out.

Thus the boys were born. They were twins. The stranger took one of them, put him down near the ashes, and as he did so said, "You shall be called Ashes-Chief." Then he took the other, stuck him behind the lining of the lodge, and said, "You shall be called Stuck-Behind." Then the man went away. He carried a small lodge, with the skin of the running-fisher, for a flag.[1]

After a while Smart-Crow returned from his hunt, bringing much buffalo-meat. As he came over the hill near his lodge, he saw no smoke rising from the smoke-hole. "Now," he said to himself, "I know what has happened. I knew that woman would invite the stranger in." When he entered the lodge, he saw Ashes-Chief lying by the fire. While he was looking at his wife's body he heard the other infant crying behind the lodge-lining.

Now Smart-Crow was very angry, and rushed out in pursuit of the stranger. He followed his trail and soon overtook him. As he came up, he said to the stranger, "Now I shall kill you." "My friend," said the stranger, "I will restore her to you." "I do not believe you," said Smart-Crow. "My friend, I tell you I will restore her," repeated the stranger. "I cannot believe it," said Smart-Crow. "My friend," said the stranger, "I will restore her to you." "You are a liar," said Smart-Crow. Then the stranger began to sing a song. The words of this song were as follows:—

> "I am a great medicine [powerful].
> Everything in the ground hears me.
> Everything in the sky hears me."

When Smart-Crow heard this song, he believed in the promise of the stranger. Then the stranger took the bundle from his back, and said, "I give you this lodge and the running-fisher skin." The stranger set up the lodge. There were four buffalo-tails hanging to its sides. Two of these were cow-tails, and two were bull-tails. One of each hung in front, and

---

[1] The medicine object for a painted lodge is often spoken of as a flag: *i. e.*, an emblem hung from a pole.

also behind. This lodge was called the Four-Tail Lodge. The stranger told Smart-Crow that the hanging of the buffalo-tails on the lodge would make the buffalo range near it, so that the people would always have meat. The stranger transferred this lodge to Smart-Crow. He sat down upon a stump, explained the ritual to him, and also taught him the songs. Among other things he said, "The punk which you use to make fires is made of bark, and does not kindle quickly; take puff-balls (fungus) instead, for they are much better. They are the Dusty Stars. You are to paint these stars around the bottom of the lodge. At the top of the lodge you are to paint the Seven Stars on one side and the Bunch Stars on the other. At the back of the lodge, near the top, you must make a cross to represent the Morning Star. Then around the bottom, above the Dusty Stars, you shall mark the mountains. Above the door, make four red stripes passing around the lodge. These are to represent the trails of the buffalo."

When Smart-Crow had received all of the instructions belonging to the new lodge, and had learned all the songs, he went away with it and returned to his own lodge. He picked up Ashes-Chief, and said to a large rock lying near by, "I give you this child to raise." Then he pulled down the lining of the lodge, picked up Stuck-Behind, and called out to his friend the beaver, "I give you this child to raise." So the rock and the beaver took the boys away.

The boys grew up. When they were about fifteen years old, Smart-Crow began to wish that he might have them with him again. He went out to get them back; but the boys were wild, and knew nothing about people. So, when the boys saw him coming, Ashes-Chief ran into the rock and Stuck-Behind into the beaver's house. Then Smart-Crow took some arrows from his quiver, laid them down near the rock, and concealed himself in the bushes. After a while, Ashes-Chief came out, saw the arrows, and looked curiously at them. As the boy was about to pick them up, Smart-Crow sprang out and caught him. Now Ashes-Chief had been raised by the rock, and was so strong for his age that Smart-Crow was scarcely able to hold him. He saw that his son would soon break away; so he said, "Ashes-Chief, lick my hand, and you will know that I am your father." Then Ashes-Chief licked his hand, stopped struggling, and said, "Yes, you are my father, and I will go with you."

Now Smart-Crow was anxious to secure Stuck-Behind, and advised with Ashes-Chief as to how to proceed. Finally they decided to draw him out of the beaver's house by playing the hoop-game. Smart-Crow concealed himself near the house while Ashes-Chief began to roll the hoop back and forth near the door. Stuck-Behind became curious to know about the hoop, and ventured out to play. When he was outside, Smart-Crow sprang upon him, and held him fast. Now, Stuck-Behind had been raised by the beaver, and for that reason was very hard to hold. Smart-Crow said to him, "Lick my hand, and you will know that I am your father." He did so, and recognized his father.

When the boys were at home with their father, their names were changed. Ashes-Chief was now called Rock, and Stuck-Behind was called Beaver. Rock was the evil (?) one, and Beaver the good one, as the Crow had told their father in the dream. One day Rock said to his father, "Make me a bow and two arrows." "What do you want with bows and arrows?" said Smart-Crow. "Well," said Rock, "Beaver and I wish to go out to hunt buffalo. While we are gone, you must go back to our old lodge where the bones of our mother lie, and cut a stick such as she used for stirring the meat when cooking. Wait there for us until we bring the meat." Then Rock and Beaver went on their way to hunt.

Now, at this time, the people cooked in pots of clay. These were shaped out of mud by the hands, and put in the sun to dry; then the kettle was rubbed all over with fat inside and out, and placed in the fire. When it was red hot, it was taken out, and allowed to cool. Such a pot was good for boiling. Rock told his father to take one of his mother's pots, fill it with water, and put it over the fire so that it might be ready for his mother to boil meat.

After a while the boys came up to their mother's lodge, where her skeleton lay.[1] They had a great deal of meat with them. Rock said, "Now, I shall take a little meat from each part of the buffalo, boil it in the pot, and then make medicine to put over the skeleton of our mother." Beaver said, "I shall help mother with the heart, the brains, and the marrow." Rock took up the tongue, blew his breath on it four times, and put in into the pot. Then he took up the other parts, one at a time, and did the same. The brains and marrow, however, he laid to one side, and did not put them into the pot. Rock said to Beaver, "I will help mother in two things and you may help her in the other two things." Now Smart-Crow was lying down in bed. The boys took his robe, and covered their mother's bones. Then the pot began to boil more than ever, and Rock said to his father, "Get up, call mother, and tell her that her pot is about to boil over."

The father arose from his bed, went over to the place where the robe lay, and said, "Get up, woman! Your pot is about to boil over." The bones did not move. Then Beaver called, "Mother, get up quick! Your pot is boiling over." At this there was a little movement under the robe. Then Rock called out, "Mother, get up quick, and feed us!" At this there was

---

[1] In former times the dead were often left in the lodge, while the whole camp moved to another site.

much movement under the robe, and parts of the woman's feet could be seen beneath the edge. Now Beaver called to her, which made the fourth time, saying, "Mother, get up quick! I have a heart, brains, and marrow for you to eat."

The woman sat up and drew a deep breath. "I have had a long sleep," she said, "I am very hungry: I shall eat." The boys gave her some of each part of the buffalo to restore her to life. For eyes, they gave her the inside of the eyes; for brains, they gave her the brains; for tongue, part of the tongue; for heart, part of the heart, and so on. When she had eaten all of these, she got up and set food before her children and Smart-Crow, as she had always done.

Then Smart-Crow said to his wife, "Let us move from this place, it is an unlucky place for us. Let us leave this lodge here and take the new one given me by the stranger. When this new lodge is up in a new place, make a sweat-house, that I may go through it, for we have a medicine-lodge now. I did not kill the stranger, because he promised to restore you to me, and gave me this new lodge. After all I have seen, I believe that this lodge is very powerful. You have been asleep for a long time. Your bones were bleached, now you are alive; and it is the power of this lodge that made you so. When we are old, we will give this lodge to Beaver; he is a good man. Rock, on the other hand, is no good, and he will not live long."

This happened out in the far north, when the Piegan lived there.

When the mother had put up the new lodge in a new place, she made a sweat-house. Smart-Crow put the skin of the running-fisher around his shoulders, painted his face, took off his breech-cloth and moccasins, and was ready to go through the sweat-house. Then he covered the sweat-house with the skin of the new lodge, that it also might be purified. When he came out of the sweat-house, he painted his wife and children, and, taking up the lodge, put it in place. When all this was arranged, the woman looked at the lodge, admiring it. "What are those round things at the bottom?" she said.

"Those," said Smart-Crow, "are for two purposes. They will help us to live long and to make fire quickly." When they had gone inside of the lodge, Smart-Crow said to his wife, "Now I shall teach you how to use the smudge." Then he took some moss from the pine-tree and laid it upon the fire, singing a song. "You are to do this," he said, "every morning and every night. Also you must sing two seven-songs [fourteen] that I shall teach you."

Now all this time Smart-Crow had been away from his people; but now he returned with his family and the new lodge. This created a great sensation.

Now the hoop that was used in catching Beaver was the big game-hoop. Rock and Beaver often played at this game. One day their father told them that they must not roll the hoop in the same direction as the wind. Then they went out to play. Now Rock said to Beaver, "There is no reason why we should not roll this hoop with the wind. Nothing will happen if we do." "Oh," said Beaver, "our father requested us not to do this, and we should obey him." However, Rock paid no attention to what he said, and started the hoop in the direction of the wind. Now, the hoop continued to roll and roll. It would not stop, and as the boys followed along, waiting for it to fall, they were brought near a rock lodge. As the hoop rolled by, an old woman came out, took it in her hands, and invited the boys inside. They both went in.[1]

Now this old woman had some kind of power. She killed people by suffocating them with smoke. As soon as the boys were seated, she took out a large pipe with a man's head for a bowl. Then she placed a great heap of wood on the fire, and, after shutting the door and the ears [smoke-hole] of the lodge, lighted the pipe and made a great smoke. Then the old woman said to the boys, "Smoke with me." "No," said Rock. "You must," said the old woman, "because it is the custom for the guest to smoke with the head of the lodge."

Now this old woman was a cannibal, and the boys knew it. So Rock said to the old woman, "Well, I will smoke with you." But Beaver refused. Then the old woman gave back the hoop, which Beaver took and put over his head. Rock took out a yellow plume and tied it to his hair. Now both of these things had power. The hoop kept the smoke away from Beaver's head, so that his head was in a hollow place surrounded by thick smoke. The plume in Rock's hair whirled in the air, and kept the smoke from his face. Now the smoke was so thick at last that the old woman could not see. She did not know that the boys had such great power. It became so thick at last that she was almost suffocated herself. "Oh!" she said, "there is too much smoke." She tried to rise to open the door, but fell down dead. Then the boys went outside of the lodge, and called out as if talking to the old woman. In this way they made all manner of fun of her great power. Looking around, they found themselves near the rock that had raised Rock. Then Rock took an arrow from his quiver, spit upon the point, dipped it into the water, and, pointing toward the rock, asked it for help, saying, "Make the arrow do what I wish." Then he threw the arrow at the lodge in which the old woman lived. It struck at the bottom, making a hole from which the water began to flow. The stream continued to increase in

---

[1] See Kroeber, Gros Ventre, op. cit., p. 109, where this incident appears as a separate tale.

size until it carried the lodge and rock away. Then the boys went home. Rock told his father everything that had happened, and laughed a great deal.

There was a tall tree upon which grew some fine berries. The father said to them, "You must not eat those berries." Some time after, when the boys were out by themselves, Rock looked up at the tree, and said to Beaver, "Come, let us get some of those berries." But Beaver said, "No. Every time father requests us to do a thing, you do the opposite." But as Rock insisted upon getting the berries, Beaver consented. Now, beneath this tree lived a monstrous snake with a large horn in the middle of his head. When they came near the tree, Beaver was afraid, and said to Rock, "I do not wish to climb the tree. You get the berries." Then Rock began to climb the tree, and, when he was up in the branches, the snake came out of the bushes and began to climb the tree. When the snake came within reach, he tried to hook Rock; but, missing, his horn struck the tree and stuck fast. Then Rock broke the tree and twisted the trunk, which pulled out the snake's brains. This snake always killed people who came to gather berries. Then the boys took some of the berries and went home. Rock related the adventure to his father, and laughed as if it were but an incident.

Once they were forbidden to shoot at the morning-bird. Now the morning-bird was a very powerful creature; every one was afraid to do anything to him. One day when the boys were out, they saw this bird, but could not get at him as he was high in the air. Later they saw the bird near the ground, and Rock suggested to Beaver that they send an arrow after it. Again Beaver tried to persuade Rock to heed the commands of their father; but without success. So Rock shot an arrow into the bird. It fell into the branches of a tree, almost within their reach. Rock stood upon a log and tried to reach the bird; but every time he tried, the bird got a little higher. Then he got upon a limb, and finally into the tree itself. Then, as he climbed the tree, the bird went higher and higher, and the tree became taller and taller, until Beaver, who stood upon the ground, could not see them. Now Beaver felt very much ashamed that he had yielded to his brother's folly. He did not feel like going home to tell his father, so he sat down by the tree and began to cry. When this happened, the boys were men, but Beaver cried so much at the foot of the tree that he became a dirty little ragged boy again.

At this time the Piegan were out looking for buffalo, but could find none. They were forced to live upon such berries as they could find. One day an old woman was out gathering berries when she heard a child crying.[1] Looking around, she found Beaver at the foot of the tree. He was almost

---

[1] See Arapaho incident (Dorsey and Kroeber, op. cit., p. 347).

starved. The old woman felt sorry for him, picked him up and took him home.[1] She gave him to her daughter to care for, saying, "Here is my grandson. When he grows up, he will run errands for us. You must feed him." Now, as they had no meat from which to make soup for the child, the daughter gathered some old bones around the camp and boiled them in a kettle. A few days after this the chief of the camp, who had two beautiful daughters for whom there were many suitors, made a public announcement. He said, "To-morrow morning a [prairie] chicken will sit upon a tall tree near the camp, and all the young men are to shoot at it with bows and arrows. The man who hits it first shall receive my eldest daughter for a wife."

Now Beaver was a very dirty little fellow, he even defecated in bed, and every one in the camp talked about his uncleanness. When he heard what the chief said, he said to the old woman who found him, "Make me some arrows and I will try to hit the bird." "Oh, you dirty thing!" said the woman in disgust. "You are a disgrace to the camp; you would nauseate everybody. The girl would not have you anyway." The boy insisted that the arrows should be made for him; and, the fourth time he made the request, she made a bow and four arrows. All were very poorly constructed.

When the time came for the young men to try their skill at shooting, the little boy came among the crowd, wearing an old piece of skin for a robe. He was pot-bellied. His eyes were sore and dirty. The people made fun of him. "What can you do?" they said. "What brought you anyway?" So they threw dirt at him and mocked him. Then the shooting began. One after the other, the young men discharged their arrows at the bird; but no one made a hit. Beaver looked at the bird in the tree, then discharged one of his arrows, which came near hitting the bird.

Now there was a man in the crowd called Crow-Arrow, who had never been able to get a wife. He observed that the boy had some kind of power, and envied his success. Then he got his bow ready to discharge an arrow at the same time as the boy, and, in case the bird was hit, he would dispute the ownership of the arrow. When the boy discharged his second arrow, Crow-Arrow discharged his also. The boy's arrow struck the bird, and it fell to the ground. Crow-Arrow, who was very swift, ran at once to the spot, pulled out the boy's arrow and put in his own. The people, who were all looking on, said, "No, it was the boy who hit the bird." Then they all went before the chief, and announced to him that the little dirty boy

---

[1] This incident in connection with part of the preceding is a version of the widely distributed Found-in-the-Grass Myth. For a similar rendering, see Kroeber, Gros Ventre Myths, op. cit., p. 77.

had won; but Crow-Arrow insisted that it was his arrow that killed the bird. The chief looked at the small dirty boy with disgust, and said to himself, "I cannot have him for my son-in-law, even if he did hit the bird." Then he said to the people, "Since there is a dispute about this, we will try something else. All the young men shall set wolf-traps, and whoever gets a black one or a white one shall be my son-in-law."

Beaver went home and asked his grandmother to make him a wolf-trap. The grandmother said, "Oh, you get away from here, you dirty boy! No wolf would ever go into a trap you touched." But as Beaver insisted, she fixed up a trap just back of the lodge. In the evening, Beaver went out to fix his trap, and when morning came there was both a black and a white wolf in his trap. Now Crow-Arrow had set a trap also, and in the morning found a black wolf in his trap. Crow-Arrow hurried to the chief with his prize; but when he got there he found Beaver with two wolves, one black and one white. "Well," said the chief, "there is no dispute about it this time. The little dirty boy must be my son-in-law."

So the eldest daughter was dressed up, her face painted, and taken over to the lodge where Beaver lived.

Now Beaver always defecated and urinated in his bed. When the girl saw him she was disgusted, for his eyes were dirty and his abdomen was very large; but she gave him some food. He ate, and immediately defecated in the bed. His grandmother cleaned him, and scolded. After a while the girl and Beaver went to bed, but he dirtied the bed as usual. When the girl awoke, the condition of the bed caused her to vomit. The girl said she would not live with such a husband as this, and went over to live with Crow-Arrow. When the chief heard this, he was very angry, because he knew that the little dirty boy possessed some kind of power, for which reason his daughter should have kept her promise. So, to make amends, he sent his youngest daughter over to be the wife of Beaver. Now this girl was rather bashful, and when she came to the lodge where Beaver lived, she got behind the old woman, and, peeping out at him, whispered to the old woman, "I think that boy is very pretty. I shall stay with him because he is so nice, and I see no reason why my sister left him." Then she went to bed with Beaver. He did as before, but the girl got up and asked the grandmother for a piece of robe to clean the bed. She was cheerful and kind.

Now all this time the people had been without meat, and the chief sent out the young men in every direction to look for buffalo, but none were seen. Beaver said to his wife, "You are to go home to-night and stay with your mother until I send for you." He said to his grandmother, "You also must go away from this lodge and not return until I call you. You must leave me alone here." As soon as they were gone, Beaver took some yellow paint, put it in the hollow of his hand, mixed it with water, and painted his entire body. Then he took hold of his hair, pulled it down and painted it. At once be became a man, as before. Before him stood the Four-Tail Lodge of his father. In it was a dress covered with elk-teeth for his wife, also a fine white robe for himself. There were beds and other furniture in the lodge. Then Beaver sent out for the old woman, his grandmother, and when she came up directed her to wait outside of the door. Then he brought out a fine dress covered with elk-teeth, and told her to put it on. As soon as she did this, she became a young woman again. Then he sent the grandmother over to the lodge of the chief to call his wife. The young woman did not recognize the grandmother, but followed her as requested; and when she came to the strange lodge she also failed to recognize Beaver. Beaver explained to her what had happened, and told her that she was to be rewarded for her kindness to him when he was such a dirty little boy. He brought out to her a fine dress covered with elk-teeth, and, rubbing paint upon her hair, pulled it gently until it became very long. Then he sent his wife to her father. When she came in she said, "Father, my husband is about to go out to drive the buffalo over into the enclosure. There will be one white buffalo in the herd, and my husband requests that no one shoot it, but that it be roped and then knocked on the head so that no injury be done to the skin, for it is to be made into a robe."

All the young men of the camp went out with Beaver to drive the buffalo. Crow-Arrow also went. Beaver took a white rock and placed it near the edge of the enclosure, then he took up a rock colored like the beaver, and placed it on the other side. Then he directed the young men to lay rows of rocks spreading outward from these two. Then they laid down between them some buffalo-chips. As they were putting down the last Beaver shouted four times. Everybody looked around. They saw a herd of buffalo, a white one and a beaver-colored one in the lead. Then the men hid behind the rocks. This was a buffalo-drive.[1]

When the people were going out with Beaver to prepare the buffalo-drive, Crow-Arrow came upon an old buffalo-carcass. He cut out some of the spoiled meat, and carried it back to the chief to make him believe that he had the power to get meat first. While Crow-Arrow was on his way back, he heard the shouting and the noise of the buffalo going over. He ran up as quickly as he could, and saw the white buffalo already roped and about to be knocked upon the head. Looking around, he saw the beaver-colored one and shot it. When the buffalo were killed, Beaver called to his wife, directed her to take his arrows, rub them over the skin of the white

---

[1] See Arapaho incidents (Dorsey and Kroeber, op. cit., pp. 349, 355, 374, 386).

buffalo, and throw them away. These arrows were feathered with eagle-tails. As the woman threw them from her, all the young men fought for them, because they were regaided as very good medicine. When Crow-Arrow saw this, he directed his wife to take his arrows and do likewise with the skin of the beaver-colored buffalo. Crow-Arrow's arrows were made of crow-feathers. Now when Beaver's wife rubbed the arrows over the skin of the white buffalo, it was made smooth and clean; but when the wife of Crow-Arrow rubbed the skin of the beaver-colored buffalo, it did not change. So when she threw her arrows away, no one seemed anxious to pick them up. Now the wife of Crow-Arrow, the same one who deserted Beaver, felt ashamed. She came close to Beaver, and said, "I wish you would give me some of your arrows to clean the skin." "No," said Beaver. "Once I married you, but you refused to live with me or to clean me: now I shall not help you clean skins." When Crow-Arrow saw what had happened he was very angry, and went home with his wife. He was very angry be-cause Beaver seemed to have greater power than he. Now Crow-Arrow was a great medicine-man, and so he transformed himself and his family into crows, and they flew out at the top of their lodge. Then the crows flew around all of the lodges, and called out to the people in crow-language, "We shall starve you; we shall take all the buffalo away from you, and starve you to death."

After this no buffalo were seen in the country, because the crows took the buffalo over the mountains.[1] Beaver and his people were soon driven to starvation; but the crows returned, flew around over their lodges and mocked them. So Beaver called the people together in council and said to the young men, "What can you do? Has any one power to bring back the buffalo?" No one seemed to have such power. This was in the winter. Then Beaver said, "Let two young men go to the place where the beaver lives, cut a hole in the ice, build a fire and try to smoke the beaver out. Then I shall transform myself into a beaver and lie by the hole as if dead." The young men did as directed. During the night, Beaver went down to the place, transformed himself into a beaver and lay down upon the ice as if dead. Part of the skin was pulled away, and his entrails could be seen. While he was lying there, Crow-[Arrow] flew up, looked down, and said, "Oh, yes! I know your game. I know you. It is no use for you to try to get me in this way. Your people will starve. You think you are very smart, but you cannot get me. It is no use to try me in that way, because I know too much." None of this made any impression upon Beaver, who

---

[1] From this point forward, the narrative is similar to the Dog and the Stick (Grinnell, op. cit., p. 145). In that tale, Napiwᵃ, or the Old Man, takes the part played by Beaver in the above. The incident occurs among the Arapaho as a detached story (Dorsey and Kroeber, op. cit., p. 459).

looked precisely like a corpse. Then Crow said to himself, "Well, after all, I believe it is a real dead beaver." He came down and looked closely at the corpse, and pecked at the breast and eyes. They were all frozen hard: he could not make a dent in them. So the Crow took up a piece of fat from the entrails. He flew to a place and began to eat. Then he said, "Yes, it is a real beaver." Then Crow went back to the corpse and began to eat. Beaver lay still for a while, but suddenly transformed himself into a man, sprang upon the Crow and caught him. As he struggled, the Crow cried, "Let me go! let me go! I will get buffalo for you." "No," said Beaver, "you are a liar. I shall hold on to you this time. I shall surely punish you." So he broke the wing of the Crow, took him home and tied him to the smoke-hole of the lodge. Then Beaver gathered a lot of birch-wood and threw it into the fire, making a very black smoke. Now, up to this time, all crows were white; and while Crow was crying in the top of the lodge, "Oh, let me go! let me go! I will bring you buffalo surely," the smoke made him black, and crows have been black ever since. After Crow was as black as he could be, Beaver consented to let him go if he would call the buffalo. Crow promised, but, as soon as he was released, he flew to the top of the lodge and called back, "I shall let you starve, I shall let you starve. I was just fooling."

Then the people of the camp scolded Beaver. They said, "You knew that he was a liar. You knew that he would not keep his word. You should have kept him fast until he produced the buffalo." "Well," said Beaver, "I will get the buffalo myself." One of the men said, "I should like to go with you." "What kind of power, have you?" said Beaver. "Well, I have some power," said the man. "I can transform myself into a swallow, a pup, and a spider." "Well, you have some power," said Beaver, "but I have greater power. I can transform myself into anything, but you may come with me."

Now, the name of this man was Little-Dog. He transformed himself into a swallow, and Beaver became a prairie-chicken. Then they started out to look for buffalo. As they went along, Little-Dog saw Crow's camp in the distance. Then he transformed himself into a spider, and, coming up to a man belonging to Crow's camp, inquired of him the whereabouts of Crow. The man informed him that he had gone over the mountain to live, and that there was a very high cliff behind them. Then Little-Dog transformed himself into a swallow, and Beaver into a horse-fly. Together they flew over the cliff. Here they saw Crow's camp. While they were looking, Crow's people moved their camp. Then Little-Dog transformed himself into a spider, and Beaver became a pine-tree. Now the two watched a long time for the buffalo; but they saw no trace of them around Crow's camp. One day they saw Crow go away. Then they went to the place where the camp was first seen, and Beaver transformed himself into a digging-stick, and Little-Dog became a pup. After a while the young daughter of Crow came out to look around the old camping-place. She found the digging-stick and the pup, and carried them home with her. When she came up to her lodge, her mother was tanning a hide. The girl said to her, "Mother, these things were left behind when we moved camp." So the woman thought no more of it, and the girl took the two into the lodge to play. Now the girl was very fond of the pup, and carried it about in her arms, with the digging-stick stuck on her back in the way that women carry babies. While the girl was playing with the pup, as children do, she raised up the edge of the bed. There was a deep hole under it, and, holding the pup over it, she said, "Pup, do you see that deep hole? Do you see all the buffalo down there?" Now Little-Dog and Beaver looked down into the hole and saw where the buffalo were hidden. As the girl was looking over, the digging-stick slipped from her back into the hole, and pup grew into a large dog, so large that he slipped down of his own weight. The girl was very much frightened, but went away without saying anything to her mother.

So Beaver and Little-Dog fell down into the hole. Beaver transformed himself into a man, and Little-Dog became a monstrous dog. At once he began to bark and chase the buffalo, and the man ran after them shouting. This frightened the buffalo so much that they dashed up through the hole and out upon the earth. There were so many buffalo that it took them a long time to get out; so that Crow returned while Beaver and Little-Dog were still driving buffalo. Crow knew who was driving them out, and took his station by the side of the hole, waiting to kill them. However, they were not to be caught so easily. Beaver caught hold of a buffalo, transformed himself into a stick, and concealed himself in the long hair of the neck. Little-Dog became a pup once more, and fastened his teeth in the long hair of the breast of a buffalo. Thus they were carried out, unobserved by Crow.

Now the buffalo were running over the earth, they were restored to the people once more.[1]

After this, Beaver returned to his people. One day he told his wife that she must never put sagebrush on the fire as it was against his medicine; but one day his wife forgot this, and threw the sagebrush into the fire while Beaver was away. When Beaver came in, he knew what had been done. He said to his wife, "Now, since you have used the sagebrush for the fire,

---

[1] The confinement of buffalo in a cave is an incident often found in the mythology of the buffalo area. For its recurrence in this collection see pp. 123, 124.

I must leave you and go to my brother. You will never see me here again."
Then he took his white robe and a plume. He blew the plume up into the
air and rose to the sky. His brother had been carried to the sky on the
branches of a tree, and Beaver went up to him. Now they are both stars.
Every night we see two large stars side by side: these are the two brothers,
Ashes-Chief and Stuck-Behind.

2. Blood-Clot, or Smoking-Star. [1]

Once there was an old man and woman whose three daughters married
a young man. The old people lived in a lodge by themselves. The young
man was supposed to hunt buffalo, and feed them all. Early in the morning the young man invited his father-in-law to go out with him to kill buffalo.
The old man was then directed to drive the buffalo through a gap where
the young man stationed himself to kill them as they went by. As soon as
the buffalo were killed, the young man requested his father-in-law to go
home. He said, "You are old. You need not stay here. Your daughters
can bring you some meat." Now the young man lied to his father-in-law;
for when the meat was brought to his lodge, he ordered his wives not to give
meat to the old folks. Yet one of the daughters took pity on her parents,
and stole meat for them. The way in which she did this was to take a piece
of meat in her robe, and as she went for water drop it in front of her father's
lodge.

Now every morning the young man invited his father-in-law to hunt
buffalo: and, as before, sent him away and refused to permit his daughters
to furnish meat for the old people. On the fourth day, as the old man was
returning, he saw a clot of blood in the trail, and said to himself, "Here at
least is something from which we can make soup." In order that he might
not be seen by his son-in-law, he stumbled, and spilt the arrows out of his
quiver. Now, as he picked up the arrows, he put the clot of blood into the
quiver. Just then the young man came up and demanded to know what it
was he picked up. The old man explained that he had just stumbled, and
was picking up his arrows. So the old man took the clot of blood home and
requested his wife to make blood-soup. When the pot began to boil, the
old woman heard a child crying. She looked all around, but saw nothing.
Then she heard it again. This time it seemed to be in the pot. She looked
in quickly, and saw a boy baby: so she lifted the pot from the fire, took the
baby out and wrapped it up.

---

[1] This is a widely distributed tale, and very popular among Plains tribes. A footnote to
an Arapaho version (Dorsey and Kroeber, op. cit., p. 298) gives its general distribution. The
version given here is in close agreement with a Gros Ventre rendering (Kroeber, op. cit., p. 82).

Now the young man, sitting in his lodge, heard a baby crying, and said, "Well, the old woman must have a baby." Then he sent his oldest wife over to see the old woman's baby, saying, "If it is a boy, I will kill it." The woman came in to look at the baby, but the old woman told her it was a girl. When the young man heard this, he did not believe it. So he sent each wife in turn; but they all came back with the same report. Now the young man was greatly pleased, because he could look forward to another wife. So he sent over some old bones, that soup might be made for the baby. Now, all this happened in the morning. That night the baby spoke to the old man, saying, "You take me up and hold me against each lodge-pole in succession." So the old man took up the baby, and, beginning at the door, went around in the direction of the sun, and each time that he touched a pole, the baby became larger. When halfway around, the baby was so heavy that the old man could hold him no longer. So he put the baby down in the middle of the lodge, and, taking hold of his head, moved it toward each of the poles in succession, and, when the last pole was reached, the baby had become a very fine young man. Then this young man went out, got some black flint [obsidian] and, when he got to the lodge, he said to the old man, "I am the Smoking-Star. I came down to help you. When I have done this, I shall return."

Now, when morning came, Blood-Clot (the name his father gave him) arose and took his father out to hunt. They had not gone very far when they killed a scabby cow. Then Blood-Clot lay down behind the cow and requested his father to wait until the son-in-law came to join him. He also requested that he stand his ground and talk back to the son-in-law. Now, at the usual time in the morning, the son-in-law called at the lodge of the old man, but was told that he had gone out to hunt. This made him very angry, and he struck at the old woman, saying, "I have a notion to kill you." So the son-in-law went out.

Now Blood-Clot had directed his father to be eating a kidney when the son-in-law approached. When the son-in-law came up and saw all this, he was very angry. He said to the old man, "Now you shall die for all this." "Well," said the old man, "you must die too, for all that you have done." Then the son-in-law began to shoot arrows at the old man, and the latter, becoming frightened, called on Blood-Clot for help. Then Blood-Clot sprang up and upbraided the son-in-law for his cruelty. "Oh," said the son-in-law, "I was just fooling." At this Blood-Clot shot the son-in-law through and through. Then Blood-Clot said to his father, "We will leave this meat here: it is not good. Your son-in-law's house is full of dried meat. Which one of your daughters helped you?" The old man told him that it was the youngest. Then Blood-Clot went to the lodge, killed the two older women, brought up the body of the son-in-law, and burned them together. Then he requested the younger daughter to take care of her old parents, to be kind to them, etc. [1] "Now," said Blood-Clot, "I shall go to visit the other Indians."

So he started out, and finally came to a camp. He went into the lodge of some old women, who were very much surprised to see such a fine young man. They said, "Why do you come here, among such old women as we? Why don't you go where there are young people?" "Well," said Blood-Clot, "give me some dried meat." Then the old women gave him some meat, but no fat. "Well," said Blood-Clot, "you did not give me the fat to eat with my dried meat." "Hush!" said the old women. "You must not speak so loud. There are bears here that take all the fat and give us the lean, and they will kill you, if they hear you." "Well," said Blood-Clot, "I will go out to-morrow, do some butchering, and get some fat." Then he went out through the camp, telling all the people to make ready in the morning, for he intended to drive the buffalo over [the drive].

Now there were some bears who ruled over this camp. They lived in a bear-lodge [painted lodge],[2] and were very cruel. When Blood-Clot had driven the buffalo over, he noticed among them a scabby cow. He said, "I shall save this for the old women." Then the people laughed, and said, "Do you mean to save that poor old beast? It is too poor to have fat." However, when it was cut open it was found to be very fat. Now, when the bears heard the buffalo go over the drive, they as usual sent out two bears to cut off the best meat, especially all the fat; but Blood-Clot had already butchered the buffalo, putting the fat upon sticks. He hid it as the bears came up. Also he had heated some stones in a fire. When they told him what they wanted, he ordered them to go back. Now the bears were very angry, and the chief bear and his wife came up to fight, but Blood-Clot killed them by throwing hot stones down their throats. Then he went down to the lodge of the bears and killed all, except one female who was about to become a mother. She pleaded so pitifully for her life, that he spared her. If he had not done this, there would have been no more bears in the world. The lodge of the bears was filled with dried meat and other property. Also all the young women of the camp were confined there. Blood-Clot gave all the property to the old women, and set free all the young women. The bears' lodge he gave to the old women. It was a bear painted lodge.

---

[1] The preceding is similar to a version by Maclean, The Indians of Canada, 1892, p. 169. This author passes over the other parts of the story with "Kutoyis employed all his time in driving the evil out of the world.' See, also, the same author, Journal of American Folk-Lore, Vol. VI, p. 167.

[2] For a note on these lodges, see p. 92.

"Now," said Blood-Clot, " I must go on my travels." He came to a camp and entered the lodge of some old women. When these women saw what a fine young man he was, they said, "Why do you come here, among such old women? Why do you not go where there are younger people?" "Well," said he, "give me some meat." The old women gave him some dried meat, but no fat. Then he said, "Why do you not give me some fat with my meat?" "Hush!" said the women, "you must not speak so loud. There is a snake-lodge [painted lodge] here, and the snakes take everything. They leave no fat for the people." "Well," said Blood-Clot, "I will go over to the snake-lodge to eat." "No, you must not do that," said the old women. "It is dangerous. They will surely kill you." "Well," said he, "I must have some fat with my meat, even if they do kill me." Then he entered the snake-lodge. He had his white rock knife ready. Now the snake, who was the head man in this lodge, had one horn on his head. He was lying with his head in the lap of a beautiful woman. He was asleep. By the fire was a bowl of berry-soup ready for the snake when he should wake. Blood-Clot seized the bowl and drank the soup. Then the woman warned him in whispers, "You must go away: you must not stay here." But he said, "I want to smoke." So he took out his knife and cut off the head of the snake, saying as he did so, "Wake up! light a pipe! I want to smoke." Then with his knife he began to kill all the snakes. At last there was one snake who was about to become a mother, and she pleaded so pitifully for her life that she was allowed to go. From her descended all the snakes that are in the world. Now the lodge of the snakes was filled up with dried meat of every kind, fat, etc. Blood-Clot turned all this over to the people, the lodge and everything it contained. Then he said, "I must go away and visit other people."

So he started out. Some old women advised him to keep on the south side of the road, because it was dangerous the other way. But Blood-Clot paid no attention to their warning. As he was going along, a great wind-storm struck him and at last carried him into the mouth of a great fish.[1] This was a sucker-fish and the wind was its sucking. When he got into the stomach of the fish, he saw a great many people. Many of them were dead, but some were still alive. He said to the people, "Ah, there must be a heart somewhere here. We will have a dance." So he painted his face white, his eyes and mouth with black circles, and tied a white rock knife on his head, so that the point stuck up. Some rattles made of hoofs were also brought. Then the people started in to dance. For a while Blood-Clot sat making wing-motions with his hands, and singing songs. Then he stood

---

[1] For a similar incident, see J. O. Dorsey, op. cit., p. 34.

up and danced, jumping up and down until the knife on his head struck
the heart.[1] Then he cut the heart down. Next he cut through between
the ribs of the fish, and let all the people out.

Again Blood-Clot said he must go on his travels. Before starting, the
people warned him, saying that after a while he would see a woman who was
always challenging people to wrestle with her, but that he must not speak to
her. He gave no heed to what they said, and, after he had gone a little way,
he saw a woman who called him to come over. "No," said Blood-Clot.
"I am in a hurry." However, at the fourth time the woman asked him to
come over, he said, "Yes, but you must wait a little while, for I am tired. I
wish to rest. When I have rested, I will come over and wrestle with you."
Now, while he was resting, he saw many large knives sticking up from the
ground almost hidden by straw. Then he knew that the woman killed the
people she wrestled with by throwing them down on the knives. When
he was rested, he went over. The woman asked him to stand up in the
place where he had seen the knives; but he said, "No, I am not quite ready.
Let us play a little, before we begin." So he began to play with the woman,
but quickly caught hold of her, threw her upon the knives, and cut her in two.

Blood-Clot took up his travels again, and after a while came to a camp
where there were some old women. The old women told him that a little
farther on he would come to a woman with a swing,[2] but on no account
must he ride with her. After a time he came to a place where he saw a
swing on the bank of a swift stream. There was a woman swinging on it.
He watched her a while, and saw that she killed people by swinging them
out and dropping them into the water. When he found this out, he came up
to the woman. "You have a swing here; let me see you swing," he said.
"No," said the woman, "I want to see you swing." "Well," said Blood-
Clot, "but you must swing first." "Well," said the woman, "Now I shall
swing. Watch me. Then I shall see you do it." So the woman swung out
over the stream. As she did this, he saw how it worked. Then he said to
the woman, "You swing again while I am getting ready;" but as the woman
swung out this time, he cut the vine and let her drop into the water. This
happened on Cut Bank Creek.[3]

"Now," said Blood-Clot, "I have rid the world of all the monsters, I will
go back to my old father and mother." So he climbed a high ridge, and
returned to the lodge of the old couple. One day he said to them, "I shall

---

[1] This is regarded as the origin of a ceremony known as the "dance of the spirits of the
dead," or "ghost dance." The knife tied on the head is said to glisten or give off light, like a
halo (smoke), hence the name Smoking-Star.

[2] For a different rendering, see Grinnell, op. cit., p. 37. However, the swing is found among
the Gros Ventre (Kroeber, op. cit., p. 87) and the Fox (Jones, op. cit., p. 103).

[3] Grinnell's version contains another incident. After this adventure, Blood-Clot is eaten
four times by a cannibal. In each case the bones are restored to life by a little girl. After
the fourth restoration Blood-Clot kills the cannibal (op. cit., p. 37).

go back to the place from whence I came. If you find that I have been killed, you must not be sorry, for then I shall go up into the sky and become the Smoking-Star." Then he went on and on, until he was killed by some Crow Indians on the war-path. His body was never found; but the moment he was killed, the Smoking-Star appeared in the sky, where we see it now.

3. The Fixed Star.

One summer night when it was very hot inside the lodge, two young women went outside to sleep. They woke up before daylight and were looking up at the sky, when one of them saw the Morning Star. She said to her companion, "That is a very bright star. I should like him for a husband." She soon forgot what she had said. In a few days these two young women went out from the camp to gather wood. When they had made up their packs and were drawing them up on their shoulders with the pack-straps, the strap broke that belonged to the girl who said she wished the Morning Star for her husband. Every time she made up her bundle and raised it to her back, the strap would break. Her companion, who was standing by her side with her pack on her shoulders, began to grow weary. She said, "I shall go on with my load: you can follow."

When the young woman was left alone, and had made up her bundle again, a handsome young man came out of the brush. He wore a fine robe made of beaver-skins, and had an eagle-plume in his hair. When the young woman started to go on, he stepped in front of her. Whichever way she turned, he headed her off. Finally she said to him, "Why do you head me off?" The young man replied, "You said you would take me for your husband." "No," said the young woman, "you must be mistaken. I never had anything to do with you. I do not know you." "I am the Morning Star," said the stranger, "and one night, when you looked up at me, you said that you wished me for a husband. Now I have come for you." "Yes, I did say that," said the young woman. So she consented to go away with him. Then Morning Star put an eagle plume in her hair, and told her to shut her eyes. Then they went up into the sky.

Now the Sun was the father of the Morning Star and the Moon was his mother. When they came into the lodge, Morning Star said to his parents, "I have brought a wife with me." The parents were pleased with what their son had done. Moon gave the young wife four berries and a few drops of water in a little shell. These were given to her to eat and to drink. Though the young woman was very hungry, she could neither eat all of the berries nor drink all of the water, because these berries were all the food there was in the world and the shell contained all the water there was in the ocean (?).

After a time, Moon said to her daughter-in-law, "Now I shall give you a root-digger, and you may go out to dig roots; but you are not to dig that big turnip there, because it is medicine [nātōji'wā]." So the young woman went about the sky country digging roots for their food. She often looked at that fine large turnip growing there, and was curious to know why she was forbidden to dig it up. In course of time she gave birth to a child. One day, when it was old enough to sit alone, she said to herself as she went out to dig roots, "Now no one will know about it if I do dig it up." So she stuck her digging-stick into the ground under the turnip; but, when she tried to raise it, the stick would not move. When she found that she could not get the stick out, she began to cry. Then two large white cranes flew down; one was a male and the other a female. The young woman prayed to them for help to get her root-digger out of the ground. Then the Crane-Woman[1] said, "When I married I was true to my vow. I never had anything to do with any other man than my husband. It is because of this that I have power to help you. Your mother[2] gave you this digging-stick. Now I shall teach you the songs that go with it." Then Crane-Woman made a smudge, took the hands of the woman into her own, and, while she sang the songs, placed them upon the digging-stick. Then Crane-Woman pulled out the stick, and, marching around in the direction of the sun, made three movements toward the turnip, and with the fourth dug it out. Now the young woman took the digging-stick and the turnip home with her. When they saw what she had, they reprimanded her. Morning Star said to her, "What did you see when you dug out this turnip?" The woman replied, "I looked down through the hole and saw the earth, the trees, the rivers, and the lodges of my people."

"Now," said Morning Star, "I cannot keep you any longer. You must take the boy with you and go back to your people; but when you get there you must not let him touch the ground for two-seven [fourteen] days. If he should touch the ground before that time, he will become a puff-ball [a fungus], go up as a star, and fit into the hole from which you dug the turnip. He will never move from that place, like the other stars, but will always be still."

Sun said to her, "I shall call in a man to help you down to the earth." After a while a man came with a strong spider-web, to one end of which he

---

[1] In all Blackfoot narratives where animals take important parts in medicine procedure, it is assumed that they are persons in disguise, and "become as people."

[2] In all ceremonial gifts or transfers, the giver is spoken of as a father or mother, according to the sex; hence the thought is, that this digging-stick was not an ordinary gift, but carried with it ceremonial obligations.

tied the woman and the boy, and let them down through the hole from which the turnip was taken. The woman came down over the camp of her own people. The young men of the camp were playing at the wheel-game. One of them happened to look up into the sky, where he saw something coming down. Now this young man had very poor eyes, and, when he told his companions that something was coming down from the sky, they looked, and, seeing nothing, made sport of him. As he still insisted, they, in derision, threw dirt into his eyes. But after a while they, too, saw something coming down from the sky. As the woman reached the ground in the centre of the camp, some one, recognizing her, called out, "Here is the woman who never came back with her wood." Then all her friends came out to meet her, and her mother took her home.

Now, before the woman left the sky, Morning Star told her, that, since she had made one mistake in digging up the turnip, she would no doubt make another mistake, and allow the child to touch the ground before the time was up. So he advised her to make the sign of the Morning Star on the back of her lodge, so that she might be reminded daily of her duty. (The doors of the lodges at that time faced the sun, and the sign of the Morning Star was to be made upon the back of the lodge, because he always travels on the other side from the sun.)

The young woman kept careful watch over the boy for thirteen days. On this day her mother sent her out for water. Before going out, the young woman cautioned her mother to keep the child upon the bed, and not allow him to touch the ground. Now the grandmother was not so careful, because she did not understand the reason for watching the child; and while her back was turned he crawled out upon the ground. When she saw him, she caught him up, putting him back on the bed as quickly as she could. This seemed to make the child angry, for he pulled the robe up over himself. The grandmother paid no further attention to him.

Now, when the boy's mother came back, she looked around, and said, "Where is my child?" "Oh, he covered himself up with a robe," said the grandmother. The young mother rushed to the bed, pulled back the robe, and found nothing but a puff-ball [fungus]. She caught this up, and carried it in her bosom all the time.

That evening when the stars came out, she looked up into the sky. A new star stuck in the hole from which she pulled the turnip. Then she knew what had become of her child.

This is the way the Fixed Star came to be.

After this the woman painted circles around the bottom of her lodge to represent the puff-ball, or the Fallen Star [the one that came down]. She had already painted the Morning Star on the back of her lodge. This is why the people paint their lodges in the way that you see them. Also this woman brought down the turnip and the digging-stick. Crane-Woman taught her the songs that go with them and their use in the sun-dance. This was the beginning of the medicine-woman [leader in the sun-dance].

Many years after, this woman, while holding the sun-dance, made another mistake. She took some of the offerings from the sun lodge. When she did this, she died.[1]

4. SCAR-FACE.

(a) *Version by a Piegan Man.*

Once there was a very poor young man who lived with his sister. He had a chum. In the camp was a very fine girl, the daughter of a chief, with whom all the young men were in love. Now the poor young man was in love with her also, but he had a long, ugly scar on his cheek. One day he asked his sister to go over to the chief's lodge to persuade the girl to marry him. Accordingly, the sister went over; but when the girl found out what she wanted, she said that she was willing to marry Scar-Face whenever that ugly scar disappeared. She made all manner of fun of Scar-Face.

Now the sister returned and told Scar-Face what the girl had said. He was very much hurt, and decided to go away to seek some one who could aid him in removing the scar. Yet, though he travelled far, no one could tell him where to go for aid. At last he decided to go to the Sun. So he travelled on and on, and the farther he went, the blacker the people became. As he went along, he inquired for the Sun's house. Always he was told to go on until he came to a very high ridge where some people lived who could tell him the whereabouts of the Sun's house. At last Scar-Face came to this ridge. There he saw a nude man with very black skin and curly hair. Scar-Face called to him, "Where is the Sun's lodge?" "It is at the end of this ridge," said the black man. "But go back! go back! You will be burned very badly!" Scar-Face said, "Well, I shall go on anyway; it is better to die than to go back." "Look at me!" said the black man. "You can see how I have been burned black. You had best take my advice and go no farther." "Where do you live?" asked Scar-Face. "I have a cave to live in," replied the black man. "I stay in this cave when the sun is hot, otherwise I should be burned up." (It was just about sundown that Scar-Face met the black man.) The black man advised him to travel only at night.

---

[1] The account of the woman who married a star as the result of a wish occurs in the mythology of many tribes, its general distribution having been stated in the traditions of the Arapaho (Dorsey and Kroeber, op. cit., p. 338). This version agrees fairly well with the Dakota rendering recorded by Riggs, op. cit., p. 83.

Now Scar-Face went on towards the place where the Sun lived. Presently he saw a young man standing alone. The young man called to Scar-Face, "Where are you going?" "I am going to the Sun," said Scar-Face. "Oh!" said the young man. "Sun is my father, this is his house." (This young man was Morning Star.) "My father is not a good [1] man. He is not at home now, but when he comes in the morning he will surely kill you. However, I will talk with my mother, who is a good woman and will treat you kindly." Then Morning Star took Scar-Face up to his father's lodge, and addressed his mother, saying "Mother, I have brought a strange young man here. I wish him for a companion. He has come a long way to find us, and I wish you would take pity on him, that I may enjoy his company." "Well," said his mother, "bring him in. We will talk to your father when he returns; but I fear we shall not be able to keep the young man."

When Scar-Face was taken into the lodge, he saw on the ground a kind of earthen square, some cedar-brush, and buffalo-chips. This was the Sun's smudge-place. After a time the old woman, who was Moon, said to Scar-Face, "Is there anything that you especially care for?" "Yes," answered Scar-Face, "I want this scar taken from my face." "Well," replied Moon, "it is about time for my husband to come in. If he take pity on you — well, we shall see." In a little while Moon said, "Now he is coming." Then she took Scar-Face to one side of the lodge and covered him up with cedar. Now Scar-Face began to feel very warm, because Sun was approaching. He began to shift about under the cedar, but Moon whispered that he must be quiet. So he lay very still, but became very hot as Sun came up. Finally Moon said to Scar-Face, "Now Sun is at the door." Sun looked into the lodge and said, "Oh, my, this lodge smells bad!" "Yes," Moon replied. "Morning Star has a chum here." "Well," said Sun, "make a smudge with cedar."

After this had been done, Sun entered the lodge. Now Scar-Face was very hot. Finally Sun said, "Where is that young man?" "We covered him up," said Moon. "Come," said Sun, "get up." Then Scar-Face came out from under the cedar. He could not look Sun in the face. As Sun looked upon him, he knew that this was a poor unfortunate boy, and took pity on him. The heat then grew gradually less.

Now it seems that Morning Star was out on one of his journeys, and Sun waited for his return. When Morning Star came into the lodge and sat down in his usual place, Sun addressed him, saying, "My son, do you wish this young man for a companion?" Then Morning Star said that he did very much, as he wished for a companion to go about with him. He was

---

[1] The idea is, that he was firm, and not moved by pity or sympathy.

lonesome on his journeys. "Well," said Sun, "you must make a sweat-house." Then Morning Star went out and prepared a sweat-house. When all was ready, Sun went out. He had a disk of metal at the back of his head. This disk looked like brass. Then Sun went into the sweat-house and began to wipe off the metal disk. Then he brought Morning Star and Scar-Face into the sweat-house. When they were in, the covers were closed down. At last, when all was ready, the covers were raised and the light let in. The two boys now looked alike.

Now, Moon came out, and Sun said to her, "Which is Morning Star?" Moon looked at them for a moment, then pointed at one; but she made a mistake, for she pointed at Scar-Face. "Oh!" said Sun "you are a foolish woman! This is the star you mistook for Morning Star. After this, his name shall be The-one-you-took-for-Morning Star."

Now Scar-Face staid with his new companion at Sun's house. Sun told him that he could go anywhere in the sky-land except straight west or straight down: he could go in any other direction. One morning, when Morning Star and Scar-Face were out together, Scar-Face said, "Let us go that way," pointing to the west. "No," replied Morning Star. "It is dangerous. My father said we must not go there." "Oh," said Scar-Face, "let us go anyway.". Morning Star refused, but at the fourth request he said, "All right, let us go." So the two boys went in the forbidden direction, and presently they came to a place where there were seven large white geese. At once the birds attacked them. Morning Star ran, calling out, "Now you see." Scar-Face did not run, but killed the seven geese with his club, and ran home. Before he reached home, he overtook Morning Star, and said to him, "There is no danger now. I killed all of these birds."

When they reached home, Morning Star told his mother what Scar-Face had done, but she said to Scar-Face, "I will not believe you until you get their heads." So the boys returned and took the heads of the seven birds. (This is supposed to be the origin of scalping, and no one will believe that an enemy is killed until his scalp is produced.)

Some time after this, Scar-Face and Morning Star went out together as before, and Scar-Face said, "Let us go that way again." "No," said Morning Star. "It will be more dangerous than before." Scar-Face insisted, and at the fourth request, Morning Star consented. As they were going along, they saw seven cranes. When the cranes saw the boys, they took after them. Morning Star ran as fast as he could. These cranes were terrible looking birds, and Scar-Face was badly frightened; but he took off his robe and held it in front of him. As the cranes came up, they began to peck at the robe, whereupon Scar-Face struck them one by one with his club.

Now when Scar-Face reached home, Sun was there and asked where he had been. Scar-Face said that he was walking along when some large cranes took after him, and that he had killed them all with his club. "Oh!" said Sun, "I will not believe it until you have shown me their heads." So Scar-Face returned to the scene of his conflict, and brought away the heads of the cranes. When Sun saw the heads, he believed him. Sun was greatly pleased at the courage of Scar-Face, and brought out a bundle. "Here," said he, "are some clothes for you, — a shirt and leggings. These I give you because you have killed some very dangerous and troublesome birds." Then Sun took up the leggings, and painted seven black stripes on them, saying, "I make these here as a sign that you killed enemies. All your people shall wear black stripes on their leggings when they kill enemies." Then Sun sang some songs which were to go with the clothes.

After a time, Scar-Face said to Sun, "Now I should like to return to my people. I have been here long enough." "All right," said Sun. "You may go." Then Sun took Scar-Face out, put a hoop or ring of cedar around his head, and, as soon as the hoop was on, Scar-Face found that he could see down to his people. "Now," said Sun, "shut your eyes." Scar-Face shut his eyes. When he opened them, he found himself down by the camp of his people. Now in the camp at that time there were some Indians who were playing at the wheel-and-arrow game; and one of the players, looking up, saw a black object coming down from the sky. He called out, "Oh, look at that black thing!" Then all stopped to look. They saw the object coming closer and closer. At last it reached the ground, some distance from them. It appeared to be a person. Then the old chum of Scar-Face, who was among the young men playing at the wheel-game, recognized Scar-Face, and rushed up to him; but, as he approached, Scar-Face said, "Go back! Go back! Do not touch me. You must get some willows, and make a sweat-house out here from the camp."

Then the chum went back to the people of the camp and explained to them. A sweat-house was prepared. When all was ready, Scar-Face went into the sweat-house with the bundle containing the suit of clothes given him by the Sun. When the bath had been taken, Scar-Face came out, carrying the bundle in his arm. He said to his chum, "My friend Sun gave me a suit of clothes: now I will give them to you." [1]

Now this is why our people say that the sweat-house came from the sun.

---

[1] A different version is given by Grinnell, op. cit., p. 93. The writer heard this story a number of times in approximately the form given above. For an abstract with comments by R. N. Wilson, see Report of the British Association for the Advancement of Science, 1897, p. 789. This tale has not come to our notice among the collections from other tribes, though there are suggestions of it in Arikara and Pawnee renderings of the Woman who married a Star (Dorsey, op. cit., p. 45, 58) where we find the child destroying animal monsters. However, these incidents are about equally similar to the adventures of Blood Clot in our collection. The Micmac character, Oochigeaskw, seems to have nothing in common with the Scar-Face of the Blackfoot. See Rand, Micmac Legends, p. 101.

The medicine-lodge we make at the sun-dance is the lodge of the sun where Scar-Face had been. The weasel-tail suit which Scar-Face brought to his chum was just like those you see to-day. There was a disk on the back and one on the front. There were seven black stripes on the sleeves. These were for one group of seven birds that Scar-Face had killed. Sometimes the feet of these birds are painted on the shirt. The seven bands on the leggings are for the seven other birds that Scar-Face killed. Scar-Face directed that only such persons as performed great deeds were to be allowed to wear such a suit. After a time Scar-Face went back and became a star.

(b). *Version by a Piegan Woman.*

There was once a poor young man who wished to marry a girl of the camp; but every time he approached her she drove him away with contempt. So he left the camp and went out by himself, looking for power. He had a scar on his face, and when the girl refused him she said that she would not marry him until the scar was taken off his face. Now, as the young man was wandering about, he came to the place where the Sun lived. Here he saw some swans, who at once attacked him, but he killed them. This boy's name was Scar-Face. Just as he had killed the birds, he looked up and saw a fine young man. "Oh!" said the young man, "how did you manage to kill those birds? They are very dangerous, and have killed many people." "Oh," said Scar-Face, "it was no trouble for me: it was very easy." "Well," said the stranger, "I am Morning Star. I invite you to come to our house." Then Scar-Face went with Morning Star towards Sun's house; but, as they approached, Morning Star said, "You stay outside." Then Morning Star went into the house, and, as he did so, Sun said, "My, something smells bad!" Then Morning Star explained that he had found and brought home a young man who had killed the dangerous birds. He begged Sun to permit the stranger to live with them. Finally Sun consented to this, and told Morning Star to burn incense over Scar-Face and make him tolerable. When Morning Star had done this, he brought Scar-Face into the lodge. Then Sun took Scar-Face and put him through the sweat-house four times. When he came out, Scar-Face looked exactly like Morning Star. His scar was entirely gone.

"Now," said Sun to Scar-Face, "you are to go back to earth and take revenge on that woman who refused to marry you. I will make you a great medicine-man." So Sun gave Scar-Face a forked stick, and cedar for the smudge, and some feathers, and explained to him how to put up the medicine-lodge. Sun also told him to go to the Elk-Woman and get her bonnet to use in the ceremony. The killing of the swans represents the taking of scalps from enemies, and that is why coups are counted at the sun-dance.[1]

5. Cuts-Wood.

Once there was a very poor boy who was an orphan, and he went down to the side of a stream, where he sat and cried. He was very lonesome, and mourned over his hard lot. As his sister was now married, he had no relations in the world. Now Morning Star took pity upon him, and, changing himself into a boy, came down. Morning Star came up, and said, "What are you crying for?" The poor boy said, "I am feeling very badly because I have no relations. I am poor and hungry." "Well," said Morning Star, "I will show you a way to get food. Finally you will become the leader of the camp. I will get another boy, then there will be three of us to play together."

Morning Star went away, and soon returned with another poor boy. Then all went into the brush, where they began to play. Morning Star made a little sweat-house of one hundred willows. Then he made a medicine-woman's lodge. Then he went to the other side, and made a small sun-lodge. When this was complete, he dug a hole for the fire, and made the booth for the weather-dancers. Then, all being complete, they sang the medicine-lodge dance-songs. Then they went out to kill some birds and squirrels, and put them on top of the centre pole as offerings to the sun. Now the two poor boys did not know that their companion was the Morning Star. After they had played a while, he said, "I will go home and get some food for you." So he went into the brush, and came out with food. After this they played here every day, and the strange boy brought food for them. They did not know who it was. The boys learned the play, and spent most of their time at it.

One day, as the brother-in-law of the orphan was sitting in his lodge, he said to his wife, "I wonder how it is with that little brother of yours. We never see him eat anything, and he is out from the camp the whole day. We must watch him. There is something mysterious here." So the next day the brother-in-law went to the top of a hill overlooking the camp to watch the orphan. He noticed that he had a companion, and that they

---

[1] Another narrative in our collection differs from the preceding versions in that Scar-Face went out and killed two cranes, after which the Sun gave him a buffalo-skin with hair fringes to indicate that he had killed an enemy. He also took the cranes' bills back with him to use in the sun-lodge as digging-sticks. It also stated that the Sun gave Scar-Face a flageolet with four holes, with which to charm the girl he wished to marry, telling him, that when this was played she would not be able to resist the temptation to join him.

For a discussion of a similar use of the flageolet with origin myths, see Wissler, Journal of American Folk-Lore, Vol. 18, pp. 262–4; also an Arikara myth, Dorsey, op. cit., p. 188.

went into the brush at a certain place. Then he stole quietly to the place and saw that there were three boys. He heard them singing, and saw the small medicine-lodge. Then he went quietly home and meditated. After a while he invited some of the head men into his lodge, told them what he had seen, and suggested that they all go out at night to look at the place where the boys played. They all saw it, and wondered much. However, they said nothing about it, for it appeared to be medicine.

One day after the orphan-boy had grown up, his sister and his uncle advised him to make up that play; but the young man said, "It is powerful and medicine. I cannot make up a big one." They kept on talking to him, however, until he said, "Well, I will make it up; but my sister must be the woman to take a place in it, and she must make a confession." Then his sister asked him what kind of a confession she must make. He explained that in the first place she must have led a good life, not guilty of stealing, etc., and that if any man not her husband had accosted her to invite her to commit adultery with him, she must tell all of the details in the presence of the people; but if at any time she had been so accosted, and yielded to the temptation, she could neither make the confession, nor take part in the ceremony. His sister said that she had never made a mistake or done any great wrong in her life, and that she could make the confession. Then the orphan-boy promised her that she could go ahead and give the medicine-lodge, after which everybody would live long and be happy. Also the sun and moon would heed her prayers.

Now at this time the Indians of the camp had a buffalo-drive, and collected a hundred and fifty tongues. The orphan requested an old woman to get these tongues, and invite all the young married women to come to her lodge, but that only those should accept the invitation who had been true to their marriage-vows. When all these women were assembled, the orphan told them that they must confess, and that if they kept anything back their relations would die off. He told them that they had been invited there to slice all the buffalo-tongues, and that if, in slicing them, any one should cut a hole in a slice, or cut her fingers, it was a sign that she had made a mistake in her life, and had lied in making the confession. Then he painted one tongue black, and gave it to his sister. She sliced it. She did not cut it or her fingers. Then the other women sliced the remaining tongues and everyone had good luck. After this they put up the centre pole in the sun-lodge and did everything as they do now. After the sun-dance was over, the orphan went on the war-path. Now the next season, another woman in the camp wanted to make the medicine-lodge. So she got the tongues and did everything as before; and after the sun-dance was over, the orphan went on the war-path again. Every time he went on the war-path, he cut a stick and painted it black. He left these with his sister, asking her to watch these counting-sticks. (This is the way he got the name of Cuts-Wood.)

One time after the sun-dance, while Cuts-Wood was out on the war-path, his sister noticed that one of the sticks was missing. Then she knew that something was wrong. So she went over to the lodge of the woman who gave the last sun-dance and said to her, "You must be a bad woman, because one of the sticks is gone." The sister laid the blame on this woman. After a while a war-party came to the top of the hill. The people watching saw them throw a robe away. Then the sister began to cry, and when the war-party came in, the people heard that Cuts-Wood had been killed.

6. The Seven Stars.

Once there was a young woman with many suitors; but she refused to marry. She had seven brothers and one little sister. Their mother had been dead many years and they had no relatives, but lived alone with their father. Every day the six brothers went out hunting with their father. It seems that the young woman had a bear for her lover, and, as she did not want any one to know this, she would meet him when she went out after wood. She always went after wood as soon as her father and brothers went out to hunt, leaving her little sister alone in the lodge. As soon as she was out of sight in the brush, she would run to the place where the bear lived.

As the little sister grew older, she began to be curious as to why her older sister spent so much time getting wood. So one day she followed her. She saw the young woman meet the bear and saw that they were lovers. When she found this out, she ran home as quickly as she could, and when her father returned she told him what she had seen. When he heard the story he said, "So, my elder daughter has a bear for a husband. Now I know why she does not want to marry." Then he went about the camp, telling all his people that they had a bear for a brother-in-law, and that he wished all the men to go out with him to kill this bear. So they went, found the bear, and killed him.

When the young woman found out what had been done, and that her little sister had told on her, she was very angry. She scolded her little sister vigorously, then ordered her to go out to the dead bear, and bring some flesh from his paws. The little sister began to cry, and said she was afraid to go out of the lodge, because a dog with young pups had tried to bite her. "Oh, do not be afraid!" said the young woman. "I will paint your face like that of a bear, with black marks across the eyes and at the corners of the mouth; then no one will touch you." So she went for the meat. Now the older sister was a powerful medicine-woman. She could tan hides in a new way. She could take up a hide, strike it four times with her skin-scraper and it would be tanned.

The little sister had a younger brother that she carried on her back. As their mother was dead, she took care of him. One day the little sister said to the older sister, "Now you be a bear and we will go out into the brush to play." The older sister agreed to this, but said, "Little sister, you must not touch me over my kidneys." So the big sister acted as a bear, and they played in the brush. While they were playing, the little sister forgot what she had been told, and touched her older sister in the wrong place. At once she turned into a real bear, ran into the camp, and killed many of the people. After she had killed a large number, she turned back into her former self. Now, when the little sister saw the older run away as a real bear, she became frightened, took up her little brother, and ran into their lodge. Here they waited, badly frightened, but were very glad to see their older sister return after a time as her true self.

Now the older brothers were out hunting, as usual. As the little sister was going down for water with her little brother on her back, she met her six brothers returning. The brothers noted how quiet and deserted the camp seemed to be. So they said to their little sister, "Where are all our people?" Then the little sister explained how she and her sister were playing, when the elder turned into a bear, ran through the camp, and killed many people. She told her brothers that they were in great danger, as their sister would surely kill them when they came home. So the six brothers decided to go into the brush. One of them had killed a jack-rabbit. He said to the little sister, "You take this rabbit home with you. When it is dark, we will scatter prickly-pears all around the lodge, except in one place. When you come out, you must look for that place, and pass through."

When the little sister came back to the lodge, the elder sister said, "Where have you been all this time?" "Oh, my little brother mussed himself and I had to clean him," replied the little sister. "Where did you get that rabbit?" she asked. "I killed it with a sharp stick," said the little sister. "That is a lie. Let me see you do it," said the older sister. Then the little sister took up a stick lying near her, threw it at the rabbit, and it stuck in the wound in his body. "Well, all right," said the elder sister. Then the little sister dressed the rabbit and cooked it. She offered some of it to her older sister, but it was refused: so the little sister and her brother ate all of it. When the elder sister saw that the rabbit had all been eaten, she became very angry, and said, "Now I have a mind to kill you." So the little sister arose quickly, took her little brother on her back, and said, "I am going out to look for wood." As she went out, she followed the narrow trail through the prickly-pears and met her six brothers in the brush. Then they decided to leave the country, and started off as fast as they could go.

The older sister, being a powerful medicine-woman, knew at once what they were doing. She became very angry and turned herself into a bear to pursue them. Soon she was about to overtake them, when one of the boys tried his power. He took a little water in the hollow of his hand and sprinkled it around. At once it became a great lake between them and the bear. Then the children hurried on while the bear went around. After a while the bear caught up with them again, when another brother threw a porcupine-tail [a hairbrush] on the ground. This became a great thicket; but the bear forced its way through, and again overtook the children.[1] This time they all climbed a high tree. The bear came to the foot of the tree, and, looking up at them, said, "Now I shall kill you all." So she took a stick from the ground, threw it into the tree and knocked down four of the brothers. While she was doing this, a little bird flew around the tree, calling out to the children, "Shoot her in the head! Shoot her in the head!" Then one of the boys shot an arrow into the head of the bear, and at once she fell dead. Then they came down from the tree.

Now the four brothers were dead. The little brother took an arrow, shot it straight up into the air, and when it fell one of the dead brothers came to life. This he repeated until all were alive again. Then they held a council, and said to each other, "Where shall we go? Our people have all been killed, and we are a long way from home. We have no relatives living in the world." Finally they decided that they preferred to live in the sky. Then the little brother said, "Shut your eyes." As they did so, they all went up. Now you can see them every night. The little brother is the North Star (?). The six brothers and the little sister are seen in the Great Dipper. The little sister and the eldest brother are in a line with the North Star, the little sister being nearest it because she used to carry her little brother on her back. The other brothers are arranged in order of their age, beginning with the eldest. This is how the seven stars [Ursa major] came to be.[2]

---

[1] Traditions of the Skidi Pawnee, p. 115.
[2] For another version of this narrative, see The American Antiquarian, Vol. XV, pp. 200–203. In this case the incident of the bear-lover does not occur. The writer has heard several versions, and that given here is the usual form though in some renderings the seven brothers became Ursa major. For similar tales in whole or in part, see Dorsey and Kroeber's Arapaho, op. cit., pp. 152, 227, and 238; Simms, Crow, op. cit., p. 312; J. O. Dorsey, Cegiha, op. cit., p. 292; Jones, Fox Texts, p. 161; Kroeber, Gros Ventre, op. cit. p. 108. It appears that the Black-foot rendering combines two incidents often found separated in other parts of the continent, the woman with a bear-lover and the pursuit of children who become stars though both occur n a Dakota myth, (Journal of American Folk-Lore, Vol. XX, p. 195).

7. THE BUNCHED STARS.

In a camp of our people there was a family of six boys. Their parents were very poor. Every spring the people went out to hunt for buffalo. At this time of the year, the buffalo-calves are red, and their skins are much desired for children's robes. Now as the parents of these children were very poor, and not able to do much hunting, these boys had to wear brown robes or those made of old buffalo-skins. As the children grew up, they were constantly reminded of the fact that they had no red robes. The other children of the camp sometimes made fun of them because of this. So one day one of·the boys said to his brothers, "Why is it that we never get any red robes? If we do not get any next spring, let us leave the camp and go up into the sky." Then the boys went out to a lonely place to talk the matter over. Finally they agreed that, if they did not get red robes in the following spring, they would go ᵛup to the sky country. The spring hunting-season passed, but no red robes came to the boys. Then the oldest brother said, "Now I shall take you all up to the sky." The fourth brother said, "Let us also take all the water away from the people, because they have been bad to us."

Then the oldest brother took some weasel-hair and placed a little on the backs of his brothers. Then he took another bunch of hair, put it first into his mouth, then rubbed it on his palm. "Now shut your eyes," he said. Then he blew the weasel-hair up, and, when the brothers opened their eyes, they found themselves in the house of the Sun and Moon. The Sun, who was an old man, and the Moon, who was his wife, said, "Why have you come?" "We left the earth," said the oldest brother, "because the people never gave us red robes. All the other children had red robes to wear, but we had only brown ones. So we have come to you for help." "Well," said the Sun, "what do you want?" The fourth brother said, "We should like to have all of the water taken away from the people for seven days." Now the Sun made no answer to this; but the Moon took pity on the poor boys and said, "I will help you; but you must stay in the sky." The Moon pitied the boys so much that she cried. She asked the Sun to aid her in taking away the water from the people; but the Sun made no answer. She asked him·seven times. At last he promised to aid her.

Now the next day on the earth was very hot. The water in the streams and lakes boiled, and in a short time it all evaporated. The next night was very warm and the moonlight strong. When the water was gone, the people in the camp said, "Let us take two dogs with us out to the river-bed." When they came to the bank of the river, the two dogs began to dig a hole in the side of the bank. When they had dug a long time, water came out of the hole like a spring. This is the way springs were made. Even to this day, all the people have great respect for their dogs because of this. The days were so hot that the people were forced to dig holes into the hills and crawl into them. They would have died, if they had remained on top of the ground. When the water in the springs gave out, the dogs made other springs. Now the leader of the dogs was a medicine-dog. He was old and white. On the seventh day, the dogs began to howl and look at the sky. The leader of the dogs was praying to the Sun and the Moon. He explained to the Sun and Moon why it was that the boys got no red robes. He asked them to take pity on the dogs below. (This is why dogs sometimes howl at the moon.) On the eighth day the Sun and Moon gave the people rain. It was a great rain, and it rained for a long time.

The six boys remained in the sky, where they may be seen every night. They are the Bunched Stars [Pleiades].[1]

8. THE MOON-WOMAN.[2]

Once there was a woman with two children. She had a black birthmark on the calf of her leg. One day the woman disappeared, and she could not be found anywhere. After a time, her husband married again. Now the woman had been enticed away by a man who lived in the moon. This man had met her as she was going for wood. After they had lived in the moon a while, the woman said to her new husband, "I am anxious to see my children again. Suppose we go down and visit them." So the woman disguised herself in men's clothing and they both went to her former husband's lodge. They told him that they were Cree Indians, but that they could speak Piegan. The father and the two children took the strange men into the lodge and treated them kindly. The smaller of the two strangers seemed much interested in the children, kissed them, played with them, etc. The father of the children took notice of this and grew suspicious. At night, when it came time to go to bed, he also noticed that one was very slow and cautious in taking off his leggings. The next day, when both of the strangers were out of the lodge, one of the children said, "Father, that young man has teeth and eyes like those of my mother. Somehow he makes me think of mother." The father said to himself, "I believe that stranger is my former wife in disguise. I shall watch my chance and find out if this is true."

---

[1] See American Antiquarian, Vol. XV, p. 149, for another version.
[2] While this is not strictly a star myth, it may be considered as such since it is sometimes said that the husband of the woman was a star. In some versions the woman went up into the sky and became the moon.

The father now set about discovering the identity of the strangers. He began to make arrows for himself, and gave some of the material to each of the strangers. As he did so, the taller stranger said, "My friend is not good at making arrows." But the father insisted that they all make arrows, which they did. He noticed that the arrows made by the smaller stranger were very poor indeed. This stranger also kept an otter-skin drawn closely over his forehead, and in eating kept his mouth closed as much as possible. The next night the father kept the strangers up very late, telling them stories so that they might get very sleepy, and sleep so soundly that he could look at their legs without waking them, and so discover whether or not one of them had the black birth-mark of his former wife. When they were all sound asleep, he took a stick, put some grass and bark around the end, stuck it into the fire, and, using it as a torch, cautiously raised the robe covering the smaller stranger, and discovered the familiar mark on the leg. He also saw that her breasts were bound down to make her look like a man. Then he put out the light, for he knew that the stranger was really his former wife.

When morning came he invited the strangers to get up and eat; but before doing so he directed his children and their stepmother to go outside of the lodge. When the strangers arose, he stood at the door with a white rock knife in his hand, and informed them of his discovery. He addressed his former wife, upbraiding her for her conduct, and her impertinence in returning to his lodge in disguise. "Now," he said, "I shall kill you both; for you cannot get out except through the top of the lodge." Then the woman began to plead for her life, but to no purpose. Just as the angry husband was about to execute this threat, the strange man, with the woman following, rushed out through the smoke-hole like shooting-stars. As they passed out, the man threw his rock knife at the woman, striking one of her legs and cutting it off.[1]

The woman and her new husband went up in the sky to live in the moon as before, and this is why the woman we now see in the moon has but one leg.

---

[1] See Henry and Thompson's Journal, op. cit., p. 528.

III. RITUALISTIC ORIGINS.

1. The Beaver-Medicine.

(a). *Northern Blackfoot Version.*

There was a man who always went out hunting for deer and antelope.
He was camping near a big lake fringed with bushes. He had two wives.
One day the older took a pail to fetch water. She saw a young man, Beaver,
who invited her to his tent. She went. When the man returned, he asked
his younger wife for the older one's whereabouts. "I don't know. She
went to the lake for water. When I looked for her, I could not see her trail,
but only saw the pail." The man was sad, thinking his wife had gone to
another camp. He went to another camp, but failed to find her, and
returned. Then, after a night's sleep, he went to hunt early in the morning.
The younger woman went for water. She saw the older wife rising from the
water. The women kissed each other. The older said, "If my husband
wishes, I will obtain for him the beaver-bundle which Beaver will give him
for taking me away. He must burn sweet grass. All the creatures in the
water will come to his tent. He is to prepare a feast for them. Then he
is to pray to the Sun, Moon, and Morning-Star, begging them to come to
him also." The man did as he was bid. The Sun and Moon came down
and sat in this order: —

| Sun | Man | Moon | Woman |

Then the Sun burnt sweet-grass, and sang. He said to the man, "Give
me some eagle-tail feathers." These were in payment for the first ritual
song. Then the Sun sang again and asked the man for hawk-tail feathers.
The third time he sang for black-fox hides. The fourth time he said,
"Old man wants black-coyote skins." The man's second wife fed the visi-
tors. Then they untied the beaver-bundle. Sun took paint, rubbed it on his
hands, gave it to the man, and the man prayed to Sun for long life. The
Sun sang all night, giving the songs to the man. Before sunrise, he left to
rise in the east. After four nights' singing, the beaver-bundle was given to
the man. The Sun said, "Your people shall always have the beaver-bundle.
Every spring, when the leaves are coming out, you shall put seed [tobacco]
in the ground, and dance. Make a vessel of buffalo-hide. At sunset go
into a large tent and feed all the Indians. You, the owner of the beaver-
bundle, and the old men shall dance [tobacco-seed dance]."

After the feast the man was told to take a stick, dig a hole in the ground
and insert the seed, to make the oblong [altar], put dry sticks in the centre

and burn them. The next morning he was to rake the ashes, and have the little boys stand there and pray to the Sun and the beaver-bundle man to let the tobacco-seeds grow. After a month and a half, he was to send a young man with sweet-grass to look at the tobacco: the youth must burn the sweet-grass in each corner of the oblong, take out some tobacco and return it to the owner of the bundle. No one was allowed to look before. The next morning all the old men were summoned, the tobacco was dried and mixed with kinnikinnick. All prayed, then smoked. Each old man was to have his own tobacco. The bundle-owner examined the seeds, saying, "You have a good crop" or "you have only a small crop." The man who had the smallest grieved.[1]

(b). *Blood Version.*

You say you have heard the story of Scabby-Round-Robe; but he did not first start the beaver-medicine, because it is said in the story that there was such a medicine before his time. The story I now tell you is about the origin of the beaver-medicine.

Once there was a man and his wife camping alone on the shore of a small lake. This man was a great hunter, and had in his lodge the skins of almost every kind of bird and animal. Among them was the skin of a white buffalo. As he was always hunting, his wife was often left alone. One day a Beaver came out of the water and made love to her. This went on for some time, until finally she went away with the Beaver to his home in the water. Now when the man came home, he looked all about for his wife, but could not find her anywhere. As he was walking along the shore of the lake, he saw her trail going down into the water. Now he knew what had happened. He did not break camp, but continued his hunting. After four days, the woman came up out of the water and returned to her lodge. She was already heavy with child. When her husband returned that evening, he found her in her usual place and she told him all that had occurred.

In the course of time the woman gave birth to a beaver. To keep it from dying, she put it in a bowl of water which she kept at the head of her bed. In the evening her husband came in as usual, and after a while, hearing something splashing in water, he said, "What is that?" Then the woman explained to him that she had given birth to a beaver. She brought him the bowl. He took out the little beaver, looked at it and put it back. He said nothing. As time went on he became very fond of the young beaver and played with him every evening.

---

[1] Recorded by Dr. R. H. Lowie.

Now the Beaver down in the water knew everything that was going on in the lodge. He knew that the man was kind to the young beaver and so was not angry with him. He took pity on the man. Then the father of the young beaver resolved to give the man some of his medicine-songs in exchange for the skins of birds and animals the man had in his lodge. So one day, when the woman went down to the lake for water, the Beaver came out and instructed her to request of her husband, that whatever he [the Beaver] should ask in his songs, that should be done. He also stated the time at which he would come to the lodge to be received by her husband.

At the appointed time the Beaver came out of the lake and appeared before the lodge, but, before he entered, requested that the lodge be purified [a smudge]. Then he entered. They smoked. After a while the Beaver began to sing a song in which he asked for the skin of a certain bird. When he had finished, the man arose and gave the bird-skin to him. Then the Beaver sang another song, in which he asked for the skin of another bird, which was given him. Thus he went on until he secured all the skins in the man's lodge. In this way the man learned all the songs that belonged to the beaver-medicine and also the skins of the animals to which the songs belonged.

After this the man got together all the different kinds of bird and animal skins taken by the Beaver, made them up into a bundle, and kept the beaver-medicine.

(c). *North Piegan Version.*

It was about a hundred years ago a man pitched his camp away from the other people. He was somewhere in the vicinity of St. Mary's Lake. Now the man and his wife went out in different ways. They separated. As the woman was going along, she came to the place where Beavers were at work. The Beavers came out and invited her down to their lodge. When the man came home that night, he missed his wife and set out to find her. At last he discovered her tracks leading down into the water at the place where the Beavers were at work. Now he watched every day for her to appear. Every night when he was in the lodge he could hear dancing and singing. He could only hear it when inside of the lodge, but whenever he went outside he ceased to hear it. One evening when he came back from hunting, he found his wife at home in the lodge. She was burning incense. She had cleared a small spot back of the fire for this purpose. The man saw a large bundle at the back of the lodge, and as he looked at it the woman said, "That was given by the Beavers."

Now that night, when the man was sleeping, he dreamed about the Beavers. In his dream he saw the Beavers come into his lodge, and one of the Beavers addressed him, saying, "Now, my brother, you have the bundle and the medicine things; so you must learn the songs and how to paint." Then the Beavers taught him the songs, how to open the bundle,[1] how to paint, etc. All the directions for the ceremony were given by the Beavers at this time. This was just as you will see it now, because we are about to open this bundle.

There was also another dream about this medicine. In this dream it was explained that the only women who can take part in the medicine-lodge are those who have been true to their husbands. In this dream a head-dress was given for the woman who makes a vow to give the sun-dance. This was dreamed by the same man who received the medicine-bundle from the Beaver. Afterwards he had another dream, in which the elk gave him a robe. This robe was to be used by the woman who gave the sun-dance. Now, after this man had the dream about the elk, he took the robe and gave it to his wife, beause she now had the head-dress that is worn in the sun-dance. She took the robe and wrapped it around the bundle in which the head-dress was kept.

Tobacco is kept in the beaver-medicine bundle, and this tobacco must be planted every year. The woman who plants the tobacco puts on the head-dress and carries a digging-stick. Songs are sung when the tobacco is planted. This is the way to raise the tobacco to be used in the beaver-medicine.

Now we must begin, and, if you watch, you will see what the beaver-medicine is.

(d) Piegan Version.

Once an old woman and her little son were crossing the Yellowstone River when the waters were very high. They had made a raft with the skin covering of a lodge. The little boy was sitting on this raft and the old woman was swimming along at the side, holding by one hand. The raft itself was tied to the horse's tail by a rope. The husband of the woman was guiding the horse. The current was so swift that the rope broke and the raft began to float down stream. The man reached the shore and climbed up on the bank, following the floating raft. At last the woman tried to climb upon the raft, but it filled and sank. Then the man went on to the other Indians, and told them that the woman and the boy had been drowned in crossing the stream. Two days after this, he came back to look for the bodies, but found the old woman and the boy sitting upon the bank. They had been under water for two days. The old woman said that when

---

[1] To open the bundle requires an elaborate ceremony. This narrative was given as a prelude to the opening of this ceremony.

they sank the Beaver pulled them into his lodge. When they got into the lodge, they were safe. When they looked around, they saw a great many other animals there. Then the Otter said, "Here is a woman. Let us kill her and eat her." But the Beaver said, "No, this is a poor woman and a boy that were drowning. I took pity on them and brought them here." "Well," said the Otter, "they are people; they deserve to die. Let us kill them." So they argued for a long time; but at last the Beaver prevailed over all the other animals, and thus saved the lives of the woman and her child. This shows that the Beaver had some sort of power, at least power to save people. Then the Beaver told the woman that she would have great power, that she would live long, and that he would give her some songs. Now when this woman returned to her people, she started the Crow-water medicine. She is still living among the Crows and the first beaver-skin that came into her hands she kept for medicine.

Now when the man came up and found the old woman and the boy on the bank, he was going to shake hands with her; but she told him not to come near her, that first he must make four sweat-houses. When all was ready, the woman entered the first sweat-house. When she came out, they saw in it a great deal of sand and lake-grass. Each time the woman went through a sweat-house, they found sand and lake-grass in it. Thus the sweat-houses were to get the sand out of her body.

2. OTTER-WOMAN.

It was in the north. Very far north, at a place called The-Place-to-fall-off-without-Difficulty. Some people were camped there. Among them was Chief-Level-Head, (other name, Buffalo-Lodge-Pole) who was trapping beaver. This man was a great hunter and trapper. He spent most of his time in this way. He had camped there before. His relatives wanted him to stay with them, but he would not; and, taking his wife, he went away and camped by himself. His wife was Otter-Woman. One day he went out to hunt, and, on reaching camp with his meat on two dog-travois, he called his wife to come out and get the meat. No one came. Then he called several times, but received no answer. Then he, himself, took off the meat, untied the dogs, and went to look for her. As he went along he said, "I wonder if anything could have happened to her. Did she go off with some young man? Did she get scared and run away, or did she get lonesome and go back to the camp?" All this time he was tracking her along. At last he came to the place where she got water, and there he found her robe. There also was the pail made of paunch, her wooden cup, and bundle of wood. Now he knew what had happened. He saw tracks going down to the water. It was very deep. The man went into the water to follow the tracks, but lost them. He saw a beaver's house. It was a big house. Then he made a raft of four poles and followed up the tracks in clear water. He saw that these tracks led up to the beaver house. Then he knew for sure what had happened. Then he went home and cried. He made up his mind that the Beaver had run off with the woman; but he still cried and cried. He was there seven days, crying all the time. On the seventh day he thought to himself, "To-morrow I will go home"; but that night he cried as before. But a man came to him, saying, "I have been sent to you. You are to fix up a lodge, for your wife is coming to-morrow. You must not look out when she comes." He heard the man sing, "Our walking is powerful, the man says," etc. "My old home I am looking for it. It is powerful." (This means that the woman looked for her home.) Now while the woman was coming up, the strange man sang many such songs. These are the beaver-songs. When the woman came out of the lake, she wore a medicine-bonnet, and some head men [beavers] came out with her to help with the songs and to transfer the bundle. This party went into the lodge and transferred the bundle and the medicine-bonnet to the woman and her husband. The tobacco-plant and everything else was given with it. It took seven days to transfer the medicine.

Then the man and his wife went home, and the next summer he went out and planted his tobacco-seeds as the Beavers had directed. That year it grew well. Then he transferred the bundle to another man, and this man called in a friend to help him get it.

"Now it has boiled over."[1]

3. Tobacco-Seeds and Beaver-Medicine.

Once there were some men who owned a beaver-bundle. One of them went away on a journey and requested that the others await his return before planting the tobacco-seed. They did not wait. So when he returned he was very angry and aggrieved. He went out alone on the prairie, crying to himself. At last a Lizard came up and asked him what the trouble was. When he told the Lizard what had happened, it promised to help him. It directed him to go into the woods. As he went along, he met a very old man. When he had explained his troubles to him, the old man called together a great many quadrupeds and birds. These animals set to work to prepare the ground for planting the seed. The Antelope and the Snow-bird offered to give him the power of their dung to make the plants grow. As

---

[1] This expression is often used to indicate the end of a narrative.

they had no tobacco-seed, three birds volunteered to go to the sun for a supply. So they started off to the sky, and when the first cloud was reached, one of them gave out; but the cloud turned him yellow. When the next cloud was reached, another gave out; but he became red. The other bird went on alone until he finally reached the sun, and became black. This one brought down the seed. Now all the animals assembled, and proceeded to plant the new tobacco-seed. They sang many songs, and performed all the parts of the ceremony. When the seed was finally planted, they fenced in the plot with rocks and sticks, after which they all went away. The man now returned to his people with many new songs, and whenever he heard beaver-men singing, he would go into the lodge and sing his new songs, the number of which far surpassed the others.

At the end of the season, when it was time for all the people to go out to gather their tobacco, it was found that the only tobacco growing was that planted by the animals. In every other plot the buffalo had trampled everything into the earth. The man gathered his tobacco and took it home. His friends were very much disappointed over the failure of their planting. After a time, he invited them all to his lodge and gave them some of his tobacco. Then they transferred to him the other beaver-bundles and he put them together, so that now the tobacco-planting songs are a part of the beaver-medicine.

4. Crow Indian Water-Medicine.

Once a Crow Indian had a son killed in war. He was in mourning: so he took his lodge into the mountains and camped there that he might have dreams in which power would be given him to revenge the death of his son. He slept in the mountains ten nights. At last as he was sleeping, he had a dream, and in this dream he heard drumming and singing. Then a man appeared and said, "Come over here: there is dancing." So he followed the man. They came to a lodge in which there were many old men and women. There were eight men with drums. He also saw weasel-skins, skins of the mink and otter, a whistle, a smudge-stick, some wild turnip for the smudge, and some berry-soup in a kettle. One old woman had an otter-skin with a weasel-skin around it like a belt. So the man staid there, learned the songs which these people sang, and when he came back to his people he started the Crow-water-medicine. Since that time he has had other dreams: and the skins of the beaver, the muskrat, all kinds of birds, etc., with many songs for each, have been added.

This medicine has great power. If any one wishes a horse, he calls in some of the Crow-water-medicine people. Then they pray, sing, and dance.

The power of this medicine is such that after a while a man may come along and say, "I have had a bad dream. You must paint me, that the dream may not come true." Then he gives a horse as a fee. The medicine has power also in treating the sick. The people who have this medicine meet at regular times, — on Sundays and at the time of the new moon. They paint their faces with a broad red stripe across the forehead, and one across the mouth and cheeks. A rectangle of red is also painted on the back of each hand. Some wear plumes.

5. Scabby-Round-Robe.

In the olden times, when Indians danced, it was the custom for a woman who had a lover to dress in his clothes and dance before the people, telling what deeds she would do in war; it being understood, of course, that it was the man, her lover, who intended to do these deeds.

Now there was in the camp a very poor young man named Scabby-Round-Robe, who had very few clothes, and who was in love with a young married woman. Her husband had another wife, but she was very old. He also had a bundle called the water-bundle [beaver-bundle]. One time when the women in the camp were about to dance, he said to the young wife, "Why do you not dance? Surely you must have a lover, almost every woman has one. Why do you not dress up, dance before the people, and show who he is?" He did this because he was jealous of the young wife.

Scabby-Round-Robe always wore a strip of skin around his head with two magpie-feathers stuck up behind. His robe was very badly tanned and the corners had been cut off. That was the reason he was called Scabby-Round-Robe. He was very poor himself, but he had a chum who was very rich. Now one day he was out with his chum far from the camp. At this time the women were about to dance. When they began, there appeared among them the young woman wearing some of Scabby-Round-Robe's clothes. The people looking on said, "Who is that woman wearing those queer things?" Then some one called out, "Oh, those are Scabby-Round-Robe's clothes! That must be his girl." Then the people laughed and derided. Some time before this, Scabby-Round-Robe had been taken away by the Beavers, and had lived with them one whole winter. By this means he obtained some of their power. One day he said to the young woman, "If you ever do dance with the women, you must tell the people that when the waters are warm,[1] you will go on the war-path and kill an enemy."

---

[1] In the spring of the year.

Now, as the people were mocking, the young woman came forward and said, "Wait, I wish to speak." When they were quiet she said, "When the waters are warm, I shall go on the war-path and kill an enemy." Now the people laughed all the more at the thought of poor Scabby-Round-Robe going on the war-path and killing an enemy. While Scabby-Round-Robe and his chum were walking along, they heard a great uproar in the camp. His chum said, "Let us go to see what is going on." They came up just in time to hear the chief and the people make fun of Scabby-Round-Robe. Scabby-Round-Robe was very much hurt and went home at once. He said to his chum, "I shall go out on the hills, and sleep and wander about until the waters are warm. Then I shall return."

Now it happened that a Snake Indian had killed a Piegan; hence the people must go to war in the spring. So when spring came, nearly all the men of the camp went out on the war-path. Scabby-Round-Robe and his chum followed along behind, out of sight. Scabby-Round-Robe always carried a stick he had from the Beavers. From time to time the war-party drove them back, but every time Scabby-Round-Robe and his chum would follow again. They were driven back repeatedly, but persisted in following. Finally it was reported to the chief that two boys were always following the scouts, upon which he gave orders that they should remain behind. At last the scouts reported that enemies were seen on the other side of a river, the waters of which were very high, and difficult to cross. So the Piegan moved up to the edge of the stream and looked over at the hostile camp. Scabby-Round-Robe and his chum went up stream above the camp of their people. Scabby-Round-Robe said, "Now I shall kill a chief." He looked across the river and saw the chief of the Snakes talking to his people. Then he said to his chum, "You stay here upon the bank. I will cross over and bring a chief." Then he went into the water until it reached his arms, when he dived under, coming up in the middle of the stream. When he came up, his people saw him, and called out, "That is one of our people crossing!" Scabby-Round-Robe dived again, and came out near the opposite shore with his stick in his mouth. As he came up this time, the Snakes saw him; and their chief said, "I will go out and kill that fellow." So the chief waded out into the water with a long spear. Scabby-Round-Robe backed away until the water reached his breasts. Then he held the stick in front of him and sang a song. The chief approached and struck at him; but the spear stuck into the stick. Then Scabby-Round-Robe took the spear, killed the chief, took him by the hair, and dived. He came up in the middle of the stream, in plain view of his people, as if he meant to come ashore among them. Then he dived again, but came out at the place where his chum sat. He immediately scalped the chief, and gave his chum half the scalp, saying, "Take this quick, before the others get here." The whole camp rose up as quickly as they could, and began the race to count coup on the dead chief.

Now the Piegan started home.

The young woman who had danced for Scabby-Round-Robe was out in the brush picking rosebuds for soup, when a war-party was announced. A runner came into the camp and said, "Where is that girl who danced for Scabby-Round-Robe?" The people said, "She is out in the brush picking rosebuds for soup." Then they called her. She at once threw down the rosebuds and ran out to meet Scabby-Round-Robe. When she met him, he kissed her and gave her the scalp for the woman's scalp-dance. After the war-party had come in, the husband of the woman, who was a chief, took Scabby-Round-Robe to his lodge, and said, "I will give you this lodge, the woman, and my bundle of beaver-medicine: they are all yours." So Scabby-Round-Robe lived with the woman. Afterwards he taught the people some of the things he had learned from the Beavers, and you will remember that in the beaver-songs, they often say that diving is safety.[1]

6. The Elk-Woman.

(a) *Blood Version.*

This medicine-bonnet was given to a woman who was camping near the Mountains. One day while her husband was away she heard an Elk whistling in the woods. At another time when her husband was away, a man came to the lodge and asked her to go away with him. He told her that he was the Elk that she had heard, and that, if she would go away with him, he would give her some medicine. To this promise she finally consented and went with him into the brush, where he explained to her the whole ceremony.[2] He told her all about the medicine-bonnet, calling in many animals to help give the woman some power. Among these was the Crane, who offered the use of his bill to dig the medicine-turnip. He said his bill was to be carried on the back like the bunch of feathers on his own neck. Then the Crane proceeded to dig with his bill, and as he did so he sang a song, "I wish to be on level ground."

A robe made of elk-skin, used by the woman in the ceremony, is to represent the Elk himself. The bunches of feathers placed around the bonnet are to represent the prongs of the horns. There are about six bunches in all.

---

[1] Another version is given by Grinnell, op. cit., p. 117. Clark gives a brief abstract (Sign Language, p. 71).
[2] A similar incident is given by the Arikara (Dorsey, op. cit., p. 127).

In front is hung a doll with quill-work upon it. A white-rock arrowpoint and some ear-rings are hung on the side. There are also two little dolls tied on near the feathers. Weasel-tails hang down by the side. Feathers of the owl are used in making up the bunches on the side of the bonnet, while behind is hung the skin of a woodpecker (?) and part of the tail of a wildcat. There should also be part of the tail of a white buffalo tied on somewhere. All of these parts were contributed by the animals called together by the man who took the woman into the brush, and each of these animals sang a song as they gave them. The buffalo was there also, and gave its hoofs, which were tied to the end of the digging-stick.

You will see all these things upon the medicine-bonnet; but the present one used by the Blood Indians is a little different from that used by the Piegan.[1]

(b) *Piegan Version.*

You are asking me about the badger and the medicine-bonnet? Well, the badger-skin is used as a case in which to put the bonnet, but the badger-skin is a new addition to this. It was dreamed not so very long ago. This badger-skin should always be painted red, and it is necessary to go through a ceremony when it is painted. But now I must tell you about the bonnet.

There was once an Elk who was deserted by his wife. When he found that she was gone, he went out to look for her, and finally saw her in the thick woods. He was very angry and wished to kill her: so he walked toward her singing a song. Now this was a medicine-song, and he intended that its power should kill his wife. He had great power. The ground was very hard; but at every step his feet sank deeper into it. Now his wife was frightened; but she had some power also. She began to sing a song, and as she did so she turned into a woman. In her new form she wore a medicine-bonnet, a robe of elk-hide over her shoulders, and elk-teeth on her wrists. The song that she sang when she became a woman was: —

> "My wristlets are elk-teeth;
> They are powerful."

Then the woman moved toward a tree, moved her head as if hooking at the tree, and it almost fell. Now when the Elk saw what she was doing,

---

[1] By way of comment, the narrator said that the Elk did not teach the woman all that there was to be learned about it, but that later it was learned that the bonnet was to be used in making a vow, and was to be worn by virtuous women only. Once, after this woman had received the bonnet, the people were attacked by an enemy while they were camping in a ravine. The woman remembered the song, "I want to be on level ground." She went up under the fire of the enemy, and, when out on the level plain, began to dig with a digging-stick while she sang this song. This gave her people power over their enemies, and saved them from destruction.

he stopped in great surprise at her power. He did not kill her as he had intended.

This was Elk-Woman. In the sun-dance a tree or post is put up in the centre of the sun-lodge and the woman who wears the bonnet makes hooking motions at the pole, as did the Elk-Woman in the first part of the story.

7. THE BUFFALO-ROCK.

(a). *Piegan Version.*[1]

Now listen. I suppose you are asking about the iniskim [buffalo-rock], about the way we first came to get it. At a place called Elbow-on-the-Other-Side [in Canada] it was found. The woman who found it was very poor. Her name was Weasel-Woman, and her husband's name was Chief-Speaking. Well, now you will hear the true account.

At a curved cut bank called the Place-of-the-Falling-off-without-Excuse it was found. This woman was walking around there among fallen timber [logs]. Her people were all about to die of starvation. She had come out for wood, and was walking around picking up pieces of bark. Then she came to some berry-bushes on all sides of a log and began to pick white berries. Now she heard something singing. The first that she heard was "Ho-o-o-o!" as if some one were making the wing-like movement.[2] Near her was a log pointing toward the setting sun. The singing was in the log. An iniskim was sitting in a broken-out place at the end on a bed of shedded buffalo hair and sage-grass. She could just hear it sing. She stood with her head to one side, listening for a time. Then she began to pick berries again. Now she heard it:—

> "Yonder woman, you must take me.
> I am powerful.
> Yonder woman, you must take me,
> You must hear me.
> Where I sit is powerful."

Now that is the way it sang to her. As she was walking towards the place from which the sound came, she saw that the object sitting in the broken place was the one that did it. Then it said, "Ky-ja, this is where it is singing." She did not know what kind of a thing it was. She thought that perhaps it was a mouse or a bird. As she slowly removed the shedded

---

[1] Taken as a text by Dr. Clark Wissler. This myth is the major part of the ritual for the iniskim and is in general a typical Blackfoot ritual. For a narrative of the origin of this ritual in the usual form of myths, see Grinnell, op. cit., p. 125.
[2] A ceremonial gesture said to symbolize a bird. See also p. 104.

hair that covered the place, she saw it. It was a rock, a buffalo-rock. As she was standing over it, it said, "Do not take me yet. Go back and then walk slowly towards me." [It is now teaching her the songs and ceremonial procedure.] While she was approaching, it sang a song for the woman.

> "A buffalo-rock, I am looking for the place where he is sitting.
> Now I have found him. [Takes it up.]
> He is powerful.
> A buffalo-rock, I have taken him up.
> He is powerful."

This is the song when she went forward to take it up. This is the time when it told her that she should sleep out in the brush for four nights. It said, "I will show you everything about it. You, I have taken pity on you. Now you will be out four nights, and in eight nights you will get something to eat, you will sit down with great abundance."

Now when she came home again she stood outside and said to her husband, "Do not be angry. I have received something [medicine-power]. We shall have something to eat. Chief-Speaking, do not think I am double married [committed adultery]. The reason I have been sleeping out is that I have received something. It is not valuable [meaning the reverse], but it is to be the only thing [medicine] you are to live by." Her husband said, "Now where is it?" Then he saw it. "Now," he said, "she slept outside, and this one [the rock] sang for her." Then she came into the lodge. Her husband was a beaver-bundle man, and there was always a crowd of men in the lodge. He said to his head wife, "Give that woman your clothes, she who is very poor."

Now Weasel-Woman expected to receive tallow. They looked about for fat or grease, but every kind that was offered her was refused. At last they offered her some kidney-fat. Then she said, "That will do." She put it down there, then she sang. She was going to feed them all with it. She told the men to get their rattles ready. Then she sang: —

> "This man says,
> 'Kidney-fat, I want to eat it.'"

Then she sang about herself: —

> "Woman says,
> 'Kidney-fat to eat, I want to eat it.'"

In the circle was a young unmarried man who had been chosen to lead the buffalo over [the drive]. She said to him, "You sit here at the head of the lodge. I shall paint your face first. You are going to eat first, for you are to drive the buffalo." Then he sat by her. Now she was painting his face. She was going to give him something to eat, and, changing the words of the song, teach him the way he should sing it when the buffalo were being driven up; also tell him how he should stand at the edge of the declivity where the buffalo are to fall over. He was to sing four times: —

> "I want to fall [them].
> Kidney-fat, I want to eat it."

The reason for all this was that the people might be fed.

"Now," she said to her husband, "you are to handle this iniskim. Men are always better at it than women. Such things are not in keeping with the way we live. It will give you dreams [visions]. We will use it for a long time [live long]." "Yes, you are right," said her husband.

Now she painted the young man's face. Now he was about to hear the song. Her husband was making the medicine-smoke. She took the young man's hand.

> "Man says, 'Woman, iniskim, man.
> They are powerful.'
> Man says, 'Those rocks, I move them around.
> It is powerful.
> Woman says, 'Those rocks, I move them around.[1]
> It is powerful.'"

> "Good running of buffalo.
> The driver is coming with them.
> We have fallen them.
> We are happy."

(b). *Northern Blackfoot Version.*[2]

The first people, those are the ones that found the buffalo-rock. Nearly starved were all the people. A man said to his wife, "Get some wood and build a fire." She said, "I am not strong enough; I am nearly starved." "Go on," said he. "There is no firewood here." Then she arose, saying, "I shall go after firewood." She came to a place where there was wood, and, standing beside it, picked it up slowly. She was so weak that the exertion was painful. Then she heard singing, and looked around. At last she saw it. On the cut-bank's side she sat down. The thing doing the singing was the buffalo-rock. The earth was sliding down: that is how she came to see it. While it was singing, the rock said, "Take me, I am powerful." On buffalo-hair it was sitting for a bed. It stretched out its arms. In order that food might be obtained is the reason she saw it.

---

[1] Rocks marking the lines leading up to the buffalo pound, or drive.
[2] Taken as a text by Dr. R. H. Lowie.

She took it up, wrapped it in the hair and put it inside her dress. Now she knew some food would be obtained. She went back to the camp. She went to her husband's lodge. She went inside. She said to her elder sister, "Tell our husband that I shall make medicine." So the elder one said to him, "My younger sister is about to make medicine." He said, "I have faith. Let her make medicine that we may have food." Then he called out, inviting the camp. All came to the lodge, — men, women, and children, — all came inside. "There is going to be medicine," he said. To the women and children he said, "Sit here" [the rear]. "Get some tallow," said he, "just a little." Then every one looked for it. A long time they had to hunt before finding any.

Then the woman rubbed the fat on the rock. It began to sing when she did it. It sang to the woman, "Take me, I am powerful." The people all saw it. The woman passed it to them, and all kissed it. "You shall have food," she said. Then she began to sing and then to dance. All joined in the dancing. They made a noise like the buffalo. The woman sang, "A hundred shall I lead over" [the drive]. She said, "When you sing, do not say more than a hundred." Now a man said when he sang, "Over a hundred shall I lead over" [the drive]. The woman said, "We have made a mistake now. So many will go over, that the enclosure will be burst; they will jump out of it. There will be a solitary bull wandering through the camp to-night. It will be a mangy bull. No one shall kill it. Some one must go up the hill to watch in the morning. Look-Backwards, you are to go; buffalo you will see. The-One-We-Made-Look-There, also watch. From there you will see buffalo. If that bull comes to-night, we shall all be saved. If this rock fall on its face, then you will all be happy. There will be plenty of food." All went out. They were happy, because they were to receive food. The woman slept where the smudge was made. That rock made her powerful.

He came through the camp, the one she said was coming, — the mangy bull. They all knew him. They all said, "Ah-a-a! don't kill him. Rub his back with firewood." In the morning all were happy because the mangy bull came at night. They did not kill him, the one that was said to come at night. When the woman looked out, that rock fell over on its face. Then she told them to be happy, because they would have something to eat. "It would be so, if it fell on its face," she said. Looking up, the people saw many buffalo close to the camp. Then the swift young men went out and led the buffalo, many of them. They worked them into the lines. They frightened them to make them run swiftly. Then all ran over into the enclosure. Now the people ran there. Inside were the buffalo. So many were there, that the enclosure was broken down. Over a hundred were there. That is why they broke down the fence. Not many of them were killed. All the buffalo were bulls. That is why they broke down the fence.

The woman's husband took all the ribs and back-fat, saying, "With these shall a feast be made. Again my wife will make medicine." The people were somewhat happy as the number killed was small. "For a little [while] we are saved. We have a little meat," said the man.

The next night it was called out again that the woman was to make medicine. This time she gave orders that only the women were to dance, so that cows might come to the drive. So the women danced. The men tried not to make another mistake. In the morning they looked from the hill again. They were made glad by the rock falling again on its face. Again the young men went out, and all was as before. Now all in the enclosure were cows. They were all killed with arrows. None of them got out.

The people were happy now. They had plenty of meat. Every one now believed in the power of the rock. The woman who found the rock was respected by her husband.

8. Origin of the Medicine-Pipe.

The Blood Indians have had medicine-pipes for a very long time. There is one pipe among them that is so old that no one has any recollection of having heard of its being made by any one. So this pipe must be the real one handed down by the Thunder, for all medicine-pipes came from the Thunder.

Once there was a girl who never could marry, because her parents could not find any one good enough for her. One day she heard the Thunder roll. "Well," she said, "I will marry him." Not long after this she went out with her mother to gather wood. When they were ready to go home, the girl's packstrap broke. She tied it together and started, but it broke again. Her mother became impatient; and when the strap broke the third time, she said, "I will not wait for you!" The girl started after her mother, but the strap broke again. While she was tying it together, a handsome young man in fine dress stepped out of the brush and said, "I want you to go away with me." The girl said, "Why do you talk to me that way? I never had anything to do with you." "You said you would marry me," he answered; "and now I have come for you." The girl began to cry, and said, "Then you must be the Thunder."

Then he told the girl to shut her eyes and not look, and she did so.

After a while he told her to look, and she found herself upon a high mountain. There was a lodge there.[1] She went in. There were many seats around the side, but only two people, — an old man and woman. When the girl was seated, the old man said, "That person smells bad." The old woman scolded him, saying that he should not speak thus of his daughter-in-law. Then the old man said, "I will look at her." When he looked up, the lightning flashed about the girl, but did not hurt her. Because of this, the old man knew she belonged to the family. At night all the family came in one by one. The Thunder then made a smudge with sweet-pine needles, one at the door of the lodge, and one just back of the fire. Then he taught his daughter-in-law how to bring in the bundle that hung outside. This was the medicine-pipe. After a time the daughter-in-law gave birth to a boy, later to another boy.

One evening the Thunder asked her if she ever thought of her father and mother. She said that she did. Then he asked would she like to see them. She said, "Yes." So he said, "To-night we will go. You may tell them that I shall send them my pipe, that they may live long." When the time came, he told the woman to close her eyes, and once more she was standing near the lodge of her people. It was dark. She went in and sat down by her mother. After a while she said to her mother, "Do you know me?" "No," was the answer. "I am your daughter. I married the Thunder." The mother at once called in all of their relations. They came and sat around the lodge. The woman told them that she could not stay long as she must go back to her lodge and her children, but that the Thunder would give them his pipe. In four days she would come back with it. Then she went out of the lodge and disappeared.

In four days the Thunder came with the woman, her two boys, and the pipe. Then the ceremony of transferring the pipe took place. When it was finished, the Thunder said that he was going away, but that he would return in the spring, and that tobacco and berries should be saved for him and prayed over. Then he took the youngest boy and went out. A cloud rolled away, and as it went the people heard one loud thunder and one faint one [the boy]. Now, when the Thunder threatens, the people often say, "For the sake of your youngest child," and he heeds their prayers.

When the Thunder left the woman and elder child behind, he said that if dogs ever attempted to bite them, they would disappear. One day a dog rushed into the lodge and snapped at the boy, after which nothing was seen of him or his mother, and to this day the owner of a medicine-pipe is afraid of dogs.

---

[1] It is often said that the Thunder steals or seduces women. For another version of a medicine-pipe origin, see Grinnell, op. cit., p. 113.

9. The Worm-Pipe.

Now a man was out hunting. One evening he returned to his camp and was sitting on his bed smoking. A large decayed piece of wood was burning in the fire. As he was sitting there he saw a worm crawling along the stick of wood. Then he heard singing. Now the worm became a person holding a pipe with a straight [tubular] bowl. The stem was decorated. It was a medicine-pipe. The person had an eagle-plume tied in his hair. He shook the pipe-stem, and began to sing, "The fire is my medicine."

Then the worm-person transferred the pipe to the man.[1]

10. A Pipe from the Seven Stars.

The same man who got the pipe from a worm went out to hunt. After a time he decided to go up on a mountain-top to fast and sleep. He had been there four days when he heard singing from above: —

> "The Seven Stars say,
> 'My pipe is powerful.'"

> "Old man says,
> 'My pipe is powerful.'
> He hears me."

Looking up, he saw that the smallest one of the Seven Stars was singing. Then it became a person, and gave him a medicine-pipe.

11. The Black-Covered Pipe.

Once a man was camping out alone. It was when the leaves were turning yellow, and the elk are often heard to whistle. It was in the foothills of the mountains. He had been hunting here and killed four elk. Once, just after he killed an elk, he heard a Coyote call, "Wa-wa-woo-oo-oo!" Then he heard some one singing: —

> "Fine meat.
> I want to eat it."

Now he saw what it was that was singing. It was a Coyote carrying a thorn-stick wrapped in his own skin. Then said the man, "I will give you this elk."

After this the Coyote gave him a medicine-pipe.

---

[1] Grinnell (op. cit., p. 127) gives a different account of the origin of this pipe.

12. THE OTTER-LODGE.

Man-with-a-Woman-Inside-of-Him when a young man went out to a lake far in the north. This was known as Round Lake. It was very deep. He slept on the shore, but had no dreams. Then he made a raft and lay upon it. While he slept the wind carried it far out from shore. Then a Mink appeared in his dreams, and said, "Come to my father's lodge!" He heard drumming down under the water. Now the man awoke, but could not go to the lodge because of the water. So the Mink came up again and told him to shut his eyes. He shut his eyes, and upon opening them found himself under water in a lodge.[1] The otter was lying at the back of the fire in a large pile of grass from the shore of the lake. Then the Otter became as a person, and spoke to the man. He said that he would give him some power. He took up some of the grass and made a smudge, at the same time singing a song in which the following ideas were expressed: —

> "This is my lodge.
> It is a medicine-lodge.
> I will give it to you.
> The water is my lodge.
> It is medicine."

The Otter sang seven songs and at the last took up an otter-skin, held it in his hands and sang: —

> "I will have a dream when I sleep."

Then the Otter made a smudge and held his hands in the smoke. Then he took hold of the man's hand and placed the otter-skin in it. The wife of the Otter who had aided him in signing and handling the bundles, now transferred a mink-skin to the man in the same way.

The man staid with these people until he learned many songs and the ways of handling the bundle.

13. THE BEAR-LODGE.

In the old days, before the Blackfoot had horses, they were moving camp with dog-travois. A little boy was strapped to a dog-travois. The dog went to get a drink of water. He passed through some bushes. The travois was untied and fell off with the child. The dog ran off, while the boy remained sleeping on his travois. The dog caught up with the camp.

---

[1] The several divisions of the Blackfoot have a large number of ceremonial teepees to which belong bundles and rituals. The teepees are painted with designs symbolizing parts of these rituals. For a general description of teepees of this type, see Grinnell, The Lodges of the Blackfoot (American Anthropologist, N. S., Vol. III, pp. 650–668).

The boy's mother saw the dog without his travois, and went back to look for the boy. She failed to find him. The next day she said, "I shall find my boy this night." But though she searched for him, she could not find him.

The child cried at night. The Bear heard him and went to see what was the matter. He took the child to his cave. When inside, the boy looked up. He thought it was a tent, for the Bear had painted his cave on the outside with his own figure. His hind-feet were marked about the tent in front, and there were painted wings on the roof. Bear said to the boy, "You are to stay with me all winter. I shall make food for you." The child staid there all winter, and Bear transformed buffalo-chips into meat which he gave the boy to eat. He made ripe berries for him out of saskatoon-sticks. The boy grew very fast during the winter. Next fall, when the leaves were turning yellow, the Blackfoot went back near the Bear's cave. Bear, going outside, saw the Indian camp. He returned and ordered the little boy to return to his people. The boy's parents were no longer looking for him, thinking he was dead. Bear told the boy that his name was Big-Bear. He gave his name and tent to the boy, telling him to paint his lodge in the same way as his cave. He also gave him a large knife, called the "bear-knife."[1] Then he gave him some medicine. He said, "You will be an old man, for your enemies cannot hurt you. You have nothing to be afraid of." Then the Bear said, "Now go home to your father. Take this medicine, and whenever you want something you will be able to get it."

The boy went home. When he reached camp, he painted his body and face. People saw the boy, but did not recognize him. Having lived with the Bear so long, he was very wild. He said to the people, "I am the boy you lost." Then his parents knew him. He said, "I shall not hurt you, for I pity you." He staid with his parents, but grew wilder and wilder. He was a great fighter, and took away other Indians' wives. The people were afraid of him. One day they held a council and decided to kill him. They took their bows, arrows, and stone knives. Big-Bear sent his parents to the bush. Then he attacked his enemies. The people shot at and hit him; but he just rubbed his body, and there was no wound. He killed many Indians. At last they said, "We cannot kill you." Then he bade his parents go home, saying, "They are afraid of me. Let us go home."

They went home, and the people never again tried to kill him. Big-Bear now was kind to everybody. He painted his lodge and was called Big-Bear. He became a great chief. Whenever he fought, he killed many

---

[1] See narrative No. 17.

of the enemy without getting hurt himself. When there was lack of water, he merely scrunched the earth, and produced water for his parents. He lived very long. All his children were as strong as he. The tent and the knife are still here.[1]

14. THE HORSE-LODGE.

Once there was a poor man who had just one horse, a mare. It was white. The man was married. He had also a white stud colt. The colt grew to a fine size. This story is not an account of a dream, but a statement of things that really happened. In course of time the man became rich, and owned many horses. He did not ride the white mare then, but took good care of her. One day he led her down to water. While drinking, she spoke to him, much to his surprise. She said, "Father, I shall give you a lodge. To-morrow morning, when you go out to tend your horses, you will see a lodge."

The next day, when the man went out to look for his horses, he came to a lodge, on the right side of which stood his old white mare and on the left side the colt. The White Mare said to him as he came near, "You are to paint this lodge as I direct." The man brought paints, water, and buffalo-fat, and painted the lodge as the White Mare directed. On the right side he painted with white clay, the picture of the old white mare. On the other side he painted with the same kind of clay the picture of the colt. Around the top he painted the seven stars, the bunch stars and the morning star. Around the bottom he painted in red the earth and the hills, and in white the fallen stars. When the painting was finished, the old White Mare took her master into the lodge, where she taught him the songs and the ritual. Then the man took the lodge home with him and showed it to the people. This man was a Piegan. After a time he transferred the lodge and the ritual to a Blood, who transferred it to a Northern Blackfoot. Finally it was transferred back to a Piegan, its present owner, who has made use of its power for thirty years. When it was transferred to him, he gave away ten horses.

15. BLACK AND YELLOW BUFFALO-PAINTED LODGES.

One time two men were sitting on a rock by the side of a river, making arrows. As they looked down into the water they saw a lodge standing on the bottom. One of the men said, "I believe I will enter this lodge." So

---

[1] Recorded by Dr. R. H. Lowie.

he dived down into the water. When he got into the lodge he found no water on the inside. A great deal of medicine was hanging up in this lodge, and when the man came out he told all his people what he had seen. At another time the same men were camped at a place where some people saw another lodge down in the water. When this man heard about it, he dived down and entered, as before. Here, again, he saw a great deal of medicine hanging up.

Now this was the beginning of the black-and-yellow buffalo-lodges. While the man was on the inside, he was taught the whole ceremony. And when he came up, he got together all the medicine, and painted the lodges as you see them now. These two are the most powerful painted lodges we have.[1]

16. THE CROW-PAINTED LODGE.

There is another painted lodge known as the Crow Lodge. It came about in this way. One man was catching eagles on a hill. He had made a hole in which he was hiding. After a while he went to sleep. He dreamed that a Crow came to him saying, "This is my lodge. Now I shall give it to you with the medicine and songs." So the Crow transferred the lodge to the man, taught him the songs and the ceremony.

17. THE BEAR-KNIFE.

Once in the winter-time, just one month before summer, or on the sixth moon, a Sarcee was out hunting when a blizzard came down upon him. This Sarcee was of mixed blood, for his father was a Piegan. Now in the blizzard he lost the direction, because he could not see. He was feeling around in the brush and timber for shelter. He was nearly frozen, but finally he felt on the ground a warm spot. This was a bear's den. As he went in, it got warmer and warmer. Presently he heard a Bear begin to growl. Then he stopped and began to pray to the Bear. Now the Bears had a young one, a young male. And this Bear said to his father, "I pity this young man. Do not harm him!" Then the father said, "Well, all right," and the mother said the same. Then the father said to his son, "You give him some of your power first."

So the son told the young man to come in. When the man was inside, he saw it was a lodge, painted and decorated, with a bearskin for a door.

---

[1] For a more complete version of this myth, see Grinnell (Lodges of the Blackfeet, op. cit., p. 658). The same article (p. 663) contains a brief narrative concerning the origin of another ceremonial teepee.

Now he was in the lodge. At the back of the lodge he saw a rawhide bag and a lance, and on the sides were four persons and four drums. The son said to the man, "You sit at the head of the lodge" [that is where the guests are seated]: "I will sit by you." In front of the man was a pile of thorn-bushes with very sharp thorns. "Now," said the young Bear, "I will give you my knife." "All right," said the man. Then the Bear mixed some red paint in a cup of water, and said to the young man, "Now you must take off your clothes." The man did so, and sat there naked. Now the Bear took up a big turnip, and, taking some fire, put it down upon the ground before him, singing a song as he did so: —

> "On the earth I want to sit.
> It is powerful."

Then he took down the knife, held it to his breast and in the smoke, singing all the while a kind of dancing-song in which were the words, "The ground where I sit is holy," and making the sound of a bear. All this time the knife was in the bag. Now he began to sing another song, which is called the "Untying Song." Then he put the knife down. Now he made another smudge, took up the knife, and then mixed some paint in his hand. And as he sang: —

> "The ground is our medicine."

He rubbed the red paint on his hands and then over his face, afterwards scratching it with his fingers. Then he took up black paint and made the marks representing the bear-face. Then he took claws, and put one on each side of the head. Then he took paws (?) and put them on for a necklace. But before he put the necklace on he held them in the smoke and smudge, and sang: —

> "Bear-man says, 'It is medicine,
> I want it.'"

As he put it on his head he sang: —

> "Bear is looking for something to eat."

Then he caught the person next to him, as if about to eat him. (Everything that was done was accompanied with bear actions.) Then he took up the knife, held it over the smudge, and took some eagle-tail feathers for a head-dress. All this time they were sitting near the thorns and the Bear had all his regalia on. Then the Bear took up the knife, and as he sharpened it sang: —

> "My children, on the other side of the hill is a big noise.
> You get into the brush.
> I will be safe.
> I have power."

At the last words of the song he thrust the knife into the earth, and, holding it by the handle, sang: —

"I am looking for some one to kill."

Then with the knife he pretended to be about to stab the man, and, catching hold of him, threw him upon the thorns on his breast, and holding him there painted him. Then the Bear took him up again and dressed him in his own regalia. Then taking the hand of the man in his own, and both holding the paint, he began to sing, touching the paint to the man's wrist, elbow, breast, and head. Then he laid the man down on his breast, and slapped him on the back with the flat part of the knife. This he did four times with the man turned in each of the four directions. Then the Bear said, "Now you must sleep out in the timber for seven days. Whenever you pursue an enemy you must sing this song, and make the movements I do: —

'I will run after him.
He will fall.
I will stab him.'

If the enemy shoot at you, do not dodge; if you should do this, you will be killed. Do not turn back, but keep on. If you turn back, sores will break out on your body, and they will be fatal."

Now a long time after the man had gone back to his people, he was out on the war-path and in battle against the Assiniboine. One of the enemy came up to him, put his gun against him, pulled the trigger, but it missed fire. Then the man took the Assiniboine by the hair, and stabbed him with the knife. As years went on, he killed many enemies with his knife in that way. It was very strong medicine. This knife is still among our people, but there are two of them.[1]

Now it was the turn of the father-bear to give the man something, so he gave him a lance with an otter-skin hanging down decorated with feathers. Bear's claws were hung to it for bells [rattles]. The shaft of this lance was wrapped with elk-skin, and a head-dress of bear-claws went with it.

There was one thing I forgot to tell you about the bear-knife, and that is, when a man is to receive the knife, the knife is thrown at him. If he catches it, it is all right; but if he does not catch it, he cannot receive the medicine.

Then the Bear took up the lance, painted it and made a smudge as before, singing, "Bear above, says the earth is our lodge." Then he mixed the paint and painted his face as before. Then he sang another song, and as he did

---

[1] When the bear-knife is transferred, the ceremony is the same as performed by the bear in this narrative. The transfer of the knife is so rough, that no one will take it, unless forced to do so.

so struck the lance into the ground.   While singing another song he took up
the lance in the same manner as the knife, then threw the man upon the
thorns, and painted him as before.   The words in this song were: —

> "Underneath is a bear; he has sun power."

Now the lance was thrown at the man and he caught it.   If he had failed,
he would not have received it.   Then the Bear gave him the same instructions as for the bear-knife.[1]

Now it was the old woman's turn to give the man something, and she
gave him a painted lodge.   This lodge is still among the Northern Blackfoot.
On it is a picture of a bear.   The owner of the lodge wears bear-claws for
anklets, wristlets, and ornaments on his head.   He also wears a feather
head-dress and a bear-robe.   The smudge song for the bear-lodge is as
follows: —

> "The earth is our home.
> It is medicine."

The next song: —

> "My lodge I give it to you.
> It is powerful."

Then she took up the paint and sang as she painted him: —

> 'Be not afraid.
> Never turn back.
> Think of the one you kill and eat."

The woman told the man that no one must spit inside of the lodge, but he
must raise up the side, and spit on the outside.   (Same is true of the medicine-lodge.)   The medicine-bundle for this lodge was the robe and the other
objects to be worn by the man.   It must also have a bearskin for a door,
for this is the lodge in which the man found the bears.

18.   THE SMOKING–OTTER.

Once there was a white man and his wife who had for a friend a young
Indian who was not married.   The white man took the Indian off to a
great water.   They went out to a lonely island which was the nesting-
ground for many kinds of birds.   The ground in many places was covered
with feathers.   They camped there for a while.   After a time the white
man began to be suspicious of his Indian friend on account of his wife.

---

[1] The lance was buried several years ago with the body of its last owner.   During these
ceremonies the wife of the recipient of the ritual was also thrown down upon the thorns.   Once
an indecent exposure of the woman occurred when this part of the ceremony was reached, the
narration of which afterwards came to have a definite place in the transfer proceedings.

He thought that she was in love with the Indian. Now the days on the
island were very hot, and one day the Indian said that he was going down
on the shore on the other side of the island to take a swim. As soon as he
was gone, the white man put his wife into a boat and rowed away as fast as
he could. When the Indian came back, he looked around for his friend.
Seeing the boat in the distance he knew what had happened. He watched
the boat out of sight. Then he began to cry. As the man and his wife
had taken everything with them, the young Indian made a bed of feathers,
crawled into it, and mourned all night. So he lived on the island alone,
sleeping in feathers, and digging roots.[1]

One day the Indian saw an Otter and a white Swan swimming toward
the shore. As they came up, they spoke to him, saying, "My son, do not
be frightened, for we have come to take you to the shore; but you must shut
your eyes, and not open them again until we tell you. We will get to the
shore yet before the white man does." Then the swan began to sing songs.
The words were as follows: —

"The man says, 'The wind is my medicine.
The rain is my medicine,
The hail is my medicine.'"

Then the Otter sang a song. First he dipped his fingers into the water
four times, rubbed them on his hair, blew his whistle four times, and sang: —

"Wherever I lie, I hear.
The water is my medicine."

This is the way the Smoking-Otter medicine came to be among the
Indians. When the Indian was brought back to his people, he took an otter-
skin and a swan-skin for his medicine. Whenever the owner of this medicine
begins to smoke, he shakes the bells on the otter four times. Then he takes
some smoke, blows it into the hollow of his hand, and rubs it on the otter-
skin. Then he blows one handful to the otter, one to the bells, one to the
owner's heart, and one to the ground. This last is because the otter runs on
the ground. There is power in this, because the otter is supposed to have
long life.

19. The Medicine-Shields.

Once there was a man named Always-Talking and a woman named
Stepped. This woman was the wife of Always-Talking; but she fell in
love with a younger man. When her husband discovered this, he killed her.

---

[1] To this point in the narrative we have what seems a version of a Dakota myth, Riggs,
op. cit., p. 130; also Wissler, Journal of American Folk-Lore, Vol. XX, p. 196. It is interesting
to find a fragment of this myth among the Blackfoot accounting for the origin of a medicine-
bundle.

Then he went about and around the camp, telling all the people what he had done, and that they should move camp at once. This was according to the custom of that time, when women who committed this offence were killed and their bodies left unburied. So the people moved their camp far to the north, where they crossed a large river. This was early in the spring and the water of the river got very high, so high that they could not cross back again. Always-Talking had two wives left, but he mourned for his other wife, and was sorry that he had killed her.

Many buffalo were roaming about on the side of the river where the woman's body lay. There were eight buffalo who travelled by themselves, one was a cow and seven were bulls.[1] The Cow always led the bunch. As they were going along one day, they came to the body of the dead woman. They stopped, stood around and looked at it. The Cow said, "For this woman I am sorry. I pity her. You must doctor her." To this the others replied, "We are sorry too. We will do what we can for the poor woman." One of the bulls was the husband of the Cow and he said to her, "You go over to the herd and pick out seven cows to aid us in doctoring the woman." The Cow went away and came back with seven others. Now all the buffalo knew what was going on and gathered around in a large crowd.

The woman had been dead a long time, and nothing remained except her bones. As the buffalo stood around, they all became people, painted and dressed in fine clothes. They had seven drums and other medicine things. Then they began to sing a song. The words were, "We want buffalo to come to life." Then they all walked around the skeleton and pawed until it was covered with dirt and grass. They sang many other songs. Then the Cow and her husband approached the place where the skeleton was covered up, and each hooked at the place twice. Then the other buffalo did the same in their turn. Then the husband of the Cow led the buffalo around to one side and brought them up toward the feet of the skeleton. Then they hooked as before; then back again and up toward the right side of the skeleton; then toward the head. As they came toward the head of the skeleton, the husband of the Cow rushed at the heap of dirt, and the woman came to life and stood up. Then the woman took the lead of the procession and all the buffalo fell in behind. The husband of the Cow came directly behind the woman. He had great power. He would blow through his nose and all the different colored paints would come out. He blew these paints upon the woman. The other buffalo carried seven drums, and sang this song: —

See footnote p. 122

"Buffalo is going to drink.
Water is my medicine.
Buffalo is going to eat.
Grass is my medicine."

The meaning of this song was, that when the woman should drink and eat she would be fully restored to life. As the procession approached the river, they stopped three times, and a fourth time at the edge of the river. While they stopped there, they sang this song: —

"Our road is powerful.
We look for a powerful road."

Now the woman had been dead so long that she had to be given the power to drink and to eat. So the husband of the Cow put her mouth to the water with four movements, and directed her to drink by licking the water four times. Then he took a buffalo-horn spoon, painted it red and yellow, and gave the woman water from it. Then he took some dried meat, rubbed it in his hands, making four movements toward the woman's mouth, and gave it to her to eat. Now the woman was restored to life. The husband of the Cow gave her some buffalo-hair and said, "When you cross this river, go into the lodge of your husband, and if he is still angry at you, throw this hair at him, and he will die of the small-pox. If he treat you well, make him a shield, and one for each of your two brothers." The river was now very deep, and in order that the woman might cross, the buffalo made a bridge of shields over the river. The Cow told the woman to shut her eyes, and began to lead her across. She said to the woman, "When you have reached the other side, the buffalo will give you your choice of three of these shields. There are three medicine-shields here, — the first one upon which you shall step, the fourth, and the one in the centre of the bridge. You choose these, and when you get back make them." When the woman was safely across, the husband of the Cow placed all the shields before her in a row that she might choose some of them. She picked out the three shields as directed by the Cow. The Bull advised her to take others. He said, "Those you have selected have no power. The other shields are medicine-shields." But the woman still insisted upon taking her first choice, and after refusing the others four times, she was permitted to take them. Now one of the shields she took belonged to the husband of the Cow. He said to the woman, "My shield must never be put down in the house, but must hang upon a tripod. The face of the shield must always point toward the sun, and it must be moved on the tripod to follow the sun."

Now the woman started to return to her people. When she came in sight of the camp, she concealed herself until it was dark, and then went to the lodge of her husband. "Is my husband at home?" she said. "He is," a man replied. Always-Talking recognized his wife and gave her a hearty welcome. He forgave her all the past. After a time the woman told Always-Talking that he should kill three large bulls and give her the skins. When the skins were brought to her, she made three shields. She gave one to Always-Talking, and one to each of her brothers. She said to them, "When you go out on the war-path, you must take these three shields. You must never turn back until you meet enemies. If you do so, you will surely die."

This is the way the people got medicine-shields.

20. NEVER-SITS-DOWN'S SHIELD.

Somewhere on the other side of the mountains a Piegan was sleeping in lonely places. One night he slept in a buffalo-wallow and had a dream. Next day he returned to his people and entered his father's lodge. The next day he asked his father to cut a piece of skin from the belly of a bull and shrink it by heating over a fire. This done, he was to cut it round like the sun, and paint the picture of a bull and a cow on one side; also to put a fringe across the middle of the shield to represent the beard of the bull. In the centre of the piece he was to tie the head of a jack-rabbit. Then he was to take a piece of elk-horn, bend it into a hook, and tie it across the middle. Wristlets were to be made from the skin of the buffalo's nose, and dew-claws were to be tied to them. Armlets were to be made from the skin taken from the throat where the hair is long. A strip of skin from the buffalo's mane was to be taken for a necklace. Finally his father was requested to get a white horse with red ears, and to bob his tail like that of the rabbit. The horse should be made to look as much like the rabbit as possible. A whistle was to be used to imitate the noise made by the rabbit.

When the boy's father had done all this, he was directed by his son to hang the shield upon a pole on the back of the lodge, then to ride round the camp and tell all the people to stake down their lodges. "When this is done," said the boy, "I shall sing a song, and if nothing happens, we shall destroy this shield." So the boy's father rode round the camp, calling out to all the people and telling them to stake down their lodges and send a swift runner to assist his son. The whole camp knew that some powerful medicine was about to work. The women hurried out to stake down their lodges. When the father returned to his lodge, the boy dug up some dirt at the side of his bed, and scattered some light-colored dust in the hole. "This," said he, "is to represent the place where the buffalo do their pawing." The young man directed the runner to go out by the left side of the lodge and run around very fast, take the shield down from the pole as he ran, and bring it into the lodge without stopping. While the runner was doing this, the boy sang a song. He was sitting down with a buffalo-robe, hair-side out, drawn around him. When the runner came in with the shield, the boy put it on by putting his feet through the carrying-strap and pulling it over his shoulders. Then he fell over into the hole he had dug, rolled in the dust he had scattered there, and grunted like the buffalo. Then he got up and shook himself. Immediately a great storm came. It blew the dust the boy shook from himself straight up into the air. It did not blow down the lodge in which the shield was; but every other lodge in the camp was blown over, notwithstanding the fact that they had been staked down very tight. In this way, the great medicine-power of this shield became known to the people.

Once, a long time after this, the enemy attacked the camp, and the Piegan were driven back among their lodges. The boy who owned the shield sat quietly in his lodge and let them fight. His people called him to come out, but he sat still. Finally he sent for a number of young men, and when they arrived he requested them to get a number of young cotton-wood-trees and put them against his lodge. While the young men were bringing the trees, the boy had his horse brought in. The young men soon came back, and brought so many trees that they almost broke down the lodge. Then the boy put on his wristlets, his armlets, his necklace, took the shield, sang a song, rolled in the dust and shook himself, as before. This time, however, he shot straight up in the air and came out at the top of the lodge, breaking some of the cottonwood-trees, and came down astride his horse. The horse jumped four times, like a rabbit. All this time the enemy were shooting at him. As the horse jumped the fourth time, the enemy ran. The boy pursued them, striking them with the hook of elk-horn that hung upon the shield, and every man struck fell dead.

The shield takes its name from its owner, who always sat down; but the people speak of him, according to their way, as he who never-sits-down.

21. THE EAGLE–HEAD CHARM.

One day a man came to a tall tree in the top of which was an eagle's nest. The nest was made of sticks, and was very broad. The man looked up at it. He saw a buffalo-calf standing up there. "These birds have some great power," he said. "I will sleep here [at the foot of the tree] to see if I get some power." So he put his robe over his head, lay down under the tree and slept. He awoke, hearing a puff of wind. He uncovered his head and found himself up in the nest. The buffalo-calf, frightened, was jumping about snorting. Looking up, the man saw two eagles circling around the tree. They were very high and were sounding their whistles [screaming]. There was a wind. The eagles came down. The man was afraid. He took two young eagles up in his arms and cried. The female eagle said, "Let us do something for this man: he takes pity on our children." Then the male eagle struck the buffalo-calf, knocking him off the nest, and also knocking off a dead calf that was there. Then he became a person and stood before the man. The eagle-person sang songs. He had a straw in the bunch of hair at the top of his head. He told the man that this was to make him as hard to hit [in a fight] as a straw.

FIRST SONG.

"I don't want them [enemy] to kill me.
These here [the straw, etc.] I shall fight with."

SECOND SONG.

"This here, my head-top, wear.
It is powerful.
Guns for me are fun [easy to overcome]."

THIRD SONG.

"That there I am looking for.
Guns [are] my medicine."

While singing the third song, the eagle-person waved his arms as if flying around, and moved his head as if searching for the guns. At the end of it he blew his whistle four times and took the man down to the ground.

FOURTH SONG.

"Gun I want to eat [capture]."

FIFTH SONG.

"Now let me eat a gun."

While singing the fifth song, the eagle-person flapped his arms, and at the end blew his whistle. Then he said to the man, "I will give you some power." He took a feather from his tail and threw it through the body of the calf, saying, "So you can do to enemies." The man said to himself, "I do not want such power as this, to kill people." The female eagle said, "Do not give him such a power as that. Give him some other power." So the male eagle said, "Well, you will get long life and good luck."

Soon after, the man came to a place where some young men were shooting at white-headed eagles. He watched them. They killed one. He asked for the head and a wing-bone. When they were given to him, he tied the head on to his hair and made a whistle of the bone. The man soon went on a raid and got many horses. He went into many fights, but always got out safely. When a very old man, he transferred the charms and formula to a young man, its present owner, who attributes his long life and safety to its power.

22. The Pigeons.

Once an old man was in mourning for a son who had been killed on the war-path. He had gone out to the place where the body had been found. Then he went up on a high hill. This was a very lonesome place; but there were many pigeons there. The name of this man was Changes-His-Camp. The place was in the direction of the Crows. He himself was a Piegan. Now it was the fall of the year, and the old man was crying for his son. While he was doing this, he heard the turtle-doves inviting each other. He went over and joined them. They said that they would give him a society. They said that he had mourned a long time and that now he was about to get revenge. That he would move camp a few times and three Crow Indians would be killed. Then they danced, and showed him the whole thing. When he came back, he started the Pigeons.[1]

23. The Mosquitoes.

Once a Piegan lived in the woods in the far north. This was a long time ago. One day he was out hunting in timber in which there were a great many insects; but the insects were all in their holes because it was raining. The man wore a buckskin shirt, leggings, and moccasins. After a while the day cleared off, and at once the insects began to fly. They swarmed around the man so thick that he could not push them away. At last they got under his clothing. They bit him all over until he was almost dead. At last he was exhausted, and fell down upon the ground. Now the insects settled on his face, and began to work their way into his eyes, nose, and ears. His whole head was covered with them. Before he became unconscious, he heard a voice calling out, "Mosquitoes, mosquitoes, get together, get together! Your friend is nearly dead." Then the mosquitoes got together and came out in single file. The man saw that four of them were painted yellow with blue stripes across the eyes, nose, and cheeks. The others were

---

[1] The Blackfoot maintained a series of related societies for men similar to the military societies of the Arapaho, Cheyenne, Hidatsa, etc. The names given them by Grinnell are Little-Birds, Pigeons, Mosquitoes, Braves, All-Crazy (?) Dogs, Raven-Bearers, Dogs, Tails, Horns Kit-Foxes, Catchers, and Bulls. Our collection of narratives contains origin myths for a number of these. See Grinnell, Blackfoot Lodge Tales, op. cit., pp. 104, 221.

painted red. These four were called the "yellow mosquitoes," and wore eagle-tail feathers in their hair. The others wore plumes and a long feather hanging down from the head. They had a leader who wore a feather on his head, and had his face painted yellow with red bands cross it. Also four of them carried a piece of rawhide with the hair on it, upon which they beat time. They wore moccasins and breech-cloths. All the members wore eagle-claws on their wristlets, the strings of which were wrapped with porcupine-quills. They all sat down in a circle while a song was sung. Then all danced around in the direction of the sun four times, and, springing up, they dashed upon the insects, quickly driving them away.

24. The Braves.

Once a boy was out hunting squirrels with bow and arrows. He chased a squirrel into a hole, and lay near by waiting for it to come out. He waited so long that he fell asleep with his head resting on the bow. After a while he heard shouting and then a war-whoop. This caused him to wake up. He could hear the shouting, but could see nothing. Finally he looked up into the sky, where he saw many men coming down. Behind the main body were two side by side, and in the rear one man. Their robes were turned hair-side out, and buffalo-hoofs hung from the corners. One of the men carried a stick with plumes fastened to it. The men in the front row had their faces painted black. One in the centre of the front rank wore a fine suit trimmed with weasel-tails and a feather in his head. All the others wore robes. This leader carried a rattle in his hand, half of which was painted yellow and half red, with a hawk-feather hanging from the end. His face was painted half red and half yellow. Then the men all fell into single file. In the rear were four men painted black, and wearing black robes. Each carried a lance wrapped in black cloth trimmed with four bunches of crow-feathers. Their faces were painted with white streaks across the nose. Some of them carried water-vessels made of buffalo-stomachs, on their backs. All of them carried whistles. The leader was painted red, wore a red robe, and carried a spear with feathers of many colors. Their faces were painted. There were four other men, all painted white with black circles on their faces and four marks below their eyes. They carried spears with four bunches of eagle-tail feathers on them. Sage-grass was tied around the spears. One man wore a buckskin suit trimmed with weasel-tails and his body was painted white. There were two men wearing robes with the hair-side out. They wore shirts and red moccasins cut full of small holes. Their bodies were painted red with black marks

·on the faces. Their robes were kept in place by bearskin belts, and they wore arm-bands of bearskin. Each carried a red bow and four arrows, two blunt and two pointed. There was a man in the rear called Brave-Willow. He wore a robe tanned on both sides. His face was painted red with a black mark across the nose. Buffalo-hoofs were tied to the corners ·of his robe and a plume fastened at the back. He carried in his hand a willow painted red with plumes on each of the branches.

This is the way the Braves were first found out. The men with arrows were called Brave-Bears.

25. Dog-Chief.

Once there was a very nice girl the daughter of a head man, and many young men sought her for a wife. One of the men in the camp owned a very large dog. It was a brindle. One time this girl borrowed this dog, hitched him to a travois, and went out for wood. After this she borrowed him many times, and he became used to her. Whenever he came about she always fed him and petted him, and whenever she went for water he went with her. One day as the girl was going along she said aloud, "I wish you were a young man, then I would marry you." Now the dog heard and understood. That night he turned himself into a man and went to the lodge where the girl was sleeping. She awoke and found some one kissing her. She put out her hand, felt the man, and noted that his hair was fine and that he had finely shaped limbs. When he went away she wondered who it could be. She never had anything to do with other men. She had two brothers, and for that reason she did not wish to say anything about it. She thought the person might have been one of her suitors. So she thought to herself, "If he comes, next time I will mark him." So that evening she took some white earth, mixed it with water in a cup, and stirred it with a stick-weed.[1] That night the strange visitor came again, and, as he caressed the girl, she rubbed some of the white earth on his hair, on his robe, and on his back.

Now the next day there was a dance in the camp, and while it was going on, the girl went out and looked around. Though she could see every man in the camp, none of them wore the marks of her paint. Now she wondered who he could be. As she turned away, she saw a dog in the distance. It

---

[1] For a note on the wide distribution of this myth see Dorsey and Kroeber, op. cit., p. 209. The punishment of a maiden regarded by herself or her parents as of too great worth to be the wife of even the best young man in camp, is a favorite theme among the Blackfoot story-tellers. Her humiliation usually takes the same form, she marries a man of extraordinary promise, who turns out to be a creature equally disgusting. For another example in this collection, see p. 151.

was her travois dog, and as he came up she saw stripes of white paint on him, just as she had marked her strange visitor. Now she thought to herself, "It can't be the dog; but surely that is the paint. Now to-night he will come again, and I will try it once more." That night the man came again. This time she took his middle finger, and, putting it into her mouth, bit it very hard so as to cut it through with her teeth. Now she was the daughter of the chief of the tribe. The next day there was to be a dance, and she requested her father to order the young men to dance holding up their hands. Her father did this, and as they danced she looked closely at all their hands, but saw no bruises on them. As she looked away, she saw the travois dog again. As he came up, she noticed that he was lame, and when she examined his foot, she found that one of his toes was nearly cut in two. Then she went to the man and asked him for the loan of the dog to go for water. She put him to the travois and went. When out of sight of the camp, she took the dog into the brush, turned to him and said, "Here, it is you that visits me at night." The paint was on him yet, and he was very lame.

Then the dog became a man, took off the travois and stood up. He was a fine young man. He said to the girl, "Well, it was your fault, you wished it." Then the dog-man took her into the brush. The girl said, "Let us go far away from the camp. This is a disgrace to me." "Well," said the man, "I will be a dog again, and you may drive me home with the water; but to-night, when all the people are asleep, we will leave the camp and no one will ever know about this." So they took the water home, and the girl got all her things together, some food and some moccasins. When it was dark, she told her mother that she was going out for a while. When she was out of sight, the dog-man appeared and they went away together. The next morning the chief called out about the camp, asking if any one had seen the girl. Then the man who owned the dog called out about the camp, saying, "My large travois dog has gone. Has any one seen him?"

The dog-man and the girl went far off. They were gone four years. They had two children, a boy and a baby-girl. The children were real people, for the dog-man was now a person. They all returned to the camp of the girl's people, and the dog-man called at the lodge of his former owner. When he came to the door he said, "Can I stay here a while?" "Yes," said the owner. The dog-man had ten dogs with him. One day the man said to him. "To what tribe do you belong?" "Well," said he, "I belong to a tribe living far away." "Then how is it," said the man, "that you speak our language?" The dog-man replied, "Because our people speak the same language as you." Now the dog-man always wore his moccasins, and whenever he had occasion to change them, he went outside, where no one could see him. About this the people became suspicious. Whenever his wife would cook a meal, he would say that he would eat outside; and some of the people who watched him saw that he ate his meat raw. So one day his former owner said to his wife, "I believe he is not a person. Suppose we look at him when he has his moccasins off." So one time, when the dog-man was asleep, they saw his foot sticking out of the bed. He had feet like a dog. During this time the parents of the girl began to see a resemblance in the wife of the dog-man to their lost daughter. They began to have suspicions also. Now the dog-man thought to himself, "I guess they know all about it." So one day he said to his former owner, "Do you know that I am a dog?" "Yes," said the man. "Well," said the dog-man, "I am your old brindle." Now the girl went over to her parents and told them the story. She explained everything as it had happened.

Now, when the news was spread in the camp, all the men stood around and began to make remarks. They said, "Now, you see all the fine young men refused her: so she married a dog." The dog-man was very angry because of this abuse, so he requested his wife's people and the people of his former owner to move camp that night. So they moved. When they had camped again, not far away, the dog-man began to call out like a dog, and all the dogs in the camps joined him at once. Now the people were all afoot because they had no travois dogs. So they held a council, and sent four men over to the dog-man's camp to get the dogs back; but when they came there the dog-man barked, and all the dogs jumped upon the four men and killed them. Then the people begged of him to give up the dogs. At last he consented. So they got their dogs back.

Now this dog-man had a dog-skin for a medicine, which he gave to his wife's brother. This man called in a number of young men, and organized a society. This society was called "The Dogs." After a time the son of the dog-man became a chief, and, like his father's ancestors, he was a great runner. He led the buffalo over the drive, and pursued enemies in battle. His sister became a good woman, a great worker, economical, etc. These children were real persons. There were no traces of dog in them.

26. HAS-SCARS-ALL-OVER.

Once when the people were in camp the young men were out chasing buffalo. They were trying to drive them over, but did not succeed. The people of the camp were very hungry, as they had been out of meat for a long time. One day while the young men were out after buffalo again, two young women went out from the camp to gather wood. When they were out in the brush, they heard a noise over in the camp. Some one in a loud voice was telling the people to be quiet and keep close to the camp, because the young men were now driving up the buffalo. The young women heard what was said. One of them said aloud, in the presence of her companion, "Leader of the buffalo, if you will lead the herd into the enclosure so that my people may have plenty of meat, I will take you for my husband."

When the young women had their bundles of wood ready to draw up on their backs with the pack-straps, they heard a great noise. The buffalo were going over. The companion of the girl who made the vow to marry the buffalo said, "Listen, the buffalo went over. Hurry!" Every time the other woman raised her bundle of wood to her back, the strap would break and the wood fall to the ground. When this had happened four times, her companion, who was very anxious to get to the camp, left her. When the young woman was alone, making up her bundle for the fifth time, she heard some one say, "I have come for you. I want you to go with me." The young woman looked up in surprise. She saw a handsome young man finely dressed. She was frightened. She said, "No, I do not have to go with you. You have nothing to do with me." To this the young man replied, "I have killed all my people on account of you. You said you would marry the leader of the buffalo if he led them over. I was the leader of that herd, and you know from what you have just heard that I have done my part." Then the young woman began to cry and said, "Yes, I did say that. I must keep my vow. I will go with you."

Now all the people of the camp were busy butchering, and no one noticed the absence of the young woman for a long time. At last her husband and her relatives began to ask about her. Finally they learned that she and the other woman had gone into the brush to gather wood just before the buffalo were driven over. When the companion of the missing girl was questioned, she told them of the promise made in her hearing, and that she left the woman in the brush because her wood kept falling down. Then she asked the people if any of the bulls had escaped from the enclosure. Then the watchers remembered that they saw the leader of the herd spring over the fence and run away. Now every one was sure that the missing woman had gone away as the wife of the leader of the buffalo.

The husband of the woman began to make many arrows. He gathered all the different kinds of rock he could find to make arrowpoints. He made many arrows. Then he started out to find his wife. He travelled many days. One day about noon he came to the place where the buffalo lived. While he was scouting, he saw a woman going down to the river for water. As he watched her he recognized his wife. He took off his clothing and painted himself with buffalo dung and urine.[1] Then he hurried

---

[1] So that he might not be discovered by the scent of his body.

to the river, where he met his wife. He said to her, "I have come to take you home." The woman had a buffalo-horn in which she carried water to her buffalo-lover. Her husband was thirsty, and said to her, "Give me the horn that I may take a drink." Before she could answer, he took the horn from her hands and drank with it. Then she said to him, "You must wait here until the middle of the afternoon. That is the time when my lover takes a nap. When he is sound asleep I will steal away, meet you here and go home with you." Then the woman filled the horn with water and carried it to the Bull. When he was about to drink, the horn made a peculiar loud noise. He stopped, looked sharply at the woman, and said, "Some one met you and talked with you." The woman said quietly, "Well, one of your young men came down to the river, took the horn from my hands and drank from it." "Oh! all right," said the Bull as he put the horn to his mouth and drank.[1] When he had fallen asleep the woman stole away, met her husband at the river, and they started home. They went as fast as they could. When the Bull awoke and missed the woman, he called together his herd, and ordered them to look for her. They soon found the trail of the man and woman by the scent. Then the whole herd followed rapidly.

As the man and woman were running along, they looked back and saw the whole herd following them. The woman said that the leader of the herd was a very powerful medicine-man. He had been shot many times, but nothing seemed to kill him. He has so many scars on his body, that the buffalo named him Has-Scars-All-Over. When the herd came near them, the woman threw down her robe. The whole herd stopped to hook and trample it. In this way they gained a start. Just before the buffalo overtook them again, they reached a forest. The man and woman climbed into a very large tree. When they were safely seated in the branches, the woman reminded the man again that the leader of the herd was a powerful medicine-man. The man said to her, "Do you know what will kill him?" The woman replied, "I have heard him say that white flint rock is the only thing of which he is afraid." The man looked over his arrows and took out five that were tipped with this rock. While he was doing this, he heard the buffalo come to the tree. As they lost the trail, the whole herd passed by, except one old scabby bull. He was so old that he could not keep up with the others. When he got to the tree, he stopped to rub his sides against it. While they were watching him from the top of the tree, the woman said, "I have a notion to spit on that bull." "No!" said the man. "None of them have seen us, and if you keep still they will not find us." The woman,

---

[1] To this point the incidents are similiar to those in the Origin of the Bull Band, Grinnell, op. cit., p. 104.

however, took no notice of what he said, but leaned over and spat upon the bull. At once he looked up, saw the people in the top of the tree and bellowed loudly. The whole herd came back at once. The bulls began to butt the tree. The man took his arrows and shot the buffalo down one after the other. He killed so many that they lay in heaps. Now the leader of the herd was a powerful medicine-man. He began to roll in the dust. After he had rolled over four times, he got up and shook himself. As he did so the dust shot straight up into the air. Then he charged upon the tree, and as his horns struck it, a large piece flew off. As he did this the man in the tree shot a common arrow at him; but it rebounded from his side without doing him any harm. The woman said, "About the fourth time he strikes the tree, it will fall." When the leader of the herd charged the second time, the man shot a white-pointed arrow at him. It entered his head, but did not stop him. When he struck the tree, one of his horns passed through the trunk and stuck fast. However, this split the tree, causing it to fall. The moment he struck the ground, the man shot another white-pointed arrow into him. He died instantly. When the buffalo saw their leader fall, they ran away as fast as they could.

The woman came up and stood looking at the dead bull. She began to shed tears. The man looked at her in great surprise. He said, "Did you really love that buffalo?" "Yes," replied the woman.[1] When she said this, the man took out his white-rock knife and killed her at once. He returned to his people, and founded the society known as the "Front Tails." They were known by this name because each member wore a buffalo-tail upon his belt, which was hung in such a way as to be seen from the front.

27. SCABBY–BULL.

Once there was a married woman. This was in the olden times. One year the buffalo would not go over the drive. Every time they were brought up, they broke through the lines. Then, the old men consulted each other. One said, "It is curious how the buffalo act. Some one must be making power secretly." Now the husband of this woman was a head man. One day when he was talking about the strange acts of the buffalo, one suggested that they question the young men who formed the lines of the buffalo-drive as to what they observed. As they could tell nothing, they were directed next time to watch carefully, to note the leader, his age, and all his char-

---

[1] A similar tale has been found among the Crow Indians (Simms, op. cit., p. 322) and among the Arapaho (Dorsey and Kroeber, op. cit., p. 423).

acteristics. "Perhaps," said one, "you young men stick your heads up
too quickly." After the next attempt to drive the buffalo, the young men
reported that a young bull led the herd. Some said that he was middle-
aged, and one young man said that he was an old bull.

Now this woman was a fine-looking person. At one time she was the
belle of the camp. She was virtuous and industrious. About this time
the leader of the herd spoke to her. He said, "If you will go off with me,
I will lead the herd over. Then I will get out and join you in the brush."
Now the woman thought it over and said to some one, "If I had no children,
it would be with me like the woman who married a star."[1] (The bull had
appeared to her in a dream.) After thinking it over, she decided to promise
to marry him because of her people. They were very hungry, and it seemed
her duty to make the sacrifice on their account. So after a while she said
that she would marry the bull. She really just thought it, she did not
speak it. She was thinking of her children as she went out after wood.
Presently she saw the brush where she slept when dreaming of the bull. As
she was starting home with the wood, she saw the buffalo go over the drive.
She went back with her wood as quickly as she could.

After the buffalo were in, one bull got out. He was scabby and lame.
He ran right through the camp, and as he passed the woman she noticed
red on his head. Now the woman started out for more wood. As she
went out of the lodge she saw two ravens sitting close by. "Now," she
thought, "this is strange that they should be there." As she started down,
the ravens began flying around her head, telling her that the buffalo-man
was coming. Now this man always had many animals and birds around
him, — swallows, small birds, canary-birds, etc.; and while the woman
was making up her bundle of wood many birds were flying round her head.
Then she heard the brush crack, and a man stepped out. "Hold on!"
he said. "I am in a hurry," the woman replied, "I must get back to do
my butchering." All this time the birds were flying swiftly around her
head, and she lost her presence of mind, being unable to go on. "Well,"
said Scabby-Bull, "you promised to marry me in your mind. I killed all
my relations on account of you." Then the woman consented, and they
went off together.

All this time the people were butchering. The husband looked everywhere for the woman, and after a few days began to mourn for her as lost.
He cried, and called upon all living things to help him to get back his wife,
to tell him where she was, etc. As he was going about crying, he came to a
bluebird's nest in a broken tree. He cried beside the tree, and took up

---

[1] This refers to the narrative of a woman who went to the sky to become the husband of
the Morning Star, pp. 58–61.

some of the young ones in his hand, still crying. Then the Bluebird said to him, "What are you doing this for?" Then the man told the Bluebird all that had happened. "We know who it is," said the Bluebird. "It is Scabby-Bull. He is a powerful medicine-man. You cannot kill him. We can do nothing for you. None of your arrows will kill him. You must take a blunt arrow, paint it yellow, and shoot him on the crown of the head. That will make him crazy. Then you can shoot him again. That will kill him. Then you must cut him open. A canary-bird will fly out, and you must kill it also. Now go over to the other brush you see yonder. In a forked branch you will find a nest of young blackbirds. Take up one of the young ones, and begin to cry." The man found the nest as directed, and, holding one of the young ones in his hand, began to cry. After a while the male Blackbird said, "What are you doing that for?" "Well," said the man, "I have heard Scabby-Bull ran off with my wife. I have children at home like yours, and need help to get my wife back." "Well," said the Blackbird, "I can help you in one way. I can give you power to fool him. I have that power when around hawks, eagles, etc. Seabby-Bull is the leader of the buffalo herd and is protected by a number of birds. You go on to the next brush, where you will find an ant-hill. Upon it is a white stick on which an ant is sleeping. Give him food, and ask him for help." The man went on until he came to the Ant, when he did as directed. He explained all his troubles to the Ant, who promised to help him. The Ant said, "Go on to the next brush. You will find a couple [man and wife] down there. Take some of these willows for them to eat [use]. Call on them for help. These people have the power of arrows." Then the man went on. Presently he came up to an old couple, from whom he got some power. The old man said, "You take two blunt arrows. Scabby-Bull is afraid of them. You can kill him with such arrows." The old man gave him medicine, leggings, and a shirt worked in porcupine-quills. He said, "Your arrows will be as many as your quills, and will stick and hurt like quills. In the next brush you will find a very quick person. Call on him for help." The man went on. When he came to the next brush, he found a Prairie-chicken with his wife and children. So the man took some grass-hoppers and fed the chicks. "What are you doing that for?" said the Prairie-chicken. Then the man explained to him that he had lost his wife, etc. "I know all about Scabby-Bull," said the Prairie-chicken. "He is a very smart person, guarded by many birds and animals, and very hard to approach. I will help you all I can. I can scare anything that lives. [This refers to the noise as a prairie-chicken suddenly takes wing.] I will scare Scabby-Bull. You will find him by a spring. I can take you there. Now go back to the old man and ask for your arrows." When the man returned with his arrows, the Prairie-chicken said, "You must go back to the Ant and feed him again. He should give you more power. He may give you the power to turn into an ant. This Ant is the same one as the flying-ant. The buffalo and birds pay no attention to flying-ants. Scabby-Bull is protected by all sorts of things, and a flying-ant is about the only thing that can approach him." So he went back and got the power to turn into an ant. The Ant said to him, "Now Scabby-Bull is abusing your wife, because I have been there to see." When the man got back, the Prairie-chicken and he started out. After a time they saw Scabby-Bull in the distance. "Now shut your eyes," said the Prairie-chicken. At once the man became a prairie-chicken, and was flying along with the other. They saw all the birds flying around the herd. Then they alighted and began to feed with the other birds. "Look," said the Prairie-chicken, "see that herd of buffalo! Scabby-Bull and your wife are there. Over yonder is the spring where they drink." Then the Prairie-chicken said again, "Shut your eyes!" At once the man became a winged-ant. "Now," said the Prairie-chicken, "you can fly around and not be noticed." As he flew around, he saw Scabby-Bull lying with his head on the woman's lap. The woman was picking lice from his head while he was shaking his tail. Scabby-Bull was very jealous of this woman. After a while he said to her, "I shall go away, but you are to work some moccasins for me in quills. If you have not finished them by the time I return, the buffalo will dance upon you and kill you."

Then the woman set to work on the moccasins. She called upon the worms [probably ants] for help.[1] They asked her to sing a song while they worked. In this way the work was soon done. They were very fine indeed. By this time the Ant and the Prairie-chicken were back at the spring. Scabby-Bull came back to the woman, took off his left horn and sent her to the spring for water. As she took the horn, Scabby-Bull told her that if any one spoke to her the horn would make a noise. When the woman reached the spring, her former husband, who was now an ant, alighted on her ear and explained everything to her. He told her how the children at home were crying for her. That he needed her very much. Then the woman told him that she would go back to Scabby-Bull, and after he had gone to sleep she would run off. Now when she got back with the horn of water, and Scabby-Bull was about to drink, the horn made a noise. At once he accused the woman of having met some one; but she said quietly, "No, the birds were all telling me not to look." Then Scabby-Bull asked the birds. They said that they had done so.

Now, Scabby-Bull went to sleep and the woman met her husband as she had promised. Then he said, "Shut your eyes!" At once the woman

---

[1] This seems to be a part of the Red-Head narrative, pp. 129–132.

became a winged-ant. Then they flew away. The buffalo herd was so large that they were flying over buffalo until sunset and even the next day. About sundown the next day was the time the Ant had stated that he would withdraw his power. Now, as they were flying about over the herd, the birds and animals guarding the buffalo noticed these ants flying along; but when the Ant withdrew his power, they became prairie-chickens, and so they flew along day after day. At last they were clear of the buffalo, and, becoming human beings, walked on foot. As they were going along, the bluebird was flying over their heads, calling out that the buffalo were gaining on them. Looking back, the man and woman saw them coming. Then the woman threw off one moccasin. When the buffalo came up to the place, they stopped to lick it. After a time they gained on them again, and the woman threw off her other moccasin, which delayed the buffalo as before. The next time she threw away one of her leggings, then the other legging, then one garter, and then the other garter. Then she threw off her robe, then her belt, and then her dress. Each time, the buffalo stopped, but gained on them again. Now they came to a tree and climbed into the top. The buffalo were following on their trail. All passed by but one. In the rear was a scabby, lame bull who stopped to rub his back on the tree. While he was doing this, the woman said, "I have a mind to spit on him." "No, you must not do that!" said the man. "The buffalo have not seen us yet." "Oh!" said the woman, "he is such an old bull that he will not notice it." So she spat on him. Then the bull looked up, saw them in the tree and began to call the herd. Then the man began to shoot them with his arrows. He had flint-points, white-rock points, etc. All this time the buffalo were knocking pieces off the tree, and by the time he had killed all the buffalo, the tree began to tremble. Now the man had but ten arrows left, and Scabby Bull began to make medicine to charge upon the tree. When he charged, he knocked off a large piece. Then as he charged again, he said, "I shall get you this time!" All this time the man was shooting his arrows at him, but they made no wounds. At last he took up the medicine-arrow, shot Scabby-Bull in the forehead, which brought him to his knees, and with the fourth arrow he was killed. Then the man came down, scalped Scabby-Bull, and burned the scalp.

Now the woman began to cry. "What!" said the man, "did you love that bull?" "Yes," was the reply. Then the man upbraided her, reminding her of the dangers he had gone through to rescue her and the ill treatment she had received from the bull. Then he knocked her down, cut off her breasts and her genitals; then those of the bull, which he thrust down her throat.[1] So she died.

---

[1] That such outrages were in a way conventional is made probable by an incident noted by Henry, op. cit., p. 262.

28. The Horns and the Matoki.

(a) *Blood Version.*

Once a young man went out and came to a buffalo-cow fast in the mire. He took advantage of her situation. After a time she gave birth to a boy. When he could run about, this boy would go into the Indian camps and join in the games of the children, but would always mysteriously disappear in the evening. One day this boy told his mother that he intended to search among the camps for his father. Not long after this he was playing with the children in the camps as usual, and went into the lodge of a head man in company with a boy of the family. He told this head man that his father lived somewhere in the camp, and that he was anxious to find him. The head man took pity on the boy, and sent out a messenger to call in to his lodge all the old men in the camp. When these were all assembled and standing around the lodge, the head man requested the boy to pick out his father. The boy looked them over, and then told the head man that his father was not among them. Then the head man sent out a messenger to call in all the men next in age; but, when these were assembled, the boy said that his father was not among them. Again the head man sent out the messenger to call in all the men of the next rank in age. When they were assembled, the boy looked them over as before, and announced that his father was not among them. So once again the head man sent out his messenger to call in all the young unmarried men of the camp. As they were coming into the head man's lodge, the boy ran to one of them, and, embracing him, said, "Here is my father." After a time the boy told his father that he wished to take him to see his mother. The boy said, "When we come near her, she will run at you and hook four times, but you are to stand perfectly still." The next day the boy and his father started out on their journey. As they were going along they saw a buffalo-cow, which immediately ran at them as the boy had predicted. The man stood perfectly still, and at the fourth time, as the cow was running forward to hook at him, she became a woman. Then she went home with her husband and child. One day shortly after their return, she warned her husband that whatever he might do he must never strike at her with fire. They lived together happily for many years. She was a remarkably good woman. One evening when the husband had invited some guests, and the woman expressed a dislike to prepare food for them, he became very angry, and, catching up a stick from the fire, struck at her. As he did so, the woman and her child vanished, and the people saw a buffalo cow and calf running from the camp.

Now the husband was very sorry and mourned for his wife and child.

After a time he went out to search for them. In order that he might approach the buffalo without being discovered, he rubbed himself with filth from a buffalo-wallow. In the course of time he came to a place where some buffalo were dancing. He could hear them from a distance. As he was approaching, he met his son, who was now, as before, a buffalo-calf. The father explained to the boy that he was mourning for him and his mother and that he had come to take them home. The calf-boy explained that this would be very difficult, for his father would be required to pass through an ordeal. The calf-boy explained to him that, when he arrived among the buffalo and inquired for his wife and son, the chief of the buffalo would order that he select his child from among all the buffalo-calves in the herd. Now the calf-boy wished to assist his father, and told him that he would know his child by a sign, because, when the calves appeared before him, his own child would hold up its tail. Then the man proceeded until he came to the place where the buffalo were dancing. Immediately he was taken before the chief of the buffalo-herd. The chief required that he first prove his relationship to the child by picking him out from among all the other calves of the herd. The man agreed to this and the calves were brought up. He readily picked out his own child by the sign.

The chief of the buffalo, however, was not satisfied with this proof, and said that the father could not have the child until he identified him four times.[1] While the preparations were being made for another test, the calf-boy came to his father and explained that he would be known this time by closing one eye. When the time arrived, the calves were brought as before, and the chief of the buffalo directed the father to identify his child, which he did by the sign. Before the next trial the calf-boy explained to his father that the sign would be one ear hanging down. Accordingly, when the calves were brought up for the father to choose, he again identified his child. Now, before the last trial, the boy came again to his father and notified him that the sign by which he was to be known was dancing and holding up one leg. Now the calf-boy had a chum among the buffalo-calves, and when the calves were called up before the chief so that the father might select his child, the chum saw the calf-boy beginning to dance holding up one leg, and he thought to himself, "He is doing some fancy dancing." So he, also, danced in the same way. Now the father observed that there were two calves giving the sign, and realized that he must make a guess. He did so, but the guess was wrong. Immediately the herd rushed upon the man and trampled him into the dust. Then they all ran away except the calf-boy, his mother, and an old bull.

---

[1] Tales of a buffalo-child and similar tests occur in other tribes. See Simms (Crow, op. cit., p. 319) and J. O. Dorsey (Ceghia, op. cit., p. 140).

These three mourned together for the fate of the unfortunate man. After a time the old bull requested that they examine the ground to see if they could find a piece of bone. After long and careful search they succeeded in finding one small piece that had not been trampled by the buffalo. The bull took this piece, made a sweat-house, and finally restored the man to life. When the man was restored, the bull explained to him that he and his family would receive some power, some head-dresses, some songs, and some crooked sticks, such as he had seen the buffalo carry in the dance at the time when he attempted to pick out his son.

The calf-boy and his mother then became human beings, and returned with the man. It was this man who started the Bull and the Horn Societies, and it was his wife who started the Matoki.[1]

(b)   North Piegan Version.

Many Indians were in camp where they had made a buffalo-drive, but they could find no buffalo. They sent out two boys to look for the buffalo, and these two boys traced them to the south. Now one of the boys had the power of a crow and went ahead to look for the buffalo. He discovered that a person named White-Crow had driven all the buffalo away. Then one of the boys became a black crow, and when they came back to camp and told the people that White-Crow had driven all the buffalo away, the chief said, "Black-Crow, go up and talk with White-Crow, and lead him off somewhere, and, while he is away, steal the buffalo." So Black-Crow went out and began to talk with White-Crow to lead him off, but White-Crow was suspicious and wanted to go back. Then Black-Crow told him that he would go out himself to look for buffalo. When Black-Crow was out to where the men of the camp were, he advised them only to travel by night, and in the daytime to cover themselves up with grass. Then Black-Crow went back to lead White-Crow away.

Now the young men travelled along by night and finally they heard buffalo, but morning came before they reached them: so they hid again until night. Now one young man had the power of the buffalo and turned himself into a buffalo. As it was about travelling-time, Black-Crow returned and saw the buffalo in the distance bunching up, so the young man asked him to go out to see what they were doing. When Black-Crow came to the buffalo, he found that they were dancing. When he returned and

---

[1] Several informants among the Bloods claimed that many of the functions formerly exercised by the Bulls have been incorporated with the ritual of the Horns. The origin myth for the Bulls as recorded by Grinnell (op. cit., p. 104) closes with the same incidents as noted above, but opens with the initial event in the Scabby-Bull narrative, p. 112.

told the young men what he saw, they told him to go back and let them know when they danced and they would go down to see them.

The buffalo were now scattered out all around their hiding-places. One of the young men became a buffalo and the other a crow. Then they went out to see the dance. There they saw White-Crow flying around the buffalo to herd them. Then the young man who had turned into a buffalo told the crow to go back, saying, "I will stay here and become a cow, have a calf, and try to lead the buffalo away."

Now in the buffalo-dance there are two bonnets of white swanskin, one having two horns on it, and the other one horn. Then the Cow told the Calf that when the dancers hung the one-horn bonnet on a stick he could grab it and run to her. Now the Calf expressed a desire to sit by the bull with the one-horn bonnet. The others tried to keep him from sitting there, but finally he was permitted. After a time the bull with the bonnet painted the Calf's face and said, "Next time they dance, you put it on." So the Calf took the bonnet, put it on, and led the dance. He danced around in a circle. Finally, when they were all through, they sat down. Then the Calf sat down. It was his intention to run away the next time they danced.

Now Black-Crow came back and said to the Calf, "Go on with the dance; for I want to steal the dance-stick that is wrapped with swan's down." The calf wanted to steal the leader's bonnet so that all the buffalo would follow. There was still another stick, wrapped with otter-skin, and the Cow was to steal this. Now the Cow and Black-Crow succeeded in getting hold of the dancing-sticks in the same way that the Calf got hold of the bonnet. Now they all danced and the Calf led the dance, and, of course, the dancers all followed their leader. Then the Calf ran and all the herd ran after him; but the two with the sticks became tired, and stuck the sticks in the ground. Then all the buffalo lay down to rest. When the sticks were pulled up again, all the buffalo followed. In this way they travelled four nights and four days. On the fourth night, the Calf, Black-Crow, and the Cow had dreams in which the buffalo gave them power with the sticks.

This is the way in which the Horn Society came to be. All dancers must have wives, for the buffalo had wives. In every medicine-dance there are three people, — the man, his wife, the young man. The young man is the crow [messenger].[1]

---

[1] This narrative seems to be an adaptation of parts of the Twin-Brothers, pp. 50–52. For an account of a mother and son running away with ceremonial objects in a similar manner, see Crow Myths, Simms, op. cit., pp. 289–294.

29. The Kit–Fox.

Once two men were out on the war-path alone. They came to a prairie-dog town. They saw the dogs standing up, but, as they went near, the dogs went into their holes. Then they saw a woman sitting there, and one of them said, "There is a woman." So they approached her. The woman's face was painted red, with a design made by scratching with the finger. She had no dress on, but just a robe around her. She wore a plume on her head, and held a prairie-turnip in her mouth. As the men came up she said, "You are invited." Now they did not know how to get down into the holes, so the woman said, "Shut your eyes." Then in a moment they heard some one say, "Oki!" When they opened their eyes, they found they were by the side of a lodge, and when they went in they saw the Kit-Fox Society sitting around. There were many men dressed like the woman. This was the Kit-Fox Society, and a Kit-Fox man was showing the others how to perform the ceremony. He directed them through the whole ritual. This is how the men learned it.

30. The Catchers.

There was once a man called Chief-Speaking. It was his wife who found the buffalo-rock. One day she said to her husband, "You take the rock, for there will be another dream. You are to sleep on the buffalo-drive hill. It will be better for you to do this and have the dream, because you are a man and can handle medicine better than I." Now the man went out to the place and staid many nights, but he had no dream. So he thought to himself, "I think my wife has deceived me." Yet after he had been there seven days, he heard some one singing a song, and, looking round, he saw a procession. There were two men leading, each carrying a pipe. The others carried clubs with hoof rattles on them. This procession was coming down from the sun.

After this, the man organized the Catchers Society, but his wife put some of the buffalo-rock songs into the ritual.

31. The Buffalo's Adopted Child.

A long time ago, we don't know how many years ago, the daughter of a Blackfoot Indian chief was a very handsome looking girl. She was a very true girl. Many young men who had asked her to marry them were refused. Now this girl had not been with any man at any time. All at once she became in a family-way, and, when her time came to give birth to a child, she went out away from the camp, for she was very much ashamed. Then she gave birth to a baby-boy which she buried in the earth. Then she went back to camp. The next day, four buffalo-bulls came along where she had buried this child.[1] They saw it. One of the bulls said to the others, "We will bring this child to life again, and keep him for our own." The others all agreed to this. They had the power to restore life. One of the bulls began to paw and hook the dirt away from the child until it was uncovered. The second bull hooked the child around until it came to life and started to crawl away. The third hooked the child until it was a half-grown boy. The last did the same until the boy became a full-grown man. Now the Bulls said to the young man, "You can go and visit your people, and when you are through you may return to us."

So this young man went on his way to the camp. When he came to his people, they did not know him. He told them his story, and they gave him clothes, a horse, and a bow with arrows. "Now," he said, "I must go and visit some of the other Indians." Then he got on his horse and rode out. After he had travelled a long way, he saw a hawk and a rabbit. The hawk was pursuing the rabbit. When the Rabbit saw this man, it ran up and stopped at the horse's feet, saying to the man, "Brother, help me! Don't let that hawk get me. The hawk wants to kill and eat me. Help me, brother, save me from that hawk! I will give you some of my power. You will be able to run as fast as I can whenever you wish to do so." While the Rabbit was talking to the man, the hawk was flying around overhead, waiting for a chance to get the Rabbit. Now the Hawk spoke to the man, saying, "I will give you my power. You will be able to run as fast as I can fly, if you will let me have that Rabbit." Now the man said to the Hawk, "I will not let you eat this Rabbit, but I will get something else for you to eat." So he took the Rabbit with him and turned it loose in the thick timber, where he knew it would be safe from the Hawk. Then he began to look for something to kill for the Hawk. He had not been looking very long when he saw a squirrel, killed it with his bow and arrows, took it out to where the Hawk was sitting, and laid it down near the bird, saying, "You can have this squirrel to eat." The Hawk was very much pleased with this and told the man he could have the power which he had promised him before.

Now this man got power from both of them, the Hawk and the Rabbit. Then he went on his way again. He had not gone a great distance when he saw a buffalo-bull. As soon as the bull saw him, it took after him, and

---

[1] In a similiar tale among the Arapaho and Gros Ventre there are seven bulls. Also in this collection, we find seven bulls restoring life to the woman who brought the medicine shields, p. 100. The Crow rendering, however, gives the number of bulls taking part in the restoration of life as four (Simms, op. cit. p. 319.)

as soon as he knew the bull was after him, he began to whip his horse away from the bull; but, as the bull was a much faster runner than the horse, it kept gaining on him until it was almost within reach of his horse. Then the man began to use his bow and arrows, but the arrows would not faze him. The bull was nearly within reach of his horse, when the man thought of the Rabbit and called on him for help. As soon as he called on the Rabbit, the horse ran much faster, and left the bull far behind. The bull followed, however, and after the man had gone some distance his horse began to get weaker, and the bull began to gain on him as before. Again he called on the Rabbit for power, and his horse could go so much faster that he left the bull far behind. He called on the Rabbit four times; then its power gave out. Then he called on the Hawk for power, and it helped him four times. Then the bull overtook him, and hooked his horse over. The man was thrown into a washout in a coulee. Then the bull began to hook at the man, but could not reach him on account of the narrow ditch-like place he was in. Now the bull kept hooking away the earth around the man and had almost reached him with his horns, when the man saw some hawks flying around. Then he called on the hawks, saying, "Brothers, help me before this bull kills me." The hawks heard the man, flew down, and pecked out the bull's eyes.

Then the bull was helpless and could not see the man any more. Then the Bull said to the man, "Brother, give me back my sight, and I will give you my power, which is greater than that of all the buffalo." Then the man said to the Bull, "If you will bring my horse back to life, and will not harm me any more, I will restore your sight." The Bull promised to do so. Then the man told the hawks to help the Bull. The hawks flew around the Bull's head, and when they left him he could see as well as before. Then the bull went around the dead horse pawing the earth up over his back until the horse came to life again. Then the man got on his horse and told the buffalo-bull that he was going home where his fathers were.

The young man travelled many days before he found the four buffalo-bulls that adopted him. They told him that they would take him to their home. They told him that the buffalo had a big cave near the mountains, and that this cave was another country where all the buffalo lived, had lodges, and became as human beings, just like his own people. They told him that when the buffalo came out of the cave they would be buffalo, but that when they went in they became as people. They also told him about their chief. They said, "Our chief is a strong medicine-man. All the buffalo are afraid of him, and he is also very jealous of his wife. If a man even talk to her, he will kill him." When they got through telling him about this, they all started for the buffalo cave. When they reached the place they met many buffalo. They all went in, and the young man was surprised when he saw that his fathers were as men like himself, that there were so many people, such nice big lodges, and such nice land. Then his fathers took him into their lodge. Now, after he had staid there some time, he was down by a spring where all the people went for water, when the chief's wife passed by. He looked at her. She went to her lodge and told her husband that this young man was looking at her. When the chief heard this, he was very angry, went over to the young man's lodge and was going to kill him. Then the fathers of this young man said to the chief of the people, "We will fight you first; and when you kill us, then you can kill our son." Now the chief was willing to do this, for he was not afraid of any of them. Then they all turned into buffalo-bulls and went out to fight. It was not long before the chief bull had killed the four. Then he went after the young man. The young man turned into a bull, fought the chief, and killed him. Then the people said to the young man, "Now, since you have killed him, you have become our chief and may tell us what to do." The young man told them that he wanted all of them to go out of this place, never to return again, and that they would be buffalo from then on and never like people again. Then he drove them all out, and went to his own tribe. This is the reason the buffalo cannot talk any more.[1]

When the young man came to his own people, he went into an old couple's lodge, told them that as they were poor with no one to look after them, he would live with them and take care of them. The old man and woman were glad to have him. Now after he had been here a while, the Indians were very hungry for the buffalo were far away. One day the young man asked his grandmother what she would like to eat. The old woman said she wished a buffalo-calf. Just then the young man pulled off one of his moccasins and threw it down by the old woman's side. As he threw it, it turned into a buffalo-calf. The old woman began to cut it up to cook. They all ate of it. The young man did this several times. The children of the camp would come around and the old woman would give them some meat to take home with them.

Now the people began to wonder how this old woman got her fresh meat when the rest of them had none.

The chief had two daughters who used to come to see the old woman. She always gave them some meat. Now the chief thought of having this young man for a son-in-law, for he knew that he was a medicine-man. So he asked his oldest daughter to go over to live with this man, but she refused. Then he asked the youngest daughter. She went and married the young man. After the young couple had lived together for a while, the young man said to his wife, "Go ask your father to tell the people to get ready and

---

[1] For previous mention of a cave containing buffalo, see p. 52.

go out to the lines, for I shall make a buffalo-drive." Now, as I said before, the buffalo were far away, but this young man had power to bring them back to the drive. So all the people went out to the lines and waited for him. The young man was not gone very long when they saw a great herd of buffalo falling over into the enclosure. After everybody got through butchering, they went home.

Now the next day the young man said to his wife, "Go tell your father that I shall give a buffalo-dance. This dance is called the 'Bull's Dance,' and have him put up three or four lodges together so as to have a place to dance in, and to have the lodges close to the brush." The woman went over and told her father what her husband had said. The chief called out to the people, and the lodges were put up. Four lodges were joined together forming a long wall, or wind-break, open on one side near the brush. After the people had assembled the young man went there with his wife. He told the men who were going to take part in the dance what to do and also the songs. Now the young man said to his wife, while the rest were listening, "I am going into the brush, and when I come out I will show up as a buffalo-bull. I shall prance about through the crowd as if about to hook some one. When I do this, you must try to catch me by the horns. I will pretend to hook you, but do not be afraid of me, for I will not hurt you. I shall run into the brush and come out four times; and if you don't catch me at any of these times, especially at the fourth time, I shall run away for good and be a real buffalo. While I am doing this, the singing and dancing must go on. At first, when I come out of the brush, I shall be a buffalo-calf. The second time I shall be a two-year-old bull; the third, a three-year-old bull; the fourth time, a four-year-old bull." So the dance went on and the young man went into the brush. When he came out he was a buffalo-calf prancing around as if trying to hook some one. Then the woman tried to catch the calf, but it made a jump at her as if to hook, when she ran away. The calf went back into the brush and came out again. This time it was a two-year-old bull. He did the same thing, and the woman got out of his way. Then he went back and came out as a three-year-old bull, and as the woman did not catch him this time, he went back into the brush. Now the girl's father said to her, "This is your last chance. You must try to catch him, for he is not a real buffalo, he is your husband. If you don't catch him now, you will never see your husband again." So when the bull came out of the brush this time he was much larger; but the woman made for him and caught him by the horns, when he turned back into a man, and the dance stopped.

This was the starting of the Bull's Dance.[1]

---

[1] This narrative is sometimes called "The Iron Horns." It accounts for the origin of the Bull Society ceremony. It was recorded by D. C. Duvall.

IV. CULTURAL AND OTHER ORIGINS.

1. THE WHIRLWIND–BOY.

Once there was a woman who had given birth to many children, but all of them died in infancy. At last the woman said, "I will have no more children: if any more are born to me, I will kill them at once. I cannot bear to see them die as the others; and, anyway, it is no use to let them live." Now long after this, one time when the woman went out after water, she saw a small whirlwind going along. She watched it. It came directly toward her, and in the center of the dust-whirl she saw a very small boy running along. The boy said to her, "Mother, I know what you said about not having any more children; but it will be different with me. I shall be your next. When I am born, you must cut off a piece of my navel-cord, put with it sweet-grass, wrap them up, and hang the packet around my neck. Then I shall not die." When the boy finished speaking, the woman stooped over and picked him up. He was so small that she held him in the hollow of her hand, but in a moment he turned into a caterpillar.[1]

Then the woman was with child. When the time came, she went out to be delivered. It was a boy. The woman who attended her cut off a section of the navel-cord and dried it. At first they wrapped it up with the baby, but afterwards they put it in a buckskin bag and tied it on the baby's back. This baby did not die. He grew up, and when a boy of ten or twelve years (the mother had no more children), a friend of the family had a child that was always crying. There seemed no way to make it stop crying. One day this boy told his mother to take one of the bones from the right front-foot of the buffalo. She did so. When they gave it to the child, it ceased crying. Now this same woman had another child. It was a boy. He cried also, even more than the other. One day the Whirlwind-Boy requested his mother to rub some yellow paint upon the baby's forehead, then to go out and paint one of the buffalo bones yellow. When they gave this to the child, he also stopped crying. From that time on, a crying male child was always given a yellow-painted bone from the right front-foot of a buffalo, and had his forehead painted yellow. After a time the same woman had another child, this time a girl; and, like the others, it cried all the time. One day the Whirlwind-Boy requested his mother to take a bone from the left hind-leg of the buffalo and paint it red. Also to paint

---

[1] For a discussion of the peculiar association between the whirlwind and a moth see *Journal of American Folk-Lore,* Vol. XVIII, pp. 258–261.

the baby's forehead red. When this had been done, the baby ceased to cry.[1] This is the way children are kept from crying, even to this day.

Now Whirlwind-Boy would sometimes take the right hind-leg of the buffalo and paint one side yellow. Then he would go out and wander about the prairie, repeating to himself, "This bone says all the buffalo will go down the drive and over the cliff." Then he would throw the bone out in front of him. If it fell with the yellow side up, it would be as he said. At another time he would take a bone, lay a stick across it, and then drop a braid of sweet-grass. If the braid fell on the stick hanging, the buffalo would go over.[2] These things people do even to this day. When Whirlwind-Boy was a man and his mother very old, he said to her one day, "Mother, I think I shall go away before you die. I do not care to be here when that happens." His mother asked him not to go, but he was not easily moved. At last, however, he agreed to take her with him. So he called the people of the camp together and requested all to watch. He took his mother over to the top of a high cliff; then he went back some distance and became a whirlwind. When the whirlwind reached the place where the mother sat, she disappeared. No one ever saw them again.[3]

2. THE BLADDER STORY.

Once there was a very poor boy who lived with his mother. His father was dead. One day his mother was ill and was about to die, but the boy said, "My mother will come to life again." She had been gored by a buffalo and was almost dead. She had been gored in the head. The little boy said, "Give me a bladder." When it was brought to him, he blew it full of air. His mother was lying with her head towards him. He put the bladder on her head and placed some charcoal on it. Then he said to his uncle, "You must be ready to shake the lodge four times." Then he painted his mother, — a black spot on her right hand, one on the back of each wrist, and one on her forehead. On himself he made a circle at each place where he had painted a dot on his mother. Now the woman was dead. The boy took a calf robe with the hair-side up, and beat time on it as he sang,

---

[1] At this point the narrator explained that a favorite game among children was the taking by the boys of a bone from the left hind-foot of the buffalo, and going among the girls to induce them to laugh. A boy would shake the bone near the girl's face, and in as comical manner as possible say, "I know you are going to have a lover! I know it! I know it!" Now if the girl laughed, it was a sure sign that she would be a bad [unchaste] woman. If she did not laugh, she would become a great medicine-woman, true, virtuous, etc. In a similar manner, girls would test boys, but with a bone from the left front-foot.

[2] The braid of grass hanging across the stick was explained as symbolizing meat hanging up to dry, in turn the symbol of plenty.

[3] This story accounts for some of the practices in the care of children. The navel-cord amulet for boys is in the shape of a snake; for girls, in the shape of a lizard or a horned toad. It was explained that the reason why Whirlwind-Boy picked out these forms was that these animals were never sick, and enjoyed long life.

"If the bladder will not move, she will die for good." Then he said, "Mother, get up!" His uncle shook the lodge four times, the bladder moved, the woman shook her head four times and then got up. She was well again. "Now," said the boy, "you see this bladder. Whatever it is placed upon and charcoal put on it, that object will move when the lodge is shaken."

One time there was a young man in the camp with warts all over his head, face, and body. So he went to the boy with the bladder and asked to be cured. "All right," said the boy. Then he took some charcoal, sang the same song as before, rubbed the charcoal over the man, and said, "In three nights all your warts will be gone." And it was as he said. Then the boy told all the people that warts should be cured this way, and so it is done to this day.

Now there was an old woman in the camp whose son-in-law had been gone a long time. So she was left without support. She asked the boy with the bladder to use his power to get her son-in-law back. The boy took a sinew from the leg of a cow [buffalo] with part of the muscle attached. He laid it on the ground and fastened the end of the sinew with a stick. Then he put some yellow paint on the sinew, near the stick. Then he put a live coal on the painted spot, and began to sing, "Come here, come here!" etc. The fire caused the sinew to draw up, and this pulled the muscle towards the stick.[1] Now the son-in-law, in a distant camp, felt something within drawing him back to his wife's people. So he determined to return. People are still brought back in this way.

3. THE WATER–BULL.

This is a story of the water-buffalo. There was a girl who lived in the water, and it was the time when the Blackfoot got the painted buffalo-lodge. This girl was rich, for her father was a chief. One time the girl went down to the river to bathe with the others, but when they returned they noticed that she was missing. The chief sent some one about the camp to look for her, but the last place at which she was seen was the bathing-place. Now the chief told all the people that when the time came for them to move camp, he would stay until the water was low so that he might find her body. So he staid.

One day the children who were playing near the stream saw the girl put her head out of the water. She called to them, "Tell my father that I shall

---

[1] For a similar use of sinew, see Wissler, Dakota Myths (Journal of American Folk-Lore, Vol. XX, p. 128).

come ashore to-night." Now, when they told the chief, he did not believe them, but in the evening they heard a noise down by the river. There was a great roaring, and a voice called out asking them to make a smudge. So they made a smudge in the chief's lodge. Then the girl came in. They offered her food, but she refused, saying, "I cannot eat that food now, as I am used to other food." She then told them that her husband lived in the water. So her father gave her all her clothes and other property. "Now," said the girl, "my husband will give you food. The buffalo, he will drown them for you, but they will be of two colors, brown and white. Of these the white must be given back to him.[1] I will visit you every time you camp here." Now they watched her as she went out and saw her go down into the water. That night while the buffalo were crossing the river a great many were drowned and thrown upon the shore. The people found them of two colors. So they butchered them and fixed up the robes.

Now the chief said to a boy, "Go to the camp of our people and invite them to come back." When they came in, he told them what had happened, and that they all must give something to his daughter. They must throw the gifts into the water. This they did. That night the girl came out of the water again and called all the people together. They gathered around and looked into the lodge where she sat. She invited one of her friends to go down into the water with her. This friend and another went down. She gave them a black rock to hold so that they would not float. When they were in the water, the girl said, "Now shut your eyes and do not look until you hear some one say, 'Oki'!" So they went down. Some one said, "Oki!" and upon looking round they found themselves in a lodge. They were not wet and did not seem to be in the water. It was a fine place. There was a man in the lodge who sang them a medicine-song, and explained to them that whenever crossing a stream they should throw something into the water as an offering to the water-people.

When the women returned, they told what had happened, and to this day our people still throw things into the water.

4. RED–HEAD.[2]

Once there was a man who lived alone with his mother, far from other people. It is not known that he had any other relations in the world. Around this lodge and in it were many live birds and animals. The man himself had a head [hair!] as red as blood.

---

[1] To sacrifice skins of albino buffalo was the custom among many tribes
[2] Translated by Mrs. Joseph Kipp.

Once a young woman made a long journey alone. At last she came to a lodge. It was Red-Head's lodge. She raised the door-flap and saw that the lodge was well furnished with bedding and other objects made of buckskin. This young woman had just been created. She came out of the ground. She did not know how to eat, to drink, or in fact to do anything. When Red-Head came home he found her in the lodge. He told her to go out and leave him alone. The young woman was very much afraid of him. So she went to an ant-hill and began to talk to the Ants. Then she cried, and called upon the Ants for help. She begged for some kind of power to enable her to live with Red-Head and secure his good will. At last the Ants took pity on her; and one of them said, "You get us two strips of buckskin from the lodge." The young woman returned to the lodge, and stood outside until Red-Head went out. Then she went in and cut the strips of buckskin from a hide she found hanging there. She hurried away to the ant-hill and laid the strips of buckskin on it. The Ants said to her, "Now go away and do not come near us for one day. Leave us!" The next day, about the same hour, the young woman went to the ant-hill. She was greatly surprised to find the strips of buckskin beautifully embroidered with porcupine-quills. This was the first time quill-work was ever seen by the people. The Ants were the first quill-workers.[1] The Ants said to her, "Now, you go to the lodge and bring us the robe of Red-Head's mother. Spread it out for us on the ground where you stand, then leave us for another day. Do not come near us. Take the strips of buckskin we have worked for you and hide them. No one must see them now." When the young woman returned on the following day, she found the robe worked in broad stripes of porcupine-embroidery. The Ants said to her, "Take the robe with you. Sew the strips of quill-work we gave you upon the leggings of Red-Head's mother. When you have done this, put the robe and the leggings at the place where the old woman usually sits, so that she and Red-Head may see them. You are to do this when no one is in the lodge. As soon as you have put them down, go out into the brush. We shall help you again."

Red-Head came into the lodge carrying some meat. He saw the robe and the leggings lying in his mother's place. When his mother came in, he said to her, "Mother, you do very nice work." "What do you mean," she replied. Red-Head pointed to the robe and the leggings. His mother was greatly surprised to see them. She had never seen anything like them before. She declared she knew nothing about it. "That young woman must have done it," said Red-Head. "Find her and ask her to come in.

---

[1] See Simms, Crow Myths, p. 309.

I should like her to make some moccasins for me. Feed her and ask her to make some moccasins for me." The next day the old woman invited her into the lodge. When she entered, Red-Head asked her if she had made the robe and leggings that lay at his mother's place. The young woman told him that she had. Then Red-Head requested her to make him a pair of moccasins in the same way. The young woman told Red-Head that the making of quill-work was her medicine, and that no one might watch her while she did her work. If any one should look on, the power to do such work would be lost forever. The young woman took a pair of Red-Head's moccasins and left the lodge. As soon as she got into the brush, she hurried to the ant-hill. She laid the moccasins down and went away. When she returned the next day, she found them ready. She took them to the lodge. Red-Head was out hunting. She laid the moccasins on his bed. Red-Head's mother was curious to know how the work was done, but the young woman carefully guarded her secret.

When Red-Head came back in the evening, he saw the moccasins and was pleased with them. He requested his mother to tell the young woman to embroider his buckskin shirt. She called the young woman, who was out in the brush. The young woman came to the door of the lodge, but refused to enter. When she heard what Red-Head desired, she told them to hand out the shirt. This was in the evening. When the young woman took the shirt to the Ants, requesting them to work a disk on the front and back, and strips over the shoulders and on the sleeves, they said that they could not work in the dark, and that she must wait until the next day. The young woman went away as before, and, when she returned, found the work complete. The shirt was very beautiful. She took it to the old woman that she might carry it to Red-Head. When Red-Head received the shirt from his mother he was greatly pleased.

Now, the circles that had been worked upon the shirt represented the sun. This was due to the fact that this woman also had the power of the sun. A weasel gave the young woman the instructions as to the designs that were to be worked upon the shirt, robe, and moccasins. The stripes on the robe represented the trails of the weasel. The bands on the moccasins represented the place where the weasels tramped down the snow.

Red-Head was greatly pleased with the work of the young woman. He wished very much to make her his wife, but the Weasel told the young woman not to marry him. The Weasel told her to take a bone and to scrape one of the ends to a sharp point. Then to watch her chance, and kill Red-Head with it as he slept. She did as directed. Then she ran away to

the Piegan. She lived with them, and taught them how to make quillwork.
This is the way the people learned how to do it.[1]

5. THE MEETING IN THE CAVE.

Once a Snake [Indian] and a Piegan went out into the same country to
hunt buffalo. Their camps were far apart. In this country there was a
kind of cave in which scouts and hunters often spent the night. The Snake
and the Piegan were in the habit of sleeping there, but neither had met the
other. One winter evening the Snake arrived at the cave and put up for
the night. After a while the Piegan came along and began to grope his way
into the cave, for it was now dark. The Snake was asleep. As the Piegan
was groping around, he felt a person. He took the hand of the stranger
and began to shake it. Then the Snake asked him to what tribe he belonged.
The Piegan took the hand of the Snake in his own, and moved it around on
his cheek in a small circle. [This is the sign for Piegan, or the people with
small robes.] Then the Snake took the hand of the Piegan and made the
sign for Snake. [The sign is to move the pointing finger as if drawing a
waving trail in the dust.] Then the Piegan took the hand of the stranger
again and told him by signs that to-morrow they would play the stick-game.
To this the Snake replied, "Yes." When morning came, they played the
stick-game, and the Piegan was the winner. First he won the weapons
of the Snake, and then all his clothes. Then the Snake wagered his hair;
and the Piegan won this also. "Now," said the Snake, "we will stop."
So he tied a string around his head across the forehead. The Piegan said,
"I shall cut the hair close." The Snake said, "No, you won in this game;
you must scalp me." So the Piegan took his scalp. The Snake bled a
great deal and became very weak. The Piegan left him and started home.
As he approached his camp, he came over the hills singing.

---

[1] It appears from some versions that the weasel told the young woman how to make the
various articles of clothing, and what designs to place upon them. However, she did not do
the work herself, but delivered it over to the ants. In other accounts the weasel instructed her
as to the making of a man's suit. Such suits are called weasel suits because the fringes of the
leggings and the sleeves are made of weasel-skins. The weasel also gave her directions as to how
war-bonnets should be made. In most of the accounts it is stated that the stripes on the robe
were to represent the trails of the weasel. The moccasins were decorated with a single stripe
extending from the instep to the toe. This represented the track made by the weasel in the
snow. The circular design upon the front of the shirt represented the sun; the one upon the
back represented the moon.

It seems, from all the accounts, that Red-Head was a kind of Blue Beard. He killed all of
the women who came to his lodge, but also all of the men with whom he came in contact. In
one version he was killed by a man who changed himself into a woman. The birds around Red-
Head's lodge kept warning him by saying, "The woman has man eyes." Red-Head paid no
attention to this, because he wished to keep the young woman (as he supposed his guest to be),
since she appeared to have great skill in porcupine-quill work. The name of the woman is
usually given as Woman-After-Woman. This name was given her because she was believed to
have lived many lives. By this is meant that, whenever she was killed, she came to life again.

Some informants say that this woman was Scar-Face (See p. 61) in disguise, who was
sent down by the Sun to kill Red-Head. To offset the warning given by the birds around the
lodge, he hit upon the expedient of quill-work made by the ants and designed by the weasel.
This conforms generally to the above narrative, since the woman was regarded as mysteriously
created and as having power from the Sun.

After a time, the Snake in the cave revived and went home to his people. He explained to them what had happened, telling them that he had lost his scalp in a game. Ever since that time the people often speak of gambling as fighting.[1]

6. WHY DOGS DO NOT TALK.

Once a man owned a very large dog. One day when his wife went out to gather wood, the dog followed her into the brush. Now it seems that this woman had a lover who often met her when she went after wood. The dog saw what was going on. That night, when the woman's husband returned, the dog told him what he had seen. This made the dog's master so angry that he beat his wife, finally knocking her down with a piece of wood. Then he went away. After a while the woman got up and began to scold the dog. Then she beat him, and heaped all manner of abuse upon him. She took up human excrement and made him eat it. She was a medicine-woman, and used her power in such a way, that, after this, dogs could not talk. They still have the power to understand some words, but not many.

7. WHY WOMEN ARE ABLE TO STICK THE POLES INTO THE HOLES OF THE EARS OF THE LODGE AFTER DARK.

Once, when a woman named Pī′nōstsĭssī was out from the camp picking berries, she saw a burial-place. The body had been placed in a tree, but the bones had fallen down. She carefully picked them up and put them back in their places. As she did so, she said to herself, "I do not know who you are. I do not know your name. I do not know when you died. But I will put you back again. I will feed you berries. Yes, I will feed you," etc. She kept talking all the time she was at it. Now, the next time she went out for berries, she took some pemmican with her and gave it to the body. Twice again she did this. Now the ghosts[2] threw the woman into a faint, or put her to sleep, as ghosts do. While she was in this condition, she saw a girl[3] coming up to her. The woman was frightened, and called out to the girl, "Sister, now I helped you. You should do something for me. You can do much for me." Then the girl said, "I will help you in your work." She meant by this the tanning of hides, gathering of wood and water, etc. Some time after this the woman was married, and every

---

[1] This tale is part of a long narrative of adventure recorded by Grinnell, op. cit., p. 63. In a brief account by Clark (Sign Language, p. 71) Old Man is the hero of this adventure.
[2] The dead are usually spoken of as ghosts.
[3] This was the ghost belonging to the bones she had replaced.

time she had hides to tan she would call on the ghost-girl, and the work was soon done.   One dark night the lodge-poles came out of the holes in the ears of the lodge, and the woman went out to put them in.   As it was very dark, she poked the poles about without finding the holes.   Then she called upon the ghost-woman for help, and found the hole at once.   After this, every time she went out at night to put the poles in the ears of the lodge, she called on the ghost-woman, poked at a hole, and always hit it.

This is the way women do to-day when the poles will not go into the holes in the ears of the lodge: they call on the ghost-woman to help them.   They even call upon her for help when things are lost.

8.   Contest between the Thunder–Bird and the Raven.

Once the Thunder-Bird and the Raven tried their respective powers. The Thunder-Bird carried off the wife of the Raven and refused to release her upon the Raven's demand.   Then the Raven made medicine.   He caused winter with a great snowfall.   It was so cold that the only way in which the Thunder-Bird could keep from freezing was by constantly flashing his lightning.   Yet the power of the Raven was so great that the Thunder-Bird could barely keep a hole melted out large enough for his body to rest in. At last he was forced to give up Raven's wife.   Now, when there is much snow or a cold wave, the people go out and call to the Raven to take pity on the people.[1]

9.   The Raven Rescues People.

Once some people were stranded on an island.   They were in great danger there.   For want of food they were almost starved.   They ate grass. Raven took pity on them.   So he rescued them.   He brought them to the mainland.   Now the descendants of some of them are a tribe of Indians living far to the west, on the shores of the big water [the Pacific Ocean].[2]

10.   Why Grasshoppers Spit.

Once a child saw one grasshopper holding another in its embrace.   He picked them up and looked at them curiously.   Then he said, "It would be better if you bled at the nose; it would be better if you bled at the nose," etc.   He kept saying this over and over for a long time.   So it came to pass that grasshoppers now spit, or bleed at the nose.

---

[1] See Grinnell (op. cit., p. 114) for an allusion to the raven's power over the thunder.
[2] This is a mere abstract of a story formerly known among the Piegan.   However, it is given as told.

11. How Medicine-Hat got its Name.[1]

Once there was a man named Spider whose wife ran away with a man named Eagle-Bull. The woman's name was Badger-Woman. Eagle-Bull took the woman to a place on Elk River. They went down this river to a place where there was a bend in the channel, and on one side was a cut bank with a projecting point. Near by they made a shelter of logs. After a while the man told the woman that he was going to dig a pit for an eagle-trap: so he went up on the point. When he came back, he told her that he had finished the hole for the pit. Then he took some meat from the neck of an animal and went up to the trap. Then he fixed everything, put the meat on top, and went down into the trap. Now there were a great many eagles about, but every time one was about to alight on the trap, there was a sound as if some people were riding around, and at once the eagles would fly up. When the man came back home, he told the woman that he had had no luck, because some one made the eagles fly away when they were about to alight. The next day he tried again, but the same thing happened. Then he prayed to this mysterious presence, asking it to take pity on him and to permit him to catch some eagles, promising that he would give it some of the feathers. Then he went down to another place to make a trap; and when he was in this trap he heard some one singing in the old trap. Looking in that direction, he saw a medicine head-dress sticking up.[2] He could just see it. The song that he heard was, "I have power to call eagles to this place," etc. Now, while this was going on, the man heard two eagles alight near his trap, but some one scared them up as before. He staid in the trap a long time, but, not having had any luck, he went to sleep. Now in his sleep he dreamed he heard some one say, "If you kill your wife and use her for bait, it will be better." When he awoke he thought to himself, "Well, I suppose I may as well do it, for I want to catch eagles." So he went home to his camp; but the woman came out to meet him, and her manner changed his mind. He thought to himself, "Now I ran away with her, and I do not like to do this.[1]" He had a little bob-tailed dog, so he determined to use it for bait. He killed it, and carried some of the meat to the trap again. Now, while he was waiting, the dream-person spoke to him again, telling him that he did not eat dog-meat, and asked again for his wife. Now, when the man went home, he made up his mind to get sight of

---

[1] The name of a place in Alberta near the present site of Medicine-Hat, the name of the town having been derived from the aboriginal designation. A different narrative will be found in Skinner's Myths and legends beyond our Borders, (1899). In this account the name is taken from a war-tale of a Blackfoot chief who lost a medicine head-dress and with it his power in a fight with Cree Indians. It will be observed that our narrative accounts primarily for the origins of eagle-trapping.

[2] This was a feather war-bonnet of the Dakota type.

this mysterious person. So when he awoke in the morning he got up, went out at once and looked around. He saw many birds, some perched and others walking around. By watching them, he discovered that it was a raven that had spoken to him. This raven became a person. It was a woman, and she wore the head-dress he had seen sticking from the trap. Now this woman appeared before him and said, "I have been trying to help you. My man here wants a woman to eat."

Now Eagle Bull was very much discouraged. He did not know what to do about it. So he passed by the camp and down over the ridge, looking for buffalo. Once when he turned back, he saw an Assiniboine. He approached him, and finally they met. The Assiniboine was nearly starved. He had been looking for buffalo, but failed to find any. Eagle-Bull pretended to take pity on him, and invited him to his camp, saying, "I have plenty of meat. I can feed you." The Assiniboine said, "All right, but first I must get a drink." So they went to the water, and when the Assiniboine stooped down to drink, Eagle-Bull knocked him on the head with a stone and killed him. Then he butchered him. When he came home, he said to his wife, "Now I have some bait for the trap." When he went out again to the trap, he put half of the bait on the old trap, saying, as he did so, "Here is human flesh for bait." Then he went into the other trap and placed bait upon it. The eagles flew down. Finally the pit was full of birds. So he called his wife over and told her to take them to camp, and all day she kept taking them over. Now all this time he could hear the dream-person in the other trap singing, as if he were greatly pleased. The words of the songs were, "I am eating a person. I give you all the eagle-trap power." Once the dream-person said to him, "You are to trap four days, and then quit. Put all the eagles around your camp; but the catch of the last two days you are to put around in the inside of the lodge."

Now the husband of the wife was looking for her. He knew what had happened. He followed their trail, found their camp, and watched from a distance. He had another wife, whom he told of his discovery, and promised her that he would not kill the runaways, but steal up and catch them. The runaway woman had taken a young child. This was the reason he hunted for her. So he stole quietly up to the camp and saw that they were cooking meat. He came quietly to the door and stood there looking in. Then he spoke, saying, "You have many eagles." At this, Eagle-Bull and the woman sprang up badly frightened; but he called to them, "Do not run. I shall not do you any harm. You, my wife, can have this person for your husband; but I want the child." Then Eagle-Bull said to him, "My friend, if you want your wife back for a time, it is all right with me. Then she can come to me again." "No," he replied. "Well," said Eagle-

Bull, "you see there are a great many eagles inside and outside. Take your choice." The man chose those on the outside. "Now," said Eagle-Bull, "I will give you this power also." So he transferred it to him. He said, "You must kill a coyote and use it for bait; when so used, you must turn the head to the sun and the feet to the north. (Before this time, antelopes were used.) Before you go into the trap, you must sing my song, and, standing on the south side, call out, inviting the wolf to eat and smoke; also the ravens, the crows, the magpie, the eagle, and other birds, to come and get something to eat.[1]" Now when Spider did all this he caught many eagles.[2]

Now, some time after this, Spider got power from a magpie.[3] He fed the magpie's children, and they told him to go to that place to trap. So the next year he said to his wife, "We shall go back to the place and trap eagles and feed the magpie-children." So they started. The All-Comrades tried to stop him, but he told them that he was only going after some arrows and would soon come back. As soon as he was out of sight, he went over to the place, caught many eagles, and returned to camp. Two days after he had done this, he was caught by a man who wished to sell a medicine-pipe.[4] The object of his selling was to find out where the man caught his eagles. Spider had many good horses; so he said, "There are my horses and some good travois-dogs, you can have them for the pipe." "Oh!" said the seller, "I do not want such things for the medicine-pipe. I do not want anything like that. I will just give it to you. But there are two things I want to know. I want to know where eagles are caught, and how to get them. I just want to know something about them. Don't give me all the power for eagle-catching; keep some of it for yourself. You may need it. I should like to know the place for three years." "Well," said Spider," you can use it four years." "All right," said the man.

So when autumn came Spider showed the medicine-pipe man the place, how to catch eagles, and fixed him up. They stole out of camp so that no one would follow them. "Now," said he, "you must feed the magpie-children. They are the ones that helped me. If they are gone, you must put food for them anyway. In the winter you must put food in the brush to feed their children."

Now the ridge where this happened is called "Praying for Medicine" (si'kāpĭs'tānĭ).

---

[1] The names given to the birds in this invitation call are descriptive of their feathers, and not the usual names of the birds. A similar mode of speaking is often employed in prayers to the spirits of former medicine-men and other distinguished men.

[2] Eagle-Bull just saw the medicine head-dress. It was not given to him because he did not kill his wife, as directed. He did offer some of the woman's skin after the dog was refused. I forgot to tell you that at the time. — NARRATOR'S NOTE.

[3] This was given as an additional incident, and does not refer to the incident from which Medicine-Hat in said to have received its name.

[4] This refers to a ceremonial procedure by which a man is forced to receive by transfer important medicine-bundles.

V. MISCELLANEOUS TALES.

1. THE LOST CHILDREN.

In the time when the Indians had no horses, and travelled on foot and with dog-travois, many boys and girls went out on the prairie near the camp to play. One small boy who was the son of a medicine-pipe man passed some shells. The children greedily grabbed them, leaving none for him. As they would give him none, he cried, and on reaching home complained to his father. Now the father was an important man in the camp, and it made him angry to think that his child had been treated in this way. So he ordered all the people to move camp quickly while the bad children were out at play, thus leaving them behind.

In the evening these children returned to the camp. Some of the larger girls were carrying babies on their backs. When they came in sight of the former camp, no lodges were to be seen. They looked about on the ground, each at the place where their parents' lodges had stood, picking up the tools and other small objects that had been left behind in the haste. The children said among themselves, "They have only gone a little way, leaving these things for us to carry." So they followed along the trail of the moving camp, shouting every now and then that their parents might know they were coming. After a while they heard an old woman calling to them. They went over to her lodge. She lived by herself. She invited the children to stay with her, telling them that their people must have deserted them. When night came, the old woman directed them to sleep with their heads toward the fire. She said they must do this, else the mice would come in during the night and eat their hair. Now this old woman was a cannibal. One of the girls had a little brother who had always shown some kind of power. She directed him to watch the old woman during the night, and if he saw anything suspicious to bite his sister's ear. During the night the old woman arose, took a large knife, and began to cut off the heads of the children. Then the baby bit the ear of his sister, causing her to wake up. The sister took the baby in her arms, and begged the old woman to spare their lives. She promised to be a slave to her if she would spare them. The old woman finally agreed to this. After a while the old woman asked the girl to go for water. "I will take my brother with me," said the girl. "No, leave him with me," said the woman. "No," said the girl, "I must take him along with me, because he needs washing." "Well, all right," said the woman, "but be quick about it."

When the girl came to the edge of the river, she saw an Elk's Head [skull] lying there. She said to the Elk's Head, "You repeat over and over these words, I am cleaning my little brother." He was to do this so the old woman in the lodge would think that the girl was trying to get through as soon as possible. Then the girl saw a Water-Bull moving along in the stream. She called to him, saying, "Will you please take us to the other side?" "I will," replied the Water-Bull, "if you will pick the lice from my head, and kill them with your teeth." "Well," said the girl, "I will do that, if you will take us across." Then the Water-Bull came to the shore and laid his head in the girl's lap. At once she began to louse him. She took some beads, put them into her mouth, and, each time she picked a louse from his head, she bit on a bead so that the noise made by crushing them might deceive the Water-Bull. In this way she succeeded in making him believe that she killed the lice with her teeth. When the lice had been picked from his head, the Water-Bull placed the children upon his back and swam toward the other shore. All this time they could hear the old woman in the lodge calling out, "Hurry up, girl! I need that water." Each time the old woman said this, the Elk's Head would answer, "I am busy cleaning my little brother." When the Water-Bull reached the other side of the river, the children found themselves near the camp of their people.

Now the old woman got very angry because the girl did not bring the water, but kept calling out that she was busy cleaning her little brother. So she ran down to the river to see what the trouble was. When she came there, she saw nothing but an Elk's Head lying on the ground, which kept saying over and over, "I am busy cleaning my little brother." "Oh, it's only you!" said the woman, "that makes all this noise." With that she took a stone hammer and smashed the skull to fragments. Then she looked out into the river, and, seeing the Water-Bull swimming along, called out to him, "Take me across the river?" "I will, if you will pick the lice from my head," said the Water-Bull, "and kill them with your teeth." "Yes, I will do that," said the woman, "if you will hurry, for I must catch those children." So the Water-Bull put his head in the old woman's lap, and she began to louse him, killing the lice with her teeth. "They have a bad taste," she said to him. "You are a dirty, miserable beast! This is a very disagreeable thing you made me do. Now hurry and get me across this river." The Water-Bull took her upon his back, but, by the time he reached the middle of the stream, he became very angry at the old woman because she had spoken of him as a dirty beast. So he dropped her into the stream and she was drowned.

Now, when the sister with her little brother saw the camps of her people, she was afraid to go among the lodges. So she waited until the middle of the night, then, with her baby-brother upon her back, searched for her mother's lodge. When she found it, she went to the side of the sleeping, woman, and, putting her hand on her face, said, "I have come." Now the mother of the children was afraid, because the medicine-pipe man had ordered all the people to have nothing to do with the bad children. So she pretended not to know her children. She called out as if she were frightened, saying, "Some strange children will not let me sleep. They are not my children. I never had any children." When the father of the children heard his wife's remarks, he also called to the chief of the camp, telling him that some strange children were disturbing the camp. The chief ordered the children tied to a tree, and the whole camp to move away at daylight, leaving them to die. Now there was a poor old woman in the camp, who lived alone in a little ragged lodge. She had a dog with very long hair, and for this reason he was called Shaggy. When the old woman heard what had been done to the poor children, she was very much troubled. She called Shaggy to her side, and said to him, "My dog, when the camp is about to move, hide yourself in the brush, and do not make a sound, or pay any attention to me when I call you. When the people are out of sight, untie the poor children bound to that tree." The next morning, while the people were busy breaking camp, the poor old woman was running about looking for her dog Shaggy. She called him, and looked everywhere. She asked everybody she met, if they had seen her dog Shaggy. At last everybody was ready, and the chief said to her, "Come on, grandmother! Do not trouble yourself about your dog. He will surely follow on our trail." So the old woman went on with the people, mourning all the time for her lost dog Shaggy. Now, Shaggy waited in the brush until the sound of the moving camp could no longer be heard. Then he came out, went up to the children, gnawed away the thongs with which they were tied, and hurried on to overtake the camp.

Now the sister knew that it would be useless to follow her people. So she remained at this place to care for her little brother. The little brother became the object of some kind of power, and in a single day grew up to be a young man. As they had nothing to eat, the young man said to his sister, "I will make a buffalo-drive. You must stay in your lodge and not look out. If you look out, I will leave you." So the young man went away. After a time the sister, sitting in her lodge, heard a great noise. The sounds reminded her of people driving buffalo. In her surprise, she looked out. She saw no one except her brother standing there. "Did I not tell you to keep inside of the lodge?" he said. The sister took back her head, and did not look out again. She heard the same noise as before. After a while she heard her brother call, asking her to come out. When she looked around, she saw dead buffalo everywhere. "Now sister," said the young man, "you must hurry with your meat. You must dry as much as you can. Also take some of the meat and lay it around on the places where the people camped. Put some of it down where each lodge stood. Do not forget to put a large piece on the spot where the old woman's lodge stood." The young man started on a journey, leaving his sister busy with the meat. After a time he came to the camp of his own people. In the evening he walked through the camp-circle until he came to the lodge of the poor old woman. When he entered, he found Shaggy asleep and the old woman almost starved. He gave a piece of meat to each of them. The old woman told him that the people of the camp had had nothing to eat for a long time. The next morning the young man went out among the people and invited them over to his camp. He told them that he lived alone with his sister, but that he had enough meat for all of them. No one except the old woman and Shaggy knew who the young man was. The people were very glad to receive this invitation, and moved back to their old place at once. They found meat everywhere. At the place in the camp-circle where each lodge was to be, they found meat enough for a whole family. But there was one place where no meat was to be found. This was the place for the lodge of the young man's father and mother. Every one had meat except them. The young man invited his parents into his lodge. When they came in, they saw many pieces of fat hanging over their heads. "Now I shall cook some meat for you," he said, as he put a very tough hard piece into the pot. "In the meantime you may lick the fat hanging over your heads." When the meat had cooked for a long time, and had become harder than ever, he took it out of the pot, and said, "Now you shall have some meat." Then he threw the meat at his parents, striking them, and killing both.

After this the young man and his sister lived with their people.[1]

2. THE WOMAN WHO GOT MEAT FROM THE CLIFF.

Once there was an old woman who was very poor, and she slept out in the open for want of shelter. One night she slept by a cliff with a piece of dried meat and fat for a pillow. While she was sleeping, the rats came down and ate all her meat. When the old woman awoke and wished to eat, she found her meat was gone. The meat had been wrapped in cloth, and she saw some of the wrapping at a hole in the rocks. So she sat down there to find out who took her food. She said, "I wonder who stole this dried meat. I needed it very much. The people in the camp will not give me anything,

---

[1] For another version, see Grinnell, op. cit., p. 50. For a Gros Ventre rendering, see Kroeber, op. cit., p. 102. Also an Arapaho tale, given with a note on its distribution, Dorsey and Kroeber, op. cit., p. 293.

and now I must starve. I wonder who could be so mean as to take this,"
etc. Then she began to cry, and finally went to sleep. Now the woman-rat
down in this hole took pity on the old woman and began to scold the man-
rat. She said, "Now it was you who took the old woman's meat, and you
must feed her." "Well," said the man, "that is easy. We will fix it so
that she will get food, and so that the people will be her friends, because some
day they will need her." Now the rat's nest was made of shedded buffalo-
hair, and the man-rat gave this to the woman, saying, "Take a small piece
of this, put it under any flat rock, and when you turn it over you will find
dried meat." So the old woman took the nest, put it into her bosom, and
went to her own camp. She went to the fireplace and made a fire. Then
she took a bit of buffalo-hair, put it under a flat stone, turned it over, and
found her dried meat. Then she began to cook it. Now some of the children saw her, and said, "Let us go over and see what that poor old woman
is doing. Let us see if she is starving. Our mothers said we must not go
over there, because she must be dead by this time." When the children
came up to the old woman, they saw that she had a great deal of dried meat.
There were four of the children, the oldest one a girl. The old woman
said to them, "Sit down here and I will feed you." So she gave them a
great deal of dried meat, with fine back-fat. The children could not eat it
all. So the old woman said, "Take it home with you." When the children
came home, their mother said, "What have you been doing? You must
have been eating dried meat." Then they told her all about it.

A few days after this the children said among themselves, "Let us go
over to that old woman again." As they came up they saw her cooking
dried meat. The old woman asked them to sit down, and gave them more
meat than before. When they came home with what they could not eat,
their mother was much surprised, and said, "Why do you not invite that
old woman to live with us?" The old woman came over and lived with
this family. They always got food from her. She became very old, and
one day they went away and left her again. Now she had a little bag of
calfskin, which was always full of dried meat and fat. She fed the children
all they could eat, for the bag never became empty. Now, when the people
went away and left her, she was angry. She waited until the camps were
seventeen days away. Then she made medicine so that the people could
find no buffalo. In a short time they were starving. One night the old
woman put the calfskin bag down in front of her, opened it and began to
sing, "Children, come here, I will give you food. I will give you pemmican."
That night all the children ran back to the old woman. They got there in a
single night. They said, "We are hungry. We heard your voice and we
came back." They all sat around eating, but the calfskin-bag was never
empty. The children said, "Now all the people will come after us."

The next day, when the people awoke in the camp, a man called out,
"All the children have gone back. We must follow them. That old woman
must have called them." So the people all went back. The woman gave
each child a small bunch of buffalo-hair, and told each one to go up to the
cliff and put it under a rock, and then come back to her, as they must get
meat ready for their parents. Then she sent the children back. When
they turned over the rocks, they found large packs of meat. The children
took their meat and put it around in the places where their parents' lodges
always stood. Now some of the people were coming over the hill. The
children met them, and told them that the old woman gave them some
meat. After this, the people were afraid to go away and leave the old
woman. She said, "If you leave me again, you will starve to death." So,
when they moved, they always took her with them, carrying her on a dog-
travois, with a very strong dog. Finally the woman died, and left her meat-
bag with a woman, and also her power. This woman was lucky with it.
She was the girl who first invited the old woman over to live with her.

3. BEAR–MOCCASIN, THE GREAT MEDICINE–MAN.

There was once a man named Bear-Moccasin, who had a chum called
Chief-Old-Man. The reason why the former was called Bear-Moccasin
was that he wore bearskins on his feet. He also wore a bear's ear on the
head and a claw, but he gave them and some paint to Chief-Old-Man.
Now Bear-Moccasin had powerful dreams. He said to Chief-Old-Man.
"The reason I am going to do this is because you are a good friend of mine,
I know you will help me. You will have a dream on account of having done
this." "Well," said Chief-Old-Man, "whatever it is, I will do it." Then
Bear-Moccasin told him what to do if anything should happen. Bear-
Moccasin put his robe down on the ground, saying, "Let this robe be the
same as myself." Then Bear-Moccasin took up some paint and began to
paint himself, saying as he did so, "If I am killed, paint me in this way,
and put the robe over my body." Then Bear-Moccasin explained the use
of the pipe and the bear-claw and taught Chief-Old-Man the songs. When
all this was done, Bear-Moccasin took a loaded gun, told Chief-Old-Man
that an evil spirit gave him great power, and that it came from above. Then
he shot himself. Now Chief-Old-Man did as directed. He painted the
body, sang the songs, held the pipe to the corpse, and Bear-Moccasin came
to life. Now Bear-Moccasin had a dagger, and, painting it, he planted
it point up, in the ground. Then he began singing, and threw himself
down upon the knife. Chief-Old-Man sprang upon his back and jumped
up and down until the knife came through. Now he was dead again.

Then Chief-Old-Man sang the songs, took the pipe, and did as before. Bear-Moccasin sprang up again all well. There was not even a scar. Now Bear-Moccasin took the knife and handed it to Chief-Old-Man. Then he painted his neck. Chief-Old-Man cut off his head and threw it down upon the ground. Then Chief-Old-Man took the head, fitted it to the body, covered it with the robe, sang the songs as before, took a gun, painted it and the bullet, and shot Bear-Moccasin in the head. Then he got up. In the next trial, Chief-Old Man shot seven arrows into Bear-Moccasin, and as he fell he broke some of them. Then the robe was placed over the corpse and the pipe placed in its mouth, Chief-Old-Man saying as he went away, "Well, this is your smoke." As Chief-Old-Man was going along, he looked back and saw Bear-Moccasin following him, smoking. As he came up, he showed Chief-Old-Man all the arrows, telling him that two had been broken. Now, in the next trial, Chief-Old-Man took a stone hammer and an elk-horn whip-handle, and with these he beat Bear-Moccasin to death. Then he covered up the body with the robe, sang the songs, and put the pipe to his mouth as before. This time Bear-Moccasin came to life, but the upper part of his body was like that of a bear. In the next trial, Chief-Old-Man took a new sharp axe and a new lance. With the lance he stuck Bear-Moccasin through and through, and cut him up with the axe. (Bear-Moccasin had told him before this to scratch his left foot with a bear-claw, but to get his horse ready and go quickly to the top of the hill, and not to come back again until he was called.) Now Chief-Old-Man held his bridle in one hand, scratched the left foot of the corpse, leaped on his horse and rode off. Bear-Moccasin sprang to his feet, made a noise like a bear, wrestled with the trees, etc. After he had been a bear for a while, he lay down and became a man, calling for Chief-Old-Man to come down again. The tests were now finished. Bear-Moccasin told Chief-Old-Man that if at any time he should be killed, and a piece of his body, however small, could be found, he could be brought to life again. So they went home.

After a time they went out with a party of their people to hunt buffalo. While they were chasing buffalo, some white men came along with a party of Snake Indians. They pursued the Piegan. Now Bear-Moccasin had a gun and arrows. The others were not well armed. So he told them to run. All this time he was butchering a buffalo, and said, "I will finish this before I run." He was soon surrounded by the enemy, all of whom were shooting at him. But he kept on with his butchering and paid no attention to them. Then a white man came up with a sword and thrust it into Bear-Moccasin; but he rose up and killed the white man, and then went on with his butchering. Now there was a Piegan woman with the Snakes who explained to them who this man was. Then they realized that it was useless to attack such a man, and went their way. Now the party that was with Bear-Moccasin went home, because they thought he must have been killed. After a while they went back, and, while they could see nothing of their enemies, they could see Bear-Moccasin still at his butchering. When they went up to him, they saw that he had no wounds, and the only thing he said was, "Here, I have killed this white man."

Now Bear-Moccasin had great power, and he could take a woman from any man. No one dared to talk against it, and every one was afraid of him. So he raped and seduced at will. One day he saw a very nice woman in camp, and decided to try her. Now his friend, Chief-Old-Man, said, "Do not bother with that woman, for she is the wife of our chief." Bear-Moccasin replied, "I must have her." To this Chief-Old-Man said nothing, but he was not pleased. Now, when this woman went out for wood, Bear-Moccasin met her. There was an old woman with her. Bear-Moccasin took hold of the young woman and asked her to go with him. As he was pulling and coaxing her, the old woman said, "Now you ought not to do this. This is a terrible thing for you to do, because she is the wife of the chief. You are a very powerful man, but this you ought not to do. If you must do this, you can have me for the sake of letting her go." "No," said Bear-Moccasin. Then the young woman spoke up and said, "Well, I suppose he must have his way, but first let me tie this horse up." Then, with Bear-Moccasin standing by, she began as if to hobble her horse, talking to the other woman, telling her to get some wood ready to take to camp, but not to mention to any one what had happened, because of the disgrace. Then she said to Bear-Moccasin, "You go on into the brush and I will follow." As soon as Bear-Moccasin started into the brush, the young woman sprang upon her horse and rode away. Now Bear-Moccasin was very quick. He caught hold of the travois; but the horse had a good start, and he was not able to hold on. The woman galloped to the camp, and told her husband, the chief, what had happened.

Now, after a while the men in the camp went out to hunt, and the chief saw Bear-Moccasin go with them. Then the chief went out also, and as he was coming home he saw Bear-Moccasin butchering. He rode up quietly, shot Bear-Moccasin full of arrows, then shot him with a gun, and finally cut him to pieces. Now no one in the camp was angry. In a short time, Bear-Moccasin walked into the chief's lodge, saying, "Here, I bring you some of your arrows." Then the chief thought him a great medicine-man indeed.

Bear-Moccasin had another friend, whom he also advised what to do in case he was killed. However, this friend went to the chief and said, "If you ever kill Bear-Moccasin again, take out his canine-teeth and burn them."

One day the same two women were out again for wood when they saw Bear-Moccasin coming. As he came up to them, he said to the young woman, "You got away once, but I shall lie with you just the same." Now everything happened as before, and the young woman agreed to go with Bear-Moccasin. He took hold of her sleeve to lead her along; but she took out her knife, quickly cut the sleeve and ran away. As she ran, she called out that she would tell the chief. Bear-Moccasin said that he would wait there for him. So she told her husband, the chief. Now the chief was very angry. He began to make medicine for loading his gun, and when he got it ready he set out, the woman carrying an axe and a hatchet. Soon they came up to the place. Bear-Moccasin was lying down by the brush as if asleep. The chief shot him, then took out his canine-teeth, and cut his body into small pieces. Then he burned up the canine-teeth. Now the friend of Bear-Moccasin came to restore him to life, but, when he saw that the canine-teeth were gone, he said, "I will not try to bring him to life again. He may do much harm. He has done much harm already, and the blame must rest with him." Now Bear-Moccasin was dead for good.

———————

There is another story which seems to be a version of this, or the reverse. Once a young man had a dream that he came to life again after being dead. He explained the dream to his chum, and requested him to try it in case he should die. Then, to test his power, he tried to rape the wife of the chief in full view of the camp. The people called out, the chief ran out with his knife, and killed him. His body was cut up and burned. The people took care to burn up everything. So, when the fire was out, the chief ordered them to move camp, and everybody to march over the ashes, so that every trace of the young man might be wiped out. Now, after the camp had moved some distance, the chum of the dead man hid in the brush. The chief, however, watched the place to see if any one should come; but, as no one came all day, in the evening he went away. As soon as the chief was gone, the chum came out of the brush and hunted through the ashes. At last he found a very small piece of bone. He painted the bone, put the robe over it, and put a pipe there. Then taking four arrows, he shot an arrow up so that it would fall on the robe. Each time he did this, he shouted, "Look out! the arrow will hit you;" and each time the robe would move to one side. As he shot the last arrow, he ran away, but the dead man rose up and chased him. Then the young man who had been dead went on to the camp. It was now night. He went into the lodge of his mother. He sent her over to the lodge of the chief to get some food. She was to ask the chief for some of the food that was for him only. This puzzled the chief, for all the food he sent over was refused. At last he understood that it was the woman that was asked for. This he refused. Then the young man went over, killed the chief, cut up his body and burned it, and marched the people over the ashes. After that he took the chief's wives, and became the chief himself.

In still another version, the chief was forced to go around kissing all the dogs in camp, and, as it was very cold, he froze to death.

4. The Split Feather.

A long time ago, when the buffalo and deer were plenty, the Blackfoot Indians made their living by hunting. As the Indians usually camped at one place for many weeks, game would become scarce so that the hunters must ride for two or three days before they could find anything to kill. This medicine-man was very fond of hunting, and the greatest part of his time was spent in this way. He always left his wife at the camp. Now this man had the power of a feather, of which no one knew. He began to think that his wife had not been true to him, that she had been going with some other man. As he had the power of a feather and could use it in this case, he thought he would try it on his wife. So he got up early one morning, and told his wife that he was going out for another hunt, and would not return for two or three days. His wife got up and went out to get some wood to cook his breakfast for him. While she was out, he took this feather, split it down to about its middle, and placed it under their bedding. His wife came in and made the fire. After he had eaten the meat which she had cooked for him, he started out, riding one horse, and leading another which he used for a pack-horse. When night came, his wife sent word to her lover, who was a young single man. This young man came over to her, and she told him that her husband had gone away that day and would be gone for two or three days, so he could visit her that night as he had done before. The young man agreed to this. They occupied the bed under which the feather had been placed.

The next morning, before the sun was high, nearly everybody in the camp had gathered around this woman's lodge. Those unable to get inside were standing around the outside of the lodge. It was learned that the man and woman were fast together, and all night they had tried to separate. No one could assist them. The father of the young man was running about, calling on the big medicine-men of the tribe for help; but they could do nothing, as it was beyond the range of their powers. Some of the older men advised the father to bring out his best horses and weasel suits [buckskin suits decorated with strips of white-weasel fur], and make ready for the return of the woman's husband, so that he might meet the wronged man, tell him what had happened, give him presents to pay for what his son had done, and beg for his life.

The old man went home and got four of his best horses and the best things he had. These he brought to the lodge. Nearly everybody staid at the lodge, waiting for the hunter to return. They wanted to see what he would do when he came back. It was late in the afternoon when the hunter came in sight of the camps. He knew right away what had happened, because he saw so many people around his lodge. Now they advised the old man to go out and meet him, and tell him about it before he reached the camp. So he got his horses and things and started out. He told the wronged husband all about the trouble. When he got through with his story, the husband said he would take the horses and things, and that he would not kill the young man. Then they both went to the lodge. The husband got off his horse and went inside. He saw his wife still lying in bed with the young man. He asked some of the men standing by to lift the couple off the bed. When this was done, he lifted the bedding, picked up the split feather, held it up so that all might see, then pulled it in two and threw the pieces into the fire. At once the young man and the woman were released. The young man went out with his robe over his head and face, for he was much ashamed.[1]

5. THE TREACHEROUS WIVES.

Once a man had two wives of whom he was very jealous, so jealous that he pitched his lodge far out from any camp. He had a habit of sitting upon a buffalo-skull on the top of a high hill. Naturally his wives became very lonesome, and wished to get back to their people. So they decided to make way with him, and one day they dug a pit on the top of the hill where he usually sat, covered it with willows and turf, put the buffalo-skull back in its place, and arranged everything as it was before. The next day the man went out to the top of the hill as usual, and sat down upon the buffalo-skull. As he did so, the cover of the pit gave way and he fell to the bottom, beneath the brush and earth. The women watched from the camp, and, when they saw him fall, took down their lodges and moved back to the camp. When the people saw them coming in, they said, "Where is your husband?" They replied, that, as he had been gone eight days, he must have been killed.

---

[1] Recorded by D. C. Duvall. In some versions a piece of sinew tied in a knot was used instead of the feather. For an Arapaho rendering of this narrative, see Dorsey and Kroeber, op. cit., p. 458.

Now the man was at the bottom of the deep pit, and unable to get out. A gray wolf happened to pass by, and, hearing some one in the ground, spoke to him. The man explained to the wolf how he had been deceived by his wives, and begged to be released from the trap. The gray wolf promised to help him out if he could. So he set to work digging a tunnel toward the bottom of the pit; but, when he had almost reached the man, he went out and called together all the wolves and coyotes. When they were all assembled, the old gray wolf had a talk with them, explaining that a man was caught in a deep hole, and that he had taken pity on this man. He wished to have him dug out, and promised to give him as a son to the first one to reach him by tunnelling. The gray wolf himself promised that he would wait until all the other wolves and coyotes were in their holes to their tails before he began to dig. As soon as the wolves and coyotes began to dig, the old gray wolf went to the hole which he had already dug, and, as soon as the others were in to their tails, he rushed down into his own hole, soon reaching the man. Then he drew him out, set him down upon the ground, and called in a loud voice, "Ho-o-o! Ho-o-o! Wolves and coyotes, you need not wear out your nails digging for the man, because I have him out already." This gray wolf had great power for he was the chief of the wolves, so the man became his son and went away with the pack.[1]

Now the people in the camp always set traps and snares around the buffalo-drive to catch wolves. They had done this always, but now they began to notice that all the traps and snares would be sprung and the bait taken, without catching a single wolf. The reason was, that the man (who was now a wolf) would go around to all the traps and snares and spring them, after which the pack would eat the bait. The people knew nothing of this. Sometimes when the people heard the wolves at night, they noticed a strange voice among them, and, as they listened from night to night, they thought it sounded more and more like a person. They began to talk about it, and said, "There must be a person with the wolves who throws our traps." When they came to this conclusion, they decided to keep watch during the night until they found out why the traps were thrown. One night the watchers saw a large wolf go to the traps and throw them, after which the pack came up and ate the bait. Then the people decided to capture this man-wolf. When he came the next night to throw the traps, a large number of men surrounded him and roped him. He fought and bit viciously, but they succeeded in dragging him into a lodge. When they made a light, they saw that he was a man with wolf hair and claws. Then they began to consider whether any of their people were missing, and at last they remem-

---

[1] A similar incident occurs in an Arikara tale, Dorsey, op. cit., p. 102.

bered the husband of the two women, and noticed that the wolf had eyes like this man. They called in his two wives, who recognized him at once. Now the people kept the man with them, and gradually got him back to human ways. At last he became to all appearances a man again. After a time he again took his wives out from the camp, where they lived alone. One day he went out to visit the chief of the wolves. Now the wolves and coyotes became as people and lived in a large camp. The chief of the wolves invited the man to move over and camp with them. There were a great many arrows lying on the ground around the camp of the wolf-people, and the chief of the wolves warned the man as follows, "My son, you must not pick up any of the arrows you see on the ground around here, for they are mine." One day, a long time after, the man forgot the warning of the chief of the wolves, and picked up one of the arrows. Immediately it became coyote-dung; and all the camp, except the man and his wives, became wolves and coyotes again. Now the man was very sorry, and went to the chief of the wolves to make amends. He finally offered his two wives to them. Then the wolves and coyotes set upon the two women and ate them. Thus they were punished for their evil doings.[1]

6. The Woman who Married a Snake.

Now, in the olden times the Indians were travelling near the Sand-hills. One man had two wives, one of them very beautiful. The whole camp was moving. The horse ridden by the handsome woman was dragging lodge poles. Some of the poles slipped out and were lost. As they rode out of some brush and small cotton-wood-trees near the hills, she noticed that some of her poles were missing. So she said to the others, "I have lost some of my poles. You go on while I go back to find them." So she rode back and soon found the poles. As she was picking them up she saw her people disappear through a gap in the hills. As she started on, a young man met her. He wore a buffalo-robe with the hair-side out and a yellow plume in his hair, and his face was painted yellow. He was nicely perfumed. As she tried to pass on, he headed her off, and, whichever way she turned, he stepped in front of her. "What are you doing this for?" she said. She did not know him, and thought he must belong to another tribe. "I want you for my wife. I am a widower," said the young man. Then the woman began to feel dizzy, and very soon became unconscious. When she came to herself, she was in a lodge. It was a kind of underground hollow place. Chil-

---

[1] For another version, see Grinnell, op. cit., p. 78. An Arapaho rendering occurs in Dorsey and Kroeber, op. cit., p. 447.

dren were crawling around everywhere. "These are my children," said the young man. Now she saw that they were all snakes. One little snake crawled up to the woman. She picked it up tenderly, and began talking baby-talk to it. So she staid there. After a time she had two children, — a boy and a girl. Now, when the Snake took her, her horse went on and at last overtook her people. When the people saw the horse come back, they knew something had gone wrong. They followed back on the trail, speculating as they went along as to what could have happened. At last they came to the place where she had tied up her poles. Then they found her trail, but soon lost it. They looked all around, but could find no trace of her. Then they found another trail, but could not follow it. The chief said, "We shall camp here five days in order to search for the woman. Let the young men look carefully out in the brush; let everybody look for her." So they began to hunt.

Now, on the morning of the second day, the snake-man told the woman she could go home. He gave her some medicine. He said to her, "You must not lie with your husband. You must never pack meat, neither must you pack wood. Whenever you pass this place you must bring me some tripe, berries, and intestines." Then she started home. As she came up from below, the people of the camp saw her. To the first man she met she said, "I shall go out some distance from the camp. Tell my husband to make a sweat-house outside." When the sweat-house was ready, she went in. When she came out of the sweat-house, they noticed that there was water in it. Then she told the people what had happened to her. She explained to them what the snake-man had forbidden her to do. After this she lived with her husband; but, whenever she passed that place, she spent a few days with the snake-man. Now, one time when her people had killed a great many buffalo, she forgot her promise and packed some meat on her back. As soon as she started to carry it, she remembered, threw it down and ran to her lodge. She became very ill at once, and soon died. They buried her; but her body disappeared. She went back to the snakes.[1]

7. THE WOMAN WHO MARRIED FILTH.

Once there was a young woman very much sought by young men. She was quite a belle. One day as she went out for wood, she saw some human excrement. It was most extraordinary. "Bah!" she said, "That is a pile. I wonder who could have done it." This was in the fall. It was frozen hard.

---

[1] A part of this tale appears in a conglomerate Sun and Moon Myth recorded by Grinnell (Journal of American Folk-Lore, Vol. VI, p. 46). There is also a slight resemblance to an Arapaho narrative, Dorsey and Kroeber, op. cit., p. 441.

Next day when she went after wood, she smelled something sweet and pleasant, and as she was looking around she saw a handsome young man. He wore a white buffalo-robe. She fell in love with him at once and thought to herself, "I shall marry him." So she asked him to stop. "Why?" said he, but kept on going. Every time she said this, he repeated the question, without stopping. She ran after him, caught hold of him, and began to embrace and kiss him. All this time she was saying, "I will marry you. I like a handsome man." (At first sight of him she was nauseated.) "All right," said the man. She went home alone and told her father and mother to go out of the lodge, for, she said, "I am married to a man. I shall bring him here. He suits me: at last I have found one that will do."

The next day all the men of the camp went in to see her husband. They thought him very fine indeed. They congratulated her. She lived with him all winter and kissed him all the time. When spring came, he complained of not feeling well. Now she was frightened, and wished to call in a medicine-man, but he would not consent. He said that it would be of no use, because he was going to die. While they were talking, a man in the camp saw a black cloud in the west, and called out, "Ho-o-o-o-! We shall have a big Chinook." When the husband heard this, he kissed his wife farewell, telling her that he must die. They had a child: it was a boy, and still in her womb. He said to her, "Let us go out to walk, away from the camp." As they went along he caressed her, telling her to take good care of the child he should never see. When they were out from the camp he said, "I shall go into the brush." The woman called after him. She said, "I want to see you again." He turned back to look. As she hurried up, she said, "I love you, I cannot let you go," etc. She tried to kiss him, but he smelled bad. Then he ran. He was thawing out. The woman pursued him. After a while, she saw him fall. Now it was thawing. There was water everywhere. When she got to the spot there was nothing but excrement. The child became a chief. His name was Excrement Chief.

8. THE WOMAN WHO MARRIED A HORSE.[1]

One time when the camp was moving, one of the women walked behind with a travois. Some of her lodge-poles came loose and fell out on the ground. She stopped to fix them as the main body of her people disappeared over a hill. While she was tying up the poles, a very handsome young man approached her. She started on, but he stopped her by getting in front of her. "Why do you stop me?" she said. "I have never had anything to

---

[1] The narrator claimed to have this from the Crows, but it was known among the Piegan as an old tale. For a Gros Ventre rendering of this tale see Kroeber, op. cit., p. 114; see, also, Dorsey and Kroeber op. cit., p. 437.

do with you." "Well," said the man, "I want you to go with me." So the woman had to go with him. When the people camped, they missed the woman, and, not being able to find her, concluded that she had been lost or captured. A long time after this, these people were camped again near the place where the woman was lost. Some of the people saw a large herd of wild horses near a small lake, and they noticed a person among the herd. When this was reported to the camp, all the men mounted horses and went out to investigate. They surrounded the herd, cut out the horses, and roped the person. It was a woman. She had no clothing, and her body was covered with hair like that of a horse. She was very wild, and struggled in the rope. As the herd of horses ran away, they heard a colt among them neighing as if for its dam. The men took the woman back to the camp, where some of her relatives recognized in her the woman that had been lost some time before. She was very wild, had lost the power of speech and the knowledge of all human things. They kept her in the camp a while, but finally her former husband gave up all hopes. "It is of no use to keep her," he said. "The only thing we can do is to send her back to the horses." That evening they turned her loose, and she was never seen again.

9. The Woman with a Sharpened Leg.

There were two women married to the same man. One of them was very jealous of the other. She went into a near by lodge and staid there alone. The lodge belonged to them. The family heard her pounding on something. All this time she was cutting down and sharpening her leg. At last she made it very sharp. While she was pounding, the children cried out, "What are you doing?" "Oh!" she said, "I am hacking a bone." After a while, the man said to the other woman, "That woman has been pounding quite a while. Go over and see what she is doing. There are no bones over there for her to pound on." So the woman peeped in and saw what she was doing. She came back and said to her husband, "She has sharpened her leg." Now this frightened them, and the whole family ran out of the lodge. The woman with the sharpened leg called out, "Hold on! let us have a kicking-game." But they ran as fast as they could, the woman following. At last they came to another camp, and, as they ran by, a man came out. The woman with the sharpened leg said to him, "Now we kick." So they played the game. When the woman kicked a hole in his stomach, the people all scattered and ran. The woman pursued them, killing many by kicking. At last a warrior came up and struck her down with a war-club. Then they burned the body.[1]

---

[1] For an Arapaho parallel of a man with a sharpened leg, see Dorsey and Kroeber, op. cit., p. 258.

10. The Woman without a Body.

Once there was a woman whose husband had cut her head off, but the Head bounced along on the ground following him, saying, "You are my husband. I will follow you wherever you go." So the Head went on with him, and when they stopped, it fixed up the lodges and the camp just as before. The head was a fast worker, but when dressing hides it did it under cover. Yet it was done very quickly. The Head told the man that no one must watch her while doing this. Now there was a boy in the camp who was very curious, and one day he looked in. The Head always kept her digging-stick with her and, when she saw the boy, she picked up the stick, saying "You have done wrong." Then she chased him, overtook him, and beat him to death. When the people saw this they all ran. She pursued them. They fled across the river. The Head jumped in, and floated down with the current.[1]

11. The Man Cut in two below the Waist.

A long time ago, two war-parties started out, one many days before the other. Then the other party went out, and after travelling for several days came to a river where they camped for the night. One of the young men went after some water. As this man was about to dip for the water, some one spoke to him. Looking all around, he saw a man without any legs. This crippled man said that he was one of those who started out first, and that all of his party were killed off except himself. He promised to pay the listener well if he would take him home. To this the young man agreed, picked up the crippled man, and packed him to camp. When the others learned of this, they all made up their minds to go back: so the next morning they all started for home. The young man carried his crippled friend on his back. The other men tried to keep the young man from taking the cripple home. They said that he would scare all the children in the camps if they saw him. Now when they would feed this crippled man, his food would drop through to the ground. At last they came to a big river which they had to swim, so they put the cripple on a raft, and all the rest swam. Soon they all got tired, and, dropping the ropes of the raft, swam to the shore. Then the crippled man and his raft floated down the river. The end.[2]

---

[1] There is in this the suggestion of an incident in a Sun and Moon myth recorded by Grinnell (Journal of American Folk-Lore, Vol. VI, p. 47); further we are reminded of the Rolling Head found among various Indian tribes. See Dorsey and Kroeber (op. cit., p. 70), Also Wissler, Dakota Myths (Journal of American Folk-Lore, Vol. XX, p. 196).

[2] Recorded by D. C. Duvall.

12. THE GHOST-WOMAN.

One time a young man travelling alone was sitting by his camp-fire at night eating. When he had finished, he took off his old worn moccasins, and, thinking to himself how it would be if he were at home, he threw them to one side, saying, "Old woman, mend them for me." After a while he looked around for his moccasins, but they were gone. Then after a while he saw them again, and noticed that they had been mended. "Now," he thought to himself, "this is strange. I will try it again." So he said, "Old woman, get a lot of wood. The fire is about to go out." After a time some wood was piled up in the lodge. After a while he said, "Old woman, I am going out. You get some bedding and fix up a bed while I am gone." When he came back, he saw a bed made up of sage-grass. He lay down as if to go to sleep, but determined to watch to see who this person was. Now, when the fire was out, he heard a person come in. This person said, "At which side shall I sleep?" He replied, "At the side next to the lodge." This person was a woman and she seemed very nice. Now he had a wife. In the morning the woman said, "Now I shall get up and make a fire, but you must not look at me." After a while, when the fire was burning, the woman said, "Now you get up and cook." After a while the man was ready to get up, but he saw no one. Then he said, "Old woman, get some water." And, although he saw no one, the water was soon there.

Then the man started home, but when night came, he camped. He said, "Old woman, fix up a war-lodge." [1] Then he lay down to wait. When this was done, he said, "Old Woman, make a fire and cook." After a while, when the fire was ready, some one said, "Now the fire is ready. You can cook." When the man had cooked, he offered some meat to the woman, but she said, "No, I shall not eat yet." Then the man asked the woman to get wood and make a bed. Everything happened as before. The next day they went on, and camped as usual. On the fourth night the man was to see her for the first time. She said, "In the morning I shall eat." Now, when morning came, the man looked around the lodge, and saw a very handsome woman sitting there. The woman said, "I shall live with you, but you must never strike at me with fire." [2] So he went back to his people, and all went well with them. He lived with the woman for a long time, but one day he became very angry at her, and, taking a stick from the fire, made as if to strike her. As he did so, the woman pulled her robe over her head. Then the man remembered what she had said, and quickly

---

[1] A strong shelter of poles for security against a night attack.
[2] A similar caution occurs in a tale recorded by Grinnell, op. cit., p. 131.

raised the robe. There was only a skeleton beneath it. Then he wrapped up the bones and buried them. Now it has boiled over.

13. Fed by a Ghost.

Once a man was camping alone [with his family]. He had gone out to hunt by himself. In the night they heard a voice saying, "My mother wants to use your pail." Then the man said to his wife, "Woman, let them have it." After a time the pail was brought back into the lodge, and they heard a voice saying, "You can eat what is in it. It is meat." Now when they looked into the pail they found a piece of an old lodge-cover that had been boiled. After a while the Ghost came again and said, "You did not eat it. I will give you something else." "No," said the man, "we do not need anything else. We ate it." He said this because they had hidden it. "Well," said the Ghost, "I want to borrow the pail again." So the man said, "Woman, let him have it." After awhile the Ghost brought the pail filled, and said, "Here are some ribs and tripe." Now, when they looked into the pail, they found some very old bones and sticks of wood, with no meat. The man said, "I am hungry, but I cannot eat that." "Well," said the Ghost, "I shall send out a young man to kill some game." Now the next morning, as the man was going out of the lodge he heard some one say, "Here is meat." On looking around he saw a buffalo-cow lying on the ground. Then he began to butcher. Now he was happy because he had something to eat. Now it has boiled over.

14. Fed by a Coyote.

Once a young man and his little brother were travelling, and got lost on the prairie. They were out of food and were starving. One day they saw a Coyote eating. They approached him. Both of them were thin, nothing but skin and bone. The young man spoke to the Coyote and said, "Give my little brother something to eat, and when I hunt I will always leave the entrails for you to eat." "All right," said the Coyote, "you will be safe." Now the Coyote had very little left when the young man came up: so he said to them, "You stay here and eat until you are strong, then I will take you home." There was a ridge near by, and the Coyote said, "I will see that you get more food, but you must not watch me. Now shut your eyes." After a while they heard the Coyote singing, "I am looking to the west for something to eat." [This is sung in a low soft chant, like all songs in children's stories.] "Now come over here," said the Coyote. So they opened their eyes and went over. The Coyote had a buffalo-calf. He cut it open, butchered it, and then they ate. So it went on from day to day. The Coyote travelled along the ridge toward their home. Whenever the Coyote looked toward the west and sang his song, meat would fall over the ridge toward them. Thus the Coyote took them home.

15. Riding the Buffalo.

Once there was a white man who was a rancher. He had a great many tame buffalo, some of which he rode as if they were horses. One day his unmarried daughter found a skeleton on the river-bank. It had been washed out during the high water. She took the skeleton home and requested her father to make a sweat-house and doctor the skeleton. She said, "If the skeleton comes to life, and it is a man, I shall marry him. But if it is a woman, I shall have her for a chum." Her father finally agreed to try his power. The skeleton came to life as the result of his doctoring. It proved to be a Piegan Indian. So the girl married him. Now these white people lived upon frogs and turtles. As the Piegan could not eat such meat, they asked him what he would like. He told them that his people always ate buffalo. So his white father-in-law killed some of his tame buffalo for him to eat. Now, after a time, the Piegan began to long to see his people. So he asked his father-in-law if he might go. His request was granted. So he set out with some of the tame buffalo. He rode one of them, and his wife another, while the other buffalo followed behind. As he came near the camp of his people, some one called out, "Buffalo are coming!" When they looked out, they said, "People are riding upon them." When they came near, some one said, "That looks like the man who went away and never came back." Now, the Indian staid with his people a while, and then decided to go back to his wife's father and mother. He took his old father and mother with him, and the Piegan never saw them again.[1]

16. The Kutenai Black–Tail Deer–Dance.

This story came from the Kutenai Indians.[2] Long ago in their camp one of them died. The one that died was a man true and good. After he died, his spirit went away to the land of the dead to find out what was there.

---

[1] For a similar tale, see Grinnell, op. cit., pp. 25–28.
[2] For many years the Blackfoot and Kutenai Indians have visited each other and exchanged a few ceremonies. The most important one acquired by the Blackfoot seems to have been the Black-Tail Deer-Dance, a ceremony to aid in hunting deer. The narrator was the chief director of this dance among the Piegan.

When he had been there a while, the spirit told him to return to his people
and tell them what was there. He had been dead seven days, and his body
was badly decomposed; but the spirit of the dead took his spirit down to its
body and he came to life. He came to life in the midst of his friends. Now
it was this way: the watchers around the body heard a noise inside of the
corpse, but all the while the spirit of the dead man was sitting near, saying
that he was trying to sing. So they quickly unwrapped the body. Then
the man opened his eyes, and, looking at them, said, "I have come from
the land of the dead. I have come to teach you more songs and prayers."
Then he rose and picked up a small bell. Now all the people were very
hungry, for they had nothing to eat for a long time. The man said, "Now
we will dance." So he led the dancers round in a circle, and, keeping time
with the bell, sang the songs he had learned when in the land of the dead.
When the dance was over, the people rested while he prayed for them.
Then they danced again. They all slept that night, and when they awoke,
the man who had been dead said, "I know all about power. I saw it in my
dream. You can believe that there is such a place." Then the men went
out to hunt and brought home a great deal of meat, and after that the dance
was called the "Black-Tail Deer-Dance." Now every one takes part in
this dance before he goes out to hunt. They dance in the evening and at
night they can see in dreams where game is to be found.

Once again when a Kutenai Indian was out in the mountains, he was
buried in the snow, but his dog got him out. The man, however, was dead.
The dog went home and by his action induced the man's wife to follow.
The man had been dead four days. The woman carried the body home.
There were two children in the family and they had nothing to eat. The
woman said to the children, "Now your father is dead. We shall starve.
We cannot get away." Now that night the woman remembered the story
of the man who went to the land of the dead, that he came to life again by
singing songs, etc. Then she prayed that her husband might be brought
to life and food given them. While she was doing this, two young men
came in suddenly and told her that the spirits would help her. They said,
"Let us have a dance that your husband may get back his life." So they
began to dance, and danced all night. When daylight came, they stopped.
One of the young men stood at the head of the corpse and the other at the
foot. The one at his head covered the face of the corpse with a black cloth.
The one at the foot touched the dead man on the breast. Then the one at
the head took off the black cloth and the corpse opened his eyes. Then one
of the young men walked on his chest until he became alive. One of the

young men gave him a cross and directed him to pray to it and never to part with it. Now in the Black-Tail Deer-Dance they sing the same songs they sang that night.

Again, in very ancient times there was a woman who had the skin of an otter with the skull fastened to it. She was a medicine-woman. One day she challenged the others as to whose medicine was the strongest. She said, "Let us see who can kill others by touching them." Then the woman took a small pail of water, put in some earth, and, taking a mouthful of the mixture, sprinkled it upon the head of the otter. Then she stood by the door where the people were dancing, and, holding out the otter-skin, spat water from her mouth towards the dancers, and whoever was struck fell down dead. When they were all dead, she took some branches of the pine-tree, placed them on coals of fire, and held the otter-skin in the smoke. Then she rubbed the otter-skin and the people all came to life again.

One time last winter [1902] I visited the Kutenai Indians. I was dancing the Black-Tail Deer-Dance with them. One of the dancers said to me, "Now look at my body." So I watched his body, and as he danced a large cross appeared on his breast and a similar one on his back. As soon as he stopped dancing, the cross disappeared. Then we began to dance again. This time he said to me, "Now look above and below." When I looked down at his feet, I saw the cross on the ground: when I looked at his head, I saw the cross above, with rays like the sun.

17. THE HORNED–TOAD AND THE FROG.

There were two lakes near each other. A Horned Toad was going from one of them to the other to see his girl. His girl was a Frog. At last he got to the lake and coaxed the Frog to go back with him. So they started off. The Frog went very fast and the Horned-Toad was panting behind calling out, "Wait! Wait!" All this time it was raining very hard. After a while the Frog said, "Let us go back. It is too far. We shall never get there." "No," said the Horned-Toad, "it is not far." When they were about halfway over to the lake, it stopped raining. Then the sun came out very hot. It was very, very hot. The Horned-Toad began to give out. He seemed about to have a sunstroke. So the Frog passed water over his back. This revived him for a little while, but soon he began to weaken;

and the Frog did as before. In this way they managed to get along until the Frog reached her limit. Now the Horned-Toad was nearly dead. The Frog was holding him up, and struggling along, crying. When they were nearly dead, it began to rain again. Then they started on much refreshed. At last they reached the lake. Then they were married. Now it has boiled over.

18. TURTLE GOES TO WAR.

Once there was a lake with many camps on its shores. This was a long time ago. One day a Turtle came to the shore. He went up to a lodge, crawled into it, and found a woman asleep. When the man came home, he saw his wife's head in the centre of the lodge. Her head had been cut off by the Turtle. He saw the Turtle trying to pull it toward the back-rest, but it was too heavy for him. As he pulled he sang, "Turtle has hair [head]." The Turtle held the head by the braids.

Now, the people laid hold of the Turtle. One of them said, "We will make a big fire and burn him in it." Then they began to make a big fire. All this time the Turtle was trying to get away from the people who were holding him, to get into the fire. Then the people said, "He must belong in there. The fire must be his place." Then some one said, "Let us smash him between two rocks." When the Turtle heard this, he ran and got upon a rock himself. When the people saw this, they said, "He must have come out of the rock. He is too willing. Let us hang him." So they brought a piece of sinew and made a loop; but the Turtle took it out of their hands and put it around his neck. Then the people said, "He is too willing. We cannot kill him that way." Then some one suggested throwing him into the deep water. As soon as the Turtle heard this, he began to cry and pull back. The people said, "Now we have it. We have found out what will kill him." So they threw him into the deep water. When the Turtle was in the centre, he came to the surface, floated on his back and then on his breast, singing, "Turtle has a scalp! turtle has a scalp!" [1]

19. THE WARRIOR'S DILEMMA.

One time when a war-party went out, they sent a young man ahead to scout. It was dark. As he was going along he saw a lodge all by itself. He went up quietly and looked in. There was no one in the lodge except a man, his wife, and a little child. The little child could just walk and was amusing itself by dipping soup from the kettle with a small horn-spoon.

---

[1] This is a common myth in the Mississippi basin. See Cegiha Myth, J. O. Dorsey, p. 271; Wissler, Dakota Myths, (Journal of American Folk-Lore, Vol. XX, p. 126).

The man and his wife were busy talking and paid no attention to the child. Now the child happened to look up and saw the man peeping through the hole, and at once toddled over to the kettle, dipped up some soup in the spoon and held it to the man's lips. He drank it and the child returned to the kettle for more. In this way the child fed him for many minutes. Then he went away. As he was going along down to his party, he thought to himself, "I do not like to do this, but I must tell my party about this lodge. When they know it, they will come and kill these people. Now this little child fed me, even when I was spying upon them, and I do not like to have it killed. Well, perhaps I can save the child; but then it would be too bad for it to lose its parents. No, I do not see how I can save them, yet I cannot bear to have them killed," etc. So he sat down and thought it over. After a while he went back to the lodge, went in and sat down. While the man was getting the pipe ready, the child began to feed him again with the spoon. After he had smoked, he told the man all about it. He explained to him how he had come as a scout to spy upon them, and that he was about to bring up his war-party, but that they had been saved by the little child. Then he directed the man to go at once, leaving everything behind him in the lodge.

Now, the man was very thankful, and offered to give him a medicine-bundle and a suit of clothes; but the young man refused, because he knew that his party would suspect him. Then the man suggested that he might place the bundle near the door, behind the bedding. When the war-party came up and dashed upon the lodge, he could be the first to capture it. (All the important property of the lodge is always kept at the back, opposite the door, and, when a war-party rushes in, the swiftest runs to this place.)

Now the young man went back to his party, told them he had found a lodge, but that he had not been up to it or seen any one. Then they started out at once, and, when they came near the lodge, they set up a whoop and rushed upon it. Now the man kept to the rear, and as his companions were counting coup on the various objects in the lodge, he stood at the door looking around. At last he picked out the bundle and counted coup on it. Now his companions were suspicious, and they said, "Oh! we know how you did this. You warned the people so that they went away, and then you hid these things by the door, that you might get them." They accused him and threatened him, but still he denied any knowledge of the people, or as to how the bundle came to be there. Yet the people were always suspicious of him, and he was always looked upon as the man who betrayed his war-party in order to make a capture.[1]

---

[1] This narrative and the one that follows usually provoke a discussion, in which some condemn all or parts of the scout's acts, while others defend them. Such tales are looked upon as ethical puzzles to which no satisfactory answers can be given. So far nothing of this kind among other tribes has come to our notice.

20. A Warrior's Duty and his Love.

Once a scout going out from his party saw a camp. There were just two lodges. He stole up, and in the smaller one he saw a woman alone. She was beautiful, and struck his fancy. He went back and waited. At midnight he crept into the lodge and spent the night with her. In the morning he went away.

He was the leader of the war-party, and on one pretext and another kept them under cover while he made nightly visits to the woman. He did this for four nights. Then his feeling for the woman began to assert itself. He thought of plans to save her. He might lead her away and kill the others; but they were doubtless her relations and she would mourn for them. Then, if he married her, they would be his relations. Yet he was the leader of a war-party, and had discovered an enemy. At last he brought the woman and her relations to the camp of the war-party, telling them that he had married the woman. Then they went home, and though she was of hostile tribe, they lived together.

21. The Wolverene-Woman.

These Indians have a belief that there are animals with power to change into human beings. Of these the wolverene is one. It often happens that when a man is out hunting, or sitting alone by his campfire, a very handsome woman will come up. Now if he offers her some of the entrails from his butchering, she will take them daintily between the thumb and the forefinger and then throw them away. This is the sign by which she may be known. Should the man take up his gun, the woman will run away as a wolverene. On the other hand, should he allow her to come into camp and engage in familiarities, evil will follow. As soon as he gets home and smells the fire of the lodges, he will fall down dead. Sometimes he will only faint when he smells the fire of the lodges; but even then he will never be the same person again. When men go out to hunt, they are often reminded to keep a lookout for the Wolverene-Woman. When a woman is out alone, the Wolverene-Woman will appear as a fine young man. If the woman permits herself to be seduced, it will be bad for her. As a rule, her people will never hear of her again; but, should she start back to camp and smell the fire of the lodges, she will surely die.[1]

---

[1] For another example of the effect of camp-smoke, see Grinnell, op. cit., p. 133. This is not a formal narrative. While the wolverene is a well-known mythical character, there are no specific myths in which it appears. The Deer-Woman of the Dakota, and the Wolf-Woman of the Pawnee, described by Bush Otter, seem to embody the same conception as is expressed in the above (Eleventh Annual Report of the Bureau of American Ethnology, pp. 480, 481).

22. SEVEN–HEADS.

These Indians have a myth of a seven-headed person who made a business of devouring young women. One time a man came along where some animals were disputing over a piece of meat. The man settled the quarrel, and in return they gave him some power. With this power he went and killed Seven-Heads, after which he married a princess. Then the thunder stole her, but he rescued her by killing a lion, then an eagle which flew out of the lion, then a rabbit which came out of the eagle, then a dove which came out of the rabbit, etc. This story is believed by the Indians to have been brought in by the French.[1]

23. THE SAND HILLS.

Once a man was hunting buffalo near the Sand Hills. That is where the dead go. He killed a buffalo, and when he went up to butcher it, he saw a man come towards him, whom he knew to be a dead man. He was very much afraid so he said to the dead man, "Now I will divide up this buffalo with you, but first I must go back here and bring up my pack-horses. You can go on with the butchering." The man lied, for as soon as he reached his horse he mounted and galloped away. A long time after this, the man was back in the same part of the country, and thought to himself, "I will go to get the arrow-points I left at the place where I killed the buffalo." When he came to the place, he found the skeleton of the buffalo and also his arrow-points. As he looked up, he saw the same man he had seen before. The man spoke to him, and said, "My friend, where have you been? I have been waiting for you all this time." This frightened the man so much that he sprang upon his horse and galloped away at great speed. Shortly after he returned to his camp, he took sick and died.[2]

---

[1] The above abstract was recorded by D. C. Duvall. For note on the distribution of this narrative, see Kroeber, Gros Ventre Myths, p. 57: It is interesting to note that our Blackfoot informant expresses the same opinion as to the origin of this myth as attributed to Mrs. La Flèche, an Omaha, J. O. Dorsey, op. cit., p. 126.

[2] See Grinnell, op. cit., pp. 125, 132.

INDEX